BOOKS   BY

Rick R. Reed
====================

Obsessed

Penance

A Face Without a Heart

Twisted: Tales of Obsession and Terror

In the Blood

IM

Rick R. Reed

Quest Books

Nederland, Texas

ISBN 1-932300-79-1
978-1-932300-79-6

First Printing 2007

9 8 7 6 5 4 3 2 1

Cover design by Donna Pawlowski

Published by:

Regal Crest Enterprises, LLC
4700 Hwy 365, Suite A, PMB 210
Port Arthur, Texas 7764

Find us on the World Wide Web at
http://www.regalcrest.biz

Printed in the United States of America

Acknowledgments

Sincere thanks to my publisher Cathy LeNoir for her faith in me; to Lori L. Lake for her friendship, guidance, and hand-holding; to Sylverre for her excellent editorial expertise; to Donna Pawlowski for her inspired cover design; and to attorney Carole Longendyke for technical advice.

For brucifer712
I'm your man...online, offline, everywhere

Chapter
One

WHEN TONY LOGGED on to the Men4HookUpNow website, he didn't know that this would be the last time he would type in his screen name and password, the last time he would scroll through thumbnail-sized pictures of men in various states of undress, or the last time he would read an instant message.

Tony didn't know that logging on to Men4HookUpNow.com would be one of the last things he would do.

Ever.

The simple blue and white instant message box was a blank canvas, containing only a list of provocative screen names: musclestud, pnpjock, pozpup4u... And any one of these screen names could spring to life by sending Tony an instant message, or, as everyone called them, an IM. Anyone could arrive within its simple frame: a college football player, a construction worker, a truck driver, or just a man in tight jeans and engineer boots.

There was a pinging sound, and a message appeared on the screen. Tony leaned forward to see who had come to call.

And *whoosh*, a real man came through cyberspace, delivered like a gift. The box held only one word, "hi," yet Tony felt its author could see through his monitor, see him there in his living room wearing only a pair of boxer shorts, see the porno playing on his TV screen.

"Come on, man," Tony whispered, fingers poised above the keyboard. "Hi? Can't you do better than that?" He wanted someone with a bit more personality this languid August night, so he hit the Delete key and banished the guy into limbo, where someone else might take his "hi" with a little more encouragement. Tony began a scroll through the "Available Now" guys, reading the inane descriptions ("Let this hot, beefy muscle boy serve you. I'm 6'2" red hair, green eyes, former All-American football player"; "Aggressive bottom looking for well-endowed top men. I'm into just about everything except for scat and I know how to take orders"; "looking to party with a hot stud"; "straight-appearing and acting";

"Negative...UB2") and stopping if one of the thumbnails caught his eye, especially if the guy had the courage to show his face.

Tony idly stroked himself as the images paraded past. He asked himself why he was bothering with going online. For Christ's sakes, here it was, Saturday night. Couldn't he throw on some jeans and head down to Halsted Street? At least in a bar, he would know for sure what the guy looked like if they decided to hook up (rather than seeing a cock shot and hoping the guy had a nice face, or trusting a face pic a decade old). This way, all he had to work with was exaggeration, living in a world where "stocky and football player build" meant fat, where 38-year-olds tried to pass as 29, where any bald guy could lay claim to looking like Bruce Willis, where average meant so hideous you might as well hide under a rock.

The instant message box popped up.

`"Hey, what's up?"`

Well, at least better than "hi." Tony keyed in:

`"Just real horny. Looking to hook up."`

If the horny part weren't so true, Tony wouldn't have been able to keep himself from laughing. Trying to put a macho façade on his typed words, trying to make himself sound like he had an eighth-grade education, made him feel idiotic. A queer Stanley Kowalski.

`"Know what you mean, dude."`

So the guy was playing the macho game with him.

`"So, man, what do you look like?"`
`"28. Black. Blue. Nice lean muscular build, work out about 3 or 4 times a week. Nicely defined pecs. Good tan. Hairy chest. 8 inches cut, real thick. You?"`

Tony felt himself transported. It was like the guy got into his head, reading the ingredients for his perfect fantasy man. His dick started to rise with anticipation and he found his hand moving up and down the length of it, almost of its own accord. He clicked on the instant messenger list, on the guy's screen name, "jock4play" and was disappointed to see no pictures in his profile. Still, if the description was accurate... Tony typed in:

```
"Yeah, I'm 32. I've got dark blond hair, green
eyes, moustache, goatee. Smooth swimmer's build.
Work out a lot, too. Um. Got about seven, cut,
shaved balls. Check out my pics."
"You a top or bottom?"
```

There wasn't even a pause, so Tony wondered if the guy had bothered to look.

```
"Pretty open. I pretty much like it all. Pretty
versatile. How about you? What are you into?"
"I'm a top, dude. Lookin' for a good bottom boy."
"I can do that."
"Yeah?"
"Sure. Whereabouts are you, man?"
"North side."
"Yeah, me too. I'm in Rogers Park, Touhy and
Ashland."
"I'm not too far from you."
```

Tony swallowed his common sense as the image of his fantasy man took over.

```
"You wanna come over?"
"You like to party?"
"Yeah."
```

Tony loved little more than getting high and getting down.

```
"Tina's here."
```

Tony eyed the little glass pipe, its bottom crusted with black residue and white powder. His nerves—right along with his libido—were in overdrive.

```
"Poppers?"
"Got 'em."
"Hmmm. I could be interested."
```

Tony looked briefly at the TV, where a hairy-chested drill sergeant had a lithe blond "private" bent over his desk. He wanted to get things moving, so he typed:

```
"You wanna call me?"
"Sure. Number?"
"555-7654; it's my cell. Call me right back.
Okay?"
```

Was that too pushy? Many times, they never bothered to call. Many times, they said they would show up and never did. But once in a while, it all came together.

His cell chirped. He flipped it open. "Hey."

"What's goin' on, dude?"

"God, I just need some dick. You interested in hookin' up, man?"

"The sooner the better."

"Got somethin' to write with?" And Tony got busy, giving precise directions to his apartment.

Precise directions to a stranger.

After he hung up, Tony felt flushed, a deep burning radiating from chest to face. His heart pounded as if he had just done a big hit of poppers. God, the guy sounded incredible! He suddenly knew why he was doing this as opposed to going out to a bar. When the site worked, it worked. There was no bullshit, no game playing. No eye contact for an hour, no fumbling for something to say and then sounding like a dork. When it worked with the site, it was simply two lusting men getting together and pleasuring each other. They didn't need to say a word. *Then why not a bathhouse?* Tony asked himself, wandering around the apartment, folding up newspapers and throwing magazines in the wicker basket he stored them in. He remembered Man Universe and the last time he was there. It was okay, he guessed; there wasn't the usual amount of bullshit. He thought with a grin of the open doors and the guys lying within, naked on their stomachs, the white moons of their asses a focal point, the bottle of lube and poppers on the little table beside the bed. But the bathhouse lacked one thing the Men4HookUpNow offered: the element of surprise. Having someone show up after making an online connection, there was always that breathless moment when you opened the door to see what you were getting. Even if you had seen photos, it was always a crap shoot. A grab bag. And that's what made it so exciting. The gamble made the rewards all the sweeter. And, hey, if you lost one time, you just said "sorry," closed the door, and got back online.

There was no shortage of hot guys online.

Or at least adequate ones.

Tony glanced at himself as he passed the mirror in his dining room, grateful he had worked out earlier in the day, grateful for the fact that he never had to exaggerate. His blond hair was buzzed and his muscles had good definition. His lips were slightly pouty, giving his face an aura of innocence defiled...details in his face combined to form a very pleasing contradiction. Sleazy and at the same time babyish, childlike.

Tony never lacked for admirers.

And sometimes, he wished he did. He thought of *him*, the asshole who was always around, the one who, after three dates, couldn't handle his request to be just friends.

But think of that another time! A party was coming up. And Tony wanted to make sure this party was of the all-night variety.

He headed for the kitchen, to take the poppers out of the freezer. He held the little brown glass bottle up to the light and shook it; it was about at the halfway point, certainly enough to see him through the evening.

In the bedroom, he placed a couple of towels on the nightstand, along with a bottle of Wet. In the portable CD player, he put in Delirium (great fuck music) and made sure the votive candles were adequate enough to burn for the hours he planned on taking with this guy, if he was as good as he sounded.

Tony turned to the mirror once more, running his hand through the blond spikes, making them stand on end. He flexed his biceps and was pleased at the image the mirror threw back.

He reached in his dresser drawer, pulled out his metal cock ring, and slid it over his dick and balls. He strapped a metal band with studs around his right arm "Perfect," he whispered to his grinning reflection.

Blood pounded in his ears. A line of sweat formed at his hairline and under his arms.

He couldn't wait.

The buzzer sounded.

Tony walked slowly to the intercom box in the front hallway, not wanting to appear too eager. Desperation was never pretty.

It sounded once more before he placed his hand on the talk button. "Yeah?"

"It's your buddy from online."

Tony pressed the button marked "door" and then the one marked "listen" so he could hear the guy coming in. He hoped he wouldn't be disappointed.

It was hard to tell, but the guy's voice didn't sound quite as deep as he thought it had when the guy called his cell. Perhaps the intercom was just distorting his voice a bit.

But there was something else. No, it couldn't be...but the voice had a familiar cast to it. Tony wondered when the day would come when he ran into someone he knew from Men4HookUpNow.

Perhaps the day was today.

But the familiarity of the voice didn't have pleasant associations.

Imagination. *Tony, bud, you're imagining things.*

Anyway, there was no time to think about that now, not with the guy tapping on his door.

Tony peered through the peephole.

And saw nothing.

He didn't like that. But the guy was probably standing to the left or right of the hole, that's all. Good sense deserted Tony, usurped by lust.

He opened the door and the color drained from his face. "What the hell are *you* doing here?"

Chapter
Two

THE BODY, THEY had said, was a mess. A bloody, gut-wrenching mess. The gallery of ghouls had assembled before Ed even got there: two uniforms, the medical examiner, a department photographer and an evidence technician.

Ed Comparetto had been in the detective division of the Chicago police department for just two years, and reporting to scenes like this still caused his gut to tighten with apprehension. He recognized the lurid dichotomy: the desire to flee and the even stronger desire to see what had happened, the carnage that had been wreaked.

This time, this hot August morning, where the temperature was already nearing 95 degrees and the humidity was higher, Ed had no great desire to hurry inside. He dreaded what he would find in the little one bedroom apartment, dreaded it enough that his palms were sweating and an iron band was tightening across his chest.

But he knew, from the practice he had already gone through, as first an officer and then a detective, that others didn't need to pick up on the fear and the queasiness. It was all a matter of appearing confident, of putting one foot in front of the other and training his dark brown eyes on whatever atrocity he was forced to greet.

He would tell others that it got easier, and would joke along with the other guys after hours, making black humor of corpses sitting for days in bathtubs, housing project stabbings and gunshot victims riddled with holes like a slab of fucking Swiss cheese. Except Swiss cheese holes didn't have gunpowder burns around the edges.

He steeled himself, taking a deep breath, getting down deep. Even though no one would say it to his face, Ed knew that they were all looking for telltale signs of weakness, to expose him as the pansy they all knew he was. Ever since he had publicly "come out" in a *Windy City Times* article on gay officers on the Chicago police force, there had been a certain coldness toward him. Nothing overt, save for the rose someone had once tenderly placed on his desk, but enough reticence for him to know that his action had caused a change in how his peers and even his superiors regarded him. He supposed it could have been worse, but Ed still sensed they were all just waiting for a fall, so they could say he didn't really belong with them, not with real men, men used to dealing with murder and mayhem on a daily basis.

And now one of his own had fallen, which was probably why his supervisor had called him at 6:30 that morning, exhorting him to get out and investigate this new case. He'd answered the phone while still clutching at the pillow beside him as if it were a person. Perhaps Ed's homosexuality could finally come in handy. Maybe Ed would have some secret knowledge which could make him know, at a glance, why a 28-year-old bartender in Rogers Park had been stabbed, mutilated and God knows what else.

Inside, inside, he urged himself, *get it over with.*

He crossed the threshold. Lingering in the air was the smell of butyl nitrate, and the first thing he spotted was the little brown bottle, overturned on the rug. The smell, with its powerful association with sex, brought an almost surreal aspect to the crime scene. He noted too, the small glass pipe on the desk, the baggie for the world's tiniest sandwich, and the butane torch. At least the victim didn't have to worry about getting arrested for possession, or an overdose.

Ed had seen the room a hundred times before: the second-hand furniture, the 25-inch TV screen, the decent stereo system, plants, framed Chicago Film Festival posters on the wall — all the trappings of a downwardly mobile gay boy.

The thought of this particular gay boy, Tony Evans, suddenly overwhelmed Ed, gave to the surroundings a sense of poignancy. Tony would never again sit on these chairs, water these plants, or gaze upon the muscular bodies depicted on his posters.

Tony was in the bathtub, and Ed turned right and headed back along the little hallway that led to the bathroom. Outside the room, a young uniform, his ruddy Irish complexion drained of color, held his stomach.

"You wanna take it outside?" Ed squeezed the guy's shoulder. "Go on, now. You'll feel better."

"I'm supposed to tell you the guy who found the body is here. He's waitin' outside."

Ed nodded. "Good. I need a minute alone, so why don't you run on outside."

Ed watched the officer's retreating figure with more than a little longing, wishing he could go along. But the bright yellow rectangle that was the bathroom's entrance beckoned to him. He already knew this much from his supervisor: that the victim's friend had discovered his body in the bathtub, where the water was stained deep crimson from all the blood; that the victim's penis had been severed from his body and jammed up his ass; that the fingers from the victim's right hand had been removed and had not been found at the time his supervisor had phoned; that a phone cord had been wrapped around his neck, and had been, most likely, the instrument which had brought about death.

Knowing all of this made nothing easier. In fact, it made Ed's legs suddenly fill with lead; taking each step was work and he was grateful for the fact that he would have at least a few minutes alone with the body.

He breathed in again, noticing how his exhalation came out with a quiver. He would have to watch that. Taking a notebook and pen from the inner breast pocket of his sport coat, Ed forced himself to enter the bathroom.

The first thing he noticed was his own reflection in the medicine cabinet mirror above the sink. His dark features, brown eyes, and short, curly black hair made a sharp contrast to the paler than usual pallor of his skin. His breath was coming in small short rasps. He took a while, studying his reflection, because he didn't want to look around. As long as he stared into the mirror, the corpse in the tub had nothing to do with him. All the things he had already heard about the condition of the body were nothing more than words, cold, clinical, as precise as they could be.

Ed knew the body would be a whole 'nother story. Corpses had a way of bringing everything into sharp focus, giving all the forensic terminology and police lingo dimension and reality. And the worst part: one glance was all it took to make it real, to bring home the fact that this was a person who had suddenly lost everything. And for what? For a reason no one might ever know — no one save for the person who was out there now, a nameless fiend, licking his wounds and remembering. He had to be remembering.

Ed looked.

His mouth went dry. His scalp itched. He reached out to grab the sink, to clutch its cold porcelain edge. *Steady, steady.*

The tub appeared to be filled with blood, the water exposing the pale body beneath its surface through a red filter. Blood, in little Jackson Pollack flecks, spattered the tile wall above the tub and Ed found himself concentrating on these tiny constellations of gore, again training his eyes away from the atrocity in the tub.

The blond hair still retained its sheen; death had not caused the myriad spikes to fall. But the hair was the only thing that remained remotely human about this, this thing in the tub. The phone cord, like a coiled snake, still hung limply around the neck, slipping down toward the shoulders. A pale ring of red encircled the guy's neck, a ghost of former abuse. His eyes bulged outward, staring up at the ceiling: blue filmed over with yellow, bearing mute, yet horrified, witness to their owner's final hours. The body was already starting to bloat and the wounds inflicted on it looked clean, bled dry, barren holes through which life had passed.

Ed turned and let out a small choking sob. He stifled it quickly, stiffening his spine, gathered in his breath, and headed out.

At least the air would not be suffused with death outside, even if it was hot, even if it was so sticky it was almost palpable.

And he could talk to the friend who had discovered the body. What would he say?

THE GUY WAS a mess of a different sort. From a distance, he appeared almost a boy, no more than fourteen or fifteen years old. A lithe body, at best only 5'5" or 5'6", topped with a shock of golden hair hanging straight and almost covering his eyes. As Ed drew nearer, the eyes revealed themselves to him in all their pain: red-rimmed, the palest of blue irises floating in a bath of warm wet; salt tears tracked down his face.

An officer murmured something in the boy's ear and the boy tried to rein in his tears, straightening his shoulders and drawing in great quivering breaths. He met Ed's eyes, waiting with an expression revealing both curiosity and despair.

"Hi, my name's Ed Comparetto." Ed moved closer and extended his hand as he reached the boy. The hand that barely gripped his was small, the bones beneath the pale soft flesh like bird bones, tiny and fragile. "I'm a detective with the Chicago police department, homicide division."

The boy—and Ed mentally corrected himself because this was no boy at all, but a man—the man was perhaps as old as his mid-thirties. Close-up, tiny crow's feet surrounded the red-rimmed eyes and the face had a certain weathering that came only with age.

The man nodded, mutely, as if he didn't know what to say.

"What's your name, sir?"

"Timothy. Timothy Bright."

Ed jotted the name down, wondering if it was real. It sounded too much like someone you'd see as one of the dancers in some Broadway show. "Timothy, would you like to walk over here and sit down? You'd probably be more comfortable."

Timothy followed as Ed led him to a stoop next door; a big maple provided a little shade, but not much relief from the heat. Ed waited as Timothy drew in a few more quivering breaths, listening and hoping that soon the time would come when the breathing would return to normal and he could proceed with his job. Already, he knew the potential existed to invest too much in this case, and he wasn't interested in comforting Mr. Bright, who looked as though he needed it.

"So, Timothy..." Ed cocked his head. "It's okay if I use your first name, isn't it?"

Timothy nodded, and Ed was once more amazed by the pale eyes; so pale they appeared almost colorless vessels through which light passed.

"I understand you were the one who, um, discovered the body? Is that right?"

Timothy sniffed and wiped his nose with the back of his hand. Ed handed him a Kleenex from his breast pocket.

"Why don't you tell me about that?"

The voice that began, hardly more than a whisper at first, had a reed-like quality, a breathy womanish voice that must have caused poor Timothy no end of grief.

"Tony was my friend. I've known him since the day he moved in. Six months ago. Still spring...a warm day, sunshine like you would not believe. Yet there was still a chill underneath it all, as if the weather was a lie. Which it was, of course. Spring is like that."

The more Timothy talked, the more wooden and monotone he became. Ed began to wonder if he would need some treatment for shock before the day was through. And he didn't want to slow down the wandering words, didn't want to make this guy face the suffering that lay in wait for him like a razor-toothed beast of prey.

"I noticed him right away, well, because I notice a good-looking man, which Tony was." Timothy paused; a car with a loud muffler passed. He shrugged. "I guess these aren't the kinds of things you want to hear about."

"I want to hear whatever you think is relevant. Take your time."

"Well, anyway, I thought I'd be bold, because that's just how I am, and I walk right up to him and I go, 'Howdy, stranger, looks like you could use some neighborly help.' 'Cause, see, he was all alone and trying to lug furniture off this U-Haul. Sure, I felt sorry, but my reasons for offering to help were entirely selfish.

"Anyways, the two of us sort of became friends after that. Went out a coupla times or two, but you know, things just never went in that direction.

"We kinda got in the habit, a ritual you might call it, of having breakfast together on Fridays. It happened once or twice by coincidence and then we just sort of decided to always do it. It's so hard to stay in touch with friends, y'know...unless you make a little effort."

Ed traced a line across his pad. "So that's why you came over this morning?"

"Yeah, of course." Timothy stopped, eyes welling again. He stared at a squirrel across the street, watched its twitching tail as it clung to the side of an oak. He sighed. "I had my own key, so I just went up. Lots of times, with Tony being a bartender and all, he might not be up yet. So he gave me a key and I would come in, have a cup of coffee, read a magazine until Tony got up." Timothy laughed. "Sometimes, he never did get up. But that was okay with me. Because that's how it is with good friends. You know?"

Ed didn't know, but he said, "Sure."

"So I didn't bother ringing the doorbell or anything. I just let myself in and hopped right up the stairs." A smile had played about Timothy's lips, a smile borne up by memory, by a closeness, perhaps, that had once existed and would never exist again. As Ed watched, the smile disappeared. Who could smile, remembering recent events? Timothy hung his head and pressed the palms of his hands against his eyes. "Shit," he whispered.

Ed leaned close, so the warmth of his arm pressed against Timothy's cool, frail, bony arm, hanging out of an oversized T-shirt sleeve. "Take your time."

Timothy shook his head. "I don't know if I can do this." His voice had suddenly gone hoarse.

Ed placed a hand on Timothy's shoulder and squeezed. "Sure you can."

Just when the pause seemed to linger a little too long, as if Timothy would never find his tongue and speak again, he started: "You know, I've always believed I have psychic abilities. Nothing too loony or anything, but now I doubt it. Because I felt nothing as I went up the stairs. Not a thing. You know what I was thinking about?" he asked, then, more urgently: "Do you know what I was thinking about?" The voice became shrill, forcing Ed to give some sort of reply.

"What?"

"I was thinking about how I wanted pancakes! *Pancakes,* and Tony was lying in there..." Timothy bit his lower lip, and Ed could see how hard he was trying to hold everything back.

Ed also knew how much the guy wanted him to let him off the hook, to tell him he could do this later if he wanted. But his newly honed detective's instincts told him that if he did that, details would be forgotten or rearranged by a cooler and more rational mind. But the details that seemed bizarre or out of place could be just the information Ed might need to put the puzzle together. "Just go on. It'll do you good to get it all out."

"I put my key in the door and went in. It was quiet in there, but I just figured Tony was sleeping. That's the way it happened half the time anyway. So I sat down. There were a coupla magazines on the coffee table, so I put up my feet and started working through the *Gay Chicago* classifieds. You wouldn't believe some of the bizarre shit people will advertise for, shit they'll do for strangers sight unseen." Timothy stared up at the white-hot sky, as if the rest of his story were written there.

Ed glanced at the same sky and felt cold in spite of the heat, imagining Timothy Bright in the living room, while a corpse lay in the next room, mutilated and steeping in his own blood.

"Um, so I got up to get some coffee. I knew where everything was and I knew Tony wouldn't mind. I knew Tony would need a cup when he got up, just as much as he'd need a smoke..." Timothy's voice caught and he choked back a sob. He bit his lip and continued. "Anyway, on my way out to the kitchen, I decided I needed to pee before I got started."

And that was when Timothy Bright's face went blank. It was almost as if some sort of cover slid down over his features; color and emotion drained from his face and his eyes went utterly blank. He began to tremble.

In spite of himself, and knowing it was against everything he'd learned as a detective on the force, Ed slid his arm around Timothy, gave his shoulder a hard squeeze.

The action did not faze Timothy Bright. He continued to stare with a deadness in his gaze that was chilling.

After a while, he turned to Ed. "I'm sorry, but I really don't think I can go on." He bit his lower lip to quell the trembling. "I can't relive this. I'll go out of my mind."

Questioning like this was always the hardest part of Ed's job. The homosexuality the two men shared made it harder, for some reason Ed couldn't quite fathom. He wanted nothing more than to tell Timothy Bright to forget it, to go home and mourn the loss of his friend. "Timothy, you have to go on. Number one, it's going to do you good to get it out." Ed shook his head, hating his job for just a moment. "And number two, because if you don't, I'll have to take you down to the station, which will probably be a lot less pleasant than sitting here." All of this was true, but it didn't stop Ed from feeling like a ghoul, a traitor. "Just take your time. When you're ready, I'll listen. And, hey, if you wanna cry or anything, don't be embarrassed. It happens all the time."

Timothy stared at him. He nodded slowly. "I had to pee, and I turned around. I went into the bathroom, expecting nothing more than Tony's usual mess." He started crying then, really crying: warm tears flowing and his nose running. "What do I need to tell you this for? You saw yourself, didn't you? Tony was lying there in the tub in his own blood, with his dick cut off and his fingers cut off. It felt like he was looking at me, staring at me. Do you know how that felt? Could you even imagine? I thought he was looking at me. Me! As if I could help him or something."

Timothy lowered his head and covered his face. His shoulders moved up and down with the force of his grief. After a while, he was again able to talk. "That's when I walked into the living room and called 911." He laughed, but there was no mirth in it. "I never called it before; I thought it was a stupid TV show."

"Did you notice anything odd, anything unusual?"

"You mean besides Tony's bloody corpse in the bathtub?" Timothy shook his head. "Sorry. I don't know. I got kind of upset, you know. I wasn't exactly taking in the details."

"I know it's hard, Timothy."

Timothy massaged his temples. "I don't know. The phone felt sticky."

"Sticky?"

"Yeah, tacky, you know. I don't know why. I don't know what that has to do with anything."

There was activity to the east of them then. Neighbors and passersby had gathered outside. Channels Two, Five and Seven had all managed to get wind of what was going on while Ed interviewed Timothy and had pulled their vans up amid the whirling blue lights of squad cars and emergency vehicles.

They were carrying the body out, sheathed in an opaque black plastic bag. Timothy looked too, and the sight caused him to suck in his breath. "Oh God," he whimpered. "Oh no. Oh no."

Ed stood and groped in his inside breast pocket for a card. He held it out for Timothy; when he didn't take it, Ed pressed the card into his hand, curling his fingers around it. "You hang on to this. If you think of anything else, call me. Day or night. My cell is on there, too, so you can call me there, too. And..." Ed bit his lip. "And, um, don't plan on going anywhere for the next few days. Okay? I'm afraid we'll be needing to talk to you again."

"Sure." Timothy clutched the card and stared at the pavement, where a group of red ants swarmed over a melting Popsicle.

Chapter
Three

I LOG ONTO Men4HookUpNow and wait. The cascade of men appears: little thumbnail portraits of guys all over the city of Chicago, all online and all looking for love...in poses that would make their mamas gasp.

I scroll through them, looking for the right one, when I'm interrupted by the little blue and white IM box. I read.

```
"How's it goin', man?"
```

I type.

```
"Pretty good. Just kicking back, stroking. You?"
"Same here. Where you at?"
"Lakeview."
```

Boys' Town. Homo Central. How many guys in this part of town are on this very site, right now? Just waiting, waiting for someone to come over and fill the void.

```
"Cool. I'm on the north side, too.  How old are
you?"
"37."
```

I stare at the instant message box for a few minutes and, when there's no reply, close it. Guess I was too old for this one. That's okay. There's others. Always others. So many who are willing: if I did this shit seven days a week, I'd never run out of prospects. Amazing. Amazing how easy it is. A new box pops up.

```
"Hello. What's going on, buddy?"
"Just horny. What are you up for tonight?"
"Looking for a good top guy."
"That'd be me."
"Yeah? What do you look like?"
```

Already the anticipation. I'm halfway home.

"6'2", about 200. Blond, buzz cut. Goatee,
tattoos, pierced nipples and navel. Real hot
muscular build, good definition, work out with
free weights every day. Got about nine inches,
six around."
"Wow. You sound hot."
"So I've been told."
"Why no pics on your profile?"
"I have to be discreet, you know? Job, stuff like
that."
"That's cool. So what are you into?"
"Pretty much a top. Like getting serviced. Love
getting my dick worked on, rimmed, fucking."
"You like rubbers or bareback?"
"Skin to skin. No other way for me, man."
"Good answer."
"Can I call you?"

Our cyber conversation, just like the last one, ends here, with
me asking the wrong question. The guy's a coward. No matter. Lots
more to pick from...
Another IM box pops up.

"Hey, what's up?"
"Not much. Just feeling kind of horny. Looking to
hook up?"
"Definitely, dude. Where are you?"
"North side."
"That's cool. What are you into?"
"Pretty much a top. Looking to get serviced."
"Yeah? Well I'm pretty much a bottom and fuck,
I'm horny."
"Great. Maybe we can take care of that."
"You wanna get together?"
"Sure. Let's do it, man."

Can I make an aside here? All these mans, buddys, and dudes
make me want to puke. Plus the fact that—when you first meet
them—most of these guys talk like they have an eighth-grade
education. What is this? They want you to think they're truck
drivers, construction workers, professional athletes, when the truth
is most of them do something "creative" or they work at Lord &
Taylor in the cosmetics department. Enough about all this. Let's see
how easy this one will be.

```
"Got a number?"
"Sure. 555-9908. Call me right back, okay?"
"Sure thing, dude."
```

Punch in number. The guy answers after one ring. Desperate?
I say: "So how's it goin'? You wanna do this?"
"Yeah. I need to get fucked."
Oh, the subtlety. "You sound like my kind of guy. You *are*
looking for company, right?"
"Actually, I was looking to go out."
"Aw, fuck. I really have to go out, too. Well, guess it's back to
square one."
"No! I mean, wait a minute. Maybe I could have someone over.
It's just that I've got a roommate and I'm not sure when he'll be
back."
I've already made the sale, just about. I know I can close this
deal. "Doesn't he know?"
"Well, yeah, but I don't want us to get interrupted."
"Got your own room?"
"Yeah, sure."
"So we close the door. If he comes back, he comes back.
Wouldn't he be cool about it?"
"I guess so."
A little pressure, now, make him think he's losing it. "Look,
maybe we should wait 'til another time..."
"No, it's cool. Why don't you come over?"
"You serious? Because I'm really sick of all the bullshit that
goes on online."
"Me, too. I wouldn't jack you around. Got a pen?"

LAKE SHORE DRIVE at night has its own excitement,
especially when one is hurtling toward a rendezvous with an
unknown destiny. On one side of my car, Lake Michigan bears
silent witness to the streams of cars heading north and south,
headlights like glowing insect eyes, piercing the night. The other
side of the highway is crowded with high-rises, their glass, chrome
and concrete rising into the night: hives of activity within, quiet
sentinels without.
I have a cold bottle of Samuel Adams between my legs, a
Marlboro burning in the ashtray. Normally, beer and cigarettes are
not my vices. I care about my health, you see. But these are props,
the same as the deeper-pitched voice I use, same as my word
choice, which is much less sophisticated than someone with an MA
in English from the University of Chicago. The beer and cigarettes

are part of my costume. Tonight I wear faded, ragged Levi's 501s, the crotch faded, the buttons moving in an inverted question mark, emphasizing the bulge in my crotch.

When did gay men turn into no-charge prostitutes? Has it always been this way?

Whatever. I'm also wearing a Bulls T-shirt, the sleeves cut off raggedly, the neck cut low.

I take a swig of the beer, letting its cold bitterness snake down my throat, and turn up the tape player. Ironic. Leonard Cohen is singing, "There Ain't No Cure for Love."

I press down on the gas; ahead is my exit: Irving Park Road.

When I arrive, I see the apartment is a red brick six flat, identical to others all over the city. I ring the buzzer, and the guy doesn't even bother to ask who it is. No difference. We never exchanged names anyway.

Trudging up the stairs, waiting for the shotgun-cocking sound of a lock being turned, a chain sliding back into place. Someone waits to admit me. Someone I don't even know.

What a friendly world this is.

A door opens above.

What waits upstairs?

I round the bend and I see him. Nothing like his description, but who expected different? I am nothing like what I told him. No matter. As long as you're male and reasonably young and acceptable, you're in.

The guy has a good body and his lips curl into a grin as I head toward him, dragging on my Marlboro. He's wearing a pair of black bikini briefs. His moment of glory: this is what he's worked for all those long hours at the gym. Finally, someone to appreciate the shaved and defined pecs, the smooth washboard belly, the bulging biceps that I just know he will somehow maneuver to flex for me.

But he's much older than what I had expected. Mid-40s probably. His reddish-brown hair is thinning and the blue eyes are framed by crow's feet (a bottle of "eye-revitalizing" cream is in his medicine cabinet, I bet). The goatee, a desperate ploy to make himself look younger and hip, is embarrassingly ineffective. A cougar tattoo snakes down one of his arms.

"How you doin'?" I exhale a cloud of smoke and pass him as he opens the door wider to admit me.

"Great. Now that you're here."

The apartment is small, crowded with "contemporary" furniture: a black leather grouping in the living room, chrome and glass tables, spare jagged-looking twig and dried flower arrangements. On the walls, Herb Ritts posters of absurdly pumped-up young men in various settings: a garage, on the seashore.

The guy leads me into the bedroom. Platform bed, comforter thrown back, striped sheets. The nightstand holds the tools of his true trade: a plastic cup full of condoms he probably never uses, a couple of little brown bottles filled with butyl nitrate, a leather cock ring, a metal cock ring, and a large pump bottle of Wet. On the lower shelf, a stack of neatly folded, but ragged, white towels.

A dresser faces the bed and atop it, a color TV and DVD combination. On the screen, a wildly muscled dark-haired guy tries to sit on one of those orange traffic cones. Amazingly, he's beginning to succeed.

I grin.

The guy drops the black briefs and sits on the bed. Hoarsely: "Why don't you get undressed, man?"

"Why don't you do it for me."

Instant supplicant, he's on his knees before me, working the buttons on my jeans. I'm sure his eyes are glistening. Already his breath is coming faster.

I push his hand away. "Hold on." I lift the goateed face up to my own and look in his blue eyes, where nothing but desire and trust mingle. "I want you to lie down on the bed. Lie on your stomach."

He gets up and does as he's told. The half-moons of his ass practically glow in the darkness. A thin, whiter line disappears in his crack, where his thong was. The definition in his arms shows up perfectly as he raises his arms above his head to clutch the pillow.

His legs are parted, waiting.

"I just need to do something real quick. You stay right there." I look back at him as I exit the room. "You're a good boy, right? Do what you're told?"

"Yes, sir."

In the kitchen, I go quickly through the drawers until I find the one with the knives. For the first time, I get hard, and I think of the blood pumping, filling the spongy cavities.

The blood. Essence of life.

I strip down, leaving my clothes in a pile on the kitchen floor. I hope that I don't bring any cockroaches home.

I hold the butcher knife I chose to my side, concealing it with my arm, and head back to the bedroom.

He still lies there, waiting and trustful, thinking he's about to be penetrated.

And he is.

I move quickly to the bed and the guy is perfect: he closes his eyes, pulling the little brown bottle to his nose and inhaling deeply, for what seems like about 30 seconds in each nostril. Then he moves the little bottle to his mouth and inhales through that as well.

Just as I raise the knife, he turns to hand me the bottle of poppers. He sees the knife in my hand and for a moment, he doesn't know what to think.

What's wrong with this picture?

The confusion registers in his eyes, then it's replaced by terror. He half sits up, scuttling to the other side of the bed. "What are you doing?"

"Nothing, man. Don't get so excited. Can't we just do a little fantasy scene here?" I smile and imbue that smile with kindness and a hint of mischief. I'm able to keep calm. I want him to be reassured. It will be so much easier to enter him if he's relaxed.

Visibly, he grows calmer. His features relax, but a hint of wariness remains in his eyes.

"I kind of get into fantasy." I let a small laugh escape, as if I am embarrassed by this admission. "Couldn't we maybe pretend we're doing a little force scene here? I want to rape you, man."

He chews on his lower lip, and I notice he's gone soft.

"Look, we don't have to do this if you're not into it." I put the knife on the floor. "I just thought it would be kind of exciting." I smirk. "Did you really think I'd hurt you?"

"Well, no, of course not."

Of course he thinks I wouldn't hurt him. I suppose that's what everyone thinks.

Until someone *does* hurt them.

"Look, maybe we should just forget this. Not everybody is into the scene." I laugh. "But it can be kind of fun."

The guy's thinking; I can see it. And I know I've got him now. He rolls back over on his stomach, hugging the pillow. "Sorry," he says. "You just can't be too careful these days. Know what I mean?"

"Really."

He wiggles his ass at me. "Why don't I pretend to be sleeping."

"Perfect." I pick up the knife and move toward him.

In the background, a guy on the screen moans and shouts: "Oh shit, man, I'm gonna come!"

Chapter
Four

GREY LIGHT OF early morning filtered in through mini-blinds: slats of pale across the sheets. Ed turned, his arm reaching out grasping, clutching the pillow. In his dream-muddled mind, he hoped the pillow would be the man he used to grasp.

Before he even opened his eyes, his mind flooded with images of Dan: the long, lean form, the sandy blond hair, the large features that made his face seem more alive. Fingers played across the linen of the pillowcase, longing once more to feel the satin of Dan's chest, the hardness beneath.

Ed sat up and rubbed his eyes, disgusted. Would he never be over this? Would the sick longing in his stomach never vanish? It had been three months since Dan had packed his belongings, six months since Ed had told him to leave. Shouldn't it somehow be easier, since Ed was the one doing the dumping? And yet, he was taunted with dream images of Dan, always seen from afar; in his sleep, Ed was always trying to catch his eye, to offer him a smile.

But Dan never looked.

Ed rose from the bed, casting a glance back at the tangled mess of sheets, damp from perspiration in spite of the early morning chill coming in through the window.

Just as he was feeding a bag of rapidly rotting pears into his juicer, the phone chirped. Ed froze; today was his day off, and lately the phone had been silent. A weary nausea rose up in him, and with it a knowledge that it was the department calling. He checked the LCD on the receiver and saw he wasn't wrong. *Don't pick up.* He felt certain that bad news waited to be released by the touch of his hand on the receiver, quieting the ringing but opening a Pandora's box of untimely death.

Just as he was about to lift the receiver, an image from a month ago exploded in his brain like colors behind his eyelids. Timothy Bright, the strange, waifish little creature who had discovered the body of his friend, the hurt soul who couldn't seem to collect himself enough to hide his pain from the authorities.

There had been another so-called gay murder in the interim.
David Westhoff, a fixture around the north side, the area known as
Boys' Town, the kind of man most guys had availed themselves of
at least once, though they would never admit it, even to their
closest friends.

There were no leads in that murder either. Just gore and grisly
violence, a trail of senseless death leading nowhere.

"Hello."

"Comparetto?" The raspy, cigarette-scarred voice of his
superior, Roy O'Farrell, came through the line, urgency shading his
simple question. A quick image of the man flashed through Ed's
mind's eye: a balding, 47-year-old with a pot belly and a florid Irish
face, all the clichés of the Chicago south side Irishman, complete
with a drinking problem.

"That's me. What's up, Roy?" Ed paced, toying with the
buttons on the blender. He waited to hear that another of his
brothers had been found, mutilated, the hatred telescoped out on a
defiled body.

"I know it's your day off, but the Chief wanted me to ask you
to come in. It won't take long."

An alarm went off inside Ed. Roy never called detectives in on
a day off, unless something was very wrong. Had Ed goofed up
somewhere? Was a reprimand in store? Something worse?

"What is it, Roy?" Ed felt a cold finger of dread work its way
up his spine. In spite of being a detective, Ed always found a
mystery unappealing: unanswered questions were often the
harbingers of bad news.

"We just need to have a talk."

"Can't it wait? I've got a million—"

"No, it can't wait." O'Farrell sounded tired. "Please, Ed, just
get down here."

Ed needed to know if his premonition had been right. "Has
there been another murder?" he asked, praying for a negative
answer.

He got his wish. "No, not that you'd be concerned with,
anyway." Roy barked out a brief, sardonic laugh. Ed could hear
him light a cigarette. "There's a fuckin' murder every day," he said,
his voice barely audible. "Just get down here as soon as you can."

"I'm on my way."

The ride to headquarters seemed to take longer than usual: the
number of slow drivers spreading out across Lake Shore Drive
dramatically increased, the number of city workers repairing
potholes and flushing out sewers multiplied. Ed toyed with the
radio, glancing over his shoulder at the lakefront, did anything he
could not to think about what awaited him at headquarters. But he

couldn't help himself; there was a feeling of foreboding he couldn't shake. When he had first come out and the department knew, there had been some fear that he would be shunned. And he had been...a bit. He'd thought, or hoped, that would all vanish when people saw he was the same old Ed Comparetto, doing the same old honest day's work. Yet the sense the department was always looking for a slip-up somewhere on his part had never gone away. Roy O'Farrell had always been a to-the-point, direct sort of man, never one to play up suspense or couch his terms in anything less than bald talk. The fact that he wouldn't tell Ed what was the matter could only mean one thing: something was very wrong.

Ed weaved through the city traffic, heading south on Michigan Avenue to Roosevelt Road, where the grey home of Chicago police headquarters rose from its drab, sensible neighbors.

What the fuck's wrong now? Ed swallowed, wished he smoked so he'd have something to do.

O'Farrell's office was a mess, the color and grain of the wood of his desk long forgotten, buried under stacks of files, memos and the various detritus that came in on a daily basis. Ed had often wondered how the man managed to stay on top of things as well as he did. Even though regulations were against it, his office was clouded with cigarette smoke; a blue haze hung perpetually near the ceiling. The office smelled of coffee and tobacco.

"Why don't you close the door, Comparetto? Then grab yourself a seat. Want some coffee?"

"No, thanks." Ed sat, certain that adding caffeine and the acid from coffee to his already irritated stomach would put him over the edge. The 'close the door and have a seat' routine set Ed's nerves on edge: it was what superiors usually did when they were about to fire someone. Ed gave a sickly grin and tried to joke. "You're not gonna let me go, are you?" Surely not...

O'Farrell didn't look happy, and he didn't respond to what Ed hoped was a jesting question. But then, O'Farrell never looked happy. Today the grim, grey light outside revealed an increase in the number of worry lines around his mouth and eyes. Leaning forward in his squeaking desk chair, O'Farrell lit another cigarette and directed a plume of blue-grey smoke at the ceiling. Then he met Ed's eyes. "Look, I'm not gonna beat around the bush. They've asked me to let you go. I'm gonna need your badge and your piece."

For a moment, it seemed all the activity in the office just outside the closed door ceased. As if everyone was listening. Ed swallowed hard. *Oh my God, I'm right.* Ed knew he should be feeling something: anger, loss, confusion. But instead, there existed within him only an emptiness, devoid of color or shade. His mouth was

dry and there was an uncomfortable dampness beginning at his
temples. They had finally found a way to get rid of him.

But how?

O'Farrell waited for him to say something. And Ed wished
more than anything he didn't have to. His old fight-or-flee response
was on the blink. He wanted nothing more than to just sit here and
do nothing, say nothing. But O'Farrell waited; the script would not
proceed without Ed's input. "Why?" he finally managed to
mumble.

O'Farrell bit his lip. "You could say that we're not happy with
your progress on this gay killer thing."

"But, Roy—"

O'Farrell put up a hand to stop him. "Hear me out." He shook
his head. "Look, Ed, you've done a fine job up until now, with
everything. I couldn't have been more pleased with your
performance. Why you had to go and let the world know you were
gay was kind of a dicey choice, but I stood up for you when there
were grumblings about it. Anyway, that's most definitely beside
the point."

Was it? Ed wondered.

"But no one could have done more than I've done on this case.
Look at the file. I've tracked down every lead, gone through each
victim's personal life from A to Z, talked to everyone from
boyfriends to bartenders to dry cleaners. No one could have—"

"That's not the problem."

"What?"

"Most of your work has checked out—"

"What do you mean: checked out?"

"I mean that we can't have detectives falsifying witnesses."
O'Farrell shrugged.

"What the hell are you talking about?" Ed wanted to roll over
and wake up; none of this could possibly be happening. He didn't
have a clue as to what O'Farrell was talking about. Falsifying
witnesses? What the hell was that? He'd heard of falsifying expense
reports, but witnesses? Ed wasn't even sure what that could mean.

"I'm talking about Timothy Bright."

Ed rubbed a hand over his damp face; had the office always
been this warm? It was eerie that he had just thought of the elfin
Mr. Bright this morning.

"What about him?"

"You tell me."

"Don't play games. I'm freaked out enough as it is."

O'Farrell stared down at his desk, slowly shaking his head.
"All right. I'm not going to put you in the position of admitting
anything. Why don't we just say you resigned? I'm sure that's okay

with the brass. I already talked to them about it. You can have a few days to get your things together."

The room was beginning to move, slowly, nauseatingly revolving around him. O'Farrell was dismissing him, as if they'd already made some sort of insane gentleman's agreement that both would pretend things had been thoroughly discussed. But Ed still had no idea what O'Farrell was getting at. "I don't know what you're talking about, man. I really don't."

O'Farrell's eyebrows came together. A smirk raised the corners of his mouth. He let out a slow sigh. "I wanted to make this brief, spare you the embarrassment." He paused to light another cigarette from the butt of the last. "One of the first witnesses you said you talked to, a Timothy Bright, doesn't exist."

"What?"

"No one named Timothy Bright existed at the address you listed on your report."

"Okay, so maybe the address was wrong. Maybe he moved."

"It's all been checked out, Ed. We've searched through records for the entire Chicago area and come up with blanks. By the way, I insisted the search be undertaken when this whole pile of shit came to light. I wanted to find Timothy Bright."

"And you came up with nothing?"

"There were some Timothy Brights, but none that matched your description."

"I can find him."

"No. If he could have been found, we would have found him. Well, we did find him."

Ed blew out an exasperated sigh. "I'm following none of this."

"There *was* a Timothy Bright and he *did* live at the address you gave us and he *did* match your description, but that Timothy Bright was killed over two years ago."

"So someone's pretending to be him. Maybe the guy I talked to was the killer. That occur to you?"

"Of course it did. Listen, Ed, I tried to do everything I could for you. Things just didn't pan out. Look, I don't wanna talk about this anymore. You can appeal the decision, but we've got everything backed up...solid. I don't know why you did what you did, or how you even knew about this Bright character. Maybe he was a friend of yours?"

"A fellow fag?"

"Aw, don't pull this crap with me. People get tired. Sometimes when they get tired, they make like they're doin' their job when they're not. That's what happened, isn't it? But the sad thing is: a slip like that sends you out the door."

Ed couldn't think. His stomach churned, and coherent thought had suddenly become a vestige of his past. Without another word, he stood and walked from the office, not stopping until he got outside, where he could disappear into the cool air and the sounds of traffic, disappear into a world that no longer had any order.

ED DROVE THROUGH late afternoon traffic, oblivious to the cars around him, oblivious to the darkening clouds gathering in a pewter sky, foretelling rain.

He had been on his way home. That was his original intention: to hole up inside his Edgewater apartment, pull the blinds, and sit on the couch, no music, no TV. To sit and feel nothing seemed better than surrendering to the turmoil, anger and fear that bubbled just beneath the surface. His dog, a Rat terrier named Mia, would sit silently beside him, offering quiet comfort and demanding nothing. She always sensed when something was wrong.

What else had he to lose? Six months ago he was in a relationship with which he was happy; six months ago he was in a job that was fulfilling and had a career that looked promising.

Now, all of it was gone. It was funny how one could never truly guess what would happen...life kept itself interesting by offering an endless array of surprises.

Suddenly, the idea of sitting alone in his apartment seemed too much. It was the last thing he wanted.

Ed had never been much for drink, but today it seemed visiting a bar would be the appropriate course of action. His father had often drowned his sorrows, and his example had inspired in Ed a dislike for alcohol, smoke, dim lights. But drowning his sorrows suddenly had a lot of appeal. Especially the drowning part. Ed signaled, cut across a lane of traffic and exited Lake Shore Drive at Belmont.

The Round Up was Chicago's only gay country and western bar. And the only reason Ed decided to stop there was because there was handy parking in a nearby Walgreen's lot. Well, and the fact that watching men dressed as cowboys swirl and parade each other around a dance floor might prove amusing. Ed gave a nervous hiccup of a laugh as he thought of it, heading up Broadway.

Not that anyone would be dancing in the middle of the afternoon, he reminded himself. In fact, the place would most likely be empty.

The last image his brain produced as he pushed through the heavy wooden door was of himself, alone at the bar, with empty shot glasses crowded around him, a bottle of Rolling Rock slipping from his fingers. He would then be picked up by an older, fat man who would take him home and rape him.

"Sounds like the perfect ending for the perfect day," Ed whispered as he entered the dim interior.

Surprisingly, the place was not as empty as he imagined. In fact, it was quite lively. Happy hour was just beginning. A buffet was laid out at one end of the bar. Dolly Parton was singing "Two Doors Down."

Ed briefly considered turning around and heading back to his car. But too many eyes had already spotted him, and to do so would make him look like a fool, some closet case afraid to come inside.

He made his way to the bar and ordered a shot of Jack Daniels with a Rolling Rock. If he was going to drown his sorrows, he was going to do it right.

Three bottles of Rolling Rock and three shots later, Ed found he had almost forgotten the events of that afternoon. Although his dismissal and the loss of his career hung over his head like some large-winged dark bird, the alcohol had wrapped the trauma in gauze, making it fuzzy and distant, something that had happened to someone else.

The bartender, a young blond named Owen, set another green bottle of Rolling Rock down in front of him.

"I didn't order this."

The bartender smiled. "I know you didn't. It's from an admirer."

Ed turned the bottle slowly in front of him. One more beer was the last thing he needed. "Who?"

Owen winked and shrugged. "I'm not supposed to say."

Weariness suddenly washed over him. Another time, he would have been flattered. "Look. I don't want it." He shoved the bottle back across the bar.

"C'mon, it's already open. I'll just have to pitch it anyway."

Ed grabbed the bottle and turned on his stool, surveying the crowd of urban men done up in cowboy duds. Most were busy: engaged in conversation with friends while all the time trying to see who else was there and who might be casting glances at them.

But none were looking at Ed.

He took a swig from the bottle. The beer no longer tasted good. Bitter, it only served to increase the nausea that was welling up in him, stronger with each passing moment. On unsteady legs, Ed stood, holding on to the bar to maintain his balance.

He didn't want to be sick, not here in front of everyone. It would definitely not be the ideal way to cap a lousy day.

He slid into his jacket. Owen came up to him. "Leaving so soon? Before you've even figured out who your admirer is?"

A wave of nausea rolled over him. "Yeah," he whispered.

"Well, he told me to give you this." Owen held out one of the Round Up's business cards. Ed took it and turned it over. On the back a name and phone number was scrawled: *Timothy Bright, (847) 555-8976.*

A surge of adrenalin coursed through Ed; his nausea vanished, and he scanned the crowd once more for a small blond man, one who looked boyish from a distance, but headed toward trolldom close up.

No one fitting the description was in his view. Ed turned back to Owen, his eyes mutely appealing.

"He already left."

"What did he look like?" Ed's mouth was dry and his words came out thick.

"Short guy, couldn't have been more than 5'4", 5'5". Blond hair, mid-thirties, I'd guess." Owen leaned over, whispered, "I think you could do better."

Ed tried to smile, but knew the effort came out more as a grimace. Why was everything suddenly becoming unreal?

"Thanks." Ed slid the card into his pocket and headed out the door.

Chapter
Five

JOEY MANTEGNO WAS probably one of the most popular staffers at the Chicago Police Department's Central headquarters. Petite, only about 5'2" and weighing in at around 100 pounds, Joey's youthful face was graced by reddish-brown hair that curled around her face, wide-set large green eyes framed by thick black lashes, and a ready smile. Many detectives and officers found a daily excuse to go in and request information, whether they needed it or not. Never mind that she was happily married to an attorney, lived in Kenilworth, one of Chicago's most exclusive suburbs, and had three children, ranging in age from seven to thirteen. There was always hope that such a beautiful soul might suddenly need to shore up her self-esteem by inviting the attentions of one of Chicago's finest.

When her phone rang early on Monday morning, Joey had just completed filing the records on a drawn-out rape case that had finally been solved when the perp confessed over the weekend, after the 86-year-old woman he raped died at Cook County hospital. For Joey, such gruesome incidents were her daily fodder, and although her heart was sympathetic, her intellect prevented her from becoming too heavily weighed down by the heinous acts she witnessed each day from her basement office.

"Good morning."

"Joey? This is Ed Comparetto."

Joey's heart sank. She had heard what had happened to Ed before she left on Friday, and had brooded about it all weekend. Ed was not only one of the force's best and brightest detectives, he was a good friend, too. The two had shared many lunches together, and Joey knew all about Ed's break-up and the resulting despair. She knew the last thing he needed was to lose a job he valued. She had intended to call him and let him know that if there was anything she could do to ease the situation, she'd be happy to. But like most good intentions, it got swept away by the tide of demands of her own personal life.

She wondered why he was calling her now. "Ed? How are you, honey? I'm so sorry about what happened. There had to be a screw-up somewhere."

"Yeah, a colossal one. When I find out what it is, I'll let you know."

Ed's voice had lost its vitality and came out almost in a monotone. Joey had heard he falsified a witness statement, but was certain the Ed Comparetto she knew wasn't capable of such a thing. If anyone went by the book in these large granite headquarters, it was Ed.

"What can I do for you today?"

"A simple favor. I was wondering if you could get together some information for me on a murder that took place about two years ago. Sorry, I don't have exact dates. But I do have the name of the victim."

"Ed, you know I really shouldn't—"

"I know you really shouldn't and I wouldn't ask you if it wasn't really important."

Joey laughed. "Just because I say I really shouldn't doesn't mean I won't. God knows it's how I ended up married with three kids."

"See? 'Shouldn't' shouldn't be in your vocabulary."

"I guess you're right. So, who do we got here?" Joey pulled a legal pad in front of her and grabbed a pen.

"The guy's name is Timothy Bright. Lived up in Rogers Park, on Paulina, I believe. And I know it was around two years ago that the guy was killed."

"What do you need to know?"

"That's what I don't know exactly. Maybe it'll come clear to me when I have more information."

Joey wondered if Ed needed a rest.

"If you could just get me exact dates, places and so on, I'll take it from there."

"Hey, Ed, you know I'll do my damnedest." Joey scratched her head. "But, honey, in case you haven't heard the gossip, you've been let go. What do you need this for?"

"It's a long story. And one that, in all fairness, I should tell you about. But right now, if I just clue you in on what I know so far, you'll think I'm completely nuts."

"Sweetie, I already do."

They both laughed. Ed went on. "But listen: this is really important to me. Maybe if I can find some answers—and this guy could lead me to them—I could save my job. Let me just say that this Bright character is the reason I lost my job. So, if you could be an angel and help me out, you might be doing me a bigger favor than either of us realizes right now. I guess I just have to ask you to trust me on this."

"No one trusts you more. Listen, you know I could get in some real hot water for doing this, but that's not the problem. It may take me a little time. I don't want any inquiring minds wanting to know why I'm spending department time on a two-year-old case."

"Sure, Joey. I understand. I also understand that you'll do your best for me."

"Oh, if only you'd get over this gay thing, you'd see what my best really was."

"Harlot."

"Slut."

"Thanks a lot, Joey. I'll talk to you soon."

"You better."

ED HUNG UP the phone, blew out a sigh, and looked around his apartment. Mia sniffed anxiously at his legs and he knew he should take her out. Outside, the sky was the shade of blue that only autumn brings: rich vibrant color, so deep that Ed felt if he could reach high enough, he could touch the sky.

But he had no interest in going out and enjoying the Indian summer day. In other times, he and Dan would have hit the lakefront on mountain bikes or roller blades.

But those were other times.

Ed fingered the Round Up card in his hand, looking at the scrawled blue ink on the back.

"Timothy Bright, who the fuck are you?"

He pressed the Talk button on his cordless and punched in the numbers. Listening to the distant ringing, he pictured Timothy Bright, perched atop a piece of furniture, an imp, waiting for his call.

After three rings, a woman answered. "Hello." From one word, her deep voice told Ed a lot: she was cultured, probably affluent, and definitely not an evil little man who was turning his life upside down.

"Good morning," Ed stammered. "Could I speak to Timothy Bright, please?"

There was long pause on the other end, and Ed feared the woman would hang up. "Who is this?" she whispered.

"My name's Ed Comparetto. Timothy Bright gave me this number. He wanted me to call him."

"What is this? Some kind of joke?"

"No, ma'am. Not at all."

"I don't think this is amusing in the least."

"It's not intended to be, ma'am. Do I have the right number?"

"No, Mr. whatever the hell your name is, you most assuredly do *not* have the right number. I don't have time for this."

"Wait! Please don't hang up. I really don't mean to trouble you and I'm not playing a prank. Do you know of a Timothy Bright?"

The woman didn't answer, and Ed was already anticipating the click that would separate them when she said, "Timothy was my nephew."

Ed nodded and then felt stupid because she couldn't see and he didn't know what else to say. "I see."

There was another long pause. "No. You see: my nephew has been dead for over two years, so I don't see how he could possibly have given you this number. Unless, of course, you hang on to numbers for a very long time before calling."

"I'm sorry, ma'am. I didn't mean to upset you."

"I have to go."

"Is there any chance I could talk to you? Just for a few minutes? I could explain why —"

"Good-bye."

Ed's mouth was poised with more persuasion when he heard the click. He looked over at Mia, who was pawing at the door.

"All right, all right. I'm coming."

JOEY CALLED BACK later in the day, when Ed had given up on hearing from her. After all, it was almost five o'clock, and Joey was not big on overtime.

"Hi, honey. I got the information you wanted."

"Great."

"This is no pretty picture."

"I didn't expect it would be."

"No. I mean, this is really ugly. And I really want to know why you need this information."

"Is that a condition?"

"Of course not. I'm offended, Ed."

"Oh, don't be." Banter with Joey was fine, in the real world. Ed no longer lived there. "What did you find out?"

"Why don't I stop by on my way home and fill you in? I don't want to be staying here late, and I don't want anyone to overhear and start asking questions."

"That's fine. My calendar is pretty clear these days."

"Not funny. I'll be there in about an hour or so."

It had been a long time since the buzzer in Ed's apartment had sounded. The noise jarred him. Mia yipped and ran to the door.

Joey was like a visitor from another country. Just seeing her made Ed feel suddenly excluded from almost everything he had ever known. She brought with her all the memories of working for the force, all the hopes and ambitions Ed had had when he started working there just a few years ago. Now, she was like a member of an exclusive club to which Ed had been permanently denied access.

"Come on in, come on in. Grab a chair. Can I get you anything?"

"Coffee?"

"Coming right up."

After they were settled in, Joey pulled a sheaf of papers from her purse. "I could get fired if they knew I took these out of Records."

"I appreciate that, Joey."

"Two years ago, August. That's when Timothy Bright was murdered." Joey thumbed through the papers. "August 17th, exactly."

"What happened?"

"No one knows." Joey looked down at the floor and sipped her coffee. "I can see why you're interested."

"What do you mean?"

"I mean that this killing echoes real well these new killings, the ones you were working on before they, um, let you go."

"Similarities?"

"Similarities, hell. It's almost an exact replica of what's happened with the two killings from the summer and a couple of weeks ago. Mr. Bright was found, after several days, by his landlady in his bathtub. The water in the tub was red with blood. Mr. Bright's penis had been severed and inserted into his rectal cavity." Joey looked up at him, her face flushed. "I'm quoting from the report." She paused. "He had been strangled, but the coroner's report showed that the strangulation marks occurred after the guy was dead."

"That's a difference. The first guy, Tony Evans, was strangled to death. Mutilation was post-mortem."

"Right. The coroner's report showed Bright died from a perforated rectum. When that happens, all kinds of poison can — "

"I know, I know."

"The case was closed after a year. No one could find a clue. No motivation, nothing left behind. A big zero."

"Kind of like the more recent killings."

"Yeah."

"Anything else?"

Joey tapped the papers. "It's all in here. The victim's parents were dead. His only relative was an aunt up on the North Shore. He had no close friends that anyone could find. No enemies either, I suppose. Chalk it up to random insanity."

"Random insanity? Somehow, I get the feeling there's more to it than that."

"There usually is." Joey sipped her coffee and set it on the floor. She scratched Mia behind the ears and looked out the window at the darkening sky. "I hate to cut this short, but I've got to be getting home. Family obligations and all that crap."

"Understood." Ed rose from the slingback chair.

Joey shrugged into her windbreaker and caught his eye. "You gonna tell me why you wanted this information?"

Ed dug in the pockets of his jeans and pulled out the Round Up card, now tattered and worn from Ed's having handled it so much. He handed it to Joey.

She took it from him and examined it. When she saw the name and phone number on the back, she gave Ed a blank look. "I don't get it."

"A bartender gave me this card. He said it was from the person who sent me a beer."

Joey cocked her head.

"That was yesterday."

"Someone's playing a joke."

"Why would they want to do that? And how would they know I had any association with Timothy Bright?"

Joey shrugged.

"You know, don't you, that Timothy Bright was the first person I interviewed last August when the killings began? He discovered Tony Evans' body. And: I asked the bartender to describe the person who gave him the card."

Joey's face reflected confusion, and it wasn't much of a leap for Ed to understand why. This whole scenario seemed too bizarre and ghoulish to be believable. Joey cocked her head. "So you're saying this person who gave the bartender the card looked like Timothy Bright?"

"Yep."

"So, have you called the number?"

"Yeah. The woman who answered said Timothy Bright was her nephew."

"So this person had some knowledge of Bright."

"Of course, but who the hell is it?"

"Was Bright the person that got you in trouble with the force?"

"Yeah." Ed hung his head and whispered, "I just don't know what's going on."

Joey put her arms around him and squeezed. Her lithe form felt strange in Ed's arms, almost insubstantial. But comforting nonetheless.

Ed pulled away. "There aren't any photos in with those papers, are there?"

"Sorry, I couldn't get anything like that. Besides, from the report, any crime scene photos would make the victim look pretty damn unrecognizable." Joey reached for the doorknob. "If there's anything more I can do to help, you just call me. Hell, call me anyway. We can still do lunch."

"Sure thing."

Ed watched Joey walk out the door and back into her normal life. Again, he felt excluded. He went to the couch and sat. He picked up the papers, knowing they would only add to his confusion.

Perhaps somewhere, there was a clue.

Chapter
Six

MILT WEINSAP LIVED alone. He was the kind of man to whom appearances meant everything. The way he had decorated his little one-bedroom apartment was demonstrative of his love of appearances. The Edgewater apartment, just blocks from Lake Michigan to the east and the domiciles of several gangs to the west, had the look of a place one would expect to see leaping from the pages of some interior design magazine, its glossy pages bearing testimony to an almost slavish devotion to style and cleanliness.

As Milt fluttered around the living room, straightening magazines and making sure the bleached oak furniture and white sofa and chairs revealed not even the tiniest speck of dust or dirt, he kept one ear alert for the sound of the buzzer downstairs, the one that would let him know his gentleman caller had arrived. He stood back and surveyed the living room, liking the way the Deco sconce light fixtures gave a muted glow to the room, filling it with a warmth that at once flattered the almost minimalist design of the furniture and imbued the room with the kind of warmth that seemed sensual, almost erotic. Milt tiptoed into the bedroom where the overstuffed goose down white comforter had already been pulled back, revealing beige pinstriped sheets and a pile of matching pillows. The cherry wood, Jenny Lind furniture bore a high gloss. The mini-blinds had been opened enough to admit a dull yellow light from the sodium vapor lamp outside his window. Candles had been placed around the room, pillars, columns, and tapers on almost every available surface, awaiting the touch of Milt's sterling silver lighter. Milt knew that then the room would dance with light and shadow, flickering and giving the room the coziness of the private den of some wild beast.

Milt happened to catch a glimpse of himself in the mirror by the bed and was pleased with what looked back at him. Milt was a small man, but recent workouts had toned and hardened his 5'10" frame, giving definition to his abdominal muscles, enlarging and separating his pecs and subtracting the love handles from his sides.

His short red hair, buzz cut, complemented the goatee he had completed growing only a month or two before and the jade green contact lenses he had just put in.

He was 45 years old and had no intention of letting Mother Nature make him look any less appealing.

Milt crossed the room and pressed the key to shut down his Dell laptop. He didn't like the thought that it was this very device that was bringing him his gentleman caller. It was like some sort of electronic fishing lure. Milt would have preferred to have been discovered on a walk along Foster Avenue beach, just blocks away from his apartment, the wind off the lake giving his face a ruddy glow: irresistible.

But sometimes, Milt thought, we did what we had to do to make our dreams come true. Who said that one's true love couldn't be met in cyberspace? Why, Milt knew that while he was busy prospecting online, someone as desirable as he could be doing the exact same thing.

Milt slipped into his paisley silk robe and slid into a pair of black Calvin Klein boxers.

He had been through the routine before, so many times the routine had been fraught with disappointment. It seemed no one who showed up at his door was ever appreciative of all the care he took in making sure his apartment was clean, or even the care he took with his own personal hygiene, making sure he smelled of soap and perhaps just a hint of Tuscany cologne. It seemed all they ever wanted to do was copulate like animals, sometimes leaning against his front door, pants down, waiting to be serviced.

And Milt would comply. Hoping, always hoping, that after it was over and the animal was tamed, his suitor for the night would stay on and share a cup of Earl Grey with him, the two basking in a warm afterglow while the CD player spilled out Oscar Peterson.

But they never stayed. In fact, they often were out the door before their pants were completely zipped, leaving Milt alone to clean the semen from his chest.

And yet Milt considered himself an optimist. Each time he made a new "date" online, he hoped this one would be different. This would be the one who would compliment him on his refined taste, his mannish good looks, the one who would take him in his arms and stare into his eyes and tell Milt how fortunate he was to have logged on to Men4HookUpNow (his first time!) and gotten so lucky. Perhaps he'd even say they should wait to consummate their new relationship, because Milt was special and he wanted it to be much more than a quick sexual encounter.

And then there were the other online experiences, so many of those other experiences, where he'd get an instant message or e-mail asking for specific directions to his apartment, even giving Milt an estimated time of arrival and then the man would never show. Many nights, Milt had waited anxiously by his window, ears perking up each time a car parked in front of his building, sometimes even watching with enthusiasm as a lone male exited his car, and then his enthusiasm would sink as the male would walk to another building.

About this caller, Ed felt different. He knew he wouldn't be one of the game players. He knew this caller would show up. He recalled the manly voice, with just a hint of boyishness, asking him all sorts of questions before he made a decision as to whether he should pay Milt a visit. The kinds of questions designed to get to know Milt better, designed to make sure Milt was conveniently located, in short the kinds of questions someone serious about getting together would ask.

The buzzer sounded, and Milt's heart gave a small lurch.

Everything was at the ready. Everything was perfect.

This time it would be love, Milt was certain.

Milt hurried to quiet the buzzer, letting the person below in without asking for identification. No one else would be coming to call at this late night hour. He leaned on the Listen button, hearing the metallic bark of its release downstairs and the creak and slam of the glass-and-wood-framed door down below. Butterflies beat against his ribs as he imagined the heavy step of carpenter's work boots coming up his stairs, rounding the landing.

Milt stood poised at the keyhole, watching. Soon, a distorted figure appeared in the glass. For a moment, Milt's heart sank in disappointment. The man outside was not the burly blue-collar man Milt had hoped for, but a short boyish-looking man whose face was topped with a mass of messy blond hair, in need of a comb and a dollop of gel.

But Milt knew it was the inner soul of the man that counted, and he turned the deadbolt so that his caller would realize he was now on the right floor.

Milt took a breath and swung the door open. He smiled.

"Milt?" The voice that came out of the boy/man was higher than the one he had been enraptured with on the phone. No matter; the same thing had happened several times before. The fact that the voice was pitched slightly higher than the voice on the phone proved only one thing: that the caller wanted only to make a good impression.

And this was a quality Milt admired in a man. After all, impressions were so important.

"Hi," Milt said and swung the door open wider.

The man was shorter even than Milt, almost elfin. He looked

harmless as he swung by Milt. With him came the smell of cigarettes and beer, and in spite of his usual aversion to such scents, Milt was enchanted with the smell, conjuring up as it did images of men in bars, smoking and swilling beer while balls on a pool table cracked in the background, overlaid with the voice of Patsy Cline singing "Crazy."

Milt closed the door. "Ray?"

The man smiled, and his face was lit up by it. His teeth were two perfect rows of white, glorious. The smile changed his entire face, bringing out a radiance and, Milt thought, a depth and decency not immediately apparent.

"Hello," Milt said. "Can I get you something to drink? I have a nice bottle of Chardonnay chilling in the kitchen."

"Chardonnay? My favorite. Bring me a glass, would you?"

"Coming right up." Milt hurried into the kitchen, where two Waterford crystal wineglasses chilled in the freezer. He removed them and took the wine, already uncorked, from the top shelf of the refrigerator. Good wine should be allowed to breathe, Milt thought, listening to the *glug glug* sound of the wine as he filled each glass.

"Here you are, Ray." Milt handed him his glass and thrilled at the electricity that went through the two of them as their fingers briefly touched.

Ray clinked his glass against Milt's. "Cheers," he whispered, and his pale blue eyes met Milt's for the first time. Milt could see a quiet fire dancing in those eyes and was certain that fire spoke of an intelligence and grace he had searched for all of his adult life.

Maybe, just maybe, this was the one.

"Would you like to sit down?"

In response, Ray grabbed a coaster and set his wineglass on the coffee table. "What I'd really like to do is kiss you."

Milt closed his eyes for a moment, then set down his own glass. He noticed his hand was trembling, ever so slightly. Milt moved closer, wondering how the faded jeans Ray wore would feel pressed against the shimmering fabric of his robe.

When Ray's arms encircled him, Milt was pleasantly surprised. Even though the man was small, his grasp and reach were those of a much larger man, all-encompassing, engulfing.

Milt surrendered to the embrace. The hot touch of Ray's lips on his neck blocked out all thought and the stubble of Ray's beard on the sensitive skin of his neck caused Milt to feel flushed.

He was sure love had arrived.

After they finished their wine, Ray took Milt's hand and led him into the bedroom. Quickly, Milt dropped his robe on a Queen Anne chair in the corner of the room, then hurried about, lighting all dozen candles. When he was done, he switched off the

overheard and stood back, satisfied, as the room filled with a
warm, flickering glow.

He stared into Ray's eyes with what he hoped was a
meaningful expression, conveying more than mere lust. He hoped
his look said, "You are special. You are the one I could be happy
with."

He felt that Ray picked up on his meaning as he crossed the
room to take him, once more, in his arms. Milt surrendered to the
tight embrace, surrendered as he felt Ray's thumb hook into the
elastic waistband of his shorts and slide them slowly down over his
thighs, his knees, until they were in a heap that Milt kicked away.

And then the passion rose and Ray was kissing him all over,
wetting his face, throat, chest and stomach with his tender,
fluttering kisses.

"Lie down on the bed while I get undressed."

Milt lay across the white comforter, his ass white in the
flickering glow of the candles. He watched himself in the mirror,
trying to imagine how inviting he must look to Ray.

And Ray was there in the shadows, slowly removing his
clothing, revealing a body whose definition was sharpened by the
half light. His tousled blond hair was a warm glow in the flame.

Milt couldn't wait for the moment when he would feel the lithe
yet manly form stretched out of top of him, his sex pressing
insistently against him.

This time would be like no other.

This time would be *making love.*

Ray bent over, fumbling in the pocket of his jeans. Milt closed
his eyes for a moment, appreciating the consideration of this man.
Obviously, he had brought his own condoms, so unlike so many
others of his suitors, who defiled his ears with terms like
"bareback" or "fucking skin on skin."

This one, however, was thoughtful, considerate. Milt wiggled
against the comforter, feeling its downy warmth beneath him and,
he hoped, making him look more inviting.

Milt glanced into the mirror once more and froze.

He let out a little groan and tried to right himself but for a
moment, was paralyzed.

Ray did not have a condom in his hand, but a large hunting
knife.

Milt twisted over, drawing his knees to his chest, covering his
quickly withering erection. His mouth had suddenly gone dry and
it was with great effort that he formed the words. "What are you
doing?"

It was then Milt saw the face he had seen as kind twist into the
face of a demon with a simple, yet demented, smile. "Just getting

my knife out. My trusty Bowie." Ray winked. "It'll make things more fun. A little role-playing is all. A little rape scene." He barked out a short laugh. "You didn't think I was gonna hurt you, did you?"

Milt's throat felt constricted. His heart pounded. "No, uh, of course not. Y'see, I'm not into anything like that." With a mighty effort, Milt managed to work some spit down his throat. "I think you better go now."

"Why, sweetie? When the party's just beginning?" Ray moved closer to the bed, weighing it down at one side with the pressure of his knee.

Milt scooted backward, making himself into a little ball, spine rigid against the headboard. He was panting now; perspiration trickled down his sides from his armpits. The bed was against the wall, and the only way he could get off of it was to go toward Ray, something he desperately did not want to do.

"I want you to go. Please." Milt hated the way his voice had suddenly become so whining. There was no authoritativeness, no force behind it. It was the voice of a scared little boy: high, wheedling.

"I wouldn't hear of it. The party's just beginning."

"Put the knife away. You're frightening me."

"Come on. A boy like you...you probably appreciate a big old knife." Ray lifted the knife so its stainless steel took on added brightness in the candlelight. "A big old *piercing* knife." He chuckled and Milt cringed at the sound of the laughter, unconnected to anything he had known as human.

Why hadn't he listened to himself when he had first started going online? He had told himself then that these were strangers and you didn't know who you were letting into your house. But it had been a year of such alliances, and nothing bad had happened. The fear had disappeared, proven wrong by scores of no-shows and men just wanting to get off quickly and without involvement.

And now the fear was twisting inside him, an unwelcome parasite, making his stomach churn and his heart race, blood pounding in his ears.

With one deft motion, Ray sprawled across the bed, knife aloft. He plunged the knife downward, just missing Milt's thigh as he scurried away, the knife buried in his comforter and mattress, sending up a spray of feathers and foam dust. Milt managed to get to his knees, crawling and grunting, heading toward the footboard.

The second time the knife came down it glanced off Milt's shin, and the warmth of his own blood set off new alarms. For just a moment, he thought of how the blood would stain the $300 comforter and the sheets beneath it.

He gripped the footboard, trying with desperation to use it to hoist himself out of the bed and screamed as the knife plunged in deep this time, just at the top of his buttocks. "Please, no," he whispered.

But Milt did manage to propel himself somehow over the footboard and landed in a heap on the hardwood floor. Something cracked in his wrist and he winced, but ignored it, scrambling to his feet and running for the door.

The next knife-blow hit him as he reached the front door. He felt it break through the skin and muscle of his back, the blade's penetration white-hot, searing, delivering to him a pain unimaginable and breathtaking.

Milt slid to the floor, curling into a little ball, right there by his front door. His breath was ragged and wheezing. "Please, sir," he whimpered. "Please don't hurt me." Milt scrunched his eyes together as he watched Ray raise his knife once more.

Chapter
Seven

HELENE BRIGHT KNEW, as she went toward the back of her bedroom closet, this little exploration was not a good thing. Almost accusing, the cardboard moving box had always sat at the back of the closet, next to orderly rows of shoes, beneath rows of dresses and blouses. The box contained nothing more than letters, old photographs, report cards, and other documentation of life: the papers and other detritus used to prove we exist. They meant nothing, really, when life passed. Perhaps they meant nothing when we lived.

But they meant something to her, and as she crouched before the box, gingerly holding out her hand in an offer of peace as if warily approaching a wild animal, she questioned whether doing this would do anything more than louse up what was already a lousy day. Opening the box, she pictured herself a matronly Pandora, clothed in the vestments of Chicago's North Shore. But unlike Pandora, she knew what the box contained.

Her memories. All the papers, photographs and records conjured up mental images. Images she had longed to submerge, sink beneath the acquisition of clothing, antique furniture, gourmet foods, bottles of wine that carried price tags in the hundreds and sometimes even thousands, cars, more. When acquiring things did not blot out the memories, she always had her trusty Dunhill cigarettes and a Bloody Mary at the ready (just as she did now).

Kneeling against the hardwood floor, she set the half-drunk Bloody Mary to her right and put her cigarette between her lips. Pulling the box out from under the row of dresses sent up a small cloud of dust.

She stared at it uncertainly, almost as if she didn't know what it contained. Her heart pounded; she feared its contents, thought opening it could release scabrous, long-nailed fingers that would grab her face, rend her flesh and cut off her air.

Why did she have to look in the box anyway? It had been years since she had leafed through its contents, years since she had even thought about her nephew, Timothy. A conscious act of will had ensured she didn't think about him and the horrible way he had died. She had spent most of her energy these last few years blocking out the memories, trying to sever any ties, emotional or otherwise, she had with him. It hadn't been easy. When she had been able to keep him out of her conscious, everyday thought, he would creep into her slumber late at night, small hands poised above her face, ready to strangle or soothe; she never stayed asleep long enough to find out which. On those nights, she would awaken, bathed in sweat and panting, sometimes even beating her frustration into her pillow. "I've failed! I've failed!" she would cry into the empty room, knowing the phrase went beyond merely failing to keep him out of her mind.

She slid her fingers under the top of the box and lifted the lid. Failed? she thought. Had she failed? Would a jury of her peers convict her? She had tried to do her best by him. Was it her fault he turned out to be a, she could barely even think the word, let alone say it aloud: homosexual?

Some would say it *was* her fault. She lifted out the photograph from its place on top of everything else. Seeing his face again brushed away the mental cobwebs that had formed around his image, bringing into sharp focus his beautiful, waifish features. She sucked in some air as too many memories came rushing back. A ravaged apartment, walls splattered with blood. Mysteries never to be answered, mysteries certainly never to be probed by her mind, which was too tired and, she could admit, too relieved that everything was tied up prettily in the end, in spite of the tragedy. "Too pretty to be a boy," her friends always told her, sometimes in front of Timothy himself, as if this were supposed to be some kind of compliment.

There we are, she thought, sliding the side of her hand across the satin grain of the photograph to free it from its screen of dust. "My, how I loved you," she whispered to the blond image below, the bright blue eyes, like frozen sky, staring back at her. She held the picture away from her, remembering.

His eighteenth birthday. She had worked for weeks, making it special. Dinner at Charlie Trotters, followed by a play afterwards at the Palace. What had they seen? It didn't matter. Afterwards, she had instructed the driver to take them down to Lake Michigan. They walked along the lakefront, hand in hand, looking more like lovers in the moonlight than aunt and nephew.

And I liked giving that impression.

That night, the air had been warm, the moon a sliver of pewter hovering over the waves, sending out a sheath of brilliant white across the gently rolling water.

She took a big swallow of Stoli and tomato juice. Were her hands trembling?

She remembered standing by the dark water and thinking *if only...* If only this moment could last, if only age didn't separate us, if only familial ties, forged in blood, could be undone...

The photograph had been taken earlier, before they had gone out: Timothy so handsome in his navy blue Brooks Brothers suit, she in her glittering Bob Mackie dress, black hair pulled back to show off the white sheen of her skin and large greenish-brown eyes, the eyes of a cat.

She didn't think she was flattering herself to say their age difference wasn't all that apparent. Even though she had been more than twice his age at the time, she still looked like a girl, still blushing, pert nose turned up with surgical precision.

It was after he had gone, just two years later, that she had begun to age.

She slid the photograph back into the box.

Why had that bastard called, looking for Timothy?

Why couldn't the past lay dead, like her nephew?

She slammed the cover back on the box, stood and kicked it back into the shadows, where it belonged.

Perhaps tomorrow she would come up here and take everything out and burn it. After all, the memories it contained had nothing to do with her life now, nothing at all. She was as far removed from that box as she was from the Sahara. She didn't know why she hadn't done it years ago.

Besides, what the box contained could, in the event something unforeseen should happen to her, start a whole string of probing questions. Questions neither she or anyone near her would ever be prepared to answer.

But right now, it was time for another Bloody Mary.

Chapter
Eight

PEOPLE IN CHICAGO are of two opinions on the main branch of its public library. Some of them love its large, imposing red brick structure, topped with what look like huge greenish metal gargoyles and filigree, making the building unique among Chicago's other architectural treasures. Those same people would say that a city as large as Chicago should have such an imposing structure, a testimony to Chicago's intellectual life. Others hate it, thinking the structure is an embarrassment, gothic and shockingly modern all at once, a waste of taxpayer dollars when a perfectly good structure existed before, right on Michigan Avenue.

Now, as Ed made his way through the streets of the Loop to enter the library's quiet portals, he was not thinking of architectural innovation or even the need for such a building. He wondered what he would find, as he scanned microfiched images of old *Chicago Tribunes*, looking for answers.

Ed made his way quickly to the periodicals section of the library, then felt lost among all the materials there. He was ashamed to admit to himself that he'd never been here and didn't know where to begin.

"Can I help you find something?"

Ed turned at the sound of the deep, slightly raspy voice, and saw a young man, tall, with dark, curly hair, his face enhanced by a reddish mustache and goatee. The young man wore jeans, hiking boots and an off-white cable-knit sweater a size or two too large. Ed's first impulse was to refuse the offer; after all, he had been a detective with one of the largest police forces in the country and should be able to figure things out for himself. And who was this guy anyway?

"You work here?" Ed asked, sizing up the young man, noting his youth and his casual dress. Shouldn't an employee wear something more official-looking?

The guy gave him a lopsided grin, his full lips turned up at one corner. "Five years. Is there something in particular you were looking for?" The guy's blue eyes seemed to flash for just an instant and Ed had to wonder if there was more than a solicitation for help going on here. As always, he wondered how obvious his sexual orientation was. Ed was about to dismiss the guy when he looked around once more, daunted by the imposing stacks of periodicals, the drawers upon drawers of newspapers and magazines.

"I wanted to check out a couple old *Tribunes*. Could you point me in the right direction?"

"What did you need?"

"August 17th, a couple of years ago. I'd just like to see all the papers around that time."

"Not a problem. Why don't you grab a seat at one of the readers," he motioned to rows of carrels with microfiche readers, "and I'll get you set up."

"Sounds great." Ed was relieved. This might go much quicker and more easily than he had thought. Ed made his way over to a seat near the end of a row and arranged his pen and legal pad on the wood surface of the desk. He could feel eyes on him as he sat and glanced up. His new helper was looking back at him. When he saw Ed staring, he turned quickly and disappeared.

It didn't take long. The guy came back within moments with a small box. He dropped it on the table in front of Ed.

"You know, don't you, that I'm really not supposed to do this."

"What?"

The guy shrugged and smiled. The smile changed his face completely, making him look like a little boy. Ed turned to stare at the blank screen of the microfiche.

"I mean, we're supposed to get these requests in writing, on ridiculous little slips of paper, and then process them in order."

"I didn't ask for any favors."

"I know you didn't. The boxes are all labeled. Do you know how to work the machine?"

Ed was about to respond that of course he knew how, then realized he didn't. A trip to the library had turned into a small exercise in humility. "Why don't you show me?"

"I'd be happy to." That smile again. "After all, I do have all the answers. I'm a librarian."

Ed waited.

"You were supposed to laugh."

"Oh."

The young man flicked the machine on and explained to Ed how to load the film and scan through the various pages. It seemed simple enough.

"Thanks a lot."

"I'll be right over there at the desk if you need anything else."

"Thanks."

"My name's Peter Howle."

It took Ed a moment to see the extended hand, with its long fingers, the veins standing up in sharp relief against the smooth, white skin. His knuckles were coated with dark, coarse hair. After a moment, Ed shook the hand.

"Got a name?"

Ed snorted out his own small version of a laugh. "Ed."

"Okay, Ed. I'll be right over at the desk."

"Thanks again."

Peter stood behind him for several uncomfortable moments before walking away.

Ed whispered to himself. "Jesus."

It didn't take him long to find what he was looking for. Timothy Bright's death was front page news. Ed stared for a long time at what appeared to be a college yearbook photo. Even though the photo was grainy, reduced to dots too large to provide much of a fine resolution, Ed could see that the man identified as victim Timothy Bright was the same man he had talked to when he investigated the first murder last summer. There was, even in the poorly reproduced photograph, the same air of boyish innocence, the boyishness carried almost a little too far for someone his age.

Ed hadn't even read the accompanying story and already he was chilled. This *was* the same guy he had talked to, there was no doubt about it, and yet here Timothy Bright was, in front of him, dead, in a newspaper two years old.

His detective's instincts failed him. How could this be? An amazing case of look-alikes, made even more improbable by the fact that the look-alikes shared the same name?

Ed's stomach churned, the unreality of the situation slamming into his psyche, making him queasy, making him want to forget the whole business. He wanted to stand and go back to his apartment, open today's *Tribune* and just look for a new job.

But that wasn't an option. How could he leave this behind? He had to find out what was going on. This all seemed impossible, but it had happened. It had happened to him; he knew he had spoken to this person.

Maybe the Timothy Bright Ed talked to was a ghost, appearing because he had died the same way one of his brothers had died and he wanted to point Ed in the right direction. Maybe this ghost had a message from beyond that would finger the killer, who was, perhaps, the same twisted individual who had murdered Timothy Bright nearly two years before.

Bunk. Timothy Bright was alive when Ed spoke to him. Ed had

put an arm around him and the flesh and bone beneath his arm felt as solid as his own. No ethereal wisps of ectoplasm, but blood, muscle, hair and bone.

And all that physical reality was perfectly embodied in the neatly boxed photograph on the front page of a two-year-old *Chicago Tribune*, with its simple, yet chilling caption, "Homicide victim Timothy Bright."

In spite of the queasiness and dizzying cold fingers touching his spine, Ed turned his attention to the story, forcing his eyes to scan the type. The story told him basically the same news Joey had brought him the other day, but it was fleshed out with detail Joey may have been too embarrassed to admit. Things like how the victim was found nude, with evidence of sexual molestation. That his rectum had been perforated by a sharp object, which was the injury the coroner had determined had killed him. Post-mortem stab wounds and evidence of strangulation.

Ed swallowed, mouth suddenly dry, tasting of cotton. The same signs of hatred of gay men he had witnessed the day he met Timothy Bright were all here in this story. Timothy Bright looked like the victim of a fag basher from hell, much as his "friend" Tony had appeared to be such a victim, floating in his bathtub of gore.

Other details: the victim's apartment was in a state of disarray, almost looking as if it had been ransacked. Blood-spattered walls and signs of struggle.

Near the end of the story, Ed found that Timothy Bright was survived by Helene Bright of Wilmette, his aunt and former guardian.

A voice came back to Ed, buzzing with what now seemed a macabre intensity through his telephone. "Timothy Bright was my nephew." Ed noted the name on his legal pad. He could find Helene Bright and, like it not, she would talk to him.

"Find everything you need?"

The voice startled Ed enough that he jumped. He turned to find Peter Howle standing behind him. Peter leaned over and looked at the screen. "Pretty gruesome stuff."

"Yeah, very gruesome," Ed mumbled. "I think I've got all I need...at this point." Ed didn't want that to be taken as a double entendre, so he added: "Thanks a lot. You've been very helpful."

"All done?"

Ed massaged his temples. "I guess so. Although I don't know if I'm any less confused than when I came in here."

Peter laughed. "I don't know if *I'm* any less confused than when I came in here."

"Yeah, well, I guess we've all got our problems."

"Want me to put this stuff away for you?"

"That would be great."

Peter leaned over to flick off the microfiche. Ed watched as the image of Timothy Bright faded, then died. He wished he could make the image fade as easily from his mind.

"If you need any more help with your research, give me a call." Peter held out a Post It note. His phone number was written across the yellow surface.

Ed didn't want to be rude. He took the paper and stuffed it into his jacket pocket. He then swept his pad and pen into the black leather backpack he had brought with him and stood.

"Thanks again."

"Any time."

Ed left the library with the feel of Peter Howle's eyes burning into his back and the image of Timothy Bright's photograph burning into his memory.

Chapter
Nine

FROM HELENE BRIGHT'S Journal, April 28, 1977

What a day this has been. I'm tearing my hair out with the luncheon I'm planning at the club, the derby party I'm trying to get finalized here, and the assorted sundries I'm responsible for in just keeping my life on track. And then little Timothy, dear sweet child that he is, has been accused of something by one of the neighbors that I simply refuse to believe. Still, I find myself having to deal with a crying child and a disgruntled mother.

The Watsons three houses down recently "adopted" this horrible little creature, a Great Dane puppy. Why someone would want to take this horse of a slobbering beast into their home is beyond me, but people's pet choices have always eluded me. Animals are for zoos, not peoples' homes. I would never own one myself: the smell and the hair alone are nauseating and threats to our general well-being. To the point, though: Claire Watson came pounding on the door about 11 o'clock this morning, saying she had something she wanted to show me. She was obviously distraught, eyes red rimmed and just this trembling cowering demeanor that I found totally inappropriate. I was in the middle of going over the menu for the Derby Day party and had to put that aside to traipse down the road to this woman's house. She said not a word the entire way there. And when I asked her what the matter was, she would only say, "You'll see."

When we arrived at the Watson's Tudor fronted monstrosity (ah, the tackiness of the nouveau riche), I found her son, Brian, sniveling on the porch. I asked him what the matter was and before he could even respond, Claire pulled me inside the house. Pulled hard enough to hurt my arm. I was shocked. I snatched my arm away from her and glared. "What's the matter with you? You hurt me."

Claire gave only a snort of laughter in response, laughter that was mirthless and cold. By this point, I was beginning to feel worried. I still hadn't a clue as to what was going on and had even considered turning on my heel and going home. Busy as I was, I had no time for mysteries and games of suspense. I'll leave those to the trashy paperback crowd.

"Follow me," Claire instructed and I was taken aback. Who did this woman think she was? I asked her that very question, becoming more and more peeved by the second.

"I believe I'm a concerned mother. And when you see what I have to show you, I hope you'll be a concerned aunt." Her eyes were almost sparkling with outrage. She added, "That is, if you have a shred of decency in you."

I was so dumbfounded by this treatment that I didn't say anything. I followed her mutely down a hall done up in totally inappropriate modernist prints and crowded with tacky, overpriced reproduction furniture.

Claire switched on the light at the top of the basement stairs. "This won't be pleasant, but I felt you needed to see it," she said before descending the stairs.

I followed her down and I have to admit was beginning to feel a wee bit nervous. There was an odd, very distasteful smell coming up from the basement and when I commented on it, Claire said only, "It gets worse."

Inside the laundry room, I finally discovered what all the fuss was about. It appeared someone or something had gotten hold of their Great Dane puppy. The creature lay dead in a pool of blood on the concrete floor, its brown eyes staring at nothing.

Claire seemed to be watching me as I took in the corpse. Its belly had been slit open and, along with a tremendous amount of gore, its entrails had been pulled out. Ropes of intestine lay near the dog's stomach, sticking to the darkening and rapidly congealing blood. I felt my bile rise and raised a hand to my mouth, fearing I would vomit.

"Pretty horrible, isn't it?"

I nodded, feeling too sick and weak to say anything at that particular moment. Finally, I did manage to say, "I've seen enough. Can we get out of here?"

Claire led me out of the laundry room and into the finished part of the basement where the Watsons had one of those rooms people are calling 'family rooms.' She was decent enough to let me sit on the couch; she sat in a chair across from me and stared. That's all: simply stared. Her eyes were once more brimming with tears and her lower lip was quivering. What did she want me to do? Console her? Wrap my arms around her and tell her everything would be all right?

What she told me next had to be a lie.

"Brian says Timothy did this."

I laughed in spite of my churning stomach. Timothy has to be one of the gentlest boys around. I've seen so much rough housing among the neighborhood boys and Timothy would never even take part in any of that. So how could he possibly have done something like this? "That's preposterous," I told her. "I think you should check again with your own. That's not my Timothy's handiwork, you can be sure of that, Claire."

She regarded me again with a look of disbelief.

"Brian loved that dog." And then she broke at last into tears. "He's been begging us for the last year to get him one."

"Oh, you know how boys are."

Her eyes widened as if I had just said something shocking. But I wasn't about to sit there and let her accuse Timothy of something of which he just is not capable.

"Brian told me that Timothy told him he wanted to see what the dog looked like on the inside. He used the butcher knife from the block in the kitchen."

"No, that's not possible," I said, standing on legs that I must admit were a tad bit unsteady.

Claire stayed where she was, staring at the floor. Her voice was barely above a whisper. "Brian says this isn't the first time he's done something like this. He says Timothy has tortured insects and the Timmons' cat turned up missing a couple of weeks ago. I think you should ask Timothy about that."

"I'll ask him nothing of the sort." How dare this woman say such a thing! With each passing moment, I was growing more and more outraged. The nerve of this woman knew no bounds. I kept seeing the dog and it was making me more and more ill. I needed to get outside, where the air didn't stink of blood and entrails.

I headed for the stairs.

"You'll have to pay for this, you know." Claire shouted at me as I headed up the stairs.

"I'll pay for nothing. This was not the work of my nephew. I think you better look carefully at your own household before accusing innocent neighbor children," I shouted back. "Timothy is about the gentlest boy you'd ever want to meet. And you know it."

And with that, I hurried from the house.

I can't write anymore. I did not, and will not, ask Timothy about this disagreeable matter. I don't want to upset him.

Perhaps tomorrow will be a more sane day. I hope so.

Chapter
Ten

MARK DEITRICH HOPED the guy didn't show up. He had been disillusioned so many times in the past by guys whose pics were, well, overly flattering. And the one on the way didn't even have a pic.

Mark was suddenly very tired of all the online games and even the games played in the bars, superficial and never what he really wanted. Besides, a sense of weariness washed over him, filling him with a lethargy that bordered on comatose. He wanted nothing more than to just hop into bed, curling up with the latest Stephen King and letting those fantastic nightmares lull him off to sleep. He would awaken the next morning hopeful. Tomorrow he would meet someone who was in it for more than just the sex. That would be the start of a relationship, the first he'd had with a man in his twenty-six years.

Mark went into the bedroom, shooed his two cats, Chloe and Purdy, off the bed, and pulled back the comforter. He kicked off the grey Nike shorts he wore and looked at himself in the mirror over the bed.

Why couldn't the guys online be honest? So many of them, when they did bother to show up, were disappointments, nothing like their pics or profiles. Didn't they realize they would be found out as liars as soon as their prospective "date" opened his door?

He guessed they were like salesman, hoping against hope that once they got in the door, he could be persuaded.

But they never could persuade Mark. More often than not, he tried to muster up an apologetic expression before saying the line that would send them away. "Sorry. I think I'll take a pass."

He would have respected them more, he thought, if they had tried to argue. Even if they had called him a jerk. But they were all wimps, and if they didn't tell him that the situation was "cool," they would at least walk away, wordless, head hung low in disappointment. Mark knew he was good-looking, everything he claimed online, and coming so close to finding what he was sure they were seeking had to be hard for them. *Listen to you! Ever hear of modesty?*

But he wasn't about to sleep with a guy just because he'd bothered to make the trip to his front door. It was the guy's own fault, anyway, for not being honest.

Mark pulled the covers up around him. He was on page 676 of *Insomnia* and wanted to get through it. Why did King have to write these long tomes that took him weeks to read? He had three other books waiting and it seemed the pages just kept coming, no end in sight. But he was too far along in the book to just put it aside.

The buzzer sounded. "Oh shit," he whispered, throwing back the covers and setting his book on the nightstand. He was tempted to just let it sound a few times, inducing in him a guilty nervous tension, and not answer it. The guy would go away eventually. Where had his horniness disappeared to?

Still, he couldn't just leave his visitor down there. That was exactly the kind of behavior he abhorred. He slid into his shorts and went to the front hallway, where he pressed the intercom buzzer.

"Who is it?"

"It's Ray, from online."

Mark buzzed him in, wondering if this guy would be the blond muscle-boy he promised. Fat chance.

He waited by the front door, thinking the guy would have to be an Adonis for him to do anything tonight. There was no anticipation as he imagined the elevator bringing the guy up, only dread. *But hey, get through this and you can crawl back into bed and let sleep overtake you. Another night alone, chalk it up.*

A tentative knock.

Mark peered through the peephole and saw nothing. *This does not bode well*, he thought, imagining the guy stepping back, out of view. *If he was everything he said he was, he would not hide from my view. He would step proudly up for inspection, if he had any confidence in his looks.*

Oh well, I didn't really want anything tonight anyway.

Mark swung the door open.

The guy looked like a little elf. In spite of that, Mark was certain he was much older than the 27 years he had said on the phone. 37 was more like it, and that was giving him some credit.

No sugar tonight, Mark hummed mentally. "Listen, I'm really tired. I think I'll take a pass. Sorry."

The guy's reaction was swift and unlike the responses Mark was used to seeing. Sure there was a hint of disappointment, but the way his blue eyes came alive told a tale of rage, too dark for him to even consider letting this stranger in.

The guy was scary.

"Are you sure? You wouldn't have to do anything. Just lay back and let me take care of you."

Mark shook his head. "Sorry, man, another time, maybe. I just don't think I'd be much fun." He started to close the door.

The guy put up his hand to stop Mark from closing the door. Mark was surprised...and a little taken aback. *I guess he's not used to getting an argument. Well, he'll get more than that from me.*

"You won't be disappointed."

"No, man, it's you who'll be disappointed. Really." Mark put a hand to his forehead, as if thinking. "Look, why don't you give me your number and I'll call you later in the week."

"Sure you will."

This was the kind of reaction Mark had wished for. A guy with some spunk. Only there was nothing pleasant about this. Mark wished he had just stayed in bed. Why did he always have to be a decent guy? It was a curse he carried around with him.

"Really. I've got to go." And Mark pushed the door closed, listening with relief as the door latched.

He looked outside the peephole and could still see the guy out there. *He's probably coming up with a new tack. Well, fuck him.*

As soon as Mark had turned away from the door, the knock sounded. He sighed and stared at the door, waiting for the knock to repeat itself. It did. "Go away, man. Enough."

The guy's reply came, muffled, through the wood. "Hey, man, it's cool. I'm sorry if I came on a little strong. Can you just let me in to use the bathroom? I'll be out in two seconds."

Mark gnawed at a hangnail, wondering what he should do. Common sense told him to just leave things alone, crawl back into bed, and try to get some sleep. But the part of him that his mother had always prevailed on to have good manners and to be a gentleman also spoke up. And, in the end, Mark listened to the voice of his mother. Where was the harm in letting the guy use the bathroom? After all, he had driven all the way down here at Mark's request. It was the least he could do. "All you need to do is use the bathroom, right?"

"That's it. I'll be out in two seconds."

Mark wearily opened the door, thinking he was stupid for doing so. But how could he be so cruel to send the guy on his way without even having the decency to let him use the john?

The guy passed him, giving him a look that was more than dirty as he headed into Mark's apartment. Mark wished, again, he had just left him there. "Which way?"

Mark pointed to the hallway on his right and watched as the guy disappeared into the bathroom. It was quiet in there, too quiet, and Mark began to get anxious. He hurried into the bedroom and picked up his book. He knew sleep would be elusive after this encounter. He plopped down on the couch and opened the book. The lines of type failed to line up.

What's he doing in there?

In moments, his question was answered as the door opened and the guy emerged, naked and grinning.

Oh no, Mark thought, standing, and then his guts constricted as he noticed the guy was holding a knife in his right hand. Jesus Christ, what was this?

Mark backed up, book still in hand. When the guy got close enough, he swung the heavy tome at his head, feeling it connect.

The guy staggered backward and the surprise was apparent on his face: his mouth in an "O" and his eyes wide.

"What's the matter?" Mark asked, panting now, adrenalin pumping in him like a drug.

The guy rushed at Mark again and succeeded in nicking his arm with the knife. A bright crimson spot of blood appeared on Mark's forearm. Mark raised the heavy book up again and brought it down on the guy's own forearm.

He gasped in pain and dropped the knife. It clattered to the hardwood floor. He looked up at Mark with an expression Mark could only describe as crazed fury.

"Get the fuck out!" Mark screamed, stooping to grab the knife. He had it now and brandished it in his would-be attacker's face.

Whimpering, the guy rushed to the bathroom to gather up his clothes.

"I oughta cut your fucking guts out right now! What's wrong with you?" Mark's voice quivered with rage and terror.

The guy skirted around Mark, his bundle of clothes clutched close to his chest, and ran for the door.

Mark slammed the door behind him, then leaned close. He heard the guy muttering outside, "I'll get you. I'll get you, you son of a bitch."

Chapter
Eleven

ED RESTLESSLY MOVED from one channel to the next. A hundred and fifty stations and nothing worthwhile on any of them. In that other life, the one he had just a few months ago, it didn't matter how many channels he had. Cable was a luxury he often thought of getting rid of, since the TV was on so little. Back then, his job filled so many hours — hours he sometimes cursed, but was ultimately glad to have put in, the work being interesting, never knowing what each new day would bring. And then there was Dan, and when he wasn't working, the hours were filled with him. He thought, of course, of their lovemaking first, but also thought of the simple happiness they'd had: the walks by the lake, the hours of conversation, planning their future together, the hotly contested games of racquetball, the board and card games they played, the friends they visited. Ed thought, with more than a little sadness, of how we really don't know what waits for us around each corner. Life was filled with surprises, and just when you thought you were settled, it threw a new curve your way.

He switched to ABC. The local ten o'clock news was just beginning. The lead story caused a jolt to run though Ed, making him sit up on the couch and lean forward. Sheila Martin, Channel Seven's amber-haired anchor, was looking into the camera, her carefully made-up face assuming an expression of sobriety and concern. "Richard Lewshevski, head of the Chicago Police Department's Detective Division, announced today the formation of a task force to investigate a spate of recent killings in Chicago's gay community. Since last August, three gay men have been brutally murdered in their homes. The victims have been identified as Anthony Evans, 23, David Westhoff, 42 and Milton Weinsap, 38. All of the men were victims of stab wounds and strangulation. Further details are being kept confidential by the department. None of the victims' residences bore any signs of forcible entry. Lewshevski stated that, since nothing was missing from the victims' homes, robbery has been ruled out as a motive. Richard

Byers is on the city's north side with more."

Ed watched as Richard Byers, a young black reporter with close-cropped hair and a well-groomed mustache, stood in front of Carlisles, a popular gay bar on Halsted Street. Ed couldn't remember when he'd last been there, probably with Dan for happy hour many months ago. The bar's mahogany- and glass-fronted façade looked unreal on video, like a set from a movie. "Thank you, Sheila. I'm standing in front of Carlisles, one of the city's more popular gay gathering places. Halsted Street, the hub of the city's gay community, is quiet tonight. I've spoken with several men and have discovered that Chicago's gay men are living in fear. Tonight, talk inside the bar centers around the three dead men, and who will be next. The Pink Angels, a voluntary protective group in the neighborhood, are upping patrols, and several men have commented they are using extreme caution when meeting strangers. All of the victims, except for the first, lived within a one-mile radius of Halsted and Roscoe, where I'm standing right now."

The station cut back to Sheila Martin, who concluded, "In a statement released just this morning, the Chicago Police Department has announced that formation of the task force to track the killer is just about complete. The mayor has appointed several of the city's north-side detectives, along with circuit court judge Martin Anger, the city's first openly gay elected official, to serve. Lewshevski said that, with the combined efforts of the force, the killer will be caught soon. Leads are coming in from all over the city and Lewshevski is confident that one of these leads will bring detectives a break in the case."

The news was interrupted by a commercial for Aleve pain reliever and Ed hit the Mute button. It always seemed the volume went up when commercials came on, and it also seemed that Ed was finding more and more in his life to be annoyed with. Lewshevski was a pompous asshole, more caught up in appearances than doing any real good, and Ed scoffed at the idea the killer would be apprehended soon. He knew, from his own work, and from what Joey Mantegno had told him, that the force had no idea, none whatsoever, who was doing these killings.

But I do, Ed thought, feeling a tense rigidity in his back. Timothy Bright. The name haunted him now on a daily basis. He couldn't even confide his concerns to anyone in his former department, because they had already sanctioned him for his association with the deceased.

And now the killings were big news. Ed flung a pillow from the couch across the room, knocked over a plant and began massaging his throbbing temples. He felt powerless, angry, and it seemed he would never discover anything more than he already knew.

And now his brothers were dying; slow, horrible deaths, Ed was sure. Deaths marked by terror.

The phone rang. Ed picked it up. "Hello."

"Ed? Is this Ed Comparetto?"

The voice was unfamiliar and male. "This is he."

"Hi, Ed, this is Peter." A pause. "From the library?"

"Oh sure, how are you?" Ed rolled his eyes.

"Good. Listen the reason I was calling is you, well, I don't know if it matters or not, but you left behind your pen when you were here the other day."

"I did?" Ed hadn't noticed.

"Yeah. It's a pretty decent pen, a pewter Cross fountain pen, and I thought you'd like it back."

Ed didn't own a Cross pen, fountain or otherwise. He was partial to Bics, the cheaper the better. Either that, or a pencil. He started to tell Peter that the pen wasn't his, then thought of the guy's face, the way he smiled and how helpful he'd been. Maybe, especially since his days were lately filled with nothing but TV and brooding, he shouldn't be so hasty to cast away this opportunity. "Oh?" Ed didn't want to say the pen was his, but he didn't quite want to close the door, either.

"Yeah. I brought it home with me for safekeeping." There was a long pause and Ed felt for the guy. Who hadn't been in this situation before? This call had nothing to do with a pen. "I was wondering if I could get it back to you."

"That'd be great." Ed was suddenly feeling generous. "When do you work again? I'll drop by the library."

"Actually, I'm off for four days."

"Oh."

"But I was thinking maybe I could meet you someplace. Um, maybe we could have a drink or something and I could give you your pen back."

"Well, my schedule's pretty open. When's good for you?" Ed could feel the relief at the other end of the phone.

"How about tomorrow night?"

"That would be just fine. How about Carlisles, say nine o'clock?"

"Sure. I'll see you then."

As soon as he hung up the phone, Ed thought of hitting the automatic callback code and calling the whole thing off. What was he doing? He was in no state to be meeting people, gloomy and preoccupied as he had been lately.

A little voice inside chided: *You might get rid of some of that gloom if you got out and met someone, maybe, God forbid, even got laid.*

"Oh shut up," Ed whispered to the little voice, and grinned. He flipped the sound back on and switched to another channel. It was time for *Roseanne*.

IT WAS EIGHT thirty the next night and Ed still hadn't left his apartment. He recalled his high school days, when he was still into heavy denial and was still dating girls. He was feeling the same kind of sick nervousness now, queasy with anticipation. Part of him wanted to stay home; there was laundry that needed doing and a new Ruth Rendell Inspector Wexford mystery was on his end table, waiting to be opened. Hell, the guy would get over being stood up. It happened to everyone occasionally.

But Ed knew, damn himself, that he was too decent of a guy to stand anyone up. And it was too late for calling him and making an excuse. Peter had probably already left for the bar.

Ed took one last look at the Rendell book, a longing look, he thought, and stood.

In the bathroom, Ed checked himself out. The strain of the past few weeks had changed him. He could have sworn he looked older; there were new lines he'd never noticed around his eyes. He yanked a grey hair from his coarse black curls. His skin didn't quite retain the olive/tan hue he'd always gotten compliments on. Rather, he looked sallow in the light above the medicine cabinet mirror.

At least the clothes were all right: a deep forest green corduroy shirt Dan had given him last Christmas and a pair of well-worn blue jeans showed off his broad shoulders and slim hips. "At least I haven't lost that," he said to his reflection. Ed quickly brushed his teeth and went to get his keys, wallet and brown leather bomber jacket.

CARLISLES HAD A good crowd. Not so many people that you were crushed against other bodies as men restlessly moved from the front of the bar, to the back, where a dance floor and a room with pool tables competed for attention, but not so few as to seem sparse. It was always nice to have the sound of laughter and conversation around you, especially when you didn't have a clue as to what to say to your date for the night.

But Peter wasn't a date, not really. He was merely returning an item a library patron had left behind.

Right. And Timothy Bright is a very nice guy.

As Ed began to scan the faces in the crowd for one topped with curly, reddish-brown hair and marked by a well-trimmed mustache and goatee, his feelings began to war. When he didn't see Peter in the crowd, relief and disappointment coursed through him all at once.

He stepped up to the bar and ordered a Rolling Rock, still searching in vain for Peter. He encountered a few interested glances as his eyes met those of strangers across the bar and even got a few smiles. It made Ed wonder how many of these guys would go home with him tonight, merely on an introduction and few minutes' conversation. Sadly, he knew there were far too many. Even with a publicized gay serial killer on the loose, there were still far too many men willing to take a chance with a stranger. It was how Dahmer got by, how Larry Eyler got by, and how John Wayne Gacy ended up with a cemetery in the crawlspace of his northwest-side home.

Ed took a swig of his beer and headed toward the back. Perhaps Peter would be there. Again, Ed felt conflicting emotions: half of him hoped he wouldn't be there (then Ed could go home and curl up in bed with the latest adventures of Chief Inspector Wexford) and half of him was sick with dread that he'd be stood up (adding to an already bad case of flagging self-esteem).

Peter was not on the dance floor. Nor was he shooting pool. He was not standing along the wall that lined both areas, drink in hand, an optimistic smile beneath the reddish mustache.

Ed looked around once more. There were a lot of people here, and perhaps he'd just missed him. But a careful survey of all the men present did not reveal Peter Howle.

"Hello, stranger. Looking for anyone in particular?" Ed turned and there stood Peter, a Budweiser in his hand, grinning.

Ed was shocked at how pleased he was to see him and couldn't hold back the large smile that spread across his face.

"I was beginning to think I'd been stood up."

Peter cocked a thumb over his shoulder. "Bathroom. Beer and a pea-sized bladder make that part of the bar a very popular place for me."

Ed nodded, still grinning, and didn't have a clue as to what to say.

"Want your pen?"

"Oh sure, sure." Ed waited for Peter to reach into his jeans pocket. But Peter didn't do anything.

"You didn't really lose a pen, did you?"

"I never said I did."

Peter shook his head, smiling. "A little ruse of mine. I thought if you were interested, you'd play along. I wasn't even sure you were gay, so I didn't know what I was letting myself in for. I can't tell you how relieved I was when you suggested meeting here." Peter looked Ed in the eye and Ed noticed how pale blue his eyes were. "You're looking good tonight."

"And you." And he did look good. Peter wore a pair of cargo pants, a black T-shirt and a white, open Chamois shirt over it. He still had on the same hiking boots he'd worn in the library the day they met.

"Wanna go up front and sit down?" Peter offered, and Ed was grateful to follow. It gave him time to think of something to say.

It was amazing how quickly 2:00 a.m. and last call came along. Ed wanted to tell Peter how grateful he was to him for getting his mind off his problems for a night; it had been so long since he'd had a few hours freedom from the mess his life had become. But he didn't want to whine, and he didn't even know if Peter was ready to hear the twisted tale of the last few months.

The two had spent the entire evening discussing everything from movies, to books, to music, and neither had brought up the subject of work. Peter knew, and loved, Ruth Rendell, but was more partial to her Barbara Vine stories of psychological suspense, while Ed preferred the mysteries and police procedurals that Ed used to feel such a part of.

"Want another?" Ed indicated the brown bottle in front of Peter.

"Nah. I've just about filled my quota. You go ahead."

"No, I'm fine."

"Should we get going then?"

The "we" sounded awfully familiar and Ed wondered if it was a veiled invitation. But how to ask?

"Yeah. Early morning?"

"Not at all." Peter winked. "I told you on the phone: I'm off for four days. Remember?"

"Well, do you need a ride home?"

"I'd love a ride home. The el is my car, you know." And then, abruptly, Peter grabbed Ed and pulled him close. Ed was too stunned (and, he had to admit, aroused) to do anything but hug back, enjoying the warmth and firmness of another man's body pressed against his, a feeling that had been absent for far too long. Peter whispered in his ear: "What I'd really love is a ride back to your place."

Ed pulled back, trying to look surprised, but smiling too much to pull it off. "Aren't you the forward one?"

"Hey, I believe in taking the bull by the horns, or horn, in this case."

Ed laughed. He wouldn't have guessed it before he went out tonight, but he was ready for this. Maybe it *was* moving too fast. And maybe he should listen to the critical little voice he'd heard earlier, the one that talked about how many of these guys would easily go home with someone they barely knew. But Peter was kind and intelligent and besides, he was great-looking.

Ed shut off his own response before it got going too far. The one that told him that that was exactly the kind of thought Tony Evans, David Westhoff, and Milt Weinsap might have had just before they were murdered.

Ed dug his keys out of his pocket. "Let's go. I lucked out. I'm parked just up the street."

ED WISHED HE'D cleaned up his apartment. He'd grown accustomed to the scattered newspaper sections and magazines that littered the living room, the half-filled glasses and mugs on the coffee table, the way one mini-blind was slightly askew and the plants in need of watering. Now, as he switched on the light and saw them through fresh eyes, he was embarrassed. What shape were his sheets in? Ed thought of the kitchen sink, filled with three days' worth of unwashed dishes.

"What a dump!" Peter said, in his best Bette Davis voice. Ed was grateful that his best Bette Davis wasn't even close.

His quip helped break the tension. "Sorry. I really wasn't expecting company tonight." Ed set to gathering up the newspapers and magazines, folding his arms around them and heading toward the wastebasket in his den.

"Aren't you the pessimistic one?" Peter grabbed him by his shoulders and maneuvered himself in front of him. "Here, let me help you with those." Peter gently pulled the newspapers from Ed's arms.

He flung them to the floor. "There," he whispered, pulling Ed close. "Much better, don't you think?"

"Works for me."

Their mouths met in a kiss. Ed closed his eyes, trying to force out the image of Dan that went with this familiar feeling. He grabbed and held Peter tight, grinding his lips into the other man's, feeling the wonderfully rough texture of Peter's facial hair on his skin.

Peter was a good kisser, Ed thought, as images of Dan dispersed, relegated (he hoped) to the realm of memory, where the present could wash them away. Peter's body was lean and hard and, as Ed moved his hands up and down his back, he felt flooded with warmth. He could feel Peter's hardness against the front of his jeans and Ed ground his hips against Peter's.

When they broke from the embrace, both were breathing heavier, and Peter's pale blue eyes were alive in the half-light. "I've wanted this since I first saw you." Peter stroked one side of Ed's face. "I have a feeling this might be a little too fast for you."

"Don't worry about it." Ed pulled Peter against him once more, kissing first his eyes, then his nose, the reddish stubble on his chin, and finally moving back to his lips. "I suppose I should tell you I haven't done this for a while."

"Married?" Peter kissed Ed's left earlobe and it caused a deliciously cold shudder to move down his spine.

"Five years. His name was Dan."

"How long since you broke up?" Peter's hand brushed across Ed's crotch.

"Months and months. Too long."

"A sensitive guy. I like that." Peter unzipped Ed's pants and snaked inside the opening. "Very sensitive." He gave Ed's cock a squeeze.

It had been so long. So many empty nights, alone with the DVD and a lubed-up hand. Ed was afraid the evening of romance would be over all too quickly if Peter kept rubbing and squeezing the way he was doing right now. Gently he broke away from him. "Why don't we go into the bedroom?"

Peter followed him, taking off his shirt as he went. Ed lit a candle that had lain, untouched, for far too long on his nightstand. It sprung to life with the touch of the match and shadows began to dance on the eggshell colored walls.

Peter sat on the bed and began unlacing his hiking boots. His back was strong; as he bent and straightened, undoing the laces, a topography of musculature danced across the smooth surface of his skin, bisected by the orderly rows of bumps that were his spine.

Ed longed to kiss each bump. He hurried to undress, then got on the bed behind Peter, where he fulfilled his wish, licking and kissing his way down Peter's back.

Peter laughed softly. "Tickles," he whispered. At last, he pulled off the boots and threw them into a corner, where they landed with a thud and disappeared into the shadows. His pants followed, landing in a bunch.

He turned to Ed and their first naked kiss was electric. Ed suddenly realized how much he had missed this, not just the lust part—although there was no denying that that was a huge part—but the simple physical closeness of another human being. He pushed Peter down on the bed and covered his body with his own. Peter was hairy where Ed was smooth, and the textures together made Ed close his eyes and moan.

Peter's penis was pressing insistently against his belly. Ed reached down and stroked it, the silken curve of it hot in his hand. Moving downward, Ed kissed his neck, chest, stomach and finally took Peter in his mouth, swallowing him all the way down, until his nose was nestled in reddish-brown pubic hair and Peter's balls were brushing his chin.

Peter dug his hands into Ed's dark curls, pulling hard, and thrusting into Ed's mouth.

The shadows on the wall, once separate entities, became one. As the two moved, pleasuring one another, cracks of light would appear in the shadows, showing the small separations as they switched positions in order to gain or give access.

Ed moved between Peter's legs, running his hands over the hard muscular thighs, rough with coarse hair, then pushing them back toward his stomach. In the flickering light, their eyes met and Ed wordlessly asked permission.

Peter nodded. "Got a condom?"

"Of course."

After a short pause, the shadows on the wall merged and became one once more.

ED AWAKENED, HOURS later, to the sound of thunder. The room flared briefly with blue-white light, and rain pelted his bedroom window. Warm under the covers, Ed turned sleepily, throwing out an arm to snare Peter as he did so.

But all his arm connected with was the pillow. He opened his eyes to discover he was in bed alone. The thunder crashed once more, closer now, followed immediately by the flash of lightning. The storm outside left him suddenly feeling cold in spite of the warm protectiveness he had felt only seconds ago.

He sat up. The apartment was silent. Perhaps Peter's small bladder and the beer he had consumed earlier had awakened him. That had to be it.

Ed swung his legs over the side of the bed and wandered into the living room, where Peter's shirt still lay in a lump on the hardwood.

He looked to the bathroom. No light.

There was no one in the bathroom.

No light was on anywhere else in the apartment. Ed moved toward the kitchen; the doorway there was a black maw. He had always hated that his kitchen was devoid of windows.

As he headed into the darkness, thunder grumbled and the lightning flashed once more.

In that one instant, he saw Peter, his eyes alive with terror. Someone, Ed was sure, stood behind him, holding him in an embrace that was anything but loving. Another brilliant flash and crack of thunder revealed the face of Timothy Bright over Peter's left shoulder.

It also showed the glint of a knife at Peter's throat.
Ed screamed.

"Hey, hey. Wake up."

Ed roughly pushed Peter away from him and opened his eyes. The sheet atop him was damp and the images from his dream dispersed, leaving him panting and with a vague feeling of paranoia washing over him. For minutes, it seemed Timothy Bright was still in the apartment, waiting just outside the bedroom door.

He turned to Peter, whose eyebrows that were furrowed with concern. "You were screaming. A kind of low, muffled sound, but screaming. Are you okay?"

"I think so."

"Want some water?"

"Yeah." Ed pulled the comforter close around him and sat up in bed as Peter went for the water.

When he came back with a full glass and a full measure of concern on his face, Ed took both with gratitude. "Remember when I was in the library? When we first met?"

Peter slid under the sheets. "Of course."

"I think it's time we need to discuss that. We haven't talked about our work yet." And with that, Ed poured out the whole story.

Peter listened without interrupting, concern growing on his features.

The two said nothing for a while.

Then Peter spoke: "I think both of us might have a connection to these killings."

"What?" And Ed began to wonder how well he knew this guy in bed next to me.

"I have a friend. His name is Mark Deitrich. I think he may have had a very close call the other night."

"What are you talking about?"

"I think he had a very nasty little meeting with the guy who's doing these murders."

Ed looked to the window, which was dry. He nestled his head on Peter's chest, not wanting to know more, but said, "Tell me."

Chapter
Twelve

IT HAD BEEN a real heavy-duty workout, a real ball-buster. Mark had spent the entire afternoon at Bally's at Century City Center on North Clark, starting off with 45 minutes on the Stair Master, moving on to an hour of free-weight work, making his muscles burn with bench presses, curls, flies and presses and then followed it all up with 30 laps in the pool.

Now, as he sat back, his head resting on the side of the hot tub, letting the hot bubbling water flow around him, loosening tightened muscles, he found he still couldn't relax.

The guy had paid him a visit three nights ago. Three nights ago was stamped indelibly in his mind, like something burnt on the soft pink tissue of his brain with a brand. It was like there was a movie running in his mind and Mark was unable to find the switch to turn off the projector. He saw the guy coming out of his bathroom over and over again, the knife flashing now with a surrealistic glint, like something out of a TV ad. It made Mark queasy, his stomach roiling and churning, just to think of it.

And if he didn't have to think of it, wasn't compelled by some very unwelcome force, he wouldn't. He had called in sick the next day, after spending a sleepless night, lying awake on the couch, all the lights on, listening for the sound of breaking glass, the metallic click of someone picking his lock. Someone coming back to finish the job.

He had thought for quite a while of calling the police. After all, what had happened was attempted murder, and the guy should be found and punished. Who knew what he had gotten up to since, especially when the urge to kill was not satisfied with Mark? And, of course, there were those stories floating around now about a gay serial killer.

But that little twerp couldn't be the culprit. Mark shuddered to think that if he was, he had been far too close for comfort. And then the guilt rose up: what if the guy was the killer? By not coming forward, Mark feared he was an accomplice. By not telling someone, Mark was allowing him to go free, free to kill other guys.

But Mark thought of the inevitable questions that would follow. Why did he let this character in his house? How did he know him? How long had he known him? Why were there no signs of forcible entry?

The story was news. And if Mark came forward as the "one that got away," he knew the media would be all over him.

And what gave him almost as much horror as the attempt on his life was the reality of his homosexuality being made public. He flashed on his mother in Deerfield, picking up the *Chicago Tribune* and seeing his picture on page one, tied up in the tawdry mess. "Mark Deitrich, an avowed homosexual, a flaming faggot, a queer." He could see the look of distaste crossing her kind features, and then watched her collapse onto the family room sofa, head in hands, asking where she had gone wrong.

The picture hurt. He could never do that to his family. They had a certain standing in the community, and the Dietrich boys, with their superior athletic prowess and winning ways with girls, would become laughingstocks. How could his mother ever go into Macy's without hearing whispers behind her back? How could his father ever shoot eighteen holes at his club again without being subject to cruel jokes about his pansy son? And his brothers would automatically beat his ass to a bloody pulp if they knew their youngest sibling was a fag.

No one, other than a few close friends, knew he was gay. Mark dated girls, traveled in straight circles. On Saturday night, you would not find him on Halsted Street at one of the several gay bars there, but at the Cubby Bear or any of the other dozen straight bars that dotted the neighborhood around Wrigley Field. These were the places where Mark felt comfortable.

If he needed a guy, he had always been able to log onto Men4HookUpNow (but no more! not ever, ever again). On a few risky occasions, Mark had visited Man's Universe, the bathhouse on North Halsted. Lights were low there, and it was relatively simple to get in and out with a quick sexual encounter. As long as no one saw him coming out of the smoked glass doors...

The water bubbled and Mark returned to reality. It seemed that for a while everything had stopped and he had left the health club completely. He glanced down at his watch and saw that twenty minutes had passed. Mark had no idea what had transpired during that time.

He looked down at his chest, which had become reddened from the hot water. He stood and reached for his towel.

He would call Peter when he got home. Peter was the only person with whom he could talk about his "dark side," as he called it, and Mark needed to muse over what had happened to him once more. It didn't seem like it, but he knew talking through it would probably be the only way he could return his life to some semblance of normalcy. As long as Peter didn't get on his case again about going to the cops.

That was just out of the question.

As Mark headed for the showers, a question Peter asked him nagged at him, causing him to feel cold and a queasy nausea to rise up in him.

"What if he's not done with you yet, man? What if he has no intention of letting you live to tell?"

Mark drove north along Clark Street. Everything looked different now, the buildings rising up in an almost threatening stance. All the people moving along the sidewalks suddenly had blackened hearts, minds filled with malicious intent.

Mark's muscles ached. He could not wait to get home. There, he could lock his doors and feel safe in his little one bedroom. There, he could pick up a book (he was almost through with *Insomnia*) and try and lose himself among the character's lives. Lives that were threatened indeed, but not in any real sense, not like Mark's. Besides, reading lately had been an exercise in futility. He would read a line or two of type and then the images would appear once more to torment him.

He considered, waiting at a stop light where Clark and Halsted merged, finding a liquor store. He could down half a bottle of something (Captain Myers? Jack Daniels?) and maybe that would make the images go away.

Near his house, there was a little corner liquor store. Mark had never known its name; the neon sign outside read only *Liquor*. Mark didn't drink much. Even when he went out, he stuck to beer, and often not even that; a bottle of Evian usually suited him just fine.

But he couldn't stand seeing that little guy coming out of the bathroom with the knife again. Couldn't stand the way it made him feel: how he had even at times trembled, palms sweaty, heart pounding out a tribal beat.

As Mark locked his car and crossed the street, he thought again of the knife. It was a hunting knife; he and his brothers had used a similar one to gut the deer they bagged when they went hunting in northern Wisconsin. That was when he was a teenager; it had been years since he had innocently enjoyed the outdoors with his brothers and father. Now, his memories of hunting were clouded with the scent of blood and the terrified look in the eyes of the buck or doe they were tracking. He felt a kindred spirit with deer now, knew their fear. Images of deer entrails emerged from memory, and with them a vision of his own, the little guy a mad, tiny troll, pulling them from his gut while he laughed with glee, whispering the word "faggot" over and over.

Enough. If this liquor knocked him out and made him sleep through the night for once, he would be happy. Damn the resulting hangover that was certain to appear the next day.

In the liquor store, Mark bought a fifth of Jack Daniels and a bottle of Canada Dry ginger ale. He intended to drink until he couldn't stand it anymore.

He was lucky. As he pulled up to his building, someone was just pulling out, and he claimed the spot only steps from his door. He treasured such spots now more than ever; walking along outside, unprotected, was a new terror. He recalled the other night, returning home from a game of racquetball, how he had to park two blocks away.

He had sprinted the entire distance to his door, casting nervous glances over his shoulder.

Later, much later, Mark awakened in the dark. He was sprawled across the couch in the living room, Stephen King's book lying on the floor face down, several pages bent. His face felt shiny with sweat and his mouth seemed as if it had been lined with gauze. The room was gently spinning, around and around.

Mark hopped from the couch and ran to the bathroom, where he splattered the toilet bowl, inside and out, with brownish bile, tears flowing down his cheek. Afterwards, the tears continued to flow and Mark crouched on the floor, sobbing, feeling as if nothing would ever return to normal.

Why did he, he wondered, have to be gay? This never would have happened if he hadn't simply resisted his impulses. He had resisted them all his life and had done a damn good job for the most part. He blamed himself as much as he blamed the mad little troll who wanted to kill him.

The darkness had swallowed him once more. As Mark came to, his face against the cold tile of the bathroom floor, he groaned. His stomach felt as if it had taken on a life of its own, moving restlessly back and forth, churning and gurgling.

He managed to get to a kneeling position in front of the sink, where he cupped his hands full of cold water and splashed his face, then drank and drank...

He stood on legs that felt like liquid and walked to the window. He didn't know what time it was, but it had to be in the wee hours of the morning. Traffic outside was sparse and a quiet hung in the air totally foreign to most of the day. The darkness outside matched exactly how Mark felt: dark and alone. A caul of mist lay along the ground, waiting to be burned off by the morning's sun.

He longed to go outside and breathe the cold air. His head badly needed clearing and he knew the air would be just the thing.

But he couldn't! Step out there? When the little guy might be lurking, lying in wait, to finish the job?

Mark pressed his head against the cold glass.

The sound of the intercom buzzer made him give out a small cry of alarm. The cry was totally out of character.

He stared at the buzzing intercom box as if it were an invader, as if he didn't know what to do with it.

A line of sweat started at his hairline and trickled down his forehead. "Help me," he whimpered, moving toward the little box on the wall. He pressed the talk button. "Who's there?"

There was no reply.

"Who's there, goddamn it!" Mark shouted, pushing so hard against buzzer the tip of his finger turned white.

Nothing.

Mark swallowed painfully, forcing all the moisture in his mouth, which amounted to a small drop of spit, down his throat. He sat on the couch, head slumped low.

The buzzer sounded again. Mark wished he had held on to the hunting knife, but the thing had filled him such horror that he had tossed it in a Dumpster the next day.

The loud, insistent buzz came again. Mark didn't know what to do; he felt like a prisoner in his own home.

He pressed the talk button once more. "Leave me alone!"

And just for the hell of it, pressed the listen button. "Let me in," a voice said. The voice was obviously being deepened, speaking in measured tones, trying to be commanding.

Mark turned from the intercom just as the buzzer sounded again.

"What do you want?" Mark was ashamed because tears were starting.

"I want you to buzz me in. I need to talk to you."

"Who the fuck are you?"

"Ray. From online, you remember me."

Mark's breathing was coming faster now. "Go away."

"Listen: there's something I have to tell you. You didn't understand, man. That was just a game, a little rape fantasy. I've done it before. I'm sorry you freaked out."

Mark leaned against the wall, unsure if his legs would continue to support him.

The buzzer shrieked again.

"Go away."

"Listen: I just want to talk to you. I feel just terrible."

It would be such a relief to believe that what had happened

was just the result of a misguided game. So wonderful to believe that no one really meant to stab him.

"Okay, you made your point. Now get the hell out my building." Mark's words came out hoarse. He turned from the buzzer. He was suddenly very tired; his bones felt heavy, made of concrete. His eyes burned. He was not looking forward to the morning.

Just as he reached his bedroom, the buzzer sounded again: a long, loud cry in the dark, alarming, unsettling. Mark closed his eyes and winced. "God, what have I done to myself?" he wondered.

Moving rapidly to the kitchen, Mark went into the pantry, where his bright red Sears tool box lay at the back, on the floor. He opened it and got out a sledgehammer.

The buzzer was still going as he approached it; the guy must have just been leaning on it down there.

Mark smashed the intercom, the plastic breaking into shards and falling to the floor; wires spilled out, red, green and yellow, hanging there like the entrails of a gutted animal.

"I should come down there and do the same to you," he whispered to the ruined intercom.

He went to the window after a moment or two and gazed down at the street below.

There, in the dull pre-dawn light, he saw him. The small frame, the blond head bent low against the wind. There was no doubt.

The guy had returned, and Mark wondered if he would ever go away.

Chapter
Thirteen

IT WAS IN October, 1983 when I first had sex with a man. I was fourteen years old; he was 36. I laugh when I think about it now: Aunt Helene so proud of her new beau, the neurologist. He was everything she had ever sought: a successful professional, an impeccable pedigree (undergraduate from Yale, medical school at Northwestern and a residency at Johns Hopkins), a desirable address (Kenilworth) and single. Oh yes, so deliciously single. I doubt if one human being could satisfy the peculiar desires of this man. His name was David Long and he was handsome in the way men of his standing are handsome. That is to say, he was tall, blessed with a thick crop of black hair, greying at the temples (of course!), cut short. His spectacles were round and rimless; I believe he wore them more for effect than out of any optical need. He would always show up dressed in a suit of some dark fabric, gabardine, wool, silk, in hues of navy, charcoal, black.

And he had his black side! And he was an expert at concealing that black side.

I wonder now why he, with his intelligence, grace, wit and charm, went after me. After all, here I was, nephew to the kind of woman who could improve David's social standing. A woman who would do all she could, selflessly, in helping make him into an even more respected member of the social elite. She had the right connections, she had old money, she had memberships to the most exclusive clubs on the North Shore.

What a risk I was. And yet, perhaps that was part of my allure. "Too pretty to be a boy," was what they used to say about me, and I think that was no more true than when I was fourteen. My limbs were just lengthening, my hair still retained the tow-headed silk of childhood, and when I looked in the mirror, a ten-year-old boy (girl?) looked back at me. Blue eyes, pale, framed in black lashes. My skin was the color of, excuse me the flight of fancy, alabaster, and easily as smooth. The only hair I had on my body was a small, sparse triangle of whitish-blond pubic hair and a fine, white down that crowned my arms and legs. Aunt Helene let me wear my hair long and it stopped at my shoulders.

David had taken notice of me the first time he brought Aunt Helene home. They had been to dinner downtown somewhere, and her face was flushed and she was laughing, giggling, really, when the two seated themselves in the living room for cocktails.

I wandered in, wearing a T-shirt and cut-off shorts. I had been in my room, working with some water colors, trying to paint a landscape: the rocky shore of Lake Michigan, complete with huge blue-grey waves and white sprays of water against a grey sky. I was pretty good then; at least all my teachers said so.

But I'm getting away from the real story. I came in to kiss Aunt Helene goodnight and she introduced me to her new friend. He shook my hand and it seemed his big hand engulfed mine, and it also seemed as if he held it a bit longer than the average handshake. I remember the smooth hardness of his palm against mine. I looked up at him and he held my gaze, his deep brown eyes boring into mine. I could feel myself reddening, wondering what Aunt Helene would think. Of course, she thought nothing. The moment lasted only that long—a moment—and to the casual observer, nothing untoward passed between us.

But I knew. Years of experience as a professional homosexual have taught me the secret language of the eyes, and in retrospect, I can make the claim confidently that David found me more than a little interesting.

From that first date, Aunt Helene and David began to see a lot of one another. He tried his best to befriend me and Aunt Helene was delighted with the interest he took in me, presumably to gain her favor.

I always knew there was more. The hand on the shoulder, the brotherly pats all held a darker side. It was more than once I found his gaze lingering on me as we sat at dinner, more than once his hand would swat my bottom in that macho camaraderie no one would mistake for queer.

Except I guess David wasn't queer. I think the right word is pedophile.

October of 1983: I was forced by Aunt Helene to join a bunch of "youngsters" my own age from her country club for a hay ride and a teen dance. The whole evening was dreadful, with the girls giggling as I passed them and the other boys keeping their distance, not wanting to be associated with such a pitiful example of budding masculinity.

As I stood outside the Corinthian-columned façade of the building waiting for Aunt Helene, my thoughts were on one thing: getting away from these people with whom I had nothing in common and getting home to my bed, where I could read, masturbate, and fall asleep.

I was surprised, but a part of me fully expected it, when David pulled up in his cream colored Mercedes. He tooted the horn and waved. I fell into the embrace of soft, glowing lights and the smell and feel of brown leather.

"How's it goin'?" he said cheerfully. The car radio was tuned to a classical station and something by Dvorak was playing, low.

"Fine, now. I guess I'm glad to be getting home."

"Didn't you have a good time?"

"Not really." I slumped in my seat and stared out the window. I could feel his gaze on me and it was causing weird feelings to rise up within me. I felt sick to my stomach, but there was a certain delicious twinge at being next to him. I looked over at him and he looked back, smiled.

He put his hand on my knee and squeezed. "Well, it's over now."

I noticed two things then. There was liquor on his breath (Courvoisier, if I knew David) and he didn't take his hand away. An electric current pulsed from his palm to my knee. I was afraid to breathe, let alone move. Part of me wanted him to move his hand and the other part dreaded it.

We said nothing for a long time. David's hand massaged my knee, and I'm sure he wanted to give the impression that it was absent-minded, as he concentrated on the road and hummed along to the radio.

Gradually, I came to the realization that we were not on the way home. We were heading north and the houses were becoming further and further apart as we traveled along, being replaced by copses of trees behind which an orange harvest moon glowed.

My body felt as if it were laced with wire. I sat stiffly, every muscle tight, unable to think of anything to say; even as I tried to make conversation, my mind grew blanker with each passing moment.

Finally, David, looking as casual as ever, signaled and turned off on a bumpy road. "This leads down to the lake," he said, never once taking his eyes from the road. "It's a very pretty spot. Very quiet. I like to come here and think."

I still was unsure what was going on. Perhaps this was at Aunt Helene's urging, perhaps she wanted him to make more of an effort to get to know me. Was a marriage in the offing?

He pulled to the berm of the road and shut the car off. The quiet, absolute, surrounded us. From under the seat, David brought out a sterling silver flask and took a long pull from it. To my shock, he handed it to me. "Go on..." he urged, "try it."

The liquor almost made me choke, but it lit a fire in my belly and the heat radiated up to warm my chest and face.

David stared out at the water, which reflected the moon in a brilliant swatch of silver. His hand moved to my knee once more and squeezed. When I didn't resist, the hand moved up a little further, snaking between my thighs to part them.

I took another swig of the liquor, unsure how I was supposed to respond. Maybe this was a test. Maybe Aunt Helene was trying to find out if I really was queer, if the rumors and the laughter at Loyola Academy were true. Was I supposed to react with some sort of macho bravado? I envisioned myself pushing his hand away, offended, saying something like, "Hey, pal, you got the wrong guy." David would laugh and tell me I'd passed their little test.

His voice startled me. "You got a girlfriend, Tim?" No one called me Tim.

"No. I don't seem to have much luck in that area."

David laughed to himself. "You've got plenty of time for girls. Beat off much?"

The question virtually took my breath away. I reddened and stared out the window, then laughed nervously.

"It's nothing to be ashamed of. When I was your age, I did it three, four times a day." I didn't look, but I heard a zipper and a rustling noise. "Still do, as a matter of fact." When I didn't look, he said, "You can check it out. Nothing to be ashamed of. It's a guy thing."

I looked. His penis was red and hard, a tiny pearl of clear liquid poised at the tip. I had never seen a grown man's penis before and it seemed huge. I wondered if Aunt Helene had ever seen it. He gave his penis a squeeze which caused the drop to run down the shaft. It was quickly replaced by another.

"Ever fool around with any of your buddies?"

"No. Of course not."

"Hey. It's perfectly natural. Normal. You don't have to be embarrassed."

"But I haven't."

He took my hand then and wrapped my fingers around the shaft. He reached back and reclined his seat. "Just move your hand up and down." I did what he told me and felt a bizarre mixture of warring emotions. Part of me felt sick to my stomach. The other part, the part I couldn't deny because of the stiffening in my Levi's, told me I enjoyed this.

"Why don't you take yours out...let me see what you've got."

Before I had a chance to respond, he'd undone my pants and pulled them down to my ankles. He stared. "I have a feeling you like this."

And then his head was buried in my lap and I was overcome by the feel of his hot, wet mouth surrounding me and his tongue flicking at me.

It took only seconds for me to come. David stopped moving when that happened, but didn't take his mouth away. I saw the muscles in his throat move as he swallowed.

"Let's take a walk," he whispered. "Over by those pines."

I said nothing. I pulled my pants up. I was trembling as he led me by the hand to the cluster of trees near the water's edge. Wordlessly, he undid my pants once more and pushed them down. "Bend over," he whispered in my ear, then licked it. I was too stunned to do anything but comply.

When he entered me, I screamed, feeling as if I was being ripped in two. David's hand over my mouth was swift. The pain shot through me like white-hot electricity as he thrust into me over and over; it seemed he took hours. I tried to flee, but his grip around my waist was tight and I could do nothing more than whimper into his sweaty palm.

Chapter
Fourteen

ED WAS CONFUSED as he sat alone one night, waiting for Peter to come back from a late-night shift at the library. Outside, it was cold. Frost was predicted. Sleet was rapping against the windows with what sounded like sharp fingernails. Other than this sound, the apartment was quiet. And yet, he stayed confused. It had been so long since he had had dined upon anything other than heartache and loneliness. After Dan had left, all Ed could do was fight his feelings — that he wasn't worth the love of another, that if he had done something differently, things would have worked out with Dan. And then there was the quiet manner in which he tormented himself: fantasies of Dan with another guy. The two of them laughing together, then arms around one another exchanging soulful looks. The fantasies would then turn X-rated and Ed would watch, with mounting discomfort, the two of them screwing, doing things he had once thought only the two of them would do together. Dan's lips moving down a hairy body, stopping to lick and suck genitals that were bigger than Ed's, lifting his legs for a faceless man, the want in his eyes apparent, stronger than anything Ed had ever seen. And this other man, this faceless one, would always be a better lover, would always have more stamina, always have more tricks up his sleeves to bring ecstasy than Ed could ever dream of.

But now, Ed felt guilty. Since he and Peter had met, over two weeks ago now, Ed's thoughts had turned to Dan less and less. In fact, two whole days went by when Ed was certain he didn't think of Dan once. And yet, the feeling that he was being unfaithful continued. Part of him wanted Dan to know about Peter, to see how much younger he was and how much better-looking. The other part dreaded the inevitable run-in he would have with Dan, when Peter was at his side, in a restaurant, theater, or bar.

Why did he dread such an encounter? Was he still hoping Dan might be able to work out his problems, to, in effect, grow up? Did Ed want a reconciliation? Intellectually, he had long ago decided that Dan could never be the right man for him. All Ed had to do to remind himself of this decision was to recall the stress, the tension of their relationship. How the simplest statement could bring out in Dan a black mood, where silence and cold reigned like a sub-zero winter night in Chicago. All Ed had to do to know, intellectually, Dan was wrong for him was to conjure up all the months Dan lounged around the house, not even looking for work, while Ed struggled to provide a living for the both of them. But what exists in the brain does not always correspond to what exists in the heart. And, in spite of these very rational realizations, Ed also knew there was a core of love for Dan that still burned. Indefatigable, it told Ed that things could work out and that the two of them could be together once more.

Peter changed all that. He showed Ed that a relationship could be comfortable as well as exciting and didn't need tension to make it work. He demonstrated to Ed that another man could have an interest in life and work, without being goaded into it.

Dan, and the feelings of torment he had caused for so many months, began to fade. When Ed was with Peter (and they had been together almost every night since they had met), he seldom thought of Dan, other than to make comparisons between the two. And Peter always came up the winner. With Peter, unlike Dan, Ed felt free to say whatever was on his mind. Whether it was wanting to try something new sexually or a concern Ed was having or even Ed's own private torment over the loss of his career, Peter was always there to listen objectively, never getting ticked off, never looking to find some way this would offend him, as Dan so often did.

Peter had yet to reveal the name of his friend. The one he said had been threatened with a knife after meeting some weirdo over an online hook-up site. After Peter had told him what had happened, Ed had begged him to let him talk to this friend, but Peter was leery of betraying a confidence.

"The guy is completely in the closet," Peter had explained. "His family would shit if they knew he was gay. That's why he refuses to go to the police."

"Doesn't this asshole know the guy could be this killer who's out there? Isn't he selfless enough to swallow his own fears to maybe save a life? God, how can this asshole live with himself?"

Peter regarded him coldly. This was, after all, a close friend they were discussing.

"I'm sorry. But it makes me so angry that people can play with others' lives because they're afraid of being outed."

"I've been there," Peter said. "And I'm willing to wager you have, too. He's young and he thinks he was brought up around no one who was gay."

Ed stared down at the hardwood floor. They were sitting in his living room. It was raining outside and they were listening to a George Winston CD, *Autumn*. Ed didn't want to lose his temper. This should be a pleasant moment, not one in which the first fight between the new couple broke out.

"Besides," Peter went on, "I'm trying to convince him to at least talk to you. But he's afraid. Afraid in a lot of ways. It's not just the fear of being outed. He's also afraid of getting this guy mad. He's terrified he'll come back and finish the job."

Ed had understood the rationale. And he tried not to bug Peter about it, but there was so much this guy could tell him, perhaps he could even lead him to the killer. It was frustrating, but Ed tried to put his confidence in Peter, who assured him he could eventually wear him down enough to at least talk to Ed, if not report the assault to the police.

The sleet finally turned to rain. Ed looked outside and watched as heavy smears of it fell down the glass, making the streetlights outside appear distorted, something out of a Salvador Dali painting. He got up and switched WFMT on, so he'd have some company other than the sound of the rain and the clock ticking on his mantel. There was something unnerving, something he couldn't quite put his finger on, going on in his apartment tonight. Almost a feeling of being observed. But that was ridiculous. But every time the wind blew and a floorboard creaked, he tensed. It was almost as if he were waiting for someone to appear, someone with a knife, or hands outstretched to strangle him...

You need to find a new job, he told himself, you're going crazy. He looked out the window, wishing he would see Peter's red Sentra heading up his street, looking for a place to park. He knew Peter could bring him out of his brooding as no one else could.

Mozart's "Serenade No. 10" was playing and Ed tried to close his eyes and let the music surround him. But every time he did that, images of knives and outstretched hands came at him. A blond-haired elf appeared, crying in the summer heat. A dead boy come back to taunt him and ruin his life.

And then, finally, it hit him: the connection. This guy Peter knew, his friend, had met this weirdo online. Wasn't it possible that other men had met their fate in the same way? That would explain why there were no signs of forcible entry. The guys, perhaps, had welcomed him into their homes, thinking this would be nothing more harmless than a tryst with a stranger, two males pleasuring one another. It happened all the time, although Ed had never availed himself of such easy measures. These websites were proliferating, so there must have been plenty of guys who did.

He glanced up at the clock. Peter would not be home for another hour. Ed stood and went to the wicker basket he kept magazines in. There must be an old *Gay Chicago* in there somewhere...

At last, he found what he was looking for and pulled the magazine from the stack. The back was loaded with ads for just such online services. Maybe it was time Ed found out for himself what these things were all about; maybe it was time Ed found out for himself just how easy it would be to lure someone into his home, or even better, how willing people would be to invite a stranger in, not knowing the first thing about him.

Ed moved his mouse to bring his computer monitor screen to life. He pulled *Gay Chicago* in front of him, pressed the blue "e" to launch Internet Explorer, and typed in the URL for the biggest ad he saw in the classifieds, the one for a site called Men4HookUpNow.com. Ed thought the name was ridiculous, and when he got to the home page for the site, he thought that was ridiculous too, with its cartoonishly drawn pumped-up male bodies and its come-ons. He browsed a bit and found the site had a free trial period, and Ed clicked on the blue "Open a new account" button, which took him to another screen, where he had to enter the usual personal information (Ed made all of this up); but paused when the system asked for a credit card. Even though he knew he should get with the times, he had never felt comfortable giving out his credit card number online, and he felt even less comfortable giving it to a site like this one. He gave up and hit Escape. Amazingly, another screen popped up with the words: "Welcome! Your account has been created."

Ed guessed they wanted a credit card, but if they didn't get one, they didn't want to lose a prospective customer completely. They could ask again later, after the prospect was "hooked" on the easy sex the site promised. He also thought a killer could log in again and again without ever giving out any real personal information, just making up a new name each time he wanted to do the free trial.

Ed was then led to a series of screens where he could write a description of himself and upload a picture (he decided against that option).

And then he was in.

That simple.

He scrolled through pages of pictures of men, snorting with amazement at what some people chose to put up for public consumption, pictures like the one of EdgewaterBottom, a fat guy on his hands and knees on his bed, pulling his ass cheeks apart for the camera.

"Subtle," Ed whispered.

"Hey, what's goin' on?"

A small blue and white instant message box popped up on his screen. The words floated ghostly in front of Ed. Ed imagined a tough guy, someone with a close-trimmed beard, bushy eyebrows, wearing tight jeans and a flannel shirt. He knew then that this was how it worked: the imagination filling in the blanks, hope usurping the role of common sense. He didn't know enough yet to click on the guy's screen name to bring up his profile.
Ed responded:

"Not Much. Just checking things out."
"So what are you up for tonight?"

Ed was surprised at how quickly and how directly this worked. No wonder so many guys were online. This was just one service, and Ed noticed there were fourteen pages of men online, with about a dozen guys on each page. Why bother with going out when you could order in?

"Maybe just talk, maybe get together."

Ed typed, knowing he was lying, which made him wonder how many lies took place online. How many men were, like him, afraid to hook up with a stranger, but enjoyed this sort of virtual window shopping, safe and anonymous, hiding behind their monitors?

"Yeah, well I'm definitely looking to play. Whereabouts are you?"
"North side. You?"
"Around Wrigley. What are you into?"

Ed thought for a moment.

"Um, I'm pretty versatile, open to suggestions, you know?"

The instant message screen stayed blank at his response. Ed guessed the guy he was talking to was no longer interested. *Did I say something wrong?* Ed wondered. How could versatile not be what he liked?
What are you getting offended for? Ed asked himself.
For the next ten minutes, Ed scrolled through the pages of online profiles, seeing everything from normal-looking guys

looking for relationships to hardcore leathermen looking to get fisted. The messages and photos ran the gamut from the sweetly innocent and naïve, to X-rated hardcore come-ons, where safe sex was a dirty word, and hungers went far beyond the pale.

There were a few more instant messages, but it seemed Ed always said something wrong; he didn't party, or he didn't want to "travel," or he didn't have red hair. He dogged on for a few minutes more.

Another IM box popped up.

"Hey there! Nice profile."
"Hi," Ed keyed. "What's going on?"
"Just trying to find someone real on this line. Are you real?"

What was this? Some sort of existential game? At least the guy didn't start off by telling how "fuckin' horny" he was or how he was "looking to get plowed." These kind of statements would be entered before the guy on the other end even had a clue as to what the person on the other end was like.

"As real as they come."
"You're not into games, are you? I'm getting so sick of all the bullshit that goes down on here."
"Really? Actually, and this is not bullshit, I've never been on one of these sites before."
"LOL. A virgin. That's nice. You haven't learned much about all the crap. Guys get on here and lie through their fuckin' teeth. Post pictures of other guys or of themselves taken ten years ago. Invite one over and the odds are against you that he'll even show up, or go to their place and ring a buzzer that's never answered."
"I'm sure it doesn't always work out that way."
"No, once in a while it works. But for the most part, it's sheer bullshit."
"Have you met many guys this way?"
"I wouldn't say many, but maybe one a month. On nights like this, when it's shitty outside, it can be an easy way to scratch an itch. Sort of like ordering a pizza."

Yeah, Ed thought, except what if the pizza was loaded with strychnine?

"And you just invite a stranger over? I mean, I'm not trying to make you defensive or anything, but

you don't know what you're letting in."
"Hey, we all take chances, right? Go to a bar and
pick someone up. Or get picked up. You don't know
what you're bringing back home. Look at all the
guys that went with Dahmer. You think they
suspected they were heading to their deaths? No
one thinks that way, man."
"I guess I see your point. I'm still a little
leery."
"Aw, you're full of shit, too. You wouldn't be on
here if you weren't a little interested in what
could happen. Hell, last week I had this hot
muscle boy over here. Cute? Fuck! And man, this
kid knew what he was doing."
"Good for you. But what if he turned out to be
the nutcase that's goin' around killing gay guys
in Chicago? Doesn't that cross your mind?"
"Who the fuck are you? The Gay Guardian Angel?
Listen, life's full of risks. And gay men in
particular are taking them every fucking day of
the week. Sure, the guy you brought home over the
weekend might not be a serial killer, but he
might be positive. So where does that land you?
The victim, maybe, of an innocent murderer, and
the killing is a longer, slower process. What are
you gonna do? Hide under a rock? Get security
clearance before you put a dick in your mouth?
Get with it, pal. Most of us are out there for
hot sex, that's it. The odds are against being
killed by a psycho, y'know."
"Yeah, but what about the odds of getting
infected?"
"Listen, man, if it happens, it happens. Half my
friends are poz. Nobody lives forever. You wanna
hook up tonight or just shoot the shit?"
"I think I'm still in the checking things out
mode," Ed keyed in.
"Have a good one."

Ed closed the IM box.
He clicked on the "Log out" tab at the top of the page and
clicked on the X to close his Internet connection. He felt jittery. It
would be so easy for the killer, so easy. Everything was working in
his favor. Where else could you find such an easy pool of victims so
ready to just let you in? No one would know of any connection
between the killer and the deceased and death could come quickly,
surely, and quietly.
Without a trace.

It was like shooting at fish in a barrel. Hunting had never been so easy.

Ed stared at the computer. There was a very good chance that this was how he did it.

What should he do now? Call up O'Farrell and see if he'd be interested in what he'd pieced together? He wondered how seriously he'd be taken. Ed was sure the task force was taking all kinds of tips from the public; perhaps he should just phone in his hunch anonymously. Sad to think, but it might be taken more seriously that way.

And while the department was filing and cataloging his tip along with the hundreds of others Ed was sure they were getting, he could continue with his own investigation. He still had a couple of months' severance, so he had the time and the resources.

Another idea: perhaps Peter could convince his friend to let Ed talk to him on the phone, without revealing to him who he was. Ed didn't know why he hadn't thought of this before.

Ed switched the radio from WFMT to Q101. Depeche Mode's "Personal Jesus" was playing and Ed suddenly felt energized, as if he had finally turned a corner and was now heading down the street to his redemption. He stood up and began dancing around the room, feeling better than he had in months.

Peter would arrive soon. Ed wanted to make sure the evening was perfect and that his good mood would not go to waste. Crossing to the bedroom, Ed shrugged into his jean jacket and donned a Sox baseball cap. There was a liquor store around the corner and he and Peter both enjoyed a good bottle of champagne. He checked his wallet and headed toward the door.

The phone rang.

Ed picked it up, thinking (and fearing) at the same time, that one of the men he had talked with had somehow deduced who he was and his phone number. Irrational.

" 'Lo?" He also prayed it wouldn't be Peter, saying he was too tired to come over tonight.

"Mr. Comparetto?" The voice was nasal, high, yet definitely male. Ed thought it sounded vaguely familiar.

"Yes? This is Ed."

"This is Timothy Bright."

Chapter
Fifteen

IT WAS ONE of the last beautiful days, Ed was certain, the sky bright blue, laced with a few strands of cirrus, up high. A warm wind blew out of the south, cutting the chilly undercurrent that would take its hold as the sun sank later in the west. Many of the leaves were already off the trees, lying about in heaps of auburn and deep brown, giving off a rich scent of humus, decay...the harbingers of winter. The leaves that remained on the trees were fast losing their color, yet shades of red, orange and yellow still dazzled in the play of shadow and light.

Ed was west of the city, in a forest preserve parking lot. To his west lay Schaumburg, home of corporate headquarters, brand-spanking-new houses and apartment buildings, shopping malls and chain stores and restaurants of every description. Schaumburg was a place that could have existed anywhere in the United States, and Ed thought, as he sat in his Monte Carlo, that all too soon, the rest of the country would look just like Schaumburg, one town indistinguishable from the next. Going away on vacation would be like never leaving.

The parking lot was virtually empty. A couple of cars—a taxi cab-yellow Camaro and a rusted-out pickup—cruised by every so often, but neither of the men inside resembled what his recollections told him Timothy Bright looked like.

Perhaps he wouldn't show, and with that thought, Ed took a measure of relief. He wasn't too sure that meeting Timothy Bright like this was such a good idea. He had told no one about this rendezvous, save for Peter.

"You're nuts. I thought you had more sense than going out to some woods to meet this character. Why couldn't you meet him somewhere more public, like a mall or a McDonalds?"

"I tried that. He wouldn't go for it. This was my only choice."

"What do you think he wants to get out of this?" Peter's voice was tinged with anger and concern.

"I don't know. But I need to take what I can get. This guy could

very well hold the key to my getting back my job." Ed had
snuggled closer to Peter in the warm darkness. It was still raining
outside, and right now, he felt more safe and secure than he ever
had. "Even more important, this guy could very well be the killer."

"So what are you gonna do? Talk him into turning himself in?"

"Maybe."

"Right." Peter had rolled away from him and his body had
stiffened, the armor going up.

Ed leaned close and squeezed Peter's shoulder. "Hey, are you
mad at me?"

"Listen: I just don't want to hear on the news there's been
another killing." Peter turned to Ed. "I'm just getting attached to
you." He smiled, but the smile was wary and even in the darkness,
Ed could see Peter's eyes were bright with fear.

"I'll be okay. There'll be other people around. It'll be broad
daylight. I was a police officer, remember? I can take care of
myself."

"Are you taking your gun?"

Ed flushed. "I don't have a gun anymore; I turned it in with my
badge."

Ed did wish, now, that he had a revolver concealed underneath
his denim jacket. Peter was right, and even though Ed tried to
reassure him, Ed was just as afraid of meeting this guy, if not more,
than Peter was.

But he was beginning to be afraid that his fears were
groundless. He had sat alone in the parking lot for almost an hour,
playing with the radio and trying to read that day's paper, but
unable to keep his eyes on the type long enough to digest anything.

Perhaps this was yet another taunt, like buying him a drink in
the bar and, yes, even like showing up at the scene of the first
murder and claiming he had found the body.

What was Bright's connection to Tony Evans anyway? At the
time, Ed had talked with associates of Evans, doing background,
looking for answers. But he had never explored too closely Bright's
connection, because there was really no reason to. How would Ed
have known, at the time, that the Timothy Bright he had spoken
with was officially dead? Ed decided that another tack he might
take, if he made it out of this forest preserve today (grim chuckle)
would be to revisit Tony Evans' fellow bartenders and the various
friends he had spoken with back in August to see if any of them
knew Bright.

The yellow Camaro had pulled in a few spaces down from Ed,
and Ed could feel the driver's gaze on him. A young guy in a
baseball cap was looking intently at him and Ed realized this park
must be a cruising ground. Ed looked closer, trying to see if any

blond hair was falling out of the cap, or if the face beneath its bill was kind of elfin, with a turned-up nose that made the man whose face it graced appear younger than he was.

But the guy in the Camaro had a dark mustache, dark eyes. He was probably Hispanic. Ed turned away and looked out the driver's side window, to make sure the guy got the message he wasn't interested.

And when he looked, he saw the figure in the woods. A man stood just behind where the grassy area ended and the trees began. It was hard to see his face, because the trees and the bright sunlight merged to cast a shadow across his features. But his stature was small and the hair he could see, blowing back in the wind, was blond.

It seemed the man knew he was staring. He lifted a hand in greeting.

Ed swallowed, mouth suddenly gone dry. Even without a "positive ID," Ed was sure it was Bright, standing there just behind the tree line. But what was he doing in the woods? Why not come out in the day's bright sunlight? Come out where the two of them could talk at a picnic table. And why hadn't Ed heard a car? There was only the Camaro in the lot now, the pickup having abandoned the hunt, presumably to look for greener pastures. How had Bright gotten here? The forest preserve was alone in a sea of mirrored office buildings, and even none of those was very close. Had he trudged along Golf Road, then ducked into the woods somewhere just out of sight of the parking lot?

And how deep did the woods go?

Ed felt a chill in spite of the sunlight that warmed his car. The man waved again and this time, Ed could see he was motioning him to follow. Logic told him to simply turn the key in the ignition, throw the car into Reverse, and get the hell out of there. But there burned within him a desire to know. He had to find out what was going on, and this was probably the only way.

He would be careful.

He reached down and grabbed the door handle, opening it in spite of the sensible little voice inside telling him that he might indeed find out what was going on, but this information could well be the last he'd ever receive.

Before he exited the car, Ed reached into the glove box, brought out a Philips head screwdriver, and tucked it into his inside jacket pocket.

It was better than nothing.

When the man in the woods saw him heading in his direction, he turned and started moving further back into the trees.

"Hey!" Ed called, trying to thwart this move. One thing he

didn't want to do was go deep into the woods with this guy.

But he didn't stop. If he heard Ed, he gave no indication. The figure moved rapidly, deeper and deeper into the trees, and Ed had to quicken his pace to keep up with him. Ed paused then, seriously thinking of aborting this whole mission. Peter was right. What would he get out of this encounter anyway? Ed was probably the only person who knew who Bright was and, dead or alive, knew he had some solid connection to the killings.

But common sense deserted him in the wake of wanting to know. Ed crossed the tree line, keeping his eye on the red windbreaker the man wore. Perhaps it wasn't Bright at all, just someone who looked like him. Perhaps this man was leading him into the woods for a sexual encounter. Wouldn't that be just perfect? Still, Ed supposed someone trying to give him a blowjob would be better than stabbing him.

There was a small incline in the woods and the figure dipped down into it, disappearing from Ed's view. When Ed got to the top of the rise, he could see no red windbreaker. The forest suddenly appeared empty, with nothing more than the wind rustling the few remaining leaves on the trees. Where had he gone? Was he now lying in wait behind that big oak tree just ahead, the knife gripped tightly in a sweaty palm, its blade reflecting the sun?

Or, Ed thought, feeling stupid even as he thought it, was Timothy Bright really dead and what he had just seen only an apparition? A ghost?

Ed moved further along the path, stiffening when he heard a rustling of leaves to his right. He whirled, his breath coming faster now, to see a squirrel scamper up the bark of a tree and, when it reached the security of a high branch, look down on him and begin scolding.

Ed gave out a short, nervous laugh.

He stopped. The day really was gorgeous, the sun's rays slanting down between the branches to illuminate the forest floor littered with dead leaves and twigs. Under other circumstances, a perfect day for hiking, for disappearing for hours, alone with one's thoughts, the trees providing a roof.

And then, up ahead, a flash of bright red.

"Wait up!" Ed called. He began running, the red jacket and the figure growing larger as he neared them.

He was close enough now to see the face of Timothy Bright. Ed flashed on a hot summer day and it all came back: the queasiness he had felt after just seeing a mutilated body in a bathtub full of gore. Bright was grinning at him, hands stuffed deeply into his pockets.

And what did those pockets contain?

Just as Ed was within a few feet of Timothy, he turned and ran, leaves rustling, going so deep into the trees that the sunlight became muted. Here it was a semi-darkness that surrounded them. Stillness pervaded, eerie in its absolute lack of sound. The wind had died and no longer did Ed hear the cries of birds, the humming of bees.

He chased Bright, who seemed to have an almost superhuman quickness. Before long, the trail ended and the two were passing through brambles and tree roots sticking out of rich black soil. Ed saw his foot catching on one of the roots, saw himself fall and lie there, ankle throbbing, until Bright returned to claim his prey.

But he didn't fall. And he couldn't keep up with Bright, who turned right, moving through the trees as if he had charted his course in advance.

"Why are you running from me?" Ed cried out, throat burning and lungs constricting. Heat shot up from his lungs; his legs ached.

Bright was out of sight once more. Ed stopped and put a hand to the rough bark of a maple for support. It seemed he was unable to suck in enough air. Perhaps Bright was having his fun with him; Ed couldn't permit that. If the guy wanted to talk to him that was one thing, but this asinine game was getting him nowhere.

He turned and could no longer see the parking lot. In fact, all he could see were trees. It was as if he had been transported to northern Minnesota or some other heavily wooded area.

He had lost his bearings. As his breathing returned to normal, he realized he wasn't sure which direction to head to get back to the parking lot. This was ridiculous. Who got lost in a fucking forest preserve? The wind blew overhead and Ed was gripped by a strange sensation. He didn't know if this sensation stemmed from paranoia or if it was the real thing. But he had the distinct impression someone was watching him. He turned in every direction, trying to see beyond the vertical lines of the trees, trying to make out a flash of red amidst the brown.

But he saw nothing. And yet the feeling persisted.

"Bright? Why don't you come out? What did you want me to come out here for if you were going to pull this shit?"

Ed knew the answer and an icy hand gently fingered his spine.

He looked up, thinking the little bastard might have climbed a tree and was now above him, watching, laughing, waiting for just the right moment to pounce.

But there was nothing. Sun broken up by jagged branches, nothing more.

Ed was still, listening for the sound of rushing traffic in the distance: Golf Road. When at last he picked up on that faint but familiar drone, he headed toward it, trudging through the woods, making his own path. None of it was easy.

How could Bright have virtually vanished? Ed had never believed in things he couldn't put his fingers on, had always thought supernatural notions were nothing more than fanciful ideas, the province of the mentally unbalanced.

Now, as he trudged through briars, mud, and fallen leaves, he wondered if he hadn't been too quick to deny things that were inexplicable. Timothy Bright was a dead man; he had seen it on the front page of the *Chicago Tribune*, he had scrutinized police department records. And now the man was present, seemingly of flesh and blood and then gone the very next moment.

He kept trying to move toward the sounds of traffic on the road just outside the forest preserve, but progress was getting more and more difficult. But there, up ahead, was a break in the trees and Ed could see, in the distance, a large office building, its blue glass mirroring the clouds and at the top, a bit of the sun.

Thank God, Ed thought, quickening his pace, thank God. When Peter hears about this, there will be no end to his "I told you so's." And that was all right.

He was just happy to be getting the hell out of here.

It was then he felt the blow to the back of his head. He gasped and started to reach back to where the pain was beginning to burrow into his skull like a razor-toothed animal and a warm wetness was already dampening his neck, and then everything went dark as the earth rose up to meet him.

Chapter
Sixteen

PETER CHECKED THE clock again. It was now a quarter after six and the sky outside made him even more nervous. The day's bright sunlight had faded, replaced by a band of dusky gold at the horizon, fading to purple, and finally a deep navy at the top. All in all, a beautiful sunset, but the encroaching darkness worried Peter. Ed should have returned hours ago. Peter looked again out the living room window of his apartment, hoping against hope he would see the navy blue Monte Carlo coming down his street. His gut clenched as he thought of what might have happened to Ed, clenched with guilt because he let Ed go, and because he didn't go along with him.

But Ed had insisted he stay behind, fearing that if he showed up with someone else in tow, Timothy Bright would leave. Peter had, unwisely he thought now, trusted that Ed would be all right, that he could stand up to this weirdo.

But Peter knew as well as Ed that this Bright character could be the killer who was stalking Chicago's gay men. A killer who murdered his prey with certainty and cunning. The news reports claimed that one hallmark of this killer was to never leave behind indications of struggle.

But there was no killing today, Peter insisted to himself as he paced the apartment, passing his dining room windows, which faced east, affording a view of Lake Michigan. He looked out at the horizon once more, almost dark now, save for a pale dusky light. The water looked almost black, the foam on the waves silver as it crashed into the boulders lining the shore.

Whom could he call for help? Ed hadn't been gone that long, not long enough to cause any official concern. And if something had happened to Ed, who would contact him to let him know? It could be days before he discovered anything. He realized, sadly, there would be nothing to connect him to Ed, so if something terrible had happened to the man he was sure he was falling in love with, he would have to wait to find that news out until the media released it, just like anyone else in Chicago.

Peter toured the apartment once more, too jittery to sit still. "If something's happened to him, I'll never be able to forgive myself." Peter forced himself to sit down and pick up the phone.

DARKNESS. A CHILL and dampness at his back. His head throbbed, a dull ache in the back.

Ed tried to sit up, but managed only a semi-erect posture, supporting himself on one elbow. How long had he been out? The woods were quiet now that darkness had fallen and the warmth of the day had gone, replaced by a bone-chilling wind that whistled through the treetops and made Ed hug himself, seeking warmth.

When he did manage to sit up, his vision blurred and nausea rose up in his gut, wrenching it and making him fear he would puke. He could hear the sounds of traffic on Golf Road and if he turned his head (when he did, the pain made him wince, rattling through his brain like a train), he could make out headlights just beyond the thick rows of trees.

Gingerly, he touched the back of his head. It felt crusty, hair matted with a thick viscous substance that could only be blood.

Finally, he managed to stand, but only after first getting to his hands and knees, gasping and trying, with a mighty effort of will, to hold back the queasiness and the shooting pain in his head that made him see stars.

Did he have a concussion? What had he been hit with? And, most importantly, was he supposed to be dead? He thought not; Bright was too smart to just leave him behind. Ed had seen one of his victims, and the guy obviously enjoyed bringing death and misery. At least with the first couple of victims, the killer had to have left confident with the knowledge that his victims would not stand up again.

Ed stumbled through the trees, grabbing one every few minutes for support. Finally, he reached the forest's edge and was standing on a plain of mushy grass. The four-lane road was ahead of him, swarming even now with cars, their headlights like insect eyes in the darkness.

He looked to the west and several hundred feet ahead was the shape of the wooden sign marking the forest preserve. It was there he had turned in, and just a few yards down the road was the parking lot where he had left his car.

Was it still there? Or had Bright taken it? Had he vandalized it? Ed pictured the windshield smashed, tires flattened, dents of every description in the body.

He trudged through the damp earth toward the parking lot,

thanking God with each step that he was still alive. "Stupid, stupid, stupid," he mumbled over and over again, making of the words a self-castigating litany.

He thought of Peter as he walked, and how the poor guy had probably worried himself senseless in his absence. He had been supposed to arrive at Peter's apartment in the late afternoon, no later, and the two of them were going to make a stir fry dinner together. Peter knew where Ed was going and was most likely going out of his mind now with worry, sure he had met his fate.

And he had, Ed thought, as his feet connected at last with the concrete of the parking lot. His car was up ahead and, under the sodium vapor lamps, looked untouched. Ed was relieved. His head was beginning to clear, just a little, enough so that he could drive himself to Peter's anyway. There, he could discover if he needed further medical attention. It would be only under the most dire circumstances that he would visit a hospital emergency room. He didn't want to have to explain to anyone what had happened.

He almost missed it as he reached his car, he was so grateful to just be near the vehicle that would transport him out of this mess, away from the fiasco the day had become. But, as he was fitting his key into the door lock, he noticed it: a white card stuck under his windshield wiper. Sure, it could just be a solicitation from a business, ten dollars off an oil change or something, but Ed knew it was more.

As Ed headed toward the front of the car, the eerie sensation of being watched seized him again. He turned slowly (no whirling around for him) and searched the dark woods for signs of someone standing there, just beyond the tree line, watching.

But he saw no one. Ed hurried back to the driver's side door, card in hand, and got inside, locking every door before he settled back into the seat and switched on the dome light. The handwriting was shaky, but Ed recognized it as the same he had seen on the card he was given at the Round-Up.

Timothy Bright
5800 N. Ravenswood Avenue
Ask at information for my exact location

Ed didn't know what this could all mean. But he knew one thing for certain: when he checked it out, he would not be doing it alone.

WHEN THE BUZZER sounded in his apartment, Peter jumped and let out a little cry. He was far too on edge for such noises. Had someone finally made the connection between him and Ed and come to deliver the bad news?

Peter didn't even ask who it was. He pressed the buzzer to admit whoever was downstairs, praying it would be Ed.

After listening to the creak and slam of the vestibule door through the intercom, Peter stationed himself at the peephole. No one, save for a person in uniform or Ed himself, would be getting in.

And at last, Ed did appear. Even through the peephole, Peter could see his clothes were caked with mud, littered with dead leaves and twigs. He opened the door and the face that greeted him was pale, slick with sweat. But Ed somehow managed a smile just before he fell into Peter's arms and whispered in his ear: "Please don't say I told you so."

Chapter
Seventeen

MARK DIETRICH CRACKED open the bottle of Blue Moon and put the cold beer to his lips. For once, it tasted bitter and not at all refreshing. You'd think, he thought, after five of these, they would begin to taste good. He downed the beer in three or four swallows and stood on shaky legs.

He'd been shaky ever since Peter had called him last night; on edge every moment since the evil dwarf had come into his life. Sleep was elusive; the previous night he had spent switching positions in a bed with clammy sheets. The brief few moments he did manage to sleep, he was tormented by a nightmare. The nightmare had all the earmarks of reality. He was lying in his bed, trying to fall asleep, knowing that trying to fall asleep never worked. Just rest, he thought, you are getting rest. As he was musing over the torture of insomnia, he tensed. A floorboard in his living room had creaked. The wind was whistling outside, rattling the storm windows in their frame. That's all it is, he told himself, wondering if he had remembered to lock the back door. Another creak and Mark tried his best to convince himself it was nothing more than the wind and the building settling. Then he heard another noise: something being put down on the coffee table, the clunk of plastic against wood. The creak again, and this time Mark was certain the creaking was due to a footfall. He lay in bed, his whole body one singing ribbon of steel; muscles tensed. God, he thought, this is where I die. He didn't want to look up as the footsteps slowly made their way, in the darkness, to the threshold of his bedroom. Something white and ghastly was standing in the doorway. That was when he had started to scream. Really scream, and the muffled cries of nightmare brought him full awake.

Eyes wide in the dark, he finally gave up on the idea of sleep about 3:00 a.m. and had gotten up to read Steve Thayer's *The Weatherman*, a book he had just picked up at a used bookstore. When he remembered the book was about a serial killer, he had thrown it in disgust against the wall, turning instead to his windows, where he watched the sky lighten as dawn approached. Normally, he would have enjoyed the book, but Mark thought he would be sticking to magazines and newspapers for a very long time.

Peter, his only real gay friend, had called him early last night. His voice almost quivered with worry. How had Mark's life gone from relatively easy to stressful beyond belief in a few days? Peter had explained how his new boyfriend, Ed, was missing and he feared the same guy who was on a killing rampage (as Peter called it) in the gay community might have gotten him. He told him all about how Ed used to work for the police force and the reason he'd been suspended.

"If he comes home," Peter said, letting out a long, quivering sigh, "I'd really like it if you'd talk to him. It isn't fair that you're keeping information to yourself that might help take this guy off the street."

Mark had pictured himself gently replacing the receiver in its cradle and disconnecting the phone from its socket in the wall, but knew he could never do such a thing. But Peter's request had made him so anxious he had begun to sweat, a panicky nervousness rising up in him, almost enough to engulf, to send him over the brink.

"Look, we don't even have to tell him your name. Just talk to him. Maybe nothing will come of it." Mark had known, the minute the words came out of Peter's mouth, that the enticement was nothing more than a lure. That if he began this dialogue with the former detective, he would be persuaded to do more and then...everyone would know.

But Mark had finally agreed, and it was for selfish reasons he had done so. He had never in his life felt more paranoid, more fearful of opening the door or stepping onto the sidewalk in front of his apartment building than he was now. Something had to be done to stop this creep, and maybe being outed paled in comparison to what could happen if he maintained this silence. And outed he would be if this creep got his clutches on him. Not only would his family be forced to cope with the trauma of his death, but they would also have to struggle through the shame of one of their fair-haired boys being a fag. The choice was really no choice, and he had reluctantly agreed to talk to Peter's friend.

And now he was getting ready to leave, to go outside into a city that was full of fear and uncertainty. Once he had walked down the street, shoulders back, meeting the world head on. Now, when he ventured outside, his walk was accompanied by constant looks over his shoulder and nervous jumps when a car backfired or a little boy zoomed too close on his bike.

Mark put his jacket on and checked to make sure he had his keys. He headed toward the door. If meeting with this Ed could at least somehow help in putting an end to this anxiety, he felt he would pay anything. What good was being alive when life was like this?

TIMOTHY BRIGHT SAT across the street from Mark Dietrich's building, waiting. He wore a navy blue, down-filled ski parka, warm for this bright morning, but it had served him well the night before, as he watched the lights in Dietrich's window tell a tale of insomnia. The fact that he was scared was good, but small consolation when Bright thought of the threat the frightened young man posed.

How would he get him alone? If the guy spotted him on the street, Timothy was certain he would run, screaming, in the other direction, a Midwestern portrait by Edvard Munch. But Timothy knew, perhaps better than anyone, how anonymous the city could be, and just out of sight was often as good as being alone on a mountain top.

And then he had an idea, one so brilliant he wondered why he hadn't thought of it before.

MARK LOCKED THE door behind him, and realized that for the first time in his life, locking the door was a lesser evil compared to what might await him outside. He tried to breathe deeply, because his breath was coming too fast. He had learned last term, in Psych 101, about agoraphobia, and wondered if an agoraphobe was what he was becoming.

Outside, the air was cold, the wind whipping across the lake. One block over, he could hear the roar and crash of the waves when there was a break in traffic on Lake Shore Drive. The sun told a bright lie.

His car was two blocks north and he wished he earned enough to afford a parking space, so he wouldn't have to walk this short distance. But, hey, it was daylight. Up ahead, a woman with curly brown hair pulled taut the leash of a German shepherd. "Luke, heel!" she shouted, but the dog, salivating, his pink tongue a facial ornament, ignored her.

What could possibly happen here? Even his parents had approved of this safe urban neighborhood, here on the north side, yuppification complete years before. Nothing but white faces inspired their approval.

Mark strode up the street, pace brisk. One more block and he would round the corner and his little silver Honda Civic would be waiting for him. He pictured himself running to the little car, throwing himself inside and locking the door. Safe behind metal and glass. At least for this portion of the day...

He rounded the corner. The car was where he had left it, and fortune smiled on him. Near his car, two men were talking, one an older man with a newspaper in his hand, the other man younger, wearing what looked like a hunting jacket. Mark edged by them, his keys out, and got in the car. He locked the doors quickly (power locks were never more wonderful) and put the key in the ignition. Such a small enclosed space felt good. As Mark jockeyed out of the parking space, he began to feel just the tiniest glimmer of hope. Perhaps Peter's friend would be able to help him out of this nightmare.

Mark headed east, toward Lake Shore Drive. After waiting for a light and playing with his radio for what seemed like too long, the light turned green and Mark swung left, onto the on ramp.

He joined the river of swiftly moving northbound cars.

He breathed a sigh of relief. He had made it. "Aren't you proud?" he said aloud to himself.

There was a glimmer in the rear-view mirror and Mark glanced up. The guy was there, in his back seat, pale blue eyes meeting his. His thin lips curled into a grin.

"Hello, dickhead."

Mark gasped and swerved. The last thing he remembered seeing was a Ford Explorer headed for the side of his car.

Chapter
Eighteen

FROM HELENE BRIGHT'S Journal, October 28, 1987

I wish I could go back. There was a time once when I was innocent. When the world held more than ugliness. I long to hop in H.G. Wells' time machine and just set the timer back a few years, thirty maybe. I do not long to live in another time, do not want to travel back to Roman times or England at the turn of the century. No, my wants are so much more simple. I long for childhood, when the scariest thing the world held was what was lurking in the dark under the bed, or Bela Lugosi as Dracula. It's difficult to write this. It sounds corny and cliché, but tears are blurring my vision as I struggle to put pen to paper. Part of me does not want to commit the last twenty-four hours to vellum and black ink, but I've been keeping this journal for so long, I can't withhold what's happened.

Where have all the years gone? Who could have predicted the twists and turns life would take? Who would have known all the crap with my brother would come about? After all, what happened to him and Lanta was quite premature; most of the country wasn't involved in such things until a decade later. But what happened to them was not born of innocence, but of evil, of a desire for too much. Greed...when they already had so much. Hedonism I suppose is the word. And look what it netted them.

I'm rambling, I know. There is within me a desire to hold back, to put off what must be written here.

When did the world come crashing down around me? All my life I've followed the rules, done the right thing, the charitable thing. I've never been selfish and I've never deliberately harmed anyone in my whole life. Of course, a saint is not what I've been, but the few indiscretions that have colored this admittedly sheltered life have never harmed another human being. And taking the responsibilities I've taken, well, I've written at length about that already.

Daniel and Lanta. My brother and his "woman." Well, what would you call her? Common-law wife? Live-in lover? No matter. What they're both called these days is dead. But it seemed I have been pulled into the whirlwind of their wickedness (I know it's a melodramatic term, but it's apt). I stood too close to the magnet, not of my own choice, mind you, but this closeness was predetermined by blood.

And look what's become of their union. Depravity, illness and the sickest behavior imaginable.

It's Timothy. Oh God. I guess a part of me has known for some time that he's homosexual. It was most assuredly never a conscious thought, but it's always been there, in the background, waiting to emerge. I never thought it would rear its head under such hideous, tawdry circumstances. They say a mother always knows when a son is homosexual, and I have been a mother to him. The best mother I knew how to be, thrust upon me as motherhood was. And I did the best by...well, that's another story.

I suppose the signs were always there. An objective person would say "Just look at him." But I never believed that appearances could give one away, not in that manner at least. And I've found out the hard way that appearances can be oh so deceptive. But Timothy, with his fine features, his wispy blond hair, his soft, breathy voice and his delicate bone structure was always the kind of male my grandmother called a "sissy man." And he never did join in with any of the boys at Loyola Academy, never played any sports, preferring instead to spend his time at home with us. I suppose, in my loneliness, I encouraged it. That, and his delicacy. Well, I just thought he needed the protective shell our home afforded.

It's no longer a home. These walls hold an empty shell. I must leave.

Enough dawdling. Let me report the truth then and damn the pain. Writing this and the tears I've shed will most assuredly help ease the pain. At least that's the way it works in the movies.

Timothy was with David. There, is that bald enough? Already the images come unbidden, the memories from hours ago, to torment and taunt me. They won't go away, no matter what I do.

David was fucking Timothy in my bed. I came home early from lunch with Claire O'Donnell and Jane Shondell. Early I suppose isn't the right word. When I got to the club, word awaited me that Jane wasn't feeling well and she would call to reschedule. Fair enough. I was tired and going home, spending the afternoon with people I once loved seemed like a happy alternative.

What do I see when I close my eyes? I see the two of them on my bed. Timothy is on his back, his legs thrown up on David's broad shoulders. David is between my nephew's legs, the muscles in his backside bunching and contracting as he thrusts into this boy. They didn't stop for a few seconds, so involved were they in what they were doing. And I stood frozen in the doorway, unable to scream or even speak. For a moment or two, I would even venture as far as to say I felt calm. But that calm, I know, was the result of shock. David, with his medical degree, could have told me that.

And then Timothy's blue eyes met mine and he, he...smiled. I turned *wordlessly* and left the room, heading down the stairs, not sure where I was going. Anywhere away from I had just been witness to.

I heard David struggling into his clothes while trying to maneuver the stairs.

"Helene! Wait. Please let me explain."

The very idea of his trying to come up with some sort of explanation made me nauseous. Nauseous enough to wonder if I could make it into the downstairs powder room before losing my breakfast. I slammed the door behind me and everything came up. Oh, I know, it's not a pleasant image, but it's nothing compared to the image that inspired it.

David was banging on the door and I could tell he was crying. I suppose losing his future wife in this way was the ultimate in degradation and humiliation.

I am a fool. How could I have not realized this was going on? There had been, over the past few years, so many camping trips, so many evenings alone together, and I encouraged them, relieved that Timothy at last had a suitable role model in his life. I laugh to think of it, how I encouraged their liaisons.

There was no way I would open that door and after a while, the pounding and pleading stopped. I wonder if I shall ever see David again. If he's wise, he'll keep away. If I'm wise, I'll press charges.

But that isn't the way things are handled here on the North Shore. No, we keep our shame quiet, hidden away in closets paneled in cedar.

I can no longer bear the sight of my nephew and I must send him away. He's eighteen now and can well fend for himself. Daniel left him a trust fund, money enough to last a lifetime, so I don't have to feel I'm abandoning him to the wolves. He'll survive. And I never want to think of the life that survival will mean.

And about the other...well, I think that's Timothy's responsibility as well.

And I will go on. The images burned in my brain will fade and I will go on.

I must.

Chapter
Nineteen

ROSEHILL CEMETERY IS situated on Chicago's north side. Its large, gothic gates welcome visitors off the narrow street of Ravenswood, which runs parallel to the Metra train tracks. The cemetery has graced this location for more than a hundred years and among its monuments are memorials dating back to the Civil War. It speaks of a bygone era, when people, mourning, built statues, tombs and other relics to commemorate their dead. Even though this is an urban cemetery, its grounds sprawl, covering acres and acres. Situated on this land are a chapel, several ponds, and wooded copses. It is a beautiful place to stroll on a warm day.

This day, as Ed and Peter found a spot just outside the gates, was not warm. Early November, it looked as if the days of Indian summer were nothing more than a memory, something to be treasured through the long months of frigid cold, evil winds, snow, and grey skies. Now, a light drizzle fell out of a slate-blue sky. Ed had had to use his headlights on the trip over.

The day was perfect for wandering through a cemetery, in an Addams family sort of way. The two walked wordlessly through the gates and were transported, almost magically, into another world. Gone was the large, sprawling city of Chicago; they were in a peaceful place now, surrounded by trees stubbornly holding on to the last of their leaves, brown and drooping, more and more joining their kindred on the ground below with each gust of wind.

"There's a kind of directory," Peter said, maneuvering Ed to their right, where a small house stood, looking vaguely liturgical with its yellowed cement façade and stained glass windows.

The two entered and found a sort of museum had been set up, explaining the history of the cemetery and who some of its more notable residents were. Another day, they would have lingered among the history, picking up one of the maps so they could do their own tombstone hunting.

An old woman, with reddish tinted hair streaked through with grey, sat behind a desk. A pair of pince nez glasses were perched on her nose and the glasses were attached to a chain which wrapped around her neck. She was busy at a calculator, papers spread before her on a desk. She wore a pale blue cardigan over a navy dress.

She looked up when she saw the men and smiled. "Can I help you?"

Ed looked at the piece of paper he had clutched in his hand since the two had exited the car. "Yeah. I was wondering if you could help us locate a grave."

The woman pulled a map from a drawer in her desk. "What's the name, sir?"

"Timothy Bright," Ed said, his voice coming out soft. It seemed strange to be uttering that name here, among the dead. He imagined the woman examining the map and looking up, somewhat confused, and saying that there was no such person buried there. How could there be when Timothy Bright had to be alive?

She traced a red-painted fingernail over the black and white surface of the map. Finally, she paused at a particular location. "If you follow the main road back toward the chapel, you'll find the Bright site off to your left, before you get to the pond."

"Thank you." Ed and Peter went outside once more, where the rain had begun falling in heavy drops, splattering on their faces and making them wonder what purpose this mission would serve.

They located the area quickly and, wandering among the tombstones, crypts and monuments, soon located the Bright family plot.

Peter was the one who found it. "Here it is," he called out to Ed, who was staring at a statue of a little girl encased in glass.

Ed hurried over to the line of tombstones and saw first the name Daniel Bright. He had been born in 1945 and had died in 1970. Next to him was Lanta Bache, born in 1947, died in 1970 as well. Who were these people? Did their names and untimely deaths have anything to do with what was turning Ed's life upside down now?

"Here," Peter whispered, standing by a black granite marker, which had been engraved with lilies and the name Timothy Bright. Ed stood above the tombstone, not knowing what to say. The legend on the marker was simple: "*Timothy Bright. Born 1969, Died 2003. May the Wings of Angels Enfold and Protect.*"

Ed stared at the tombstone for a long time. Finally, he said, "Yes. He really is dead."

"What about this?" Peter was staring at another marker, identical to Timothy's and just adjacent to it. Ed took a long look at the marker, wondering what the procedure for an exhumation was, picturing a backhoe and a vault broken up, a pile of dirt on the dry and yellowing grass. He imagined Bright's coffin opened, the sun a pale wafered witness. Inside, they would find nothing but a satin lining and a Bible.

Ed moved to where Peter was standing and looked down at the marker. "*Theodore Bright, Born 1969, Died 1988.*" There was no comforting epitaph on this one, but it made Ed wonder: Timothy must have had a brother, a twin. Who was Theodore, and what fate caused his early death? It seemed the family had been plagued by many youthful deaths. What had brought them about?

Ed looked at Peter, at the rain dripping off his nose and said, "This doesn't give me a fucking clue. Not one."

Peter shrugged and wiped some water off his forehead. "I think you should try to find out who this Theodore was. I think we need to do a little family history research."

Ed shrugged. He suddenly felt tired and that doing research would only lead them down another, pardon the pun, dead end street. "Let's go."

Peter took Ed's hand in his. "We'll figure this out."

"We have to," Ed said, walking more briskly now through the rain. Thunder rumbled and the sky went white with lightning. "But what if there are no logical answers?"

"There have to be. C'mon. I'm getting cold."

THE ARGUMENT BETWEEN Peter and Ed had been the day before.

"The guy's an asshole. We're never going to get anywhere with him. Damn, selfishness like that makes me so mad." It was the first time Ed had displayed his temper in front of Peter. Ed realized it was a big step in their relationship; he had always hidden his anger, ever since he was a little boy when such displays were greeted with a back of the hand from his father. He had learned to keep it bottled inside, where it was safe, where it wouldn't offend anyone. But there were times, like this one, when he just couldn't keep it in check. Lurking just beneath the surface, his anger, when it did boil over, was often too much.

Peter looked at him in surprise, never having realized the gentle voice could become so deep and...loud. But Peter was not intimidated. He had grown up in a family very much unlike Ed's, where anger was expressed hotly and freely, often over the dinner table. No one questioned it and no one got hurt by it.

The two were dressing to go out to a movie. Ed had flung the shirt he planned on wearing against the wall.

Peter wore a calm smile. "Just get it all out, honey."

The statement, uttered in a camp voice Ed would have detested under other circumstances, diffused his rage, but only a little. His head still ached from the blow he had received in the forest preserve. "I'm just saying..."

"And you've said it over and over. There's nothing I can do. I've called and called; there's no answer."

"Probably hiding out with mommy and daddy."

"Can you blame him?"

Mark Dietrich had been supposed to show up that morning. Peter had talked him into discussing what had happened to him with Ed, on the promise that it would go no further than the two of them. That is, if Ed could do nothing to help.

"I'm getting to really hate this guy."

"You don't even know him."

"Exactly."

Ed had sat on the bed, balled-up shirt in hand. His breathing was coming faster and he knew that if he didn't rein in his temper, he might do or say something he would later regret.

Peter sat next to him and massaged his shoulders. "God, you're tight. It feels like steel."

"It's just so fucking frustrating." Ed fell back on the bed, one hand on Peter's back. "I don't know what's going on, and this guy could help. He could save a life. Maybe his own."

"I think Mark realizes that. That's why he finally agreed to talk to you."

"The reason he agreed is that you begged him and he probably wants to get in your pants." Where had that come from?

"Can you blame him?"

"Certainly not."

Peter had lowered himself over Ed then and their mouths merged. Mark, at least for the next hour, was forgotten.

And now it was the next day and the guy hadn't even called. They were at Peter's apartment when the phone rang.

Peter got up from the couch, where the two of them had sat reading that day's *Chicago Tribune*. Each was looking for news on the killer, and both were hoping they wouldn't find any.

"Hello?"

Ed watched Peter as he spoke in hushed tones. When Ed heard Peter say, "That's horrible," Ed stood and come closer. "Are you sure? What hospital?"

Peter hung up the phone and stared into Ed's eyes. He bit his lower lip.

"What is it?"

"Mark was in a bad car accident yesterday. On Lake Shore."

"Is he okay?"

"No. In fact, no, he's not. He's in a coma at St. Francis in

Evanston. He's in critical condition."

Ed put his arms around Peter. "I'm sorry."

"He was probably on his way to see us."

"Fuck. I'm sorry I was such an idiot yesterday."

"You didn't know. You had every reason to think he'd blown us off."

"Is he going to pull through?"

"They didn't know."

"Who was that?"

"Ellie James. She works with me at the library. She met Mark through me; she was dating him."

"Christ."

Peter sat back down on the couch. "There's something else."

Ed joined him. "What?"

"There was someone else in the car with him. A guy — small, with blond hair."

Ed felt his spine go rigid. No, it couldn't be... Ed was unable to find words for a minute or two. Could this be the end? "Well, do they know who this other guy is?"

"All Ellie knew was that they took him to Stroger."

"We have to go check this out." Ed was already shrugging into his jacket.

Chapter
Twenty

TIMOTHY BRIGHT WAS in pain. He lay in bed, the curtains drawn. The light hurt his eyes. He experienced a curious sensation: the feeling that his head and limbs were absurdly large and heavy, so heavy in fact that to contemplate lifting them was more work than he could bear. He had never felt this kind of pain before. His back still ached from being thrown forward when Mr. Asshole did his stunt-driving maneuver.

He had been all ready, the knife in his pocket. When the pretty boy stopped at the next light, he would come up suddenly behind him, slit his throat, push him aside, and take his car for a joy ride. A joy ride to a certain forest preserve, where he would wait. When darkness fell, he would drag the body to a heavily wooded area and there he would leave it, with the hopes that the snows and ice of winter would cover it. Discovery would not be made until the thaws of spring.

If only things could have gone as he planned! But he hadn't thought Pretty Boy would be so unnerved by his appearance that he would lose control of his car.

Timothy shuddered as he remembered the *boom* of the impact, the grating of metal against metal, the tinkling music of broken glass. He'd wanted to jump from the car, play dodge 'em in the morning traffic of Lake Shore Drive and sprint off to safety. But everything hurt so much that movement was a challenge he couldn't immediately accept. And besides, the woman in the Ford Explorer — that big, shielded vehicle — had climbed down from it so quickly that Timothy had no time to move, let alone think.

So he had played possum, closing his eyes and lying still across the back seat floor. He had stayed "unconscious" all the way to the hospital, while the paramedics discussed their weekends in the front seat. He had stayed "unconscious" the whole time he was in the emergency room, while a doctor sewed up a cut in his forehead and pulled his eyelids open, looking for signs of life.

He didn't know how he had managed to pull it off, but he had.

Didn't the stupid doctors know when someone was faking? Timothy attributed their stupidity to being overworked. The low-rent hospital's ER that night was crawling with ODs, gunshot wounds, and heart attacks. There just wasn't time to check his pupils and do the other tests that might reveal his ruse. Lucky him!

PETER AND ED hurried inside the huge hospital. Stroger Hospital, just a little south and west of the Loop, was one of Chicago's busiest hospitals, treating victims of urban violence and those who could not afford to go anywhere else.

After checking at the main information desk, the two headed on an elevator to the seventh floor, where the woman behind the desk had directed them.

At the nurse's station, Ed asked, "Could you direct us to the room of a John Doe who was in an accident yesterday morning?"

The nurse, looking harried in spite of the youthful flush of her cheeks and her shoulder-length blonde hair, rolled her eyes and pulled out a log. She rubbed a hand tiredly over her eyes. "Do you have a name?"

"No. The person is this accident has never regained consciousness and had no ID."

The nurse nodded. "I know who you mean. He's in 725." She pointed down a hallway to her left. "It's down that way, three or four doors, on your right."

"Thanks." Both men hurried down the hallway. Ed wondered anxiously how he would feel when he came face to face with the person he might have spoken to back in August once again. He worried that if this was the guy, he would never regain consciousness and nothing would ever be solved.

And what if the murders continued?

But such worries were unfounded. When they entered the room, all they found was an old man lying asleep while an IV tube dripped a clear liquid into his arm and an unmade bed on the other side of the room, looking recently vacated.

Ed rubbed his temples, where a headache was beginning. "Christ, what now?"

Peter touched his arm. "Relax. Maybe this isn't the right room."

"Right. Let's go ask Miss Congeniality again."

But Miss Congeniality was gone. In her place, a fat woman with frizzy black hair sat drinking coffee. "Help ya?" she croaked when she saw the two of them.

Peter spoke this time. "Uh, yes, we just spoke to a nurse and she told us we could find the guy, the, uh, John Doe, who was involved in an accident on north Lake Shore Drive yesterday in Room 725."

The new nurse consulted the log briefly. "That's right."

"He wasn't there. I was wondering if he had been moved or something."

"No, no there's no indication of that. He should be there."

"Well, he's not," Ed said.

"Well, I wouldn't think he could have just up and walked away."

The nurse came with them to the room. When she saw the rumpled and empty bed, she looked as confused and lost as Peter and Ed.

"I just checked his stats this morning. I'm certain this is the right room."

"Well, he's not here," Ed repeated, hoping the guy's absence was the result of a bureaucratic mix-up and not something more disheartening.

"No kidding. Look, are you guys looking for a family member or something?"

"No, we think it's our friend," Peter said and looked at Ed to silence him, challenging him to disagree.

Ed said nothing.

"Why don't the two of you wait up by the nurse's station and I'll see what I can find out." The woman's dark features were creased with worry.

Ed and Peter waited for almost a half hour before the nurse returned. She sat down beside them, shaking her head before she said anything. "I'm afraid I have some bad news." She paused. "What relationship did you have to this person again?"

Peter said, "We're his friends. But we're not even sure this is the person we're looking for. Just tracking down a lead."

"Right," Ed agreed, already feeling his hopes deflate.

The nurse said nothing for a moment. "Look, I probably shouldn't even tell you this, but the guy in 725 has disappeared. No one's seen him since they came around with breakfast this morning. It looks like he just up and walked out."

"What the hell?" Ed glared at the woman.

"Listen, honey, this isn't my fault. It happens sometimes, but I wouldn't have expected it from this guy, who hasn't said anything or moved since we brought him in."

Peter asked, "Were his injuries severe?"

"That's the weird thing. He had a cut on his forehead and what appeared to be some strain on his back, but otherwise he seemed fine. The doctors don't believe he was comatose or anything, because none of their tests indicated that. We were just thinking he was in shock or something."

"And now he just walked out."

"I'm sorry."

"Me too." Ed stood up. "You can't imagine how sorry."

The nurse stood with them. "Well, look at it this way. This might not have even been the friend you were looking for, and if it was, he's at least well enough to walk out of here on his own."

"It's alarmingly comforting." Ed frowned.

Peter pulled him away. "Thank you very much." He gave Ed a shove toward the exit. "She might be right, you know," Peter said as they headed toward the bank of elevators.

"So where does that leave us? Where does that leave Mark Dietrich? Who dies next?"

"Don't think that way. This could be something else entirely."

"I wish we had such luck. But it doesn't seem to be running that way lately."

AFTER A FEW aspirins and some water, Timothy was feeling marginally better. At least he didn't feel weighed down as he had before, although his back ached every time he moved and the pain behind his right eye had not subsided.

He wished there was someone he could call. But there was no one. Aunt Helene wasn't far and she had always made an excellent angel of mercy, but a call from him would probably send her to the nearest mental hospital. The same was true of almost anyone else he used to know.

Timothy Bright was alone. And being injured like this increased the feeling, made of it some strange hulking thing that weighted him down with pain and immobility.

But there was one way to make a connection. And perhaps that way would at least take his mind off the pain and the loneliness if only for fifteen minutes or so.

He pulled himself over to the computer, and with a couple clicks of the mouse, was in Men4HookUpNow.

Who would he be today? He could be anyone. And anyone out there with whom he made contact was safe: he was too tired and in too much pain to even consider getting out of bed.

Wasn't he?

JOHN HAD NEVER actually gone online. Well, he thought, I mean, not for sex. Oh sure, he had seen the ads in the back of *Gay Chicago*, had looked at the chiseled muscles of the models there, had even fantasized about what it would be like to be with one of them. The anonymity of the whole thing intrigued him.

He looked around the small studio he occupied. It was only the one room, really, with a bathroom attached to it. Kitchen along one wall, two windows to the left of the kitchen, a table, two chairs, a futon and coffee table comprising the living room. A bookshelf held rows of Modern Library classics he had studied as an English major at the University of Illinois: *Moby Dick, The Scarlet Letter, The Sun Also Rises, Pride and Prejudice, Anna Karenina,* the whole panoply of authors he supposed no one ever read anymore, save for English majors. There was no TV. A *Colt* magazine lay open on the table.

The men from *Colt* had usually been enough for him, their hirsute, muscular forms coming alive for him as he stroked himself, picturing these same men doing things to him that he could never admit to anyone.

Lately, though, the pornography failed to arouse him. He longed for a more corporeal connection. It had been years since he had felt the warmth of flesh pressed against his.

John Austin was ugly. Another thing his apartment did not contain was a mirror, save for the one over the bathroom sink. While at the University, he had to take at least three science courses to fulfill his BA requirement, one of which had to be a lab class. John loved the "mad scientist" look of the chemistry lab, with its beakers, Bunsen burners and glass tubes. A kind of alchemy, he thought. As a junior, John had done poorly in the book portion of the class, but had looked forward to the Monday night lab sessions. It was during just such a lab session that John got creative and tried throwing together things that he didn't realize were explosive when merged. The resulting explosion did him no disabling harm, but the splash of acidic liquid altered his face forever. The hair at the front of his head never grew back, and his face had that Freddie Krueger look everyone loved to whisper about. Except this wasn't make-up; there was no removing the burned scar tissue at the end of the day. Now, John existed on big-billed Cubs caps that he pulled low on his face, hoping the shadow would spare him from distasteful—or worse, pitying—glances he encountered in the street.

Not that trips in public were that frequent. His English major and ability to work fast procured a job as a copy editor with an educational publishing house. Every week, a new book arrived via Federal Express for him to edit; he rarely had to make any sort of human contact, which was just fine with him.

John fingered the keyboard in front of him. If it hadn't been for his job, he didn't think he would have even bothered with the expense of a computer and an online service. But he needed to be available for e-mails from the publisher, and some of the smaller stuff he edited online. Once in a while, he got an e-mail from his mother in Carbondale. But this contact, John thought, was just to assuage her guilt. Ever since the accident, she could barely stomach looking at her son with his new face, the face that bore no resemblance to the rest of the Austin clan.

He could do without contact from her.

He logged onto Google and typed in Men4HookUpNow, the service that had the biggest ad in the back of *Gay Chicago*. Of course, it came up at the top of the search engine listings. He clicked on the URL and paused at the home page screen.

Where did he suppose this would get him? There was no need to post a photo of himself, no need to even describe what he looked like. A lot of these guys, he saw at a glance, listed only what they were looking for and hardly said a thing about themselves. What would a guy do when he opened the door to John's face? Would he welcome him in? Or, more likely, would he slam the door and retreat, gibbering in horror, to the safety of his abode?

There was always phone sex. He had availed himself of such measures before. John supposed he could be someone else entirely, optic fibers and imagination making of his flabby body an Adonis, with lean, chiseled muscles and a huge cock. His face would be handsome: cleft chin, wavy auburn hair, perhaps a goatee. Of course, an eagle tattoo would adorn his chest, a band of barbed wire tattooed around his 16" biceps.

But talking had all the appeal of the *Colt* magazine. Empty. Relying too heavily on his imagination. He didn't want to sublimate his consciousness to try for another sad orgasm.

And he longed for the touch of another. No one ever touched him, not even in the most casual way. He craved touch the way a man stranded in the desert craves water.

"Just because you want something doesn't mean you can have it," he said to himself.

He stared at the monitor screen, wondering how he should approach talking to someone. If he started getting anywhere with someone, should he tell him the truth? It seemed his only recourse, because if he did make some sort of connection, he wouldn't get very far. Why waste both of their times?

Perhaps a mask? John had an idea: maybe someone out there would get into some sort of fantasy scene. A rape, complete with ski mask. He imagined himself asking his potential suitor to leave the door unlatched and he would enter, cutting through the darkness, moving toward a bedroom where a warm man waited. Waited to take him into his arms, hold him and caress him, kiss him through the slit in the knitted cap.

This is what I have to do for love, John thought, the despair and dejection rising up in him like a wave of nausea. Well, you never get anywhere unless you try...

He took a deep breath and began the process of creating a screen name and online profile. He signed up for the monthly renewable billing plan because the site told him that this was the best value. Who knows? Maybe this will work out, John thought, with the optimism of the desperate.

It didn't take John long to figure out the instant messaging system. Just glance at the list of screen names of online suitors, click on one, see how they looked and sounded (although John didn't think he had much right to be choosy, he still had his likes and dislikes, no matter how unappealing he might be to others), and then click on the "IM" button next to the guy's name. He noticed there were currently twelve pages of guys online. Surely, among these dozens, he could find one other lonely soul who would go along with his needs. Perhaps a masochist, who would get off on the anonymity John was thinking about.

John sent out three or four instant messages to guys who looked promising, but all of them went unanswered (he imagined that they could see through their monitors at his scarred face; reality told him it was more likely the fact that he had not posted a photo online...almost everyone had some sort of photographic representation). He tried one more, wondering if this process was always so long and involved. *Patience.* This guy's screen name was BrightBoy and he also had not posted a pic. At least he couldn't hold *that* against John.

```
"What's up?"
```

John keyed in. And then, because he thought he should try to take control, typed:

```
"What are you looking for?"
"Looking to get together maybe."
"Me too. I'm in Buck Town."
"Looking for company or travel?"
"Either way."
"Cool. I need to stay in. What do you look like?"
```

John couldn't respond.

```
"Hello? Still there?"
"Yes. I'm 6'1", 195, brown hair and eyes."
"What are you looking for?"
"I just want to..."
```

John stopped.

"Actually, I'm looking for someone who would be
into a fantasy scene."
"Oh yeah?"

It almost seemed John could sense the other guy's interest
being piqued through the computer.

"Yeah. Would you be into a little role-playing?"
"Maybe. Depends on the part."
"I was hoping to do a little rape scene."

John thought for a moment.

"Nothing too rough, of course. Pretty vanilla,
really."
"Sounds cool. Tell me more."
"Well, I could wear a mask and you could leave
your door open and wait for me in the bedroom,
pretend like you were asleep."

John closed his eyes in self-loathing. No one would ever go for
this. It was so unsafe. Of course some guy's going to leave his door
open for a perfect stranger to walk in and have sex with him. Right.

"That could be fun."

John was shocked. He had read in the paper about the serial
killer in Chicago. Didn't this guy have any sense? Still, his loss
could be John's gain. And the desire rose up in him, the prospect of
being close to someone again, his hands exploring willing flesh, the
warm beating heart pressed against his. John typed:

"When would you want to do this?"
"Now."

John looked out his windows at the grey skies. The world
today was monochromatic, industrial buildings contrasting the sky
in various shades of their own drab grey.

"Sounds good. Where do you live?"
"Just take Lake Shore Drive north..."

TIMOTHY LOGGED OFF the computer. What was he doing? He needed to rest. But the guy online sounded so perfect, so willing, so right up his alley.

Wincing, he got out of bed and headed toward the bathroom. "Rape scene, indeed. That's my line," he whispered to himself. "We'll see who's the one getting penetrated." He giggled.

In the bathroom, he bent over, giving out a little cry at the sharp pain in his back when he did so, and splashed cold water on his face. He looked at himself in the mirror, the bandage on his forehead, the lackluster blond hair. "Not exactly my best," he whispered to his reflection. "But who gives a fuck?"

Timothy slid into a pair of navy sweat pants and managed to pull a T-shirt over his head. He put a baseball cap on over his dirty hair. "Twenty minutes, a half hour." He shook his head, thinking how this was too perfect: someone into rape. Just the kind of bastard he wanted to get revenge on.

"Revenge for killing *me!*" he shouted.

JOHN MADE HIS way north, following Sheridan Road when he reached the curve where Lake Shore Drive ended and became Hollywood. His hands trembled on the steering wheel. His face wore a sheen of sweat under the stocking cap. His stomach churned and at each light, he contemplated turning the car around and heading back to the sanctuary of his apartment. What kind of person would want to go through with this, anyway?

TIMOTHY DARKENED HIS little apartment, drawing blinds and curtains across all the windows, shutting out what feeble light the grey day had to offer.

"What are you doing?" he asked his reflection in the gilt-edged mirror in his front hallway. "What the fuck are you doing? One cardinal rule: never have anyone here."

He pulled the chef's knife from its oak block in the kitchen and went with it to the bedroom, where he placed it under his pillow. "Bastards like you make me sick. You're getting just what you deserve."

What would he do with the body? Solve that problem later. Maybe you shouldn't answer the door, that way you'll still be anonymous, the voice of reason whispered in his ear.

Timothy answered back: "I'll still be anonymous because this dude ain't talkin'. Not ever again."

JOHN MADE HIS way past Loyola University, where a group of students waited to cross the street under the el tracks. At the red light, he watched them as they passed by, laughing and talking to one another. He had been like them once, carefree and connected. The blue jean-clad boys hurried across the street, unappreciative of all they had.

All John didn't have.

When the light changed, he gunned the accelerator and sped north until he came to Estes, where he made a right and headed back toward Lake Michigan. The guy said his building was last, next to the water. A white brick courtyard building.

John located the building, but finding parking was a problem. He ended up having to park on Sheridan Road and walking back. People tried not to look at this tall man in the black ski-mask, but failed. Even though the day was damp, dim and cool, it was still far from being weather for such attire. He kept his gaze leveled at the sidewalk and hurried back to Estes, where his "date" waited.

What would it be like? John's nerves pulsed like electric impulses. What would his hands touch? What would the skin of another feel like? It had been so long since he had touched flesh other than his own, he wondered if he wouldn't come immediately, after just lightly running his fingers along someone's back.

And suddenly he felt tears well up in his eyes. Cursing himself, he wiped them angrily away, before they had a chance to dampen his mask.

He paused in front of the building, looking at the black wrought-iron gate that barred him from the courtyard. Once, he supposed the fence didn't exist. But those were safer times.

What if, when the fantasy was played out, the guy wanted him to remove the mask? What would he say? Would he do it? If he did, he was certain, it would ensure there would be no repeat performance. He supposed he could plead he wanted to keep the fantasy alive. And if the guy liked it, he might agree, and they would see one another again and again, faceless lovers bound up in dishonesty and subterfuge.

TIMOTHY PEEKED THROUGH the curtains when the buzzer sounded. Below stood a tall man wearing a nylon jacket, dark grey, and a black ski mask. What was with this guy, anyway? Timothy had supposed he would put his mask on when he entered the building, or just outside the door. Why wear it outside?

Timothy crossed to the front hallway and buzzed him in through the gate, watched his progress through the courtyard, then buzzed him in through the door to his entrance. He unlocked the door, leaving it slightly ajar, and went into the bedroom, where he lay curled, his hand lightly stroking the knife under the pillow. He put his thumb in his mouth.

Soon, the creak of floorboards heralded his arrival. The door closed, the latch falling into place. Every muscle tightened and Timothy closed his eyes to see a bright play of colors, red, yellow, orange swim beneath his eyelids.

He could hear the guy's progress down the hall, across the living room and finally the creak of the bedroom door.

And then he could feel the man's gaze on him, appraising. Would this one turn and leave?

Timothy wouldn't have it. This one was not getting out.

"I thought you'd be naked." The voice was deep and sounded odd in the quiet apartment.

Timothy didn't respond. At least not verbally. Instead, he flipped on his back, stretching as if in sleep. Casually, he pushed the sweat pants down and off, kicking them sleepily to the floor. A turn of his head and the baseball cap tumbled off, landing on the floor beside the bed. There was no way he could remove the T-shirt while pretending to be asleep.

Apparently, it was enough. The floorboards creaked as his suitor for the afternoon crossed the bedroom. Timothy could hear him breathing as he stood beside the bed.

JOHN GAZED DOWN at the body before him. It was nothing like the bodies he fantasized over in his *Colt* magazines. Almost hairless, the body was lithe and small, the legs well-muscled, the penis lying in a nest of soft, pale brown hair. The guy's face was small, too, the features elfin: turned-up nose, blushing cheeks, the full lips parted as in the breath of slumber.

Tentatively, John reached down and laid his hand on one of the legs, splayed out across the sheet. In the dim light, it was hard to discern the color of the sheets, but he could tell they were faintly striped.

The touch was electric. The skin was impossibly smooth and John sucked in his breath at the feel of it. He moved his hand down the thigh, over the bump of the knee and down, reveling in the feel of the coarse blond hair, which was invisible in the half-light. John tried to quell the trembling the touch caused, steeling and tightening the muscles in his arm...to no avail.

THIS ONE TAKES his time, Timothy thought, trying not to recoil from the touch of his warm hand, trying not to scream at the feel of the hand on his leg. It made him think of a cockroach crawling down his leg. He bit his lip and rolled over.

JOHN COULDN'T BELIEVE it. The sight of the two half moons of the man's ass before him causing his breath to quicken, causing his heart to hammer, tight, stealing his breath.

THE FEEL OF the hand on his ass made Timothy stiffen so much he had to bite his lip, bite so hard he tasted metal: the copper of his own blood. He couldn't stand being touched here, conjuring up as it did the worst memories. He gripped the knife under the pillow, curling his fingers under the shank so tightly his knuckles went bloodless and his palms slick with sweat.

JOHN COULD FEEL the tension in the man's buttocks when he touched them. Clenched tightly, the half moons became iron, muscles bunching beneath the baby-smooth white skin. He stroked, letting his fingers lie gently in the crack.

He began to undress.

WHEN TIMOTHY HEARD the rustle of clothes dropping to the floor, he became so filled with rage, his eyes snapped open and he whirled on this fucker who had come to call. The memories rushed back in, making his temples throb and his head ache. Even after all these years, the night rushed back to him with all the clarity of a motion picture.

There was Teddy, the pain in his eyes real, gasping for breath under the tutelage of forcible pain. It was his own face, Timothy thought.

JUST AS HE removed the last of his clothes (save for the ski mask), John watched as the man turned, shocked by the pale blue of his eyes meeting his own. This wasn't the way it was supposed to be.

"No," he whispered. "You're supposed to be asleep." The moment deflated the strength of the fantasy the way a pin deflates a balloon.

"Fuck you." The man stared at him, challenging.

It was then that John saw the glint of silver, dull but horrifyingly obvious even in the dark of the bedroom.

As he turned, the bedsprings creaked. John reached down for

his jeans and sprinted toward the door, nausea and terror rising up in him. The door was not far, not too far. He had to make it.

He stumbled as he left the bedroom, and with the stumble, could feel the man right behind him. Something hot and metal brushed down his back as he moved away. He turned and as he turned, he saw the man standing behind him, a huge knife held aloft in his right hand.

"No," he whimpered, reaching for the weapon.

It sliced, hot, through the skin of his palm. He tried to wrap his fingers around it, despite the pain. Just as he did so, the man yanked the knife back, slicing deep.

John gasped as the blood poured from his palm, splattering on the hardwood. Tremors seized his entire body. His head shook; an icy chill shot through him; the shit left him, splattering on the floor to combine with his blood.

He reached out to grab the man's throat with his left hand and as he did so, the knife plunged in, through his ribs.

John gasped, sinking to his knees, wondering where all the air had disappeared to.

AFTER HE WAS done, Timothy pulled the mask from the face and gazed down in horror at the brown, scarred tissue there.

"And you weren't even cute," he whispered. A single giggle escaped him.

Chapter
Twenty-one

IT WOULD BE a mess to clean up. Timothy sat panting, on the hardwood floor, knees drawn up to chest. The guy lay, brown eyes open and already filming over. They stared fixedly at a point on the ceiling. Timothy wondered if the eyes continued to see in death, wondered if the man's spirit hovered somewhere near the ceiling, watching this whole tableau and damning Timothy. It didn't matter. Timothy was already dead and condemned to hell.

Would he be able to clean the blood and the shit from the floor? What a surprise, Timothy thought, I've never seen anyone scared shitless before. The man's body was flabby; if he ever had any muscle tone, there was no evidence of that now. And his face, God, what the hell was that about? Must have been in a fire. Would anyone notice that a guy this ugly was missing? My first victim with no face.

Timothy reached out tentatively and touched the guy's penis, stroked it. He leaned over and put it in his mouth. Reaching up, he ran his hand over the guy's stomach, feeling the coarse brown hair, reveling in its texture. One of Timothy's hands was on the floor and he slid it outward until it made contact with the blood, warm and already slightly viscous. He slid his hand around in it, then lifted his head away from the guy's penis long enough to cover it with blood. Then Timothy lowered his head once more, tasting the blood and the cooling flesh beneath it. He bit into the flesh at the base of the cock, bit harder, harder, until savagely, he sank his teeth in hard enough to break through the skin.

Timothy looked down to watch the semen spurt from him, shudders coursing through his body.

"I hate you," he whispered to the unseeing eyes.

Then he lifted himself up on one elbow and placed his head on the man's chest. He fell asleep.

When he awoke about a half hour later, the body had grown much colder.

"This is a problem," Timothy said to himself, licking from his lips bits of crusted dried blood and flakes of flesh. In the past, he had always left his victims, walked away clean.

Timothy felt tired. In fact, he couldn't recall a time when he felt more exhausted. Had the simple act of killing left him this drained? The body was going nowhere; he could dispose of it later. Wearily, Timothy got to his feet and headed toward his bedroom. He had almost made it to the bed when he stopped and turned around.

Returning to the living room, he hooked his hands under the guy's armpits and dragged the body into the bedroom with him, grunting with the effort of it. A smeared trail of blood, feces, and semen marked the body's course from living room to bedroom.

Timothy squatted and tried to lift the body onto the bed. Grunted and strained with the effort. Finally, after too many attempts, attempts that made his weariness seem almost like another presence in the apartment, pushing him down, he let it drop with a thud to the floor. "Fuck this," he whispered, having not even enough energy to put breath behind his words.

He slept.

When he awakened, the darkness in the apartment was complete. Timothy leaned over and looked down at the corpse lying on the floor next to him. He reached out and lightly traced his fingers over the scar tissue on the face. "I had to."

Timothy got up from bed and stretched. He had a lot of work ahead of him.

He kept his tools under the kitchen sink. He shoved aside the red metal toolbox Aunt Helene had given him for his sixteenth birthday, in the failed hopes it would make him more macho or something, and reached back into the dark interior of the cabinet for a hacksaw. Next to the saw was a new box of blades. He pulled out the saw and put a new blade in. "Perfect," he whispered, running his fingers lightly over the serrated edge of the saw's blade. He had had little use for tools up until this point, but was grateful to his aunt for thinking of him.

Timothy returned to the living room. The floor would need a good scrubbing, that much was for sure. But right now, he had to get rid of the body.

He wished he hadn't done it. Not killed the guy, there were no regrets there. But he was sorry he had invited him home. This was how people got caught. It seemed that, sooner or later, his serial-killing brethren all fell into the same trap: they had to bring someone home. Gacy, Eyler, Dahmer...they all did it and, in England, Nilsen. And sooner or later, it was just such behavior that got them caught.

But Timothy was not going to get caught. How do you catch a

dead man, anyway? he thought and a smile played across his features. Things always have a way of working out.

He stood above the body, staring down at it, wishing there was an easier way. Aunt Helene had always referred to him as "delicate" and he supposed on that score, she was right. He had never been strong, always the sissy, always the first pinned in gym class when they practiced wrestling.

And here was this big man. How was he going to manage to get him into the bathroom, and worse, into the tub? But there was no other way: disposing of the body neatly meant he would have to do it there.

Timothy yanked the sheet from his bed and positioned it under the body. Taking a deep breath, he began pulling the body from the bedroom, through the living room, then the front hall. Finally, panting, he arrived at the bathroom threshold. He slid down on the floor, the sweat tickling as it trickled from his armpits down his sides. "Just a little further," he told himself breathlessly.

He stood once more and tugged on the sheet until the body was next to the tub. Squatting, he positioned his hands under the guy's armpits. He recoiled slightly at the coldness he felt there, mixed in with the damp, sticky feel of anti-perspirant. He breathed in deeply and grunted as he tried to lift the body of the rim of the bathtub. He managed to get it off the floor momentarily, but then the two of them toppled over. Timothy was pinned beneath the corpse, staring up into filmy brown eyes. The scarred face was within inches of his own and on impulse, Timothy stuck out his tongue and tasted the cold, striated flesh.

Enough of this. Timothy positioned his hands on the guy's chest and pushed, putting all of his weight behind the shove. The body reared up enough for him to scramble out from beneath it.

Finally, Timothy lifted the legs, flailing like pieces of wood over the edge of the tub, then got his hands under the back and was able to somehow fold the body up and into the tub, where it landed in a sort of sitting position, one arm still out, the fingers dragging on the floor.

Quickly, Timothy placed the arm in with the rest of the body, then positioned it so it was lying on its back in the tub. He stopped up the drain, took off his T-shirt and paused. Might not the blood splatter his eyes as he cut? Would the blood even splatter at all, since it was not being pumped through the body any longer?

Just to be safe, Timothy retreated into his bedroom where he found an old pair of Speedo swimming goggles in the bottom of a drawer. He slid them over his head and loosened the rubber band so it wasn't too tight.

The body looked strange lying in his tub. For just a moment,

Timothy wished that he could keep it. "Don't be ridiculous," he said aloud to himself. He knelt and picked up the hacksaw.

Grabbing a good handful of hair, Timothy lifted the head from the porcelain. Positioning the blade at the throat, Timothy giggled and said, "Believe me, you're going to be better off without this." He laughed some more, almost uncontrollably, the hacksaw wagging in his hand as the shudders of his hysteria coursed through him. "This is one trick that'll really make you lose your head," he quipped, then groaned.

"Stop it!" he screamed, his voice high and shrieking, reverberating off the ceramic tile.

He began to saw through the flesh. There wasn't much blood, as Timothy had suspected, but he could see this was going to be a tiring job. It wasn't easy working through all that muscle and bone.

Who would have thought?

Chapter
Twenty-two

SHE WASN'T CRAZY. Sure, most people who saw Annie Macomb pushing her shopping cart from Dominick's thought she was insane, the victim of urban blight, a destroyed family, a fall on hard times from which she could never recover, the downward spiral taking her further and further down until getting back up to what some called a "normal" life was virtually impossible. But Annie lived on the streets because she preferred to. There had been social workers and even, once, a TV news team who tried to help her. She remembered the pretty blonde reporter who made it her business to locate Annie's sister in Naperville. When her sister, Esther, found that she was living on the streets, she of course offered to take her in. The TV woman could arrange for some sort of vocational training. But that life, with all its trappings, was not for her. Sure, she had spent too many Chicago winter nights shivering in a store doorway, bedded down with newspapers, rags and cardboard, never enough to block out the chilling winds and snow. But on the streets, she was free. There were no alarms to be set, no timetable at all to follow. One day melded into the next with Annie scarcely noticing. Annie used to be a voracious reader: philosophy, history and biography were her favorites, and she always remembered, if not word for word, what Thoreau had said about possessions and how they chained you down. The more you had, the less free you were. Everything Annie owned was in a shopping cart, going where she did as she made her way through the streets and alleys of Chicago's north side. She realized, once she had winnowed down her possessions to an essential few, that most people were slaves to acquisition, to the care and maintenance of things that did nothing more than trap. Sure, her belly was empty from time to time, but collecting cans often helped in her quest for food. She was no wino, never even touched alcohol. Annie kept her own counsel and that was how she liked it.

On this early November morning, Annie was hungry. The last time she remembered eating was from the Dumpster at McDonalds on Howard Street and Western. And that was early yesterday afternoon. If she could gather enough cans, she could buy herself a decent breakfast: maybe even pancakes from McDonalds. When you ate as infrequently as Annie did, your stomach grew smaller and it took less and less to fill it. A couple of pancakes and sausage links could fill her for an entire day.

She had a good start on breakfast, her shopping cart already brimming with a pound or two of aluminum cans. As she headed down the alley behind Estes, she thought one more cache of cans and she could go to the recycling center, cash them in, and eat. The thought was almost rapturous.

She lifted the brown metal lid off the Dumpster. Inside were several white plastic trash bags and several heavier-gauge black garbage bags, like the kind folks used to collect grass clippings. Also in the Dumpster were many free-floating pieces of trash: beer bottles, cereal boxes, assorted newspapers and magazines. And as Annie sifted through this detritus, she spied several cans lying near the bottom of the Dumpster. Annie was a small woman, but she had her strengths. Standing on tiptoe, she began pulling out several of the trash bags so that access to the bottom of the Dumpster would be easier. When she lifted the black bags, she was surprised at how heavy they were. She grunted as she pulled each of the four bags out, and had to lean against the Dumpster to catch her breath when she was through. What in the hell was in them anyway?

Annie was tempted to just leave them alone. The few cans at the bottom of the Dumpster, she was sure, would be enough to gain her cash for a proper meal. But what if what weighed so much in these garbage bags was something valuable, something that would give her two, maybe three days' respite from sifting through other people's garbage? Annie began to untie the first of the bags, the one nearest to her.

She peered inside and saw what looked like a ham bone. She remembered the hams her mother would bake on Easter and leaned closer, sniffing. But no smoky smell of pork came out of the bag. It smelled bad in there, like rotting meat. She reached in to sort through and jumped back recoiling in horror, wiping her hands on her down coat.

Annie's mouth was suddenly very dry and her heart was pounding. What she had felt inside the bag was smooth skin, crowned with coarse brown hair.

It was no ham bone in there, Annie realized, the horror mounting within her, but a human leg. She bit her lip, trying to hold down the bile that threatened to escape through her mouth. "Jesus Christ," she whispered.

She opened another bag and saw something brown and hairy.

Annie hefted the weight of the thing, turning it. Filmy brown eyes stared back at her; the face was scarred and burned.

Annie vomited then, the yellow bile coming up to splatter on the concrete beneath her. And when she was finished, when she sat, heaving, on the brick pavement, she began to scream.

ARLISS BELL HAD lived in the back apartment in the 1100 block of Estes for thirteen years, ever since he retired from teaching English at Senn High School. With Lake Michigan so near, it was a little bit of peace here in Rogers Park, where the traffic swarmed on Sheridan Road and the el trains rumbled just a few blocks west, near Ashland.

Arliss was relaxing with his first cup of coffee of the day when he heard the shrill scream coming from behind the building. He got up, throwing the *Reader's Digest* he was perusing to the floor and rushed to his kitchen window, which looked out on the alley behind the building. Two floors down, he saw her: the bag lady he sometimes gave change to on his way back from the el. She was sitting in the alley, looking like some sort of doll, legs splayed out in front of her, several black garbage bags around her.

And she was screaming, barely pausing for breath, just a continual wail, almost a howl. "Good grief," Arliss whispered to himself, "what now?"

He went into the bedroom and donned a pair of Chinos and an old Notre Dame sweatshirt. On the way to the front door, he grabbed a white cardigan sweater from the dining room chair he had left it on the night before.

There was very little excitement on his street and as Arliss descended the stairs to his building's exit, he wondered what could have caused such hysteria in the woman, who was usually grounded, never mumbling to herself like some of them did.

Outside, the cold air hit him. The wind had picked up during the night and it ripped across the lake, picking up an ice chill from its churning waters. The waves roared, almost, but not quite succeeding, in drowning out the woman's cries.

Arliss felt he was being plunged into a nightmare. As he rounded the building, he couldn't imagine what would cause her to scream like that.

As he entered the alley, he saw it: a human head lying half in/half out of a garbage bag. He closed his eyes and opened them again, hoping for a different outcome: a rotting head of cabbage or a bowling ball, anything but the macabre specter of a decapitated head lying feet from his back door.

He didn't want to get any closer. He called to the woman: "I'm going inside to phone the police! Would you like to come with me?"

And the woman stared at him, her screaming suddenly ceased. "I can't move," she whimpered. "I can't get up. Hurry! Hurry!"

And Arliss turned to run inside and dial 911.

IT WAS THE usual pairing: old and young, experienced and novice, teacher and student. Officers Joe Taudzimio and Ellen Ryan, of the Rogers Park district, had just completed a call at 1610 W. Fargo, where a domestic disturbance had been quelled by threats from Taudzimio to the husband and placating words from Ryan to the wife.

The two officers made their way out into the cold morning, their breaths leaving a trail of vapor in the air.

"They'll be at it again before we turn the corner up at Paulina," Taudzimio said to his partner, who was only three months out of the Academy. She was a short, wide blonde with brown eyes, close-cropped hair, and a scar on her forehead. There was an air of femininity about her, almost a Rubenesque sensuality, undercut by a bulldog manner that led no one to believe she was any less vigilant than her older, football-player built, cigar-smoking partner.

"You see a lot of this?"

"*You've* seen a lot of it. Hell, it's our bread and butter. If these women would just get away..."

"Easier said than done, Joe, easier said than done." Ellen shook her head and slid in the passenger seat of the squad car.

The dispatcher called out their number even before Joe turned the key in the ignition. "Check on a possible body in the Dumpster at 1133 Estes."

"Jesus Christ," Joe said, switching on the flashing lights and gunning the ignition. "This is going to be one mother of a day."

Ellen Ryan stared out the window, wondering what lay in wait for her.

When they arrived at the alley behind Estes, an older man in a cardigan sweater was waiting for them. A bag lady, wearing a grimy red and black plaid coat, stood next to him. She looked pale, sickly in the morning light. Ellen wondered just what she had seen to make her look so ashen.

The officers got out of the car and the man in the cardigan came up to them. "I'm Arliss Bell and that's Annie Macomb." The man seemed nervous, bouncing his weight from one foot to the other, and his eyes moved all over the place: the brick pavement, the lake a few hundred yards away, the officer's eyes. "She discovered the, um, remains, about a half hour ago."

It was then that Ellen Ryan let her eyes drift to the black garbage bags lying on the alley pavement. She could see a bit of brown hair sticking out of the top of one of them.

"What happened?" she asked Arliss Bell.

He rubbed a hand over his face. "It seems there's a dismembered body in there."

Ellen felt like ice shot through her veins, although she was careful not to show it. "I'll check it out," she said, making sure to put plenty of breath behind her words and trying to calm the quaking that was beginning in her muscles. She must not show her fear, her queasiness at the situation.

"You don't have to do that," Joe said, striding toward her.

She put up a hand. "It's my job as much as yours, Joe. Right?"

"Let's both look."

As they both moved toward the bags, another squad car pulled up. Ellen ignored the slamming doors and opened the first bag, the one out of which hair protruded. She let out a little cry at the head she saw inside. It was horribly disfigured, burned almost beyond recognition. But the scar tissue was old; this hadn't happened recently.

"You okay?" Joe whispered in her ear.

"I'm fine."

Two other officers were coming toward them and Ellen opened the second of the bags.

One of the new officers, with whom Ellen had attended the Academy, began questioning Arliss Bell and Annie Macomb.

"Did either of you see anyone around the Dumpster earlier today or last night?"

Both of them shook their heads. Annie Macomb clutched a soiled handkerchief in both hands, twisting and untwisting it.

Just then the building custodian arrived. A young guy with red hair and a beefy build, his blue eyes were clouded with concern, eyebrows together and frowning. "I'm Pete Lipton. Can I help you?"

The newly arrived officers explained the situation and asked him the same question they had asked the others.

"Yeah, early this morning, one of our tenants, David Long, was carrying those bags out. I noticed because he looked like he was having a lot of trouble with them; they were obviously heavy."

"Did you say anything to him?"

"Nah. I had a lot to do today. But I remember this because he's a little guy and the bags seemed to be overwhelming him."

"What apartment is he in?" Ellen Ryan joined the grim group to her west.

"He's in 109. I got a pass key."

Joe told him, "We'll let you know if we need it."

Ellen Ryan and Joe Taudzimio hurried inside the building. "Do you really think he'll be in there?" Ellen asked.

"I've seen weirder things happen."

They waited for a moment outside the door, listening. There was no sound from within. Joe pounded on the door. "Mr. Long? Could you open the door, please? Chicago Police."

There was no answer. Joe turned to Ellen. "Why don't you run down and get that pass key?"

When she got outside, Ellen saw that vans had already arrived from Channels Five and Seven. "Jesus," she whispered. "These guys sure as fuck don't waste time."

She tapped Lipton on the shoulder and asked him for the key. "I'll have to come in with you."

"I don't think so." Ellen grabbed the key from his hand and went back inside.

"The media's already out there."

"Christ. I hope they don't fuck up any evidence."

"Well, I think the guys down there will keep them from that," Ellen said.

"Yeah, you would think that." Joe turned the key and opened the door.

Ellen didn't know what she would find when she followed her partner inside the apartment.

What they found was nothing. The apartment was devoid of character: no pictures on the walls, table surfaces clean, bed stripped to its striped mattress. She opened the bedroom closet. Rows of empty hangers.

"Looks ready to move in," she said, looking around at the sterile apartment.

Joe had moved into the bathroom. The tub and fixtures were clean; in fact, they sparkled. "Guy's a wonder with a sponge," he said.

"Well, at least we got a name."

"Yeah, if it'll do us any good. Let's go make sure the ME is on his way."

Ellen followed her partner. "Think they'll be able to find anything useful? This place has been cleaned."

Joe called over his shoulder. "You'd be amazed. Do you know what one of the most effective tools is for getting up tricky fingerprints?"

Ellen shook her head, descending the stairs behind him.

"Super Glue."

Chapter
Twenty-three

THE TEN O'CLOCK news came as a revelation. Ed and Peter were lying in bed, post-coital grins on both of their faces. The flickering glow of the TV screen and a pillar candle provided the only light. Neither of them was paying much attention to the TV screen. Peter lay with his head on Ed's chest, and Ed's eyelids were fluttering; he was about to fall into a very satisfied slumber. Both of them wished the news could have been delayed.

The news of John Austin's murder was not the lead story. In fact, the story was third in the line-up, behind a story about a series of car bombings in Iraq and a southside apartment fire. Neither Ed nor Peter really heard the first two stories, but when Andrea McClellan said, "The dismembered body of a Chicago man was found early this morning in a Dumpster on the far north side of Chicago," Ed and Peter both sat up. Ed grabbed the remote and turned the volume up. Both listened silently as the dark-haired anchor described the events of earlier that day. "Police are seeking a David Long for questioning. Long was seen in the early hours of the morning depositing several trash bags behind his Estes Avenue apartment."

"David Long? Does the name ring a bell?" Peter asked.

"No." Ed rolled over and faced him. His interest was piqued by the fact that John Austin was young and single. But the killing did not have the earmarks of the others. John Austin was not killed in his home and no mention was made of his being gay. Still, no one said he wasn't gay. And who was to say that he hadn't met David Long online?

"But this could be something. I have to find out more." Ed rolled over and looked at the clock. It was already ten thirty. "I'll call Joey Mantegno in the morning and see if I can get some more details."

ED WAS UP early the next morning. When Peter awakened, Ed had already showered and dressed, which was unusual because Ed usually liked to awaken with Peter.

Peter lay back, drifting between sleep and wakefulness, trying to rouse himself to get out of bed. Ed came in, hair still wet from the shower, wearing a Nike T-shirt and flannel boxer shorts.

"You look great," Peter mumbled sleepily.

"I just talked to Joey."

Peter sat up and rubbed his eyes. "What did you find out?"

"Interesting. Very interesting. John Austin may have been gay. Investigators are still trying to track down leads, but it seems the guy was pretty much of a loner. He was disfigured in a chem. lab accident years ago at the U of I."

"Why would you say he might have been gay? Did he have a lover? Has he been seen at a bar or something?"

"Nothing like that. The guy couldn't have possibly kept more to himself; worked at home as a copy editor. They're having a hard time finding anyone who knew this guy."

"Then what?" Peter wore a puzzled expression.

"They checked his computer. Guess what they got?"

"They didn't?"

Ed nodded. "Men4HookUpNow. It was the last site he logged onto."

"Can't they find out who he talked to through that? I mean, aren't there, like, electronic tracks left behind?"

"I already thought of that. While you were asleep, I looked into it and found out a couple things: one, they could possibly trace, like an e-mail, back to the ISP, but that's as far as it could go without a court order."

Peter swung his legs over the edge of the bed and rubbed some sleep out of his eyes. "Well, gee, if there was ever a reason for a court order..."

"Right, but I also found out that large networks assign IPs to hundreds of computers at a time, so the best one can typically hope for is to trace the IP back to the network region. It's not that hard to remain anonymous. You could just avoid using the same computer or the same logon every time you went online. Then, if you varied your connections and provided false information from the start, you're virtually untraceable." Ed walked to the window and peeked through the blinds, then turned back. "Plus, IMs are pretty much anonymous; they don't link to an IP address."

Peter sighed. "What about David Long?"

"He's the piece of the puzzle no one seems to know anything about. Beyond his address on Estes, no one can seem to discover anything. His trail leads nowhere. No previous address, no family, nothing. Joey said it's almost as if he didn't exist prior to plopping down on Estes. Neighbors they've talked to said the guy was quiet and kept to himself."

"How did this Joey person find out so much information?"

"This Joey person, as you call her, has a way of getting information out of the detectives. If you ever meet her, you'll see why."

Peter nodded and grinned, throwing off the sheets.

Ed shook his head. "That looks almost irresistible. But I've got a busy day ahead of me. I'm going to talk to a bartender partner of Tony Evans."

"Tony Evans?"

"He was the first victim. First one we knew about, anyway."

CHRIS BRYANT WAS drying beer mugs when Ed came in. The bar, a quiet little neighborhood spot in the Edgewater neighborhood of Chicago, had just opened. It was empty. One dark room, with white lights around a mirror behind the bar, a neon sign announcing drink specials, and a long, dark, wooden bar with a row of stools behind it gave the bar the appearance of bars everywhere. The bar, a place called "The Cell," could have existed anywhere in the United States; it was totally lacking in character or local color. That in itself, Ed thought, gave it sort of its own character.

When Ed sat down at the bar, Chris, a tall blond with a mustache, buzz cut, and a linebacker's build, set the glass on a draining rack.

"What can I get you?"

"Just a mineral water. Tynant's, if you got it."

"We've just got LaCroix."

"Fine."

As Chris was getting the drink out of a cooler, Ed said, "I spoke to you on the phone yesterday."

Chris's eyebrows came together; he obviously didn't remember.

"About Tony Evans."

"Oh yeah. But I already talked to the cops."

"I'm not a cop." Ed paused for a minute, staring down at the bar. It made him wince a little inside to denounce his former profession. "As I told you, I have a personal interest in the case."

Chris nodded. "I don't know what I can tell you. Tony was a nice guy; we used to work Tuesday and Thursday nights together. He seemed pretty together. I wasn't real close to him, but what happened came as kind of a shock."

"All I really want to know is one thing. Did he have a friend that you can recall, a guy named Timothy Bright?"

Chris shook his head, concentrating. "Timothy Bright? We don't usually get guys' last names when they come in here, unless we have some reason for getting to know them better."

"Guy claims to be a close friend."

Chris shook his head again. "I'm sorry, man. But I don't remember any Timothy Bright. Did he come in here much, that you know?"

"I don't know that," Ed said. Another dead end. Why hadn't he thought to dig up the old newspaper photo of Bright? It might have helped. Wasn't this always the way? Would he never find anything out about Bright? Was Bright even real? Maybe the force was right in letting him go. Maybe he never talked to a Timothy Bright; maybe he'd imagined it all. He took a swig of his water and was about to leave when he thought of the news story last night.

"Hey, did you hear about that body they found in Rogers Park yesterday?"

Chris put down another glass and looked up. "A body?"

"Yeah, they found this guy all cut up in a Dumpster."

"Shit. That's terrible. No, I didn't hear nothin'."

Ed thought it was worth a try, see if the bartender would take the bait. "Yeah, they're looking for this guy named David Long for questioning."

Chris moved to stand in front of Ed. "What was that name again?"

"David Long."

"Now *that's* a familiar name."

"Oh yeah?"

"Talk about a friend of Tony's. The David Long I know was in here all the time, bugging Tony. Guy was a creep."

Ed couldn't believe his luck. On a whim, he asked, "What did this Long guy look like?"

"Weird, man. Like a little troll. I don't mean in the sense that he was an ugly old man, like the term is so often used by these queens that come in here. But like a real troll, something out of a, pardon the expression, fairy tale."

"Describe him." Ed took another swig of water, trying to appear detached, trying not to leap over the bar and get right in the bartender's face.

"I don't know. Short. Maybe 5'6", kind of girlish features. Little pug nose, straight blond hair with bangs. Kind of delicate."

"Like an elf?"

Chris laughed. "You got it. You know the guy?"

"I think we've met."

"This isn't the same David Long the cops are looking for?"

"That I don't know. It's not that unusual of a name."

"I wouldn't be surprised. The guy was weird. I didn't exactly have him pegged as a killer, but, Christ, there was a screw loose somewhere."

"Why do you say that?"

"Guy was just always hangin' around, never ordering much of anything, just mooning over Tony. Tony had his share of admirers, he was a hot guy, but this dude's interest was definitely not welcome. Tony hated queens like that."

"Did Tony ever do anything to him?"

"Yeah, the last time he was in here." Chris stopped to laugh. "Tony told me he was going to get rid of the guy, get him off his back."

"What did he do?"

"Well, it's pretty rude. Told him he was gonna give him what he wanted. Split the little fucker in two, rape him, man, and then make sure he didn't come back."

"Rape him?"

Chris shrugged. Another customer came in, an older man in a suit. "Yeah. That seemed to set this Long guy off. He spit at Tony and then stormed out."

"Ever come back?"

"Never saw the guy again. Thank Christ."

"When was this?"

"About the middle of August."

Chapter
Twenty-four

HELENE DIDN'T WONDER, anymore, why she was alone. It had been so long since she had had a social life, a boyfriend, a family, that the lack of those things had been reduced to a dull ache, at times not even noticeable. She filled her days with books, television, cigarettes and Bloody Marys. It was the Bloody Marys, she supposed, that numbed her ache the most. By evening the memories and mistakes were nothing but a blur, no more real than the docudramas on Lifetime.

Helene Bright's house was spotless, save for the quarter- and half-empty tumblers of tomato juice and vodka that one could find anywhere: living room, kitchen counter, night table in the bedroom, back of the toilet. Spotless save for the often close to overflowing ashtrays, filled with Dunhill butts that also found a home in every room of her house.

Helene lay asleep on the couch, a Patricia Cornwell mystery open on her chest, David Letterman on the TV. Her mouth was open and a line of drool ran down her chin. Her dark hair was pulled back from her face, giving her an older, pinched look. Slack-jawed and snoring, who would have recognized this once-beautiful, wealthy woman, who could have had her pick of successful admirers? Her black sweater was littered with cigarette ashes and her black slacks on good terms with lint.

Helene eventually roused herself, lifted the remote from where it had been poking her in the ribs, and shut the TV off. She closed her book and set it on the coffee table. Cornwell's heroine, Dr. Kay Scarpetta, would have to wait until tomorrow to see if the forensic expert made it out of her latest dangerous situation alive. Of course she would; Cornwell needed to keep Scarpetta alive to keep her own bank account thriving. It was only money, and held no sway with Helene; she had more money than that author would ever dream of. Her father, with his visions of microchips and high-tech ideas, had seen to that. She wondered if her life would have been different if she hadn't been handed everything on a silver platter from when she was a young girl. Wondered even more if her brother Daniel would still be alive, and if her twin nephews would have had a different life story to tell.

Who knew? Even small changes in one's life could produce vastly different outcomes, altering paths completely. Right now, the dull throbbing behind her eyes could find respite only in sleep. She headed out of the den and toward the curving staircase in the foyer. As she headed up the stairs, she remembered suddenly when she had first seen the house; how she had conjured up the happy home she would provide for Timothy once they had moved in, the house tastefully and professionally decorated. But a house didn't bring happiness, nor did money, nor did a man.

Helene wondered, rounding the corner and heading into her bedroom, if happiness was even a possibility. She could have anything she wanted and yet all she wanted to do was die. It didn't matter that she could walk into Nordstrom, Neiman Marcus, or Barneys and buy anything she wanted. She wanted nothing.

She shed the clothes and went into the bathroom adjoining the bedroom. She appraised herself in the full length mirrored wall adjacent to the shower. Her body was bone-thin, the ribs protruding, the limbs stick-like. No one would ever want her. Not again. Those days were behind her, thank God. Still, it would have been nice to have someone to say goodnight to, someone to fall asleep next to in bed at night.

Quit the self pity, she told herself. It's not an attractive quality. On the sink was a half-empty Bloody, the water from the ice separated from the vodka and tomato juice. Helene picked it up and swirled the liquid around until it combined. Opening the medicine cabinet, she shook an Ambien from the prescription bottle there, popped it in her mouth and washed it down with the tepid, weak cocktail. "Cheers," she whispered to her reflection. "To your health." She laughed and the laugh sounded hollow, empty, resonating off the marble walls of the bath. She hoped that tonight, she would sleep through the night. The pills no longer guaranteed anything. Many nights, she found herself awake in silence, when it seemed everyone in the world was slumbering save for herself. She would smoke a cigarette and stare out the window at her back lawn, which adjoined a country club golf course. Manicured green for miles, dotted with a lake that was home to Canadian geese in the spring.

She slipped into her nightgown and pulled back the duvet. Sliding in between her Laura Ashley sheets, she closed her eyes and waited. A dull, dreamless slumber would come, overtaking her, stealing her consciousness for another night, or at least part of one and she would awaken feeling drugged and heavy and arise to begin another day of boredom. She wondered why she hadn't taken all the Ambiens and just gotten it over with.

Helene managed to sleep until a little after 4:00 a.m. But there was something different about her awakening, a difference that was not immediately apparent. Usually, she awakened slowly, her head a groggy soup, feeling almost too heavy to lift.

But today, she awoke all at once and felt no effects from the drink and the drug. Helene rolled over and looked at the clock. 4:10. She lay in bed for a moment or two, staring at the ceiling, before she realized she hadn't swam up from an unsatisfying slumber, but had been awakened by something.

She didn't know, immediately, what had awakened her, but gradually she remembered: there had been a crash somewhere in the house. Once she grasped this, she realized it had been the sound of breaking glass and it had come from somewhere below her. Everything in her tightened. Muscles became like steel and her heart pounded. She lived in one of the most exclusive neighborhoods in one of the richest suburbs in the country and yet had never experienced a break-in. Amazingly, she had never had an alarm system installed.

Suddenly, Helene was afraid. Her desire to die was a lie. She didn't want anyone to harm her, let alone kill her. She sat up in bed when she heard movement below her, a heavy footstep on the floorboards in the kitchen. She grabbed the pillow, squeezing it so tight the muscles in her fingers threatened to cramp.

With as much stealth as she could muster, she slid from her bed and went into the bathroom. She didn't turn the light on, but dressed silently, breathlessly in the dark. She found her shoes under the bed and slid into them.

There was no gun in the house and the only protection she could think of for herself, a knife, would be in the kitchen. And from what she could make out, that's exactly where the sounds were coming from.

She sat down on the bed and lifted the receiver of the telephone on the nightstand. She shuddered when she heard a dead line, no dial tone, no nothing.

Oh my God, she thought, they've cut the line. She had no way to cry for help. She cursed herself for resisting buying a cell phone.

Another sound from below caused her to jump and give out a small cry. Perhaps, she thought, just perhaps, I could slip out the front door undetected. Moving to her closet, she grabbed a coat. Her hands were trembling. She wished more than ever that she was not alone.

Helene moved down the stairs, praying a creak would not give her away. When she got to the curve in the staircase that would give her a view toward the kitchen, she saw the room was flooded with light. There was no doubt now that there was someone in her house. At four o'clock in the morning...

Let them have everything, she thought as she stepped off the bottom stair. The doorway was in front of her. Beyond it lay freedom, freedom from harm, from the kind of death she had only read about in newspapers.

She scurried across the parquet and had her hand on the doorknob when she heard a footstep behind her. Close. She sucked in some breath; her hand, which was aloft, dropped. She froze, heart pounding so hard she feared it would explode.

She didn't dare turn and look. She didn't want to see who had come to her home, who had invaded her sanctuary. She shut her eyes tight, preparing herself for the sudden blow to the back of her head, the jab of a knife, the report of gunfire...

Another footstep. Closer. She bit her lip to hold in the scream which burned in her throat. Another footstep. Helene could feel the presence of the intruder, standing silently behind her. She swore to herself she could almost feel his breath, certainly she could hear it.

Her muscles unclenched and she felt free to move. Perspiration made her body feel slick under her clothes. Think, she told herself, think.

To her right was the living room. On every wall were banks of floor-to-ceiling windows. It would be a simple matter to raise one of those windows, jump out, and head down the brick driveway. One of her neighbors would help her. Of course they would.

But the intruder was standing close enough to prevent her from doing this, especially when she had to pause to unlock the window and raise it. She imagined how a knife would feel sliding between her ribs as she fumbled with the windows. Imagined what the report of a gun would sound like in the silence of the night, wondered what it would feel like as it entered her. Would it burn?

Finally, feeling more helpless than she ever had, she screamed.

The light from the chandelier hurt her eyes with its sudden brilliance.

"Don't scream," a male voice from somewhere behind her said. A voice that was agonizingly familiar. Where had she heard that voice before? Where had she at least heard one like it?

Helene couldn't move for a few seconds. She was disoriented by the light and her fear paralyzed her. Lately, her opinion of herself hadn't been high, but she was ashamed now for being so helpless.

There was but one course open to her. She realized she didn't have much of a chance, but it was her only option. She steeled herself, breathing deep, and dashed for the living room.

She struggled to unlock the window nearest to her, the one next to the fireplace. When she opened the window, cold air rushed in. Odd, her intruder hadn't pursued her. She heard no footsteps echoing her own when she ran. She put one foot out the window and had raised her leg to follow with the other foot when she heard the voice again.

"Don't go. I'm not here to hurt you."

"Oh God!" Helene screamed. No, it couldn't be. It wasn't possible. This was a nightmare and soon she would awaken, dull grey light seeping in through her bedroom windows.

She whirled and saw him standing there in the foyer, looking as small and helpless as he had always looked. *Had looked in life.* Timothy.

"You're dead," she whispered, still poised with one foot out the living room window. She pulled her leg back in.

Timothy grinned. "One could say dead and buried. But that wouldn't be quite true, now would it?" He laughed.

Helene righted herself on the living room floor. "Timothy," she gasped. She reached out to him and with the effort of lifting her arms, saw his image go blurry before her.

She collapsed.

Chapter
Twenty-five

SHE COULD SEE herself. There was an odd reality to the image; there was no mirror to give it to her and yet, there she was. If she was looking through the lens of a camera, this is what she would have seen: her face planted in the sandy bottom of some body of water. The water was pale blue, bordering on turquoise, as if underwater lighting had been used. Her dark hair flowed behind her, a Medusa of waving black locks, lifting and twisting in the water's current. Her eyes were open and her nose was buried in the sand. She could not see her body. She knew her thoughts, which were rational enough to tell her that she could drown within minutes. Her thoughts told her she needed to turn over, that the struggling was in vain because she was making her body move the wrong way. She needed to go up, to reclaim the air that would prevent her from dying. And yet she struggled, moving downward, burying her face deeper and deeper in the sandy bottom. Rational thought told her to turn over, but whenever she tried to do so, she found she couldn't. There existed within her a dull panic, a certainty that her lungs would become iron bands across her chest and in the end, she would open her mouth, filling her lungs with water and sand.

Helene awakened from this troubled image sweating. For a moment, and only a moment, she had forgotten what had happened before she fell into this fitful slumber. And then it all came back: the intruder in the darkness, the flash of bright light, and finally, seeing Timothy. Timothy, who had been dead and buried for years. She tried to move and couldn't, and then she recalled when she had first heard of his death. It came to her as lightning, striking swiftly and surely, the harbinger of the life that was to come, a life in which she was a prisoner of her own depression.

It was August. Chicago may boast bone-numbing wind chills and feet of snow in the winter, but the summers can often be tropical, with highs hovering around one hundred degrees and the humidity at the same level. Helene had been in a different place then. Life was far from good, but she still had her friends and some semblance of a life. She played tennis, she swam, she didn't drink nearly as much. When she returned home from shopping, the light on her answering machine was usually blinking. Her mailbox held postcards and letters.

The phone call had come in the morning. Helene, in her air-conditioned refuge of a house, had just finished breakfast, her waffles accompanied by Vivaldi on her favorite classical music station, WFMT. The announcer had just informed her that the day's highs could break a record and warned that the elderly and those in poor health should stay indoors. Inside her air-conditioned sanctuary, the day outside looked falsely pleasant: a bright blue sky, with just a few strands of cirrus, the sun making everything outside look bright and clean, if one didn't look too closely at the grass, which was turning brown in spots. The sun also made a great contrast, a play of light and shadow that was remarkable. Blinding brightness merged with deep darkness under the trees.

When the phone rang, Helene was just loading her breakfast dishes in the dishwasher. Expecting it to be her friend Claire, with whom she had a lunch date later in the day, Helene was completely unprepared for the call. Later, she would think that no one is ever prepared for sudden bad news and the way it can turn one's life inside out. One never knows what awaits us around this or that corner.

"Hello." Helene's voice was cheerful, sounding almost decades younger than the voice she now possessed, one scarred by too many cigarettes and a desire not to be noticed.

It wasn't Claire. It was a man who identified himself as Michael Shaunessy, with the Chicago Police Department. Helene thought at first he was soliciting for donations or even calling to question her about a break-in that had occurred earlier in the week down the road.

Such innocent concerns were not to last long. "Ma'am, do you have a nephew by the name of Timothy Bright?"

Helene paused. She and Timothy had not been on speaking terms in many years. What now? What had he done now? And how much bail would be required to get him out of jail? Would she need to cancel her day's plans to go down to some godforsaken precinct?

"Yes, he's my nephew. Is something wrong?"

"Ma'am, I'm sorry to have to do this over the phone..." The officer paused then, and Helene's nerves tingled; everything went tight within her. Gone were the mundane concerns of the day.

"Has something happened to him?" She rushed out, breathless and her heart beginning to pound.

"Ma'am, I'm sorry to have to be the one to inform you, but a body fitting your nephew's description was found early this morning in his apartment."

"Oh God." Suddenly, Helene forgot all the problems the two of them had had in the recent past. All she could think of was how much she loved him. In anything other than name, he was her son. She had raised him, and a mother's worst fear was hearing that her child had died before her. "What happened to him?"

"It appears that he was killed."

"No. Are you sure?"

"Well, ma'am, we have every reason to believe this is your nephew. However, I would need you to make a positive ID. Do you think you can do that?"

"You mean it might not be him?" Helene was suddenly hopeful. No, more than hopeful, she was certain this was all the result of some grim mix-up, that the body discovered was one of Timothy's lovers, never mind how he ended up in Timothy's apartment or the role Timothy might have played in his death, this had to be the answer. Timothy could not be dead. He just couldn't be. She would have sensed it.

"I wish I could say so. But we're almost certain this is your nephew. Making the ID is probably nothing more than a formality, but we have to do it. Now, do you think you can help us out or is there someone else we should call?"

"No, no. I'll do it. I want to see." Helene was sure she would walk into the morgue and see the body of some other, yet similar, young man.

"We'll send a car around for you. Can you be ready in about a half hour?"

Helene was about to tell them she would drive herself, but then thought better of it. Some part of her rational mind was still functioning, and that part wondered how much longer it could maintain itself. Deep down, she knew this was Timothy, but denial overruled her and allowed her to cling to the hope that this was all some dreadful mistake. It also delayed the despair and the pain of loss which that tiny rational part told her would come eventually.

Before he hung up, Helene asked the officer, "What's happened to him?"

"We can discuss that when I pick you up."

"No, I want to know now!"

"Please, ma'am. It'll be better if I brief you in the car."

"But..."

"I'm leaving the station now. I'll see you within the half hour." And then the line went dead.

HELENE WAS TIED to a chair in her den, one of the ladder-back chairs from her breakfast set. Timothy had wrapped her in rope, pinning her arms to her sides, her ankles painfully welded to the hard oak of the chair legs.

He had said nothing. And when Helene had persisted in demanding an explanation, he withdrew a roll of duct tape from the large black bag he had brought with him.

"Do you want me to use this?"

"No, but..."

"Then shut up. One more word and you'll find yourself unable to talk."

Helene had acquiesced. She had no choice. Terror threatened to send her screaming and gibbering over sanity's brink. But for a while, shock kept her level-headed, numb. Having a dead person tie you up and breathe foul breath in your face tends to remove emotion.

Outside, the day's grey light had faded. Long shadows fell across the beige carpeting of her den. How long had she been sitting here? It must be hours now. She turned her head and gazed out the window. The sky was purple near the top, but the sun still peeked, a cauled golden ball, over the horizon, making the trees, now almost bereft of leaves, blackened silhouettes. Absurdly, she craved a cigarette and a Bloody. Food was far from her thoughts, even though she hadn't eaten since the night before.

Timothy was somewhere in the house. Occasionally, she could hear the fall of his foot, or a drawer being opened. Once, she heard the TV click on, listened to canned laughter, an argument, a scream, sports scores being announced, then abrupt silence.

What kinds of programs, she wondered, did the dead enjoy?

That awful day back in August, Officer Shaunessy stood with her outside the stainless steel doors of the morgue. The air here in this basement was cool, causing goose bumps to rise on Helene's bare arms. She didn't want to go into this room that housed the dead, didn't want to be faced with the prospect of having what little vestige of hope she retained ripped away.

He gave her a sympathetic smile. Helene wondered how many times before this balding, going-to-overweight man had been in this situation, how many hysterical loved ones he had supported on his beefy arm when they looked down at the violent end of a life. He said, "This won't take long. One quick look and I'll drive you home. Is there someone you can call? Someone who can come and stay with you?"

"Officer, we don't even know if that's necessary yet."

She caught the policeman's condescending look, a look tinged by sadness. Oh yes, he had been here before.

"Are you ready to go in?"

Helene snapped at him. "No, of course I'm not ready! I don't know that I'll ever be 'ready,' whatever the hell that means. Is anyone you bring down here ever ready?"

The officer nodded. "Point taken." He cleared his throat. "Should we go in now?"

Helene looked once more at the doors and a churning rose up in her stomach. She was afraid she would be sick. She swallowed the burning bile at the back of her throat and took a deep breath. "Let's get this over with."

The officer held the door open for her and followed her inside.

The morgue was just like she had expected, just like in the movies and the TV detective shows. Several stainless steel tables held bodies covered with crisp white sheets, a couple even had feet sticking out at the bottom of the sheet, tagged with cardboard identifiers. Along one wall were banks of large, heavy drawers, kind of like filing cabinets. *File this one under 'c' for car accident, this one under 's' for stabbing, this one under 'g' for gunshot... Oh, stop it!*

"Where is he?" Helene's voice came out in a tremble, wavering. Her legs suddenly felt weak. She feared she would faint and wanted nothing less than this public display of weakness.

The officer led her to the table furthest from them. He gripped the top of the sheet in one of his hands. He looked at Helene, waiting.

"Just go ahead." Her voice was a whisper, barely a croak.

He pulled back the sheet and Helene's hand went over her mouth, holding in a scream, lowering its impact to a gasp. The room seemed to move for an instant and Helene grabbed the steel table for support, then snatched her hand away.

The officer began to put the sheet back and she slapped his hand away. "No! I'm not ready yet." Helene leaned closer, peering down at the face. The blond hair hung back, away from his face, lank, dull, almost devoid of color. His eyes were closed, almost shriveled, around each one was dark purple tissue, savagely bruised. The lower lip was cut and another bruise ran along the jaw line. "He's been beaten."

Helene hadn't asked in the car what had happened to Timothy. She had suddenly not wanted to know and the officer, she thought, was relieved not to have to talk about it.

Shaunessy nodded. "I'm afraid so. Ma'am, I have to ask you, for the record, is this your nephew, Timothy?"

Helene shook her head, wanting to wail and holding it in. She closed her eyes and whispered, "Yes."

"SO, AUNTIE, WHAT are you thinking about?"

His appearance in the room startled her and she stared at him, her eyes wide. The contrast of seeing him alive and, in memory, dead, was almost too much. She actually wished for the comfort of insanity, wished she could just go catatonic, released from this sudden hell which was worse than anything she had ever known. She had never experienced this before, but she was at a complete loss for words...almost like forgetting how to speak.

Timothy walked up to her, grinning. She thought he was going to kiss her. His hand whipped out so fast she had no time to prepare herself for the slap that came. It didn't even sting until a few seconds afterward, when her mind had a chance to register what had happened.

"I asked you a question, Aunt Helene."

"If you must know, I was remembering when I went down to the morgue to identify your body."

He laughed at that, threw back his head and laughed, his sides shaking and his face flushing scarlet. He reveled in her merriment. "Must have been quite an ordeal for you."

Again, Helene could think of nothing to say. Even if she could, she wasn't sure she could coordinate the muscles in her tongue, mouth and jaw enough to speak. She wanted to ask him what was going on, to offer her some sort of rational explanation for what had happened. This just simply could not be. She had been inches from his bruised face in the morgue. She had attended his funeral and had stood at the coffin on another hot day in August, leaning over to whisper a prayer for his soul, trying not to look too closely at the heavily made-up face and the hair that was combed the wrong way. She had kissed his cold cheek. She had endured the flashes of cameras and the hushed voices in the background, trying to swallow her shame and grief in the presence of the media and ghoulish strangers who wanted a look at the murdered man.

"How can you be alive?" she managed to whisper.

"Who said I was?" His manner was completely wrong. He was breezy, almost cheerful. Helene thought he was enjoying himself.

She wanted to reach out and touch his flesh, to see if it gave way beneath the pressure of her fingers, if the blood would rush back in where she had gripped him, wanted more to see if the flesh was warm. She stared at his chest and noted that it moved as he took in air and breathed it out again.

Do ghosts breathe?

She remembered the slap; the hand had felt real, alive. Perhaps ghosts aren't ectoplasm, as she had read in countless gothic stories, perhaps they come back as real people.

It couldn't be. This person couldn't be her nephew, he couldn't.

Helene wished she could make herself believe this was an imposter. But she knew Timothy's face, his stance, his walk just as much as any mother knows those things about her son.

This was Timothy, of that there could be no doubt. She wondered, if she went to Rosehill, if she'd find the place where he was buried yawning open, the grave a dark and desecrated hole, the earth in an untidy pile beside it.

He leaned close to her and kissed her. Helene was too surprised to recoil. "I've missed you," he whispered.

And then he was gone and Helene was left to her ponderings in the darkness, her tongue growing dry and thick in her mouth.

Chapter
Twenty-six

ED WAS GETTING ready to leave for headquarters when the phone rang. His hair was slicked back with water, and he wore a fresh-pressed white shirt and khakis and a pair of loafers. There was electricity in the air, a sort of static tang he knew was brought on by fear. He had assembled enough information over the past few weeks, he thought, to get his old boss to take him seriously. The jangling of the phone in the living room added to his tension, making him more nervous than he knew he should have been. As he hurried to the phone, he thought the added adrenalin in his system might just be an aid to him when he pleaded his case. It would make him sharp and more persuasive.

Or so he hoped.

"Hello?"

"Ed? Ed, is that you?"

"Of course it's me, Mother." Ed rolled his eyes. "It's good to hear your voice. To what do I owe the honor?"

"What are you talking about? A mother calling her son is an honor, now, is it? Well, I guess as frequently as you call, it *is* something special."

"Sorry it's been so long."

"Well, you should be. Word has it that you've been canned. Lots of time on your hands, so don't give me the run-around about how busy you've been."

This was the last thing Ed needed, yet another morning moment to ruin his composure. He wondered how his mother, in Peoria, had heard of his termination. "Who told you about that?"

"I have my spies." Mrs. Comparetto laughed. "So what did you do?"

"I didn't do anything, Mother. It's all a big mix-up." Was it really? Ed was no longer sure of anything. "I'm working right now on getting reinstated."

"Come crawling back, huh? Begging for your job? Your father..."

"Ma! I think that's enough." His mother had been blessed (and the rest of the world cursed) with a tongue that knew no censoring. Phyllis Comparetto always said exactly what she thought. When Ed left Peoria, he thought, *God help them.* "Did you call for any particular reason?" As soon as the words were out of his mouth, Ed knew he had said the wrong thing.

"Oh, now I have to have good cause to call my son? Well, that's about what I expected."

"You know that's not what I meant. I just wondered... Oh never mind. How are you?"

"You mean other than the arthritis and the loneliness? Fine, I guess. Your Uncle Dominic is in the hospital. He had some trouble walking at your cousin Jeff's wedding. When they opened him up, they found he was filled with cancer. They just closed him back up. They're sending him home today. I thought you might want to drive down and see him. They say he's only got a couple weeks. Sent him home to die. Poor man."

"That's really a shame, Ma. Yeah, yeah, I'll come down. Maybe this weekend. I have a new friend I'd like you to meet, anyway."

"One of those faggots?"

Ed sucked in some air. "Yes, as a matter of fact, he is. Just like me."

"Oh don't give me that! Boys pass through this phase. I've been lighting a candle down at St. Nick's every week, so God will take this thing away from you."

"Mother, I'm not a boy. I don't want anyone taking this thing away from me. It's who I am. It's who you love, whether you like it or not." Ed thought of adding something particularly vicious, like telling her how he wouldn't want to stop sucking cock for all the sequins in his many ball gowns, but thought better of it. He would be the one to really suffer from such a remark.

"Well, you come on down. Let me get a load of this little friend of yours. He's probably part of the reason you are what you are."

"I thought that was Dan's job."

"Don't get smart with me, boy. I'll knock your teeth down your throat."

"See you this weekend, Ma." Ed replaced the receiver in its cradle. When the phone rang again, Ed hurried out the door. With trembling hands, he locked the deadbolt as the phone rang in the background, making his hands shake, his heart pound, and his blood pressure spike.

In the car, Ed thought he couldn't imagine how a morning could have started off worse. Just when he needed to be calm, to have all his ducks in a row (whatever the hell that meant), everything broke loose in his life.

Today, the telephone was the medium of bad news. He wished he had had it disconnected a long time ago. First there was the call, for Peter, around 7:30 a.m., from his friend at the library, Ellie. Mark, the guy who had been in the accident on Lake Shore, had died.

Peter had come back into the bedroom, his face white, lips turned down in a frown that foretold tears.

"What happened?"

"It's Mark. He passed away last night. They say he had a hemorrhage in his brain."

Ed sat up and reached out for Peter, who continued to stand still at the door to bedroom. "I'm really sorry."

Peter shook his head. "I suppose you're still going to go and talk to your old boss this morning."

Ed had been shocked at his question. What was the connection?

"Well, of course I am. What's that got to do with anything?"

Peter burst into tears then and Ed sat still on the bed, uncertain if his embrace would be welcome. Ed got up anyway and started toward him. Peter put out an arm, not to welcome him, but to stop him. "No." Peter slid into a robe and sat on the bed, his head in his hands. "When is this going to stop? Why can't you just leave it alone? Don't you see? Don't you see? This is only going to end when this maniac succeeds in killing you, too."

"This is my life, Peter. This is what I've always wanted. It's all I know. I don't want to forget it. If I can help apprehend this guy, I could get my job back."

"Your job? We're talking about your life here!"

"I'll be all right. I can take care of myself."

"Oh sure, big macho man. Well, what about the time when you came home with your head split open?"

"What do you want me to do, Peter?" With all he had on his mind for today, this was the last thing he needed. He should have known it was coming. Other cops he had known had experienced the same thing with their wives. People outside the force just didn't understand.

"I want you to forget about all this! I want you to find something else to do with your life. I want you to concentrate on *us*, instead of some sick character out there who's killing people. You keep bringing yourself in his sights, again and again. You'll never be satisfied until he gets you, too."

"No, I'll never be satisfied until I get him. And I will. And then everything will be all right. And then we can get on with us."

"Bullshit."

Ed moved close to Peter so he could look him in the eye.

"Look, you wanted to be with me, right? This is who I am. I'm not a doctor, not a lawyer, not an architect. I don't want to be anything else."

"Maybe what you are is not what I want." Peter slumped back on the bed, turned toward the wall.

Ed sighed. "I know you don't mean that."

"I wish I could be so certain."

"Will you be here when I get home?"

"No. I think I need some time to think."

"Do what you have to do. I need to get in the shower. I have an appointment in an hour and I don't want to be late."

Peter mumbled, "We wouldn't want that."

ED PULLED HIS car into a guest parking spot at the station. It felt strange to be a guest in a place he had always considered a second home.

Roy O'Farrell was waiting for him. As soon as he came into the office, Ed could feel the man's discomfort. When O'Farrell looked up from the report he was reading, his smile was false and his face looked strained. He looked, Ed thought, like someone who didn't want to be in the situation he was in.

"How you doin', Roy?"

"Could be better. This gay killer thing has got everyone on edge."

Ed sat down in one of the two chairs across from his old boss's desk. "That's what I'm here about."

"Oh yeah?"

"Yeah. I think I might have some information that could help. A lot."

"Well, shoot," Roy said. And Ed could just feel him thinking, *Humor him.*

And so Ed began, spilling out the whole story: the phone calls, the grave at Rosehill, the incident in the forest preserve, the sex line, Mark Dietrich, everything he could think of. Even as he was telling it, Ed was beginning to wish he hadn't come. It all sounded so insane.

And as Roy O'Farrell listened, his face threw up a wall. Ed could tell he was trying to think of a way to get rid of him.

When he was finished, Ed placed his hand on the supervisor's desk. "So what do you think?"

Roy shook his head. And then he smiled. The smile was falsely bright. "That's quite a tale you've got there, partner. And it certainly bears some checking out." Roy wrote something on a piece of paper. "I'll put this with the other leads we've gotten and you can be sure we'll check this out. I'll pass it along to the task force. What did you say that aunt's name was again? Helen?"

"Helene." Ed paused. "I was thinking maybe I could come back and track this down for you."

"I don't think the mood here would permit that, Ed. I'm sorry."

"But—"

Roy put up a hand to halt him. "Ed, I'm sorry. We'll check things out. Okay?"

Ed stared at the floor. "Of course. Handle it the way you see fit." He glanced up at his former boss. "You know best, Roy."

Chapter
Twenty-seven

    Daniel has phoned again. My brother, the world traveler. Who would have thought when Father sent him off to Princeton that he would be squandering his life away being a bum. Yes, a high class bum, no argument there. But he's still flopping around the world with no direction and no purpose, no thought of the future. Never mind that the places he's holing up in are exotic locales, like Paris, London, Amsterdam, and Munich.

    Today's call was from Marrakesh. I could hardly make out his words through the staticky connection. But I heard enough to disgust me. Here I am, at Vassar, trying to apply myself to my studies and he calls me up with what he thinks I will put under the category of "good news." Good news would be that Daniel was coming home, to take his place in Father's business. Good news would be that he's rid himself of that wine-swilling, drug-abusing whore he calls his "lady." Lady? If ever there was a misnomer, laying the term lady on Lanta was it.

    So the good news is that he's knocked her up. Oh, let me put it his way: "Helene. Guess what? You're about to become an auntie." What does he think? Having a baby when he has no employment, when he's squandering the family fortune away on hashish, heroin, and God knows what else is a blessed event, cause for celebration?

    It makes me ill.

    I have always looked up to Daniel. Until he met Lanta, he was a good boy, full of dreams of a prosperous future. She, with her inane hippie ways, ruined him. And now there will be a baby to tie him further down in the muck that surrounds her. Thank God, I suppose, Father has provided for us so well. Otherwise, God only knows what would happen to him and to her and that offal they will call their child.

    I asked him if he planned to marry her.

    "Marriage is for the bourgeoisie," he told me, parroting Lanta I'm sure. "It's nothing more than a piece of paper. What do we need that for when we're sure of our love for each other?"

"But what about the baby? It'll be a bastard. You'll bring disgrace to a family that's had only love for you."

"Oh, don't give me this bastard drill; that's for Victorian romance novels. Our baby will be brought up in a different kind of environment than we were. It'll have the benefit of love, and not the petty, money-grubbing ideals we grew up with. Can't you see that?"

Easy words when you have a hefty trust fund upon which to draw. I wonder how he'd feel about the bourgeoisie if his travels weren't supported by the sweat of their brow.

"No, I can't see that."

"Aren't you happy, Helene? A baby, think of it. We'll be coming home in March or April just before the baby's due. You'll change your mind once you hold him or her in your arms."

"What about all the drugs?" I asked, but then the connection became garbled.

I never knew if he heard me.

NIGHT'S DARKNESS GAVE way to morning: a grey sky and winds that whipped around Helene's house, as if they were in turmoil over her predicament. Her hands and feet felt numb, the needles tingling in them had ceased, giving way to a deadness that concerned her.

"Can't you loosen these things?" she asked him when the discomfort was reaching its peak, late in the night.

Timothy just looked at her, a strange smile playing about his lips. "Now you know how it feels to be kept a prisoner. It's not very pleasant, is it?"

"I don't know what you're talking about."

"You know exactly what I'm talking about, Aunt Helene. Have you forgotten? Should I show you the basement? Maybe that will freshen your memory."

Helene went silent.

TIMOTHY STOOD, STARING out the window of his old bedroom. A dingy grey light permeated the front yard, casting dull illumination on the pine trees that lined the red brick driveway. The flagpole in the center of the roundabout stood empty, casting no shadow.

He had been listening to the radio and had actually heard himself mentioned on the eight o'clock news report, although the name they used wasn't his; that name was buried, forgotten on the scenic planes of Rosehill Cemetery. They used *his* name, David Long's—the bastard who had defiled him. The name wasn't an uncommon one. Still, Timothy hoped the police would call on him, in his office preferably. He pictured the stunned expressions of his staff and patients when the police barged in with a warrant for his arrest.

It would never happen. Just having the same name as an alleged serial killer would not be enough to insure any kind of public humiliation. No, David Long's punishment would have to come at Timothy's own skilled hands.

And come it would. Dr. Long was the last person on Timothy's list who would pay for erasing his life.

And Dr. Long, Timothy thought with a giggle, didn't have long to wait.

DAVID LONG WAS ill. He had a whole day's worth of patients to see, but he couldn't worry about that today. "Physician, heal thyself" was a phrase that could not always be counted on, but as David Long languished in his oak sleigh bed, he wished there was a way to make it so. He lay, staring at his white walls decorated with David Hockney prints in brass frames. There was the red lounge chair, the muted champagne-colored carpeting. His window gave a stunning view of forest: oaks, pines and maples, clinging stubbornly to the last of their leaves. All that was visible to him now, however, was a dingy grey sky and a few treetops. Not that he was interested, anyway.

All night long, he had been racked by a dry, hacking cough. Nothing would come up, but each time he sought to alleviate the dry tickling it only made him wince with pain deep in his chest and ribs.

What could this be? It didn't seem like a cold. More like a form of pneumonia. Even the Smetana playing softly on the portable CD player he had in his bedroom did nothing to alleviate his misery.

He had no energy. There was no reason to get out of bed, anyway. The thought of food make him queasy; he hadn't eaten anything in two days.

Perhaps he should call Mike DeLorenze, his old friend from med school. Mike specialized in communicable diseases and he would probably be able to fix David up with some antibiotics, make him completely well within a couple of days.

But David didn't have the energy to make the call, let alone a trip down to his office. And he could think of no one to take him there.

David Long had his suspicions about what the matter was, but he buried those suspicions under all sorts of rationalizations. Yet all the clues were there, and in his darkest moments, he would lie in bed and list them: the night sweats he had had on and off for the past couple of months, the sudden loss of weight that seemed to have nothing to do with how much he ate, the swollen glands, tender to the touch, in his neck and groin, and most disturbing of all, the white patches in his mouth.

David held to the belief that these things were nothing more than the usual kinds of illness: a cold, the flu, just a little bug. But he remembered the week-long bout he had had a month ago with diarrhea and how the affliction left him drained, too weak to do anything more than to come home from his office as soon as his workload allowed and collapse in front of the TV.

He couldn't be infected with HIV, could he? He rolled over in bed, groaning as another round of coughs spasmed through him, causing him to draw up his legs in pain. He had never been a bottom. He had always used a condom when he was with another man. And those liaisons were so infrequent the past few years. How could he possibly be infected? Him, a North Shore doctor with all the trappings of the so-called good life, a position in society, respected by his peers, worshipped by his patients.

David had done what he had seen others do so many times before: ignore the pain, ignore the symptoms, and wish they'd go away. He had even told himself how the body was a wonderful machine, more capable of healing itself than any doctor could ever hope.

And yet the image remained of his face in the mirror: the dark circles under his eyes, the protruding jaw line from the loss of weight. He had nightmares about looking down at his body and seeing it covered with Kaposi's Sarcoma lesions.

He had never been tested. Denial had kept him certain he was one of the fortunate ones, one of the ones that this plague just couldn't happen to.

The phone rang and David turned to stare at it, as if he could see it vibrating with each toll. He was tempted not to answer; his arms felt too weak to make the effort to reach out and pick up the receiver. He listened as the answering machine picked it up, and he heard his own voice spouting out the familiar message.

When a high, breathy voice responded, the voice of someone definitely not female, no matter how feminine-sounding, David tried to right himself enough to pick up the phone. The voice had an air of familiarity about it, although David couldn't quite place it. He was certain he had heard the voice before.

He managed to pick up the phone, and tried to will himself to ignore the tickling in his throat which signaled another round of coughs. "Hello?" His voice was a croak.

"Dr. Long?"

"Speaking."

"I called your office and they informed me that you'd be at home today. They said you weren't feeling well. I trust I'm not interrupting your sleep."

David let loose with a string of coughs that left him gasping. "Who is this?" he managed to breathe.

"This is an old friend. Don't you recognize the voice?"

"I'm sorry," David managed to say, but the words came out a hoarse whisper.

"You remember Helene Bright, don't you?"

David froze. He hadn't heard from Helene in years. "What is this?"

"I think you know."

The voice clicked into place. But that couldn't be...

"David? Are you still there?"

"I don't have time..."

"I think you'll want to make the time."

"Who is this?" He wished desperately he had not picked up the phone. The voice was Timothy's. But David told himself he hadn't heard the boy in so long that anyone could do a reasonable imitation. There was no way to be certain that this voice matched exactly the voice of a man who had been dead now for, what was it, two years? Three?

"It's Timothy."

"That's impossible."

"Have it your way." The man laughed. "Let's just say I was a very close friend of Timothy's. Does that make it easier to believe?" The man chuckled and then went on. "Timothy confided a lot of information to me before he died." Another snicker. "Information that could be very damaging to you, or maybe damning is a better word."

"What do you want?" David's head was spinning and he wasn't sure he could remain conscious through this conversation, this harangue, whatever you chose to call it.

"I need to speak with you."

"Call my office. Make an appointment."

"That won't do, *Doctor*." There was an unpleasant sarcastic twist put on his title. "I need to speak to you right away. Today, within an hour or two."

"I can't. I'm very, very sick."

A snort of laughter. "You certainly are." There was a pause. David could feel the sweat trickling down his forehead, down his sides from his armpits. If he'd had anything in his stomach, he was sure he would have vomited.

"I repeat: I need to speak to you. Immediately. If you choose not to see me, I could reveal some very damaging information to people close to you. Raping a fourteen-year-old boy does not look very good for a doctor."

"I don't know what you're talking about."

"You know very well. Cut it out. Drop the mask, David. We both know the score. I know where you live. I'm coming out there now. Will you let me in?"

David couldn't muster any more conversation, so he whispered, "Yes."

"Good. I'm sure you'll be charmed — and quite surprised, I might add — to see me."

David let the phone drop to the floor. There was no energy left for questions.

TIMOTHY MADE HIS way north, passing through affluent suburbs like Highland Park and Lake Forest, and finally, he was on the tree-lined roads of Lake Bluff. He had traveled this route many times as a teenager, summoned by the wiles of his aunt's lover, and his own.

The car was silent, the hum of its engine barely above a whisper. He was glad Aunt Helene had invested in the Lexus. It made driving a much more pleasant experience. Although the wind whipped outside, Timothy was comfortable in an automatically maintained 72-degree temperature.

"You'd think," he said to himself, "such heat would begin decomposition." He giggled and switched on the radio, playing with the seek button and finding nothing to suit his tastes. He banished the voices of deejays and music to silence.

The driveway was barely visible from the road, just an opening in rows of pines. There was no mailbox at this point, no address marker. And yet Timothy knew the way by heart, driving from memory even after all these years.

The red brick driveway curved through the trees until, with the final curve, one had a view of the house. Red brick with cream trim and deep green shutters, it was a taste of Georgian architecture right here in Illinois. He pulled up in front of the double doors and cut the engine.

For a long time, he sat in front of the house, simply staring up at its imposing façade, which spoke of wealth, success, and a kind of quiet power. So many memories crowded into his brain. The fear, the anticipation, and the guilt of those years washed over him, leaving him feeling slightly queasy, a throwback to his teenage years, when he had spent nights in this house, doing things of which Aunt Helene could not even dream.

David Long was a relatively young man at that time, about the age Timothy was right now. He had been a handsome man, in that sort of male model way, the kind of model that would appear in a Brooks Brothers suit ad. Suave, sophisticated, with just a touch of grey at the temples. A sort of George Hamilton of the medical profession. His body firm — Timothy had explored every inch of it with fingers and tongue. Had lain in silence biting his lips as the good doctor entered him, used him, then pushed him away; pushed him home to Timothy's aunt and David's girlfriend, to spout off lies about what the two of them had done.

Timothy got out of the car. There was no guarantee David would even let him in. When David saw him, Timothy was certain that shock would impede any kind of joyful reunion or welcoming embrace. But there was no need to worry about gaining entry; a big house such as this had many means of access, and one in particular Timothy was no stranger to.

Games... They had played games, and one of them was one in which Timothy would surprise David in his sleep, playing the role of intruder. For the purpose of this game (and not because of forgetfulness, a trait David Long did not possess and abhorred in others), David had left a key in the one-horse stable that stood, needing paint, in the woods just a short walk along a fieldstone path, only a few yards away from where Timothy now stood. Timothy hoped luck would still be on his side and that the good doctor had not moved the key.

He decided not to bother with the doorbell. Much too formal. Timothy strode quickly through the trees and went back to the little stable. Inside, among the rusting garden implements, Timothy found the key on a window sill, under a trowel, just where it had always been so many years before. "You stupid bastard," Timothy whispered.

Key firmly ensconced in hand, Timothy strode with more confidence than he ever had to the front door.

DAVID DRIFTED IN and out of sleep. His slumber was troubled, his fever spiking to make him sweat, drenching the bed clothes. Fragmented images scattered with each waking, images he didn't want to consider. Most lingering was one of himself: A gaunt David staring up from a hospital bed, his eyes huge in relation to his shriveled face, his ears protruding, his hair falling out.

It was from one of these dreams that he surfaced when he heard the noise downstairs, in the entryway. He tensed, trying to hold in a string of painful coughs, and failed.

The noise downstairs stopped, as he expected. Whoever was

down there was listening, the aural antennae up, pinpointing his location in the house. There was nothing he could do but lie, gasping for air, as he heard a light tread on the front staircase. Light tread, yet heavy enough to make the oak beneath his intruder's feet creak with the pressure.

What was coming up the stairs? David wasn't really all that afraid. In different times, when his frame of reference was untroubled with thoughts of terminal disease and a slow, withering death, he might have been horrified, might have clenched his muscles in terror, mind clicking like a metronome to find a way out of what was about to happen.

But his frame of reference, like the muscular frame that had once housed his soul, had withered, gone downhill remarkably quickly over the past few weeks. He lay in bed, breathing shallow, and waited.

Someone was in the hallway. David closed his eyes, too tired for terror, too tired for little more than a vague concern. He hoped that whatever was coming would at least not be painful.

Just like in the movies, he watched the brass doorknob turn and he did manage to get up on his elbows and wonder of wonders, found his heart could still rev up with adrenalin.

"Who is it?"

His question was answered with a dramatic flinging open of his bedroom door. The heavy wood crashed into the wall behind it, sending a flurry of plaster flakes everywhere.

And then he was there and David's malaise finally took a back seat to horror. "Timothy..." He whimpered, eyes welling up, jaw gone slack.

Timothy smiled. "It's me."

Timothy's smile vanished when he saw him lying on the bed. This was not the man he had expected to see. David Long was a big, virile guy, his body a powerhouse of energy and strength. The man lying before him looked to have aged thirty years since the last time Timothy had seen him. His skin and bones outlined by the sheet covering him, his face a death mask, ghoulish, telling a tale of infirmity.

This was not what he had expected. Not at all. Timothy was confused. He was frozen in his spot, unable to move. He hadn't counted on this. "What's the matter with you?"

David Long swallowed, sucked in a big lungful of air that looked as if it didn't get down very far. "This isn't real."

"It's real, all right. Do you doubt your own eyes?"

David flattened himself against the headboard. The only things bright in his ashen face were his eyes, shimmering with fear.

Timothy took a few steps forward, watching as David

managed to draw up his knees to his chest, watching as he tried to shrink into the oak headboard of his sleigh bed. The same bed upon which he had been violated over and over throughout his teenage years. He wondered if the mattress beneath the bed linens was still stained with his blood.

There was a knife in Timothy's jacket pocket, a paring knife lifted from Aunt Helene's wooden knife block. He had selected a small knife because he wanted to make the man suffer, just as David had made him suffer when he was a boy. He touched the knife now, rubbing his thumb along the blade. All his plans were gone, usurped by the situation.

"I'll ask again: what's wrong with you?"

David swallowed again. "Nothing. A little flu. Explain this."

"Your eyes explain it all. Right? Didn't you tell me that once? Didn't you say the truth of what I was was stored in my eyes? That my attraction for other boys couldn't be denied because my sight was the — what was it? — channel for my desires? You were always so literate, David." Timothy smirked at the man on the bed.

"I came here to kill you. Slowly, in the most tortured, painful way possible. But it seems Mother Nature has already beaten me to the punch. The bitch." Timothy crossed the room and sat on the edge of the bed. "You don't have the flu. If you do, it's the worst case in recorded history."

"It's just a bug."

"Right."

The tension had vanished from the moment. In its place was an odd sadness, a despair. He had come for a fight, come thinking his tormentor would beg for his life. But how could one beg for something that had certainly lost its value?

David Long, just from the looks of him, wasn't long for this world. Timothy might even go so far as to say he would welcome a quicker passing.

Timothy wished there was a way he could heal him, make him into the man he once was, so he could steal from him something precious.

Timothy stood. "Killing you would be a favor, wouldn't it?"

David Long stared at him.

"I don't want your infectious blood on my hands."

Timothy paced. He looked out the window at the trees; in the distance, the grey snake of asphalt that was the road in front of the good doctor's house plotted a course for a speeding vehicle now and then. Everyone was oblivious to what had happened to Timothy.

And he felt the anger bubbling inside, a swarm of hornets growing in buzzing intensity. A throbbing started just behind his temples, and he reached up and clawed at his forehead as if he could rip the pain out. "How could you do this to me?"

"Do what?"

"Die."

"I'm not going to die."

"You're a master of denial, aren't you?" Timothy crossed to the dresser, where a small, round hand mirror lay, its handle lacquered with red and black Japanese characters. He picked it up and brought it near David's face. "Take a good look, Doctor, look at your own face and tell me it's not the face of a dead man."

David tried to push the mirror away, but his weakness prevented him from doing little more than making the mirror wobble in Timothy's grasp. "Look at it, damn it!" Timothy cried.

But David turned his head, squishing his eyes together.

"You won't even give me this," Timothy whispered, his words bearing an intensity that only just began to match the turmoil he felt inside. "Look in the mirror."

But David Long would not look. He kept his head turned, his eyes shut. Timothy, the mirror held in one hand, reached out with another and attempted to peel the doctor's eyelids apart. The lids parted at last, but he could do nothing to force David's gaze upon the glass.

Finally, Timothy flung the mirror across the room, where it landed with a crash. "What can I do to you?"

David Long slumped down in his bed. It would take real effort now for him to keep his eyes open.

Timothy stared at the man for a long time. There was nothing, he thought, nothing at all he could do. If Timothy believed in God, he would have said He had already meted out his punishment for David.

"You bastard," he whispered, and walked out of the room.

Chapter
Twenty-eight

Well, Daniel has finally returned home. Summer has arrived and with it the arrival of my brother and his so-called wife (although no judge or church has ever sanctioned their union). The two of them returned from Amsterdam two days ago, totally without warning. Mother was preparing lunch when a taxi rounded the bend in the driveway.

"Who on Earth can that be?" she asked, staring out the kitchen window at the Checker cab. "I'm not expecting anyone."

I left the family room to witness the two of them exit the cab, to watch the cabdriver remove their luggage from the trunk. When Daniel pointed to the house, I knew who would be paying their cab fare, even though Daniel well has the means to do so.

"Mother, you better get your bag," I called out.

I couldn't remove myself from my place at the window. They were a bohemian spectacle. Hippies, I suppose is the correct term. Daniel in his paint-splattered jeans, jersey shirt and knitted cap, Lanta in a long, flowered peasant-style dress with some sort of gauzy top that hid her weight. Her wheat-colored hair was pulled back away from her freckled face and she looked for all the world like a child.

Except for the bundles she held in her arms. Yes, I did make the word a plural. There were two bundles in her arms.

"Oh my God," I whispered to Mother. "She's had twins."

"Isn't it wonderful?" Mother gasped. She rushed from the house to greet them, wiping her hands on her apron. I don't know what's wrong with the woman; she's a disgrace. Her children are a disgrace and she acts as if it's some blessed event.

I stayed rooted to my spot, tears welling up in my eyes. Oh Daniel, my Daniel, why did you do this to me? We had shared so many dreams growing up. The two of us at the helm of Father's business, running it together, bringing new glories.

But Lanta, the bitch, came along and changed everything. Changed him, turning him from the values he had been raised on.

I watched Mother outside with them, digging in her purse to pay the cabdriver. He drove away then, a trail of blue exhaust behind him. They stood in the driveway, embracing. Their faces were bright with laughter and smiles. There was no recrimination from Mother, nothing. How could she be so blind to the shame they've heaped on the family? I wonder now if I ever knew my own Mother.

Look at her, outside in the sunlight, lifting the blankets to peer at the little creatures Lanta holds. Looking at them and grinning, as if this were something to be proud of. What will all of their friends say about these little bastards? Will she bring them to the country club and proudly introduce her grandchildren? And I can just see Lanta with them at some family gathering, she with her unstable ways and questionable morals.

As they came toward the house, I broke a plate on the kitchen floor and fled to the sanctuary of my bedroom.

Later...
They're downstairs now. I can hear their voices. Laughing, talking amongst themselves as if nothing was wrong, when nothing could be further from the truth. Father has come home and he too shocked me, accepting his son and his bitch and their wretched offspring.

Mother had been in my room, just about an hour ago, begging me to come downstairs and join them. I was having none of it. I banished her from my room, perhaps a bit too shrill, but I just can't abide this whole situation. Mother had tears in her eyes when she left the room. "Family's family," she said to me, pausing in the doorway. "If your values get in the way of that simple fact, Helene, then they're not worth very much."

I stared out the window and whispered, "Get out."

And this whole situation is much worse than you might imagine. The children, twin boys, are not normal. Mother used the words 'genetic abnormality' but I know the root of the problem. One does not ingest every manner of drug and alcoholic beverage while pregnant and expect one's offspring to come out healthy and normal. The havoc chemicals can wreak on one's body are readily apparent, I'm sure, in the twins. How did Lanta even begin to imagine they would be normal?

One, Mother says, is perfectly all right. Both, she says are beautiful, with white hair and the deep blue eyes all babies have. She said they are virtually indistinguishable. The other, she told me, is profoundly retarded. She tells me that one is very quiet and that his brain is damaged.

No surprise! How can Lanta hold her head up? If I had done such a thing, my remorse would not let me. I know I sound hateful, but the two of them will pay all their lives for their heedless lifestyles. And I can't say I feel sorry for them. If one puts one's hand into the fire, one must expect to be burned...

I want no part of the twins, Timothy and Theodore. I want no part of my brother or Lanta. I have decided to move out as soon as I can.

There must be places where normal people live and carry their lives on decently.

Father is calling up the stairs now for me to come down to dinner. In the background, one of the imps is wailing. I will not grace them with my presence.

I want nothing to do with any of them.

HELENE SAT ALONE. He had loosened the rope around her ankles and wrists before he left. Certainly, they were tight enough to render her unable to free herself, but at least now she felt warmth in her extremities, and her wrists and ankles tingled with the renewed blood flow. Outside, the sun was sinking behind the horizon, just half an orb across the grass, deepening the shadows around her and causing them to lengthen, to elongate, until they became strange twisted shapes on the parquet floor and yellow rug.

She remembered much, sitting here, bound. There was little else to do. She had been so close to Timothy when he was growing up, and there were plenty of hugs for him, plenty of new clothes from Marshall Fields, and plenty of bedtime stories. The stories were simple at first, just picture books allowing him to identify animals on their oversized pages. They had moved on to the fairy tales, and it seemed that these were the stories Timothy always liked best, especially the ones by the Grimm Brothers. The darker the story, it seemed, the better he liked it.

And now she was playing out her own dark story with him. She racked her brain, trying to find a plausible explanation for what had happened, for these recent events which had turned her world upside down. She had never believed in the supernatural. Tales of vampires, werewolves, witches and ghosts were something she'd read to him at bedtime, the stuff of trashy novels and horror movies. There was plenty to be afraid of in the real world, and she had never seen any evidence of anything beyond that scary reality.

Could Timothy be a ghost? Even with all the evidence facing her, she didn't think so. His hands, when he hit her or when he tightened and untightened her bonds, felt as real as anyone's. The palms were soft, yet the calluses below where his fingers ended were rough. There was nothing ephemeral about his touch. Weren't ghosts supposed to be wispy creatures, made up of some translucent material that one could move one's hand through with no effort? Real blood, it seemed, coursed through Timothy's veins, and his flesh had weight and substance.

And if he was a ghost, why had he aged? Oh sure, it had only been a couple of years since he died, but Helene took in that his hair had thinned more on top than when she had last seen him (a horrific flash then in her brain of a police officer lifting a sheet). There were the beginnings of crows' feet around his eyes that she was sure hadn't been there when he died.

Could this be an impostor, a look-alike usurping Timothy's role among the living? First, what would a person hope to gain by slipping into the suit of someone else's life, especially a life as twisted and unhappy as Timothy's seemed to be? Besides, Timothy was someone she had brought up from infancy; she had always thought of him as her own son. No one, save maybe for Theodore, could bear such a resemblance.

And Theodore had been dead now for many years. Even if he was alive, he lacked the intellectual capacity to wreak such havoc. Hell, he lacked the intellectual capacity to even form words. He was little more than a vegetable, barely mobile, needing constant care and attention. Theodore could do nothing for himself. There had been no surprise when Timothy had informed her that he died. Helene had always been surprised he had survived as long as he did, damaged as he was.

She thought of Theodore. He had been as beautiful a child as Timothy, perhaps in some ways even more beautiful. A pure, almost angelic light had seemed to shine in him. His blue eyes were always clear and watchful, and the impish features both brothers shared seemed to carry in Theodore a more benign look. Where Timothy was impish, Theodore was more like an elf.

What had Timothy said to her? He had said she should now understand what it felt like to be a prisoner. She pretended not to know what he meant, but she knew.

How she had taken care of Theodore was no one's business, and there was certainly never any unkindness to it. She had seen to it that he was always warm, never went hungry, and had a comfortable place to sleep. With his limited capacity, she was sure this was enough. He didn't have the ability to want for anything more.

That she had kept him away from other people had nothing to do with keeping him a prisoner. She always thought she was protecting him. Anyone as profoundly different as Theodore would have been shunned, made fun of, and tormented if he had been exposed to other children, or even other adults.

Timothy had said to her, just before all the bad things happened with David Long and he made the decision to move out, that she kept Theodore in his basement rooms because she was ashamed of him and the presence of a "drooling idiot" would seriously impede her life. He laughed at her when she said she did it only for his own protection.

Sitting here, tied down, confused and tired, she reluctantly admitted to herself that there was some truth in Timothy's accusations from so many years ago. She had always been so alone, having to raise the twins by herself, and Theodore was just too much for other people to take. He did drool, and the only sounds he could make were howling noises which were, at best, frightening. There was no need for anyone to see Theodore; they couldn't have given him anything and he would have only frightened or repulsed them. The only people who ever had any contact with the boy were Helene herself, Timothy, and the boys' pediatrician.

She had had the rooms in the basement constructed for maximum comfort for Theodore. Wasn't her heart in the right place when she had the thick pile carpeting put in and the colorful wallpaper? Was she being a prison matron when she made sure he had plenty of toys to bang around, things to spin and to stare at? She had even had a television set put in his rooms, for which he seemed to have a fascination. And she spent time with him, and made sure Timothy did, too.

Had this been cruel?

"No one even knows I have a twin!" Timothy would scream at her, over and over, especially after he reached adolescence and the fighting began in earnest.

She wondered why they needed to know. What good would it have done?

Helene closed her eyes and tried to shut her mind down. The room had gone dark now and it was frightening to be sitting here like this in the pitch, unable to move or see, wondering what horror would leap out at her next, tied down here defenseless and unable to prepare herself for anything.

IT SEEMED TO Ed that everything was falling down around him. Nothing was good anymore. First, he lost Dan (and again, even if it was by his own choice, it didn't give him any comfort; Dan was still the only man Ed had ever loved), then he lost his job through a situation so bizarre that if he had heard about it happening to someone else he wouldn't have believed it. And now Peter.

Peter had come along, forcing his way into his life with charm, a smile that electrified him, and sex that was more incredible than Ed could have ever dreamed it would be. Yet Peter was more than just a boy-toy; he had a brain, and it was possible to have more than just a physical connection with him. There was a real warmth and comfort in their budding relationship that Ed believed could have very well led to love.

But now Peter was on his way out. He hadn't come over the

night before, and their conversation on the phone, early this morning, was tense. Peter had accused him of being "obsessed," and told him that someone so obsessed could never give him the attention he deserved. Ed knew he was right, but that didn't make the words any less painful. He had told Ed he didn't want to see him anymore, at least not until he could put this whole thing behind him.

Ed pressed down on the accelerator. Perhaps seeing Helene Bright, showing up on her doorstep and forcing her to talk, would help put the whole situation behind him. If Peter could have only known how tired he was of everything connected with Timothy Bright and the murders, and how much Ed himself wanted to get on with his own life, maybe he could have come to understand why he was so compelled to put the pieces of the puzzle together, if they did indeed fit.

He glanced down at a Post-it note on the seat beside him; it held Helene Bright's address, gotten from the Department of Motor Vehicles by Joey Mantegno. "I really shouldn't do this," she had told him. "I really have no business with DMV."

"But you know people there and I know they'll be willing to help you."

Their friendship, forged in the trenches of the Chicago Police Department, was growing strained, now that they no longer had an employer in common. Ed could tell Joey didn't want to get the information for him, yet she was unable to say no. He knew he was putting her in a position where he was taking advantage of her good nature, and he hated himself for it. But there was no other way: he couldn't do this alone.

He would have to make it up to her somehow. When—not if—he got back on the force...

He turned onto the brick driveway, marveling at the luxury of the pillared house just ahead. It was large; he wondered how someone could live in such a place and feel at home. He had never lived in such opulent surroundings and was certain he never wanted to.

The house was dark, and Ed sat in the car for a few moments, thinking that his knock on the door would go unanswered. Not a single light shone from any of the windows. This was strange in itself. Even if there was no one home, you'd think in a place like this, Helene Bright would want to at least do the simplest thing one could to discourage burglars and leave a light or two on.

He cut the engine and summoned up what courage he had left. Even if she was home, he had no guarantee she would speak to him. She had been cold on the telephone when he had called, almost offended that he had mentioned her nephew. Having him show up unannounced would probably guarantee him an even chillier reception. Ed hoped his powers of persuasion would be enough to let him get his foot in the door.

Ed had, of course, considered that she could be helping Timothy. Family members were often on the wrong side of the law when it came to protecting their loved ones.

He got out of the car and approached the dark house. Its white exterior almost seemed to glow in the moonlight. He lifted the brass knocker and let it fall once, twice, three times. The house sounded hollow inside, as if it had been empty for a long time.

There was no movement from within. Ed pounded on the door, pounded and didn't stop until his frustration reddened his knuckles, leaving him tense and frustrated.

Slowly, he headed back to the car. Tomorrow was another day, and perhaps in the morning he could reach her. He knew this could be another dead end. The woman probably knew as much as Ed did about her "late" nephew's whereabouts.

HELENE TENSED WHEN she heard the low rumble of a car engine coming up the driveway. It would be Timothy, returning from whatever hell-bent mission he was on. Once, she had thought she knew her nephew; now he was a stranger to her, with the emphasis on *strange*. She had no idea what he would do to her, or even what his purpose was in returning to her and keeping her prisoner like this.

She dreaded the sound of the door opening and his quick gait across the floor. He had hit her several times already, and the slaps were often unprovoked. Tears sprang up in Helene's eyes when she realized how much hatred he must have for her.

She waited, tense, for the sounds which would herald his arrival inside the house. Waited and then tensed more when she heard the fall of the brass knocker at the front door. Someone was here! Oh, thank God.

Helene began to scream within the thick swatch of duct tape Timothy had slapped across her mouth before leaving. All that emerged from her lips and scorched throat was a loud mumble; she was sure it couldn't even be heard in the next room.

She began rocking back and forth in the chair, trying by sheer force of will to move the chair, to somehow get out of the room and to the door. She would do it if she had to slither across the front entryway, with the chair attached. She had to get out of this situation before it turned worse.

Anything could happen. And life, drab and desperate as it was, was suddenly something she longed to hang on to.

Whoever was outside was now pounding on the door. Perhaps it was someone who had tried to call and had been unable to get through, since Timothy had cut the phone lines before he left her earlier that day. The pounding grew harder and she wished, wished so much there was some way she could let whoever was standing outside know she was within.

But it was no use. She couldn't move the chair. Had she been able to do so, she would have done it long ago, crashing through the window if need be.

ED THOUGHT HE had heard something. It was too beneath his aural periphery for him to be able to discern what the sound was, but there was definitely something. He paused by the car, listening. No other sounds.

Maybe, he thought, *maybe I should just make a check.* Ed closed his car door and moved back toward the house once more. He made a circuit around the exterior of the house, pressing his face close to the windows, trying to see inside. As he got to the west side of the house, there was a tremendous bang. He moved quickly to the window from which he thought the sound had issued.

His eyes had already adjusted to the darkness. It was easy to see the figure lying on the floor. He couldn't make out much, whether the figure was a man or a woman, but he could see that whoever it was was strapped to a chair.

Ed hurried back to the front door and found it locked, as he expected. Moving quickly, he went to the back of the house, where there was another door, also locked. He pulled a credit card from his wallet and tried to jimmy the mortise lock, but discovered the door was also dead-bolted.

If it had been summer, perhaps there would have been an open window. But the house was sealed shut.

He had no other choice. He returned to the room where he had seen the figure, wrapped his jacket around his hand, and smashed the window. He shook the glass out of the jacket, put it back on, then reached in and undid the lock. By now, he could hear muffled cries coming from within the room.

He lifted the window and hoisted himself inside. Crossing the room, Ed located the light switch and flipped it.

A woman, slight in frame, with dark hair streaked through with grey, lay on the floor. In her eagerness to attract his attention, she had somehow caused the ladderback chair to which she was strapped to tip over. There was a bright crimson spot of blood on her forehead, from a wound she must have sustained in the fall. Other than that, she looked in relatively good shape.

Ed stooped beside her. She looked up at him with eyes that were bright with fear, made all the more apparent by the ashen pallor of her skin.

"This is gonna hurt," he said, knowing there was no other way. He ripped the duct tape from her mouth in one quick motion and she sucked in air, groaning softly.

"Are you all right?"

"Physically, yes." The woman stared at him as he began to unloosen her binds. "Who are you?"

"My name's Ed Comparetto. I used to be with the Chicago police force, but now I'm on leave."

"What are you doing here?"

Ed tried to think of an answer while he finished getting her untied. When she was free, he helped her to stand and led her to a love seat in the corner of the room. She sat gratefully. It must have been painful to walk, after having her circulation reduced.

"I'm looking for your nephew, Timothy Bright."

Her hand went to her mouth and she looked wildly about the room, as if Bright himself was concealed there, somewhere among the shadows. "What do you know about him?"

"There have been several murders in Chicago's gay community," Ed said. "You've probably seen something about it on the news."

The woman shook her head, staring at him. He began to feel uncomfortable under the intensity of her gaze. "I don't really pay much attention to the news."

"The first person I interviewed was a young man who gave his name as Timothy Bright. He was the one they told me discovered the body."

"Timothy?"

"I know, I know. You're going to tell me he's dead."

"Oh no, Mr. Comparetto, I'm going to tell you nothing of the sort."

Finally, Ed thought, *maybe we're getting somewhere.*

"In fact, I believe he's very much alive." Her gaze was now over his shoulder. "He's standing right behind you."

Chapter
Twenty-nine

WHAT HAPPENED THE night I was murdered? The tale has never been told. You know the adage: dead men tell no tales.

Put your mind at rest. I'm not dead. Although having the world think you are gives one a certain liberty. Death has a way of cutting all those annoying ties, allowing one a freedom to move undetected among the living, do whatever it is one wants, or needs, to do.

Three years ago, Men4HookUpNow.com was just beginning in Chicago. In its startup, the people behind this new way of meeting wanted to get people to use their service, in much the same way drug dealers want people to sample their wares. For a limited time (heard that phrase a few hundred times, right?), the people behind Men4HookUpNow.com made it a free online service. Log on all you want, chat all you want, beat off all you want, and arrange connections with strangers to your heart's content, there's absolutely no charge! In much the same way a drug dealer wants to get you hooked before he begins demanding money, the folks at Men4HookUpNow.com wanted to get desperate guys hooked on the site before they started charging.

I was one of those desperate individuals. You see, I've never been the gay fantasy image of the perfect male. While I was never a troll, I was never the type to turn a head in a bar, either. And while it's true that an average-looking man can do just fine in the old hunting game that's played out every night on the battlefields of the gay bar, I never possessed the self-confidence it takes to grab the initiative and find a man.

So my liaisons, after the fall of David Long and Aunt Helene practically kicking me out of her house, were of a decidedly anonymous nature. I haunted adult bookstores and learned what a glory hole was, how that wondrous yet crude device could be employed to give pleasure as well as to receive it. I got my homosexual schooling in public toilets and parks, anywhere where men exchanged the most intimate sort of contact, yet never went so far as to say who they were.

Men4HookUpNow.com, when it appeared, seemed to be a godsend. No more sitting for hours in the basement men's room at Marshall Fields, with my pants around my ankles, waiting for the lucky man who would come along and fulfill my most sordid fantasies. No more need to buy tokens at the adult bookstore on Hubbard Avenue and watch endless loops of gay sex while waiting for a dick to emerge through the hole in the wall. No more sitting in my car at the park near Foster Avenue Beach, where I would watch men restlessly cruise the length of the park, back and forth, back and forth, looking for something they could never really find. Not really.

Now, online, I could get a man without ever leaving the comfort of my own home. It was like shopping for clothes online from LL Bean. Only it was free and a whole lot easier.

The first time I logged on I was nervous. I had had no practice in getting to the meat of things, if you can stand the pun without groaning. I didn't know how to immediately pinpoint a location (so your potential suitor wouldn't be too far), how to discover his particular tastes (so you weren't two bottoms trying to please each other or a raunch queen with a vanilla college boy) or even how to root out those who were serious about getting together as opposed to those who just wanted to chat, e-mail, or fill up lonely hours with endless instant messages. At first, I wasn't even sure how to scroll through the thumbnail pics and profiles, looking for just the right man to suit my particular needs.

I remember that first time. My first instant message to someone. I wasn't sure what I should say. How do people start such conversations? I must have logged on five times or more before I finally had the nerve to actually IM someone; it took a couple times more before I actually hooked up with someone who was as much of a novice as I was. After talking for what seemed like hours (I had given him my phone number), I finally got up the courage to ask him to come over. As soon as I hung up the phone, I immediately regretted it. Back then, I had no knowledge of features like automatic call back. So I was stuck. He was on his way. Back then, it never occurred to me that someone would say they'd come over and then never show up.

But immediately questions began to arise: what if he doesn't like what I look like? (I didn't think it was a good idea to post a photo of myself.) What if he doesn't want to do what I want? What if I don't want to do what he wants? What if I come too soon? My encounters thus far (except for Dr. Long, who couldn't possibly count; molestation hardly being a test of sexual prowess) had been so anonymous that I never really worried about my looks and how good I was at what I was doing. They were quick, clean, and had all the intimacy of checking out at the supermarket.

But having someone in my own apartment already put things on a different level. For one, it put me in the role of host. How would I get things started? My God, I was so innocent back then! And what of Teddy, locked in his room at the back? What if he started making noises, as he sometimes did when someone came to our door? What if he started that horrible howling he did, flinging himself against the door? I'd be mortified.

I know this sounds cruel, but you have to understand: Teddy had been confined all of his life and was used to such measures.

I remember him sitting there on his bed, knees drawn up and almost covering his face, rocking back and forth. It was a habit in which he would indulge for hours.

"Teddy, I'm expecting some company." I talked to Teddy as if he understood, though I believe the fact of the matter was he was unable to discern what different words meant, let alone shades of meaning. But he was my brother, and I often talked to him, as any pet owner probably talks to their dog or cat. I think he liked the attention.

He didn't stop rocking, just went on, eyes fixed on some point only he could see.

"Teddy, I'm sorry, but I have to do this."

He began to cry, in that bawling way of his, while I straightened him out on the bed. It wasn't cruel, you see, it wasn't. Teddy didn't understand. I bound his ankles together with a belt and tied his hands across his stomach with a brown knit tie I had. My red bandanna fit perfectly in his mouth. Once I pulled his blankets up to his chin, I think he was quite content. He didn't make any attempt to move.

I felt horrible, but I couldn't let the guilt linger too long: my connection would be arriving soon. I would have to deal with my remorse later.

They say the first time you do something bad is always the hardest. It's true. This bondage scene, bereft of any sexual connotation, was to be repeated several times in the coming months. And each time I became quicker and more adept at it. Each time, I found it easier to do, until at last it became no more guilt-inducing than feeding him his oatmeal in the morning.

When the buzzer sounded that first time, letting me know "he" was here, I wasn't sure what to do. It never occurred to me to simply not answer the door. Besides, there was a war going on in my head: on one side, there was the fear of this encounter, the anxiety, and on the other, there was a real desire to go through with it, provided the guy was as acceptable as his description, picture, and voice had led me to believe.

I summoned up my nerve, buzzed him in, and waited by the front door.

When I opened the door, I was disappointed. Not that he was monstrously fat or ugly, it's just that he bore only a passing resemblance to the pic he had posted online. In the picture, he looked much thinner and younger. There was something bland about him that didn't show in the photo, a plainness that made him almost invisible. "Glen," as he told me his name was, stood about 5'10" and weighed 190 pounds. He was clean-shaven, with dark, straight hair parted at the side and cut short (badly). He wore a pair of jeans, an army green T-shirt, and nylon running shoes. If you had encountered him anywhere, you would have forgotten him minutes after seeing him.

I don't know why, but his presence made me angry. I looked at him, appraising, and I could feel the old familiar signs coming on: the pounding at my temples, the extreme restlessness, the twisting in my gut. How dare he present himself to me, looking like that? I almost blurted, "You're not what I wanted at all!" But I didn't. Instead, I stood back and allowed him to come in. I could tell he was nervous, too, but it didn't make me any more sympathetic. If anything, it made me angry. I had wanted a confident, aggressive man. Glen's eyes took in my apartment, looking at everything but me.

He came up to me, still not meeting my gaze, and kissed me. He began rubbing my cock through my jeans, and I felt nothing. I pushed him away, hard enough to make him slam into the wall behind him. He looked kind of surprised: his mouth dropped open and his eyes widened. I warmed to the look.

But then he did an unexpected thing. He laughed. "So that's the way you want it, is it?" It was then our eyes finally met. "You should have said so on the phone."

Something else within me took over then. It was as if I had become a different person. I spat on him, a long, viscous strand that ran down one side of his face.

He dropped to his knees.

Glen left late that night, wearing the bruises and welts of a good time.

And I had found a new avocation.

It went on like that for a long time; each time I grew more bold. I discovered there was no shortage of masochists out there. I did everything from fisting to water sports to scat to bondage and to the most extreme forms of discipline, the kind of discipline that's shortened to CBT in the classifieds: cock and ball torture.

And I discovered yet another purpose for Men4HookUpNow:

group sex. Almost any weekend, someone was having a party. It always amazed me how someone could invite a whole houseful of strangers over, having no more to go on than their online descriptions and photos.

I found myself slipping out to this or that north side location and enjoying myself with nine, ten, a dozen men. I liked it. I liked the elements of voyeurism and exhibitionism that were always present. During these parties, though, I always kept my sadistic side in check.

And then I began having the parties myself. After seeing that no harm came to the hosts of these parties, I grew confident enough to throw one myself.

I had had several parties before the really bad one came along. It was August. I can still remember the heat and humidity of that night. It had rained earlier in the day and the air outside was like a moist blanket, damp and unmoving.

The party was set for midnight on a Saturday. I remember that there were at least a dozen guys who said they were coming. I knew from the start it would be less than that. In general, for every three guys who said they'd show up, only one would actually arrive.

There were actually only three who showed up that night: a very young guy who was nervous but extremely good-looking, Tony Evans, and two older guys, one who had described himself as a bear, mid-forties, pot belly, hairy with wild grey eyes, and another guy who reminded me of the actor James Woods, with a wiry, thin frame, hard and lean.

The party started out pretty normal, with lots of groping and kissing that eventually led to oral sex in various combinations. One of the guys, the bear, brought some crystal meth and pot, which we all happily indulged in. I was afraid of the meth and left it alone, let the others snort the poison up their noses. I knew that drugs killed my parents and, indirectly, my grandparents, so I wasn't too keen on them. Ever. But I did smoke some pot out of a little brass one-hitter.

The night is blurry in my memory. Sometimes trauma does that to you, makes you forget. I wish I could remember more clearly what led to what and how things happened. I must admit also that it wasn't just trauma that made events that night foggy, it was also the marijuana and the languid heat, which combined to make me fall asleep.

With them still there.

When I awakened, it was to Teddy's howling. It was too loud and piercing to be coming from behind a closed door. I lay there for several minutes, too groggy to move. I was on the couch, naked, my body covered in sweat. I had a leather couch then and the feeling was unpleasant, slippery and sticky all at once. There was, too, a feeling of disorientation. I wondered if I was dreaming. The sound of Teddy's bawling was familiar and yet seemed unfamiliar in this setting.

I sat up, my skin sticking to the couch and rested my head on my hands. No one from the party was around, and I wondered if they had left. Then it hit me: Teddy's howling was too loud to be coming from behind a closed door. Besides, I had gagged him before the party started.

What was going on? I got to my feet and padded back the hallway that led to Teddy's room. The howling was interrupted every so often by a sharp intake of air and a piercing yelp.

I quickened my pace.

By the time I got to Teddy's room, everything had gone silent. I wish now I could blot out what I saw. I wish this was one of the things memory would have mercifully erased.

But memory is cruel and capricious. It doesn't seem to have any selectivity.

The three of them stood naked around the bed. They looked at me with these silly grins on their faces.

One of them spoke; I don't recall which one. "I hope he's okay."

Teddy was lying, completely unbound, with his legs parted as far as they would go.

A pool of blood was beneath his ass.

I covered my face with my hands. "What did you do?"

I moved toward Teddy. His jaw was slack and a line of drool dripped from one side. His eyes stared vacantly.

Too vacantly.

There were two thin lines of semen across his jaw. "What did you do?" I cried.

But when I turned around, I discovered I was alone with Teddy. The slam of the front door let me know my party guests had beat a hasty retreat. I was torn: should I run after them or tend to Teddy?

I didn't know yet that Teddy was dead.

I moved toward him. The way he was lying so still caused the electricity to rise within me; I could feel sparks of it flying about my spine and in my gut.

I sat down on the bed and leaned close. He wasn't breathing.

"Teddy?" I whispered, placing a hand on his chest and shaking him gently.

There was no response.

I lifted the sheet and wiped the come off his face.

I sat like that, with a corner of the sheet in my hand, for a long time. My mind was empty. I suppose I was in shock.

After a while, I don't know how long, I looked down the length of his body. When I had tied him up, he had been wearing pajamas, short blue ones with dark blue piping around the edges. Now, he was naked.

There were several red welts on his body, where, I suppose they had hit him. One in particular is burned into my memory: a red hand-print on his chest. Around the edges, the outline of the hand was already beginning to flower into a purple bruise.

It was when I got to seeing between his legs that I truly felt sick.

There was a lot of blood, pooling between his spread legs.

Oh God, what had they done? Although I already knew. Rape is such an ugly word, and I had never associated it with my twin. The two seemed mutually exclusive.

But what had happened?

"Why are you dead?" I screamed then, the world going magenta, my terror and loss peaking. What was I going to do? Although I had been asleep, I knew I was responsible for this, and it sickened me. I lifted him by his shoulders and shook him, his head flopping back and forth like a rag doll's. "Why are you dead?" I shrieked, over and over until my voice was hoarse. I flung Teddy back to the bed, staring at him. My heart was pounding and my breath was quickening.

I didn't know what to do. There was no one to turn to. Aunt Helene had abandoned me—or I her, if you listen to her side of things. I had no friends. Men4HookUpNow connections are not made of the stuff that makes up lasting friendships.

Should I call the police? There would come so many questions, and I didn't know if I was equipped to answer them.

But all of this paled when I finally looked down at Teddy and it sank in: he was dead. I brushed my hand across his face, praying I was wrong, praying for a trickle of breath from his mouth or nose.

There was nothing.

It was then I began to cry, a cry not altogether different from Teddy's bawling. Almost a howling.

After I calmed down and my breath was nothing more than a spastic heaving, as I was unable to breathe through my nose, I lay down beside him and put my arms around him.

We lay together like that until the room became tinged with grey. The sky was beginning to lighten in the east and I thought that people would soon be getting up, preparing to lead normal lives: going to church, making breakfast, making love with spouses, children coming into bedrooms to wake their parents.

A world I had never been a part of, and now, I feared, never would.

The rage took over then, blinding me, blotting out the loss (a Godsend?) and I wanted to rush from the house and track down the men who had stolen my twin's life from me.

But was it they who would be blamed?

All I knew is that I would be responsible for this. Me and my sick ways, as I could hear Aunt Helene saying.

It was then that I began beating Teddy, starting with his face, wanting to obliterate the resemblance, wanting to blot out the Teddy I had loved. I worked my way down his body, beating until the skin broke under my fists, leaving raw open wounds that bled little.

I picked up the nightstand next to the bed and brought it down on his face.

By the time I finished, the sun had risen completely, hot and unrelenting. It made of our apartment a steam room, a sauna. The heat and the copper tang of blood in the air became benchmarks of memory: something I'll never be able to banish from memory, even though I've tried. God knows I've tried.

After a while, when my breathing had returned to normal and the pounding of my heart slowed, I had an idea. No one, save for a very few people, knew of Teddy's existence. Thanks to Aunt Helene and my continuation of the family tradition, I was alone in the world, no twin or siblings.

Teddy, I thought, could be me.

I packed hurriedly and left, leaving the door to the apartment open, hastening, I hoped, discovery of Timothy Bright's body.

I would not come back for two years. Two years hidden away in a small town in Northern California, the rage and need for revenge growing, until it at last became unbearable and I knew I would have to come back.

Chapter
Thirty

ED FROZE. HELENE Bright stood slightly to his left, in front of him, and the expression on her face told a tale of terror. Her eyes were wide and her lower lip was trembling. Ed felt that she wanted to latch onto his arm for protection, but some weird sense of decorum prevented that.

"What's going on here?"

When Timothy spoke, Ed immediately remembered the voice. Everything came rushing back to the day, last August, when he had interviewed the little man, the one who had presented himself to the police as the person who had discovered Tony Evans' body.

Ed turned slowly. It came as a shock, seeing him standing there. It was like some fantasy figure had suddenly come to life, too real to be real. Timothy was grinning at him, but there was no mirth in the grin, only madness. There was something almost horrifying about the man, the way he looked so young, though the lines on his face and the thinning hair belied this false youth. His pale blue eyes sparkled with a fire that had an almost evil cast. Ed thought it was no wonder this woman was afraid.

"I asked you a question. Mr. Comparetto, is it?"

"I came to talk to your aunt. I've been trying to find you."

"I've given you ample opportunity to find me. So, far, you seem unable to do anything once you do." Timothy giggled. "This time should be no different than the rest." He cocked his head. "Well, maybe a little different." He giggled again, and it sounded so twisted it made Ed shiver, childlike and menacing all at once. "Actually, I've been waiting to run into you again. I just didn't know it would be so soon." Timothy stared at the floor. "I guess I led you here, didn't I?"

"Look: cut the bullshit. I want to know what's going on here."

"This is a private family matter."

"Timothy, I don't think..."

"Shut up, Aunt."

If Ed hadn't been standing in front of Helene, blocking

Timothy, Ed was sure the little madman would have reached out and slapped her. He could see the desire to harm her deep in Timothy's eyes and the way he stood, fists curled into balls at his sides.

Timothy stared at Ed, his eyes taking in Ed's entire compact frame. Ed wondered, was he appraising? Was he wondering right now just how to dispatch him?

Ed wasn't sure how to proceed. The idea that this guy was dead, with all the attending proof, put a bizarre and surreal curve on things that he had never dealt with in the past. He wished he had his gun with him; that would equalize things, put him in charge. But he had thought this was going to be yet another interview with someone who had known the "deceased," and hadn't come prepared for a face-to-face meeting with Bright. Besides, he had turned in his piece when he turned in his badge; it was a moot point.

"You look like you've seen a ghost."

"You're no ghost."

"It was Theodore, wasn't it?"

"Shut up, Aunt Helene. I won't tell you again."

Ed turned to look at her for some explanation of her odd remark. When he turned, he felt something heavy crash down on the back of his head. As the world slanted, he heard shattered fragments of pottery scatter around him and the tinkle of Timothy Bright's childish laughter. Ed dropped to the floor, dizzy, the back of his head sending out crimson waves of pain.

He shook his head as his eyes began to focus again. Had he been out for a second or two? On the floor were the shattered remnants of an Oriental-style vase he had noticed earlier. The vase had stood on a cherry wood stand. He hadn't thought of it as a weapon.

Ed managed to get to his knees, the pain in the back of his head screaming. His vision cleared. "Oh no, please..." he whimpered. "Please let her go."

Timothy was holding his aunt close in front of him. One arm was around her neck and Ed saw the flash of silver in the darkness: a knife at her throat.

"Believe me, Mr. Comparetto, I wouldn't hesitate to slit her throat."

"No," Ed said through a choked breath. "No, you wouldn't, would you? Killing has become easier and easier for you, hasn't it?"

"Why should I admit anything to you?"

"I know what's been going on. I know you killed Tony Evans, David Westhoff, Milt Weinsap, John Austin and, in your own way,

Mark Dietrich."

As he recited the names of the dead, Ed could see that Timothy Bright was affected. His jaw went slack and his eyes almost glazed over as he stared vacantly ahead. Was he remembering?

Helene Bright was whimpering, the blade pressed close to her throat. One move and a line of red would appear against the pale flesh. Ed didn't want to see that happen.

"All of them deserved it." Timothy Bright whispered these words, slowly and with certainty.

Ed decided that a confrontational mode would not work in this situation. "I'm sure you had your reasons, Timothy. Why don't you come with me and we can talk about it...maybe get this whole thing sorted out."

Timothy laughed. "Oh, aren't you the clever one? Please, cleverness is my stock in trade. You should know that by now." He held the knife tighter and Ed heard Helene gasp as its sharpness cut into her throat, just a little, but enough that she whimpered again, the terror within her causing her to abandon the chill façade he assumed she presented to the world on most days.

But this was not most days. Today, she saw very clearly an end to her life. Ed was sure her fear was intensified by the situation, by being held by a nephew she was certain was dead. But Ed knew Helene Bright's main fear now was not that she was being visited by the vengeful spirit of her murdered nephew, but by the fact that she was being held by someone who was insane, and thus would not be open to any kind of reasonable dialogue.

"I've cut her a little," Timothy said in a sing-song voice. "I wouldn't mind cutting her a lot. Which is just what I'm going to do if you don't get the hell out of here right now."

"What would that solve, Timothy? I'll just go call the authorities from the nearest phone." What was wrong with him? Threats like that could only land him in the morgue.

"Go ahead. By the time you do that, she'll be bleeding all over her floor, and I'll be long gone. And when you tell the authorities that the deed was done by a dead man, they'll lock you up. I'm sure everyone you know already assumes you're a few bricks short."

Ed closed his eyes. How would he get out of this horrible situation? He tried another tack. "Look, let her go. I'll be your hostage."

"I don't need to make deals. Now get out of here."

Ed felt, almost as if it was someone else doing it, his fingernails clawing into his palms. His hands were sweaty, clenched with fright and frustration. He had no bargaining power in this situation; reasoning wouldn't do him much good because the person before him was beyond that.

"I want to fuck this bitch up real bad." Timothy's breathing was coming faster now; he was almost panting. Ed knew Bright was excited by the prospect of more bloodletting.

"Why would you want to do that?" Ed took a step forward.

With his step, Timothy sank the knife deeper into his aunt's throat. She gave a small cry and suddenly Ed could smell blood; the copper in the dark air.

Ed put up his hands and moved back. "Look, Timothy, I'm sorry. I'll stay right here. Just don't hurt her anymore."

"Why should I listen to you, asshole? You're just a pawn in my game, and someone who obviously doesn't have the intelligence or the balls to get along in this world. A policeman? A detective? Hah!" And with that, Timothy ran the knife in a quick motion across his aunt's face.

She screamed.

"Quiet! Or I'll do it again."

Helene sucked in air and Ed could tell she was trying hard not to make any noise. Even in the darkness, he could see she was trembling, and her eyes were wide.

"Why do you want to do this?"

"It's a long story. Get out."

"I'm not leaving."

"I'll kill her. I swear to God, I'll cut her to ribbons."

Ed ran his hands over his face. His heart thudded uncomfortably in his chest. He couldn't leave, because that would ensure this woman's life would not last much longer. But if he stayed, the end result could still be the same.

As it turned out, the choice was taken from Ed's hands just moments later. Bright took a few steps back, holding his aunt in front of him like a shield. "We're leaving now," he said in that same sing-song voice. "You try to follow us, you take even one step towards us and this knife goes right in her throat, deep; I'll tickle her tonsils with it, you prick."

Ed watched helplessly as Timothy backed toward the door. He stood frozen as he heard them stumbling down the hall and into the foyer. Nausea rose up in him as he heard the creak of the front door opening and the slam that followed it.

Ed rushed to the window and watched as Timothy pushed his aunt into the car, then went around to the driver's side. Ed pressed his face against the glass, an involuntary moan escaping him as the engine roared to life and the car gunned around the circular driveway and down the drive, its headlights illuminating the trees on either side.

Ed slumped to the floor. He had never felt more worthless in his entire life.

Chapter
Thirty-one

FROM HELENE BRIGHT'S journal, July 20, 1970

Life marches on, twisting and turning, sickening me with its surprises. I don't even know how to begin to describe this day and what's happened. I don't even know if I can commit it to paper without tears turning the ink into one huge smudge. I don't even know what kind of person I am, writing this horror down: what kind of ghoul chronicles such ugly occurrences in a journal?

But if I don't write it down, it may never become real for me. Even now, numbness is the main emotion I feel. Numbness is what I've felt since three o'clock this afternoon, when the state highway patrolman arrived at our door. It's almost alarming, this lack of feeling. It's not quite the kind of feeling one has from day to day when nothing in particular is happening. It's more as if all of my feelings have been wrapped in gauze or cotton, buffered from the outside world and its events. It's a sick numbness, undesirable. I wish I could scream. I wish I could wail. Instead, there is only this blankness.

Perhaps writing it down will help.

The state highway patrolman arrived at three o'clock today. No, no wait; let me start at the beginning.

Today was the day Father had decided to take Lanta and Daniel up to Lake Geneva, Wisconsin, or more precisely Fontana. There, Father owns two coach houses that were once part of an estate. He had them both remodeled into apartments, one up, one down. Rental income, a good investment, the kind of thing Father is always looking to sink his surplus of money into. He retained the nicest apartment for our family. In other days, when things were different, the whole family spent many happy summer weekends at the apartment, which was just a short walk from the lake, the pier, and our Chriscraft.

Lanta and Daniel needed someplace to live with their two little imps. The one quiet, the other always wailing, his little face red and balled up into something resembling a prune. Father offered them the apartment at Lake Geneva to use throughout the winter. Lanta wants to paint and

Daniel thinks, I guess I should say thought, he had the great American novel in him. The idea seemed a good one: it would give everyone some space, some sorely needed space.

But Lanta wanted to see the place first, before she gave her final okay on the situation. Such gratitude! Oh God, forgive me for writing that.

They asked me if I would watch the babies while they drove up. "It won't be for long," Mother told me, her hand reaching out warily to touch my arm. She was still stinging from my plans to move out. I'd been looking at apartments in the city. She knew I couldn't abide the babies, and abide the way they were being raised: Lanta with her "natural" childbirth at home, breast feeding, and so far, no official registry of their birth. They might as well not exist. I wish, now more than ever, they didn't. "But the trip will be so much easier and quicker if we can just go without them. The crying gets on your father's nerves."

Reluctantly, I agreed to stay home and take care of them. I prayed they would sleep the entire time they were gone. Having anything to do with them is always most unpleasant. I have no maternal need to feed them, rock them, or worse, change their smelly diapers.

"I've pumped some milk for them," Lanta said to me before heading out the door. "It's in the fridge. Just heat it up if they get hungry."

"Right," I said, and tried to smile. Her grimace in return told me I didn't succeed very well.

And right now, that milk, like some weird life blood living on after she died, is in the refrigerator. It will be her babies' last living link with their mother.

This is hard to write. Some of the numbness is fading, like an anesthetic wearing off. My hands tremble and there is an uncomfortable swelling in the back of my throat.

Please let the babies sleep until I finish this. If I can just get it down here, perhaps I can begin to deal with it.

I watched them from the window as they took off in the station wagon, watched until the car dwindled out of sight, until the trees in the driveway swallowed them up. I felt a mixture of anger and resignation.

If I had only known it was the last glance I'd have of any of them.

The state highway patrolman knocked at the door at three o'clock. I'm ashamed to say I was beginning to get angry at my family. I had thought they'd be back much sooner and I was beginning to picture them all going in for a dip off the pier or a quick cruise around the lake in the boat. All while I was stuck at home with the children. I imagined Daniel urging my mother and father to stay, telling them something like, "Helene's with the kids. She can hold down the fort."

The knock surprised me. Timothy was in his crib, screaming. I had tried rocking him, feeding him, had even checked his diaper. Nothing would stop the screaming. Theodore lay in the crib next door, eyes wide and staring at nothing. He was silent.

I left the squalling baby to go and answer the door. I was expecting no one and wished that no one was calling right now. My nerves were beginning to cry from the onslaught of Timothy's tantrum.

I opened the door and was taken aback at the sight of the officer in uniform. A sick feeling rose up in my stomach when I saw him, the nervous expression on his face, the way he avoided my eyes, staring down at the brick porch after he'd removed his hat.

"Yes?" I said, hoping against hope he was here for some reason other than the wild thoughts that were running through my mind.

"Are you Helene Bright?"

"Yes, I am."

"Miss Bright, I'm afraid I have some very bad news."

I wanted to faint. Things got a little dizzy when he spoke the words and it suddenly seemed too hot, the flush rising to my face and burning. I didn't want to hear anymore. I knew what was coming and yet, I blotted it out. If I just closed the door, I thought, it wouldn't be so and my life could return to what it was before he knocked.

I gasped. "Is something wrong?"

"On Route 41, there was an accident."

"Are they hurt?" I didn't want to accept that it could be something worse.

"I'm afraid they were killed."

"All of them?"

"Yes. I'm afraid so, ma'am."

"It can't be," I whispered. Everything was spinning. I felt drunk. I began to close the door, even though the officer was speaking. He was asking me if there was someone who could stay with me or would I like him to stay.

I closed the door in his face and ignored his knocking until he went away.

Upstairs, Timothy continued to scream.

Chapter
Thirty-two

ED WAITED ONLY a few minutes before exiting the house and getting in his own car. He had an idea where they would go, the epicenter of this whole horrid business: Rosehill Cemetery. It was where they all were, dead or alive, and he thought it was logical, in its own mixed-up way, for them to go there.

The hour had grown late and the highways were relatively deserted. Ed's adrenalin was pumping as he sped down I-94, watching for the Touhy exit. It seemed to be taking forever, in spite of the few cars on the road. He knew it was a long way east on Touhy and each red light, of which there were many, would be an exercise in frustration and aggravation.

What if they weren't even there? Bright could take his aunt anyplace in the world; hunches didn't always pay off.

He took the curve at the Touhy exit too fast and almost lost control of the car. The tires screeched as Ed fought for control. The maneuver didn't do much for his frayed nerves; in addition to the adrenalin rush, his heart was now pumping wildly. A trickle of sweat had formed at his hairline; his hands were slippery on the wheel.

As he stopped at the first red light, fingers drumming impatiently on the wheel, he picked up his cellular phone.

HE WAS DREAMING. And in his dream, he found himself alone in a blank white room. He knew he had been put there by someone, knew in fact that he was being held prisoner there.

The room had no windows, no doors, even the usual parameters of a room—its four walls—were missing. The room curved in a circular shape, no way to discern which way anything faced. It was horrifyingly disorienting.

He could hear, dimly, Ed's voice outside the room. He held himself perfectly still, stopping his breathing to listen to the muffled voice.

Ed was screaming. He was saying something, between cries of agony, about needing help.

Peter Howle awakened, his sheets wet with sweat. Outside, the sky was that peculiar pre-dawn color that no word describes. The sky was lighter, but still seemed to retain the color of night, navy blue with no stars.

Why had he been so hard on Ed? The poor guy was doing nothing more than trying to save his own life. Peter could now see that he had no right to stand in his way.

But he desperately wanted nothing to happen to this man he was falling in love with. That was his sole reason for being so adamant about Ed's continuing this little investigation of his. The stakes were too high. Why couldn't he just find another job and forget about this Timothy Bright character? But Peter knew, deep down, that Ed's job was important to him, important to his sense of self. How could he just expect him to drop it without a fight?

Peter sat up in bed, the sheets slipping from his chest to bunch around his waist. Dim light permeated the room, enough to see the David Hockney posters on his wall, enough to see the oval-faced deco clock his mother had given him for his birthday last year.

It was five a.m.

And the phone was ringing.

Only one person, Peter thought, could be calling at this hour. He lunged for the phone and swooped it from its cradle.

"It's me."

Peter caught his breath. At least Ed was all right.

"Where are you?"

"I'm in my car, heading east on Touhy."

Peter stood and began pacing around his bedroom. The sky was getting lighter and lighter, now a pearlescent grey. "What are you doing, Ed? Why are you on Touhy at five o'clock in the morning?"

"Never mind that. I want you to forgive me."

Peter thought how this conversation could only be taking place at such an odd hour, when the good sense of day still waited to awaken. He never really meant to shut Ed out anyway; his unyielding manner on this issue was nothing more than a ruse, a hope that if Ed saw what he might lose if he stayed in pursuit of things he would give up on it...for Peter's sake.

When you love someone, you don't make them make such choices, even if it is for their own good.

"There's nothing to forgive."

"You'll see me again, then?"

Peter sighed. "I really don't have any choice. Yes, of course."

"Good. I just didn't want to go into this with the feeling I had lost you."

"You haven't lost me." Peter thought, although he didn't say it, that Ed didn't really have him yet. He had been so wrapped up in this damn case that he really had never been able to give Peter his all. "Now tell me what's going on."

"I'd rather not involve you in it."

Peter barked out a short laugh. "It's a little late for that now, isn't it?"

"I guess you're right. Still, you'd be better off just waiting for me."

"What is this? Keeping me safe? I don't need it, Ed. If this is going to be the kind of life you lead, then I'm going to have to get used to it. Right?"

"It's just better—"

"Right?"

"I suppose. Why do you need to know, anyway?"

Peter shook his head. Daylight was creeping steadily into his room and with the light, he was waffling, beginning to question his involvement with this man who was either extraordinarily dedicated or nuts. "I need to know because I care about you."

"It's a long story. I'm on my way to Rosehill cemetery."

"Should I meet you there?" What was wrong with him? Peter suddenly questioned his own sanity. He had never imagined having a boyfriend who would involve him in such life and death situations.

"No. Absolutely not."

There was a click. Peter sighed.

Rosehill wasn't that far. Peter headed to his chest of drawers for jeans and a T-shirt.

ED ARRIVED JUST outside Rosehill Cemetery at a quarter of six. He parked his car on Ravenswood and sprinted across the street.

The gothic castle façade at the front of the cemetery looked imposing against the slate blue sky. Everything was silent. No cars were rushing by; no birds were singing.

The gates were locked. It was what he had expected. But did the locked gate mean that Bright and his aunt could also not be inside?

Timothy Bright was far too clever for that. Rosehill was one of largest cemeteries, if not the largest, in the city limits. Surely, among its many borders, one could find access.

Ed looked down Ravenswood, searching for the car that had taken them away less than an hour ago...and saw nothing more than parked cars; none of which bore even a passing resemblance to Timothy Bright's vehicle. Here and there along the rows of buildings that faced the el tracks there was a yellow light in a window, indicating someone was up, about to start a normal day.

Ed wondered if his life would ever be normal again. It was hard to remember back to the time when his life was relatively unmarked by stress, a time when things were just as they were supposed to be and the only tension in his life was of the everyday variety.

How would he get past the cemetery's locked gates? And even if he did gain access, what would it gain him? Would he be able to find Bright, rescue his aunt? Or would be only be breaking into a place where he was the only living thing, save for the swans, geese and ducks that swam in the pond near the chapel, or the squirrels that foraged among the tombstones.

But there could be other life, and if he wasn't too late, Ed might find two living souls, one in grave danger and the other (just out of the grave?) twisted and with homicidal impulses.

Ed walked beyond the castle-like façade of the cemetery. A high wrought iron fence surrounded everything. Was the fence, Ed now wondered, to keep intruders out, or to keep the dead within? Were the people who managed this park-like monument to death privy to knowledge the rest of the world didn't have? Had they seen people, caked with grime, walk out of the cemetery when, for all intents and purposes, they should have lain within these fenced borders for eternity?

He traveled a great distance, the sounds of the awakening city his only company, north on Ravenswood, then west on Peterson, until he saw a break in the fence. The break was small, and he didn't know if he could fit through, but it seemed like his only chance to gain entry.

Ed sucked in his breath and worked his way into the opening. The iron of the fence pressed against his back and stomach, almost cutting off his air. He was in far enough that whether he could get either in or out became something Ed wondered about. How humiliating to be discovered here by a groundskeeper, unable to move.

He pushed, sliding himself toward the well-manicured grass and the tombstones and mausoleums to his right. And couldn't move. It was as if he had caught himself in a trap. Perhaps this was just the kind of trap the admittedly clever Mr. Bright would be laughing about now, in some other location, the blood-soaked body of his aunt lying on the floor before him.

He sucked in his breath until his lungs hurt, until he thought he could stand it no more, until he thought he might burst and let himself almost fall into the cemetery's grounds.

There was a moment when he thought it wouldn't work and then, with a dizzying loss of balance, Ed fell to the ground. *Inside* the cemetery. His shirt had ripped and there was a bright red line on his stomach, already raised, with dots of blood showing on its surface.

Ed would deal with that later. Right now, there was no time for his own pain. He got up, gasping for the air he had denied himself and began to run.

But where? This was a huge cemetery, occupying entire acres. Bright could be anywhere. The most logical place to look would be, of course, at the Bright family plot. It had seemed somewhat of a useless mission when he and Peter had visited the gravesite weeks ago; now he was grateful he knew in which direction to head.

A cold wind had blown up, and Ed remembered that forecasters last night had predicted an early snow, just flurries, but unusual for November. The prediction came true as Ed neared the Bright plot. Slants of white came down and melted as soon as they reached the earth, which still retained enough warmth to fight off its encroachment.

They had been here. Ed paused in front of the graves, panting and damning himself for being too slow. He surveyed the family plot, sickened by what he saw. The scene was unusual, having all the accoutrements of violence, and Ed wondered if what he saw was just the aftermath of a struggle or a message. More games to play...

Timothy seemed so very fond of games.

The earth above Timothy's grave had been disturbed. Seriously disturbed. The pale grass, yellow in spots, had been overturned to reveal the rich soil underneath. Soil was scattered all around the gravesite; it almost looked as if someone had dug his way out.

That much, at least is a message for me.

But the other thing Ed's detective gaze took in could certainly be evidence of a violent struggle. At the top of Theodore Bright's granite marker, there was a smear of a dark substance, almost black now, but still sticky to the touch.

Blood.

The adrenalin pumping through Ed's system seemed to ebb all at once, to wither away, leaving a vague bad taste in his mouth: disappointment that he had been too slow.

But where were they now? Ed scanned the bleak landscape, so empty and devoid of the life which was beginning to bustle just outside the cemetery's confines.

He could run the entire morning through the cemetery. And even if they were still here, which he doubted, he might never find them. The place was dotted with mausoleums, most of them ornate and bearing inscriptions that made their occupants seem somehow more noble. There were statues erected to the memory of the dead. And there were copses of trees, though now leafless, that still offered some refuge to those who sought to hide.

It was then he heard the scream. Shrill, high-pitched, and definitely that of a woman, Ed could discern that it came from somewhere to the southwest of where he was standing. Western Avenue was the western border of Rosehill and it was from this direction that the single scream came, sounding so lonely and helpless and worse, full of terror.

He remembered when he and Peter had visited, and knew there was a huge mausoleum which offered sort of a condominium-style resting place to its occupants. Imposing and crafted from grey granite, the mausoleum, Ed knew, would offer a good spot to hide. There were entrances that were shielded almost entirely from view.

Ed headed, as quickly as he could run, toward the mausoleum. They had to be there, they just had to be. He had been troubled too much by this whole scenario for them not to be. It just wouldn't be fair.

Soon the cemetery would be opening to the public. And Ed know Bright was far too smart to stick around when the cars, birdwatchers, mourners, and early morning walkers came filtering in.

The mausoleum looked deserted when he arrived. Ed took the steps up to the double doors at the front two at a time. Pressing his face against the barred glass entrance revealed nothing more than a marble interior, quiet as a chapel. Two benches stood out a little on either side of what must have been an opening to a large marble room.

Why did people spend so much on interring their dead?

The time for such questions was not now, and Ed moved quickly to the side of the building, where another entrance was located. This entrance was bordered on either side by granite blocks and pretty much blocked from view; an ideal hiding place.

Except there was no one there.

Ed backed up and repeated the process, going around to an identical entrance on the south side of the building.

Ed gasped when he saw her. At least he thought it was her. A form, shrouded in a sheet, lay on the ground near the metal doors. One of the windows in the door was boarded over by a piece or wood, proving to Ed that people did try to gain entrance.

And sometimes succeeded.

He approached the shrouded form carefully. He knew this could be just another ruse concocted by Bright. A trap to ensure Ed was taken out of the game forever. He squatted beside the still form and reached out to touch it. It seemed chilled by the air outside, but he could tell what was within was still warm.

Ed took a deep breath and pulled back the sheet.

Helene Bright's face was almost unrecognizable, so marred by bruises and cuts. When he turned her, Helene Bright slumped over on her back, her head lolling to one side.

"Oh Christ, no," Ed whispered, reaching down to stroke the crusty, bloated cheek. "Fuck... Why do I have to be involved in this?"

Helene Bright opened her eyes.

Chapter
Thirty-three

PETER DROVE. HE didn't know how he managed to gather enough coordination and sense to steer the car, but here he was doing it. Doing it in spite of the fact that his breath was quavering, two steps short of sobbing. Doing it in spite of the fact that, when he allowed himself to think for a moment of the predicament he was in, his eyes blurred with tears. Doing it in spite of the fact that his hands, every few seconds, trembled violently on the wheel.

Doing it in spite of the fact that there was a hunting knife pressed into the tender flesh just below his ribs.

He had thought he could meet Ed at Rosehill, offer him some support, maybe even some safety. He hadn't really thought that Timothy Bright would be there. He thought he would gather Ed up, bring him home and make him sleep. Things would seem more rational when he awakened.

When he arrived, he'd parked his car near the front gates and walked up to them, peered inside, searching for some sign of Ed. He hadn't noticed his car on the street and was relieved. He assumed he had arrived first and that would give him the advantage, he could at least be with Ed from the inception of this mission.

But these somewhat optimistic thoughts were interrupted suddenly, and horrifyingly, when a little man ran up to him. Peter gasped when he saw him, his clothes spattered with blood, his eyes wild.

"You have to help me, man." The voice came out a croak. The man was trembling.

"What happened?" Peter thought the face looked familiar for only a moment or two. Then it clicked. Ed's description and the newspaper photo he had seen brought everything into sharp focus: this was Timothy Bright. And he was covered with blood!

The encounter seemed surreal; Peter wanted to wake up.

"I had a wreck." Timothy was panting. "In my car. Over on Peterson. Could you drive me to the hospital?"

Peter stared at him, frozen. He wasn't sure if he should run or if he should try to detain the little man, keep him here until Ed arrived.

Wasn't this guy supposed to be dead? The thought chilled him. This person had to bear a very close resemblance, that's all.

And what about all the blood?

Peter wanted very much to run.

"Where's your car? I'd like to take a look at it."

"C'mon, buddy, I have to get to a hospital."

Peter looked him over carefully and could see no wounds, no lacerations, no bruises. The blood, he thought, had to come from somewhere else.

Peter's mouth grew dry and his heart started beating more rapidly. Would his own blood be added to the blood already staining this man?

Before he had a chance to ponder the question, the man brought out a hunting knife and poked its point into Peter's stomach. "You're taking me for a ride. I have to get out of here, now." His voice was hoarse, and there was no mistaking the desperation in it. Peter thought it useless to argue with a desperate man with a knife.

"Come on," he whispered. "My car's over here." He stopped for just a moment and glanced down at the knife. "There's no need for that. I'll do what you want."

"I just like to have some insurance." The guy grinned at him. "Now, I don't want to hear anymore out of you. What did you say your name was?"

"It's John." The guy didn't know who he was! Perhaps that could help him. Perhaps, for Ed's sake, being in the wrong place at the wrong time was exactly the right thing to do.

He pulled the car from its space in front of the Fireplace Inn restaurant, licking his dry lips, trying to force himself to concentrate on the strip of asphalt before him. He thought of Mark Dietrich, driving along Lake Shore Drive and how that drive, on his way to see Ed and Peter, had sent him down a long fall toward death. Would the result be the same for him? He thought of his family in Carbondale: his two sisters, his mom and dad. A sudden image of the funeral flashed before him, his mother inconsolable, his father stoic, wiping his bald pate with a handkerchief. His hands were trembling, the only sign of the pain the loss of his only son was causing him.

"Where do you want me to take you?" Peter whispered, his voice hoarse from fear.

"Just drive. I'll navigate."

ED SPED EAST on Touhy, heading for Ridge. He knew he could turn left there and be on his way north, to Evanston and St. Francis Hospital. There were probably other hospitals closer, but he knew the way directly to this one. He had once left a testicle there after a spectacularly painful torsion and it was the first place that came to his mind.

Helene Bright bled on the seat next to him. Every few minutes, she would waver from within the veil of pain and consciousness, mumbling something incoherent.

Finally, Ed made sense of what she was saying: "Theodore."

And then it clicked. Theodore was the brother buried next to Timothy. He had died in 1988 or something close to that.

What if it wasn't him? What if the person buried in Theodore's grave was actually Timothy?

But then who was buried in Timothy's grave two years ago?

The whole thing was so confusing, Ed longed to drop the woman off at the emergency entrance and just be done with this whole fiasco. Let the Chicago Police Department sort things out. Ed had tried, after all, to help them out, and they were having none of it. It would serve them right.

They could never solve this case. And Ed wondered if he could. But he felt he had more of a key to things than anyone, and because of that, he had to press on.

Helene Bright suddenly grabbed his arm. "Theodore," she croaked again. "Don't you see?"

"What are you talking about?" Ed tried to keep his voice even, keep it level, but the annoyance and despair made that difficult.

At a red light, he looked over at Helene Bright. She was fully awake now, and although her bruised face wore all the earmarks of confusion, she seemed coherent enough.

"What are you talking about?" Ed repeated.

"I never saw the body."

"What?"

"I never saw Theodore's body. Don't you understand?"

Ed shook his head.

"I only learned about Theodore's death from Timothy." Helene sobbed, then a cough racked and spasmed through her, leaving her gasping for air. Her ribs were probably bruised from the beating.

"So?"

"So maybe he was never really dead. At least not then."

"What are you saying?" Ed pressed harder on the accelerator as he passed from Chicago's northern border into Evanston. He asked the question even though things were already falling into place.

Helene Bright gazed out the window for a long time. Her

breathing was labored and Ed began to wonder if she would ever answer his question. Finally, she turned back to him. When he glanced over at her, a wave of pity washed over him. Her eyes were the only thing that seemed alive in the beaten face. Her skin was ashen and the bruises were already swelling and deepening to purple.

"I'm saying that there was no funeral. At least, that I knew about."

"And?" St. Francis was coming up on his right and Ed signaled to make the turn that led back to the emergency room. He needed to hear how things had played out.

"The graves were there, with markers. I bought one for each of us when my family was killed, back in 1970." She worked to draw her next breath. "There was a car accident."

Ed pulled up to the entrance. "I'll help you get in."

"Timothy called me months after Theodore was supposed to have died. I never questioned it. He hated me and would have done anything to hurt me. Excluding me from mourning over Teddy's death was par for the course."

"Let's get you inside. You can tell me more while we wait." Ed hurried around to the other side of the car, opened the door, and took Helene Bright's arm. She slid gingerly from the seat, and Ed knew she was hurting. She winced when she stood. But, once standing, she gave him a smile. "At least I'm alive."

While they waited, Helene Bright told Ed the rest. "After he told me, I went to visit the grave. The dates were there, they were engraved on the tombstone." Helene wiped a tear from the corner of her eye. The gesture was almost angry, and Ed realized this was not a woman used to giving in to her tears.

He patted her hand.

"Couldn't someone have engraved the date of Theodore's death on the tombstone for Timothy? Wouldn't that be an easy enough thing to do?"

"I suppose. But why would he want to do that?"

"*Why* is a question that doesn't apply to much of Timothy's behavior. Who knows? To hurt me, I suppose." She swallowed and Ed could see there was some difficulty there; around her throat was a necklace of small reddish-purple bruises. So, he had tried to strangle her as well.

"Then where is Theodore?"

Helene Bright looked at him, her eyes wide. "Haven't you realized it yet?"

The idea had been there since she had begun mumbling "Theodore" and it filled him with horror, but relief as well. Perhaps there was a plausible solution to this whole thing, after all.

"What?"

"It's Theodore. It's Theodore in Timothy's grave. Theodore was the one who was murdered."

Ed closed his eyes.

"I CAN'T LET you go. You understand that, don't you?"

Peter shivered in the dim light of the little barn. The guy — who said his name was David — had brought him here. David... David Long. Peter remembered that the last guy killed, John Austin, had been found outside the building where a David Long lived. He looked around himself and saw that the building, now left abandoned, thick with the smell of earth and old straw, corners crowded with spider webs, had once been a stable. There was a stall for a horse to his left; old riding supplies: a curry brush, a hoof pick, a harness, and an English saddle collected dust on hooks on the wall.

"I wouldn't tell anyone. I don't even know who you are, or what this is about."

Timothy laughed. "That's where you're wrong, my little friend. You see, I'm an astute observer. A watcher." He leaned in so close that Peter could smell his rancid breath. Peter backed away from the face, but it only made Bright draw closer. They were close enough to kiss.

"I've got a funny feeling," Timothy whispered, "you're operating under some misconceptions."

"What are you talking about?" Dread rose up in Peter's gut, icy-cold and paralyzing.

"You thought, didn't you, that I didn't know who you were?"

"Who am I?"

Timothy laughed again, laughed until he held his aching sides. Tears formed in his eyes. "You don't know?"

Peter knew what this was all about, and it removed completely from him any small sense of security he had drawn from what he thought was anonymity. His mouth went dry and he found it harder to breathe.

Timothy slapped him hard, open-handed across the face. "You know who you are. And I do, too. Does the name Ed Comparetto ring a bell?"

Peter bit his lip, feeling darkness close in all around him. Closing in, closing in, even though the sun, a cauled ball in a misty sky, shined an unflattering matte light on everything outside.

"W-what are you going to do?"

"Nothing right now. You're too choice a piece of bait." Timothy ran his hand down Peter's chest. Peter recoiled at the touch; it reminded him of a snake winding its way down his body. "Very choice," Timothy whispered.

"But right now I have some business to take care of in the big house. Can I trust you to stay here and wait for me?"

"Of course. I won't go anywhere."

"You lie so convincingly." Timothy withdrew a roll of duct tape from his jacket pocket. "What did you call yourself? John?"

Peter stared at him.

"Tell me your name."

"Don't you already know it?"

For his impertinence, Peter earned himself another slap across the face. It barely hurt; he was beginning to feel numb outside as well as within. "It's Peter."

"Peter. How appropriate. It should help me when I make a certain phone call."

Timothy stooped and began binding Peter's ankles together.

"SO SHE'LL BE okay?" Ed asked Dr. Marilyn Harris, the emergency room physician who had taken over Helene Bright's care.

The doctor combed a hand through her shoulder length salt-and-pepper hair. She looked tired, worn down by too much trauma. She nodded. "She was beaten pretty badly, but it's nothing time won't heal. There shouldn't be any permanent damage. Physical damage, that is." Marilyn Harris looked pointedly at him. "What happened? She wouldn't tell me anything."

"I don't know. I found her like this. I don't even know the woman." Ed felt as if he was betraying Helene Bright, but her nephew was still out there somewhere.

God knew where.

As Ed hurried out of the hospital, he realized Timothy Bright must now be in a state of extreme rage.

There was no telling what he could do.

Chapter
Thirty-four

THE AFFAIR HAD been brief. All of my affairs were that: too short and too free of complications. I could whine and complain and tell you that no one ever really loved me. Aunt Helene loved something that wasn't there; a dream boy she created in her warped North Shore spinster mind. David Long? I was a body, a hole to be used when he needed it. Love, or anything close, never entered into it.

Aunt Helene threw me out when she discovered the "affair" with David Long. I think that's when my hatred for her truly took root. She never questioned him, never thought for a second that he might be the one to blame.

I wanted so much for her to hate him, to punish him for what he did to me. But that would have been asking too much; that would have called in to question her judgment. She would have looked, in her own mind, like someone who couldn't be trusted to care for a child.

I wanted her to pay for doubting me. I wanted her to understand what real grief felt like.

Aunt Helene had a weird relationship with Theodore. She cared for him like some secret pet. He always had the best of everything: the best clothes, the best food, and the best toys, in hopes that one day he would be able to muster enough intelligence to play with them. Their relationship was marked by guilt; Aunt Helene never forgave herself for how she felt about him, her repulsion at the drooling, the howling, the absolute lack of a clue as to how "normal" human beings behaved.

Yet, in her own way, she loved him. Other than taking care of him, changing his shitty diapers and seeing that he got some nourishment in him, he was no trouble.

Unlike me. Me, who could never get along with the neighborhood children. Me, with the genius IQ, but the refusal to use it for pursuits that would have pleased Aunt Helene. Me, with the cruel streak. How I loved torturing small animals, watching them writhe under the tutelage of my pain, so freely given.

But I'm getting off course here. I started by saying the affair had been brief. This affair, though, was to a very specific end. And a stroke of luck brought it all about.

I met Andy Lockman just a few months after I moved out. I had yet to go online, and my sexual exploits were confined to anonymous encounters, mostly in public places, furtive and quick.

For some reason, Andy took a liking to me. We met at the park that runs along Lake Michigan from Hollywood Beach all the way down to Montrose Harbor, a distance of a little over a mile. There, on the strip of asphalt that separates grass from sand, men cruise. They've done so for years. It always seemed ill-suited for that purpose, since there are no woods or bushes or even a suitable outbuilding for these liaisons. Most of the activity there took place in parked cars. I discovered it one day while riding my bike. As I crested a hill, I noticed a parked red Mustang near an overpass. I happened to glance at the car and saw a young Asian guy sitting in the passenger seat.

A crew cut head was bobbing up and down in his lap.

From then, I tried it myself. At first, sitting in my car, waiting, waiting for someone to approach me. I didn't possess the courage to go up to someone myself and didn't even know if I could go through with it if someone did pull up alongside me. But, as with all hurdles, this one was eventually crossed, my hormones putting me on automatic pilot, removing my timidity enough.

And after the first time, as it goes with most things, it got easier.

It was probably a couple months after my first time that I ran into Andy. I was sitting in my car. It was late summer and the radio was on. What was playing? I wish I could remember, to better set the scene. I had probably brought along the *Tribune,* but who has time to read in such a situation, when the sound of a car going by forces one to glance up, in an attempt to make contact with the driver?

Such complicated mating dances.

Andy came by just about when I was ready to give up. I had even fingered the keys dangling from the ignition.

He was riding his bike, a black ten-speed. He was just a scrawny kid: tall and lanky with shoulder-length straight red hair. His face was covered with reddish-brown stubble, this before it was fashionable to have such a look. He wore a pair of cargo shorts and a Cubs T-shirt. He looked to be all of eighteen, just a little younger than I was at the time.

Andy fell for me immediately. Even though all we did in the front seat of my car was trade blow jobs, he insisted on giving me his phone number, and somehow managed to coax me into giving him mine.

And then the phone calls started. Andy would call four or five times a day, just to see what I was "up to," to tell me how much he "cared about" me. He begged me to see him.

And I did. I would come to his Evanston studio at least once a week. I had nothing but hatred and contempt for him. And each time I visited him, I pressed him further into humiliation and degradation. I would call him a "pussy boy," a "filthy queer" and a "cock-sucking faggot" while he blew me. I raped him as David Long raped me, savagely and without lubrication. I spanked him so hard, the red welts didn't leave his ass for days, sometimes deepening into bruises. I dripped candle wax on him. Tied him up. Beat him with my belt. Spit on him. Fisted him while he bit his lip to keep from crying out.

Such dubious pleasures were akin to giving candy to a child. Each step further down the road of pain and humiliation brought him closer to me.

I learned little about Andy. Conversation was not the kind of intercourse we engaged in, although I suspect Andy would have loved that. What I did learn was that he was an apprentice at a "memorial" company; he was learning the craft of engraving tombstones. He had artistic inclinations; this was an outlet for him. A dream job, if you will.

I carried this knowledge with me for weeks before I realized how I could use it to destroy my aunt. I still burned from her rejection, from her casting me from the only home I had ever known.

Wouldn't she feel just awful if she discovered that her leaving Teddy in my care had resulted in disaster? Wouldn't the guilt just eat her alive? Wouldn't she finally see the error of her ways?

The plan was simple. All it took was some of Andy's engraving tools and enough of his time to pound a date into a tombstone that already existed. Just four little numbers! I had to laugh at the beauty of the plan: it served the bitch right. I had always thought it morbid, her buying a tombstone for us when we were so young, and also wondered if it weren't some tangible proof of her wish to be free of us.

Andy was reluctant. Doing such a thing was illegal, not to mention that it would remove him permanently from the track of a budding trade. But our relationship was such that I could have made him do anything, especially if I threatened to withdraw my companionship. Andy was still too green to realize he could have gotten what I gave him in any leather bar. Just drop by the Eagle... And so he did what I asked, under the cover of a cloudy, moonless night.

Theodore's death was documented, there for Aunt Helene's weeping eyes.

I loved it.

Little did I know how handy this act would come in later.

And what, you might ask, became of Andy, our budding craftsman?

Let's just say he disappeared.

I so abhor loose ends. But you knew that, didn't you?

Chapter
Thirty-five

ED ARRIVED HOME without a clue. Where was Timothy Bright? Had this night-long episode resulted in him learning anything more? Had it advanced his investigation in any worthwhile way? He *had* learned, maybe, how a dead man could be walking around killing others. And sure, he had perhaps saved Helene Bright's life. But even on that score, he was doubtful. Her wounds were mostly superficial; she would have survived. Ed had merely been the one who had discovered her first. Once Rosehill opened its gates, someone would have found her in short order and done what he had done. All he did for her was save her from some publicity, something he knew she would have abhorred.

His apartment seemed especially empty. He wished he had asked Peter to meet him here. At least, that way, there would have been something other than scattered magazines, newspapers, and clothes to greet him when he walked in the door, exhausted and frustrated.

Thoughts of Peter endowed him with a small kernel of energy, lifting his spirits. Although lifting his spirits was a relatively easy task, since they had nowhere to go but up.

He went into the bathroom and splashed cold water on his face. He looked years older from the night, his eyes bloodshot, ringed in darkness. His face seemed to have lost some of its resiliency; it sagged.

Peter. Before he did anything else, he must call him. The poor guy had put up with so much, and he must be worried. Ed would try to make it up to him, even though it still seemed there was no light at the end of the tunnel.

Ed went in his bedroom, picked up the cordless from its base on his dresser, and punched in Peter's phone number.

Ed felt chilled as he listened to the four rings, then Peter's voice: "Hello, this is Peter. I'm not here right now. But if you leave a message, I'll call you right back. Thanks." The message, so oft-heard in the past, chilled Ed. He glanced at the clock. It was only

7:30. Peter never had to be at work before 9:00 a.m.

Where would he be at 7:30 in the morning? Peter, who loved his sleep almost as much as he loved his sex. Peter was not the kind of guy to already be out tricking around.

Fear rose up in him, like icy fingers stretching from his gut to envelop his heart, to squeeze, tighter, tighter.

Ed recalled their quick conversation earlier that morning:

"Should I meet you there?"

Oh God, he didn't.

"Should I meet you there?"

The simple words taunted him. He imagined Timothy Bright listening in on this tiny mental loop and laughing at him.

"Should I meet you there?"

Perfect. Taking Peter would be perfect. Why hadn't he insisted Peter stay put? Why hadn't he let Peter meet him someplace safe? Guilt and panic set his adrenalin to pumping. What if Peter had shown up at the cemetery before him? What if he had been there to interrupt Bright's flight from the cemetery?

It was too perfect of a windfall for Timothy Bright. He would have loved it.

Ed picked up the phone again and dialed. Heard the same now-grim message again.

"Shit." Ed hurried into the bedroom to change his clothes. There would be no rest for him, not yet.

Just as he had slipped into his jacket, ignoring the burning in his eyes and the ache in his muscles that told him he desperately needed sleep, the telephone rang.

Ed sprinted toward it, mumbling to himself, "Please let it be him; please let it be him."

"Hello."

"Mr. Comparetto?"

The voice sent a vise grip of ice around his heart. It was Timothy Bright.

"Timothy?" Ed could not let his fear or his anger or his frustration show. Somehow, he had to at least make an effort to let Bright think Ed had the upper hand. "I'm glad you called. I wanted to update you on your aunt's condition. She survived."

There was a long silence.

"Well, she always was a resilient little bitch, sidestepping death at every turn. I'll have to make sure I finish the job." Bright laughed. "Where is she?"

Ed closed his eyes. He could practically feel the cold chill of evil coming through the phone. "Now, Timothy. I thought you were smarter than that."

"Oh, my little man, you have no idea how smart I am." There

was a pause. "Your boyfriend is pretty smart, too. Isn't he?"

"What are you talking about?" *Please God, don't let him say he has Peter. Please, there's still a chance...*

"Oh, nothing."

"Stop it, Bright. I'm too fucking tired for games."

"You suck cock with that filthy mouth?"

Ed sighed. *Just come to the point.* "Where is Peter?"

"Peter and I are getting acquainted."

"So he is with you?"

"Oh yes. Most definitely. He sure is cute. I just might steal him away from you." Bright laughed again, but there was no mirth in it, only menace. "In more ways than one."

"What the fuck?"

"I just might steal him away from everyone, if you get my drift, asshole."

"He's all right?"

"About as well as can be expected. He's scared."

"Where the hell are you?"

"Tell me where my aunt is and I'll tell you where your fuck-buddy is. Fair enough?"

Ed bit his lip, tugged at his hair. God, what could he do now? Lie. "She's at Thorek Medical Center, on Irving Park Road. Intensive care."

"How easily you cave, my friend. Well, I've got to be going. Got another real hot little number to attend to here."

"Don't you fuckin' dare hang up!" Ed could play games, too. The number from where Bright was calling was captured on his Caller ID.

"Oh, I'm not going to hang up, you little queen. I don't know how you got to be a cop. You've got no balls whatsoever."

"Cut the shit. You wanna tell me where you are?"

"Yes, I do. Perhaps you and I can effect a little trade. You like trade, don't you?"

"Love it. Now, just get on with it."

"You come out here, alone, and I'll set your little Peter free." Bright giggled.

"Done. Now where do I go?"

"I'm at David Long's. Lake Bluff, Illinois, pal. It should take you less than an hour to get here. And remember two things: one, you take longer than that, let's say a half hour more, and I fuckin' kill him. Two, I see you pull up with anyone else in tow, or if anything looks suspicious, I kill him. See, I have a unique vantage point, and if anyone else is with you, he's dead. I don't care anymore about getting caught. I'll sit in jail for the rest of my life or fry in the electric chair just to have the satisfaction of taking your boy from you."

The line went dead.

Ed rushed to the door.

TIMOTHY HUNG UP the phone. He smiled; things were just too sweet. He wondered how other killers managed to get caught. His little reign of terror seemed to have no end in sight, what with his "death" over two years ago protecting him.

And once he got Ed Comparetto here and disposed of, another obstacle would be removed. It would be kind of sweet, in a way, sending the star-crossed homo lovers off to eternity together.

And then, of course, he must get to Aunt Helene. That was an issue that did cause him some concern, her lying in a hospital with all that information. She wasn't stupid, and she, of all people, could figure things out.

He wished Ed Comparetto would hurry. Timothy had a busy day ahead of him and he was eager to get started.

ED HEADED WEST once again on Touhy, anxiety mounting. It seemed this road charted his frustration and anger. His hands drummed restlessly on the steering wheel at every light, while he muttered, "C'mon, dammit, c'mon. Change."

And when he wasn't stopped at one of what he thought suddenly was an incredible number of red lights, he was speeding, gunning the car up as high as it would go without knocking off another car or hitting a pedestrian, weaving dangerously in and out of lanes in a desperate effort to clear a place for himself.

It could all be ended, right here, today. Ed wondered what it would feel like—of course, he had thought all along that if he could crack this case, he might be reinstated on the force, but now those thoughts were uncertain. They had not given him even the smallest chance to tell his side of things. They had never even bothered to listen; his years spent on the force, doing a good job, meant nothing.

Perhaps he would go into business for himself, become a private detective. The scenario certainly had its appeal, being his own boss, not having to deal with institutional politics... But thoughts like these were for later. Peter was somewhere north of Chicago and God only knew what was happening to him.

TIMOTHY SAT ON the bed with David Long. "You were the first. You were the one who initiated me. You taught me how to give pain." Timothy reached down and brushed the salt-and-pepper hair away from David's brow. "Sometimes, it even seemed it wasn't so bad." Timothy slapped David's face. "What am I talking about? You stole it all from me! Was that your plan from the start? Is that why you started dating Aunt Helene?"

Timothy curled up beside the body, which was but a shadow of what it had been before: the virile, muscular man he had once known. How much had changed. This body bore little resemblance to the one that had raped him throughout the years. The man lying beside him was emaciated, the ribs sticking out through sallow flesh. The chest, which only hours ago had labored to draw breath, was now still.

"He was going to die anyway," Timothy whispered. It had been easy to wrap his hands around the neck, easy to squeeze what life was left in David Long. He had done him a favor, really.

"I like you this way." Timothy drew his leg up over David Long's thigh, kissed the hair on his chest and closed his eyes.

"WHAT DO YOU mean, you can't give out his home address?" Ed clenched the cellular phone so tightly his knuckles were white. He had tried every tack he could think of to induce the nurse to give him David Long's home address: that he was an old friend, that he had an emergency.

"I'm sorry, sir, I just can't give you that."

"What can I say to convince you that this is a life and death situation? I really need that address; please, please give it to me."

"Who did you say you were again?"

"My name's Ed Comparetto. The truth is I'm a private detective working for a friend of Dr. Long's."

"And what is this emergency?" The nurse sounded tired. Just as Ed was about to reply, the nurse interrupted. "Hang on a second." Ed was switched into the Muzak oblivion of hold. Up ahead was the west entrance for I-94. Ed swerved onto the ramp and gunned the engine.

The nurse came back just as Ed was merging onto the expressway. She still sounded hassled and harried.

"Look, if I give you his address, you didn't get it from me."

"Understood."

The nurse recited the address and hung up before Ed had a chance to thank her.

PETER SHIVERED AS a beetle crawled up his leg. His bonds were so tight, he couldn't move. He could only sit helplessly as the insect made its crawly way up his leg. The feeling made him recoil, made him want to scream, had that been possible.

"Your boyfriend doesn't have much time left."

Peter jumped at the sound of the voice, coming from behind the darkness his blindfold imposed. He turned his head toward the direction from which the high-pitched voice came.

"I told him I'd kill you if he didn't get here on time. The way I see it, he has only about twenty minutes left."

There was silence for a few moments, long enough for Peter to think, with horror, of how he would die and the stupidity of it all being over like this. He had never thought he would die a murder victim, but then, who does? Then Peter heard something heavy being dragged across the dirt floor of the stable. What could only be a body landed beside him; he felt a head lolling on his shoulder and would have recoiled, had he the freedom to move. The cold flesh against his made him want to scream.

"Two of a kind," Timothy laughed. "That's what you'll be if he doesn't get here soon."

Peter held his breath. Death, he thought, might just be preferable to this suspense.

ED HEADED NORTH on Route 41, painfully aware of the clock on the dashboard. The fact that he had only minutes left made sweat start at his temples and armpits, every so often rolling down to tickle him like the legs of a spider.

As he headed north, the suburban landscape changed; instead of housing developments and chain stores to his right and left, there were now trees, bereft of their leaves. Traffic was light, and Ed was able to make his way easily, accelerating up to 80, 90 miles per hour. At this rate, he would be at David Long's home with time to spare.

Ed caught up to the light blue Buick too easily. Through the Buick's back window, he could see the car's driver: an old man in a hat. Not a good sign. Just as he was about to pass, a tractor trailer came bearing down on him, horn blaring to prevent him from switching lanes. Ed winced and veered back right as the truck blew by him.

"Damn."

He pulled out behind the truck, and realized the old man he had been tailgating wanted to play games. The driver could, after all, press down on the accelerator. The driver increased his pace to match Ed, zooming up to ride alongside him. Ed looked over, desperate, and caught a look at the man's face. Old, shriveled, with a yellowed mustache over thin lips, he was laughing at Ed and pointing.

How could he tell this old fool he wasn't just some young guy in a big hurry with no purpose? How could he let him know this was a situation that could have dire consequences if he didn't let him by?

There was no way, so Ed slowed and took his place behind the Buick once more, figuring he'd have a chance to get around him once the old man got reacquainted with his snail's pace and figured he had won the contest and put Ed in his place.

But that was not to be the case. It seemed suddenly that no one, not even God, wanted him to make it to David Long's house on time.

A deer, its sleek brown coat shining dully in the diffused sunlight and its eyes sparkling wildly with fear, darted in front of the Buick. The driver swerved to miss it, slamming on his brakes and skidding. The car loomed up in front of him; Ed swerved opposite to avoid impact.

The car shimmied under the pressure of the sudden turn. Ed flew off the road, headed toward a copse of pine trees at the side. The only thing that saved him was the ditch, into which the car nose-dived, coming to a sudden halt that sent Ed flying forward, the seatbelt and air bag mercifully shielding him from shattering the windshield with his head.

Ed listened as his back tires spun in the air, and the traffic whooshed by behind him.

Chapter
Thirty-six

SHE HAD BEEN with the doctor for going on twenty years. Eleanor Day had always been there for him, had watched the changes in personnel over the years, and, more disturbingly, the changes in Dr. Long himself. Those changes, it seemed, had happened quite dramatically. Each week, he had looked more and more unhealthy, his skin growing sallow as the air outside chilled and prepared itself for winter. He had lost weight until, eventually, the tailor-made suits and jackets just hung on him, his frame becoming closer to a skeleton than a healthy virile man in his late forties.

And now, Eleanor was feeling guilty. Why had she given the man who phoned minutes ago the doctor's home address? It wasn't like her; she had always been protective of the doctor; in fact, had often felt that it had been she who ran the practice.

It was just that the man had been so insistent; she could hear it in his voice as much as she could his words. And things had been so hectic. What with the doctor out sick, the calls just seemed to never stop. Dr. Michaels, Dr. Long's young partner, was making a valiant effort to see the overflow of patients Dr. Long's illness was causing. They were at her desk, wondering how long it would be before they were admitted. They were on the phone, asking when Dr. Long would return.

It seemed the man on the phone was not about to give up until he had what he wanted. The easiest thing to do, Eleanor thought in her agitation, was to just cave in and give out the address.

After all, he had claimed he was working for Helene Bright and that the situation was urgent.

Eleanor had known Helene Bright almost as long as she had known the doctor. Had watched, with jealous dismay, their romance spark and ignite, and then watched with relief as it died a sudden quick death.

She never knew why.

Eleanor picked up the phone, figuring she would use the time productively while there was a lull in the action. If this Comparetto fellow was telling the truth, she had nothing to worry about. But if he was lying, and Dr. Long didn't want to see him, she realized, with a pang of guilt, she could be in big trouble. Even though she had told Comparetto he didn't get the address from her, she figured there might be a way the information leak could be traced back to her. So, as she pushed in the buttons of Helene Bright's phone number, she thought she could at least cover her ass.

The phone rang three times before someone picked it up. The voice of a woman came through the line, and Eleanor was fairly certain this was not the voice of Helene Bright. It was higher and seemed to have more of the harshness of a Chicago accent than Helene's. This woman was from somewhere on the south side, that much Eleanor could be sure of.

"Yes, this is Dr. Long's office calling. Could I speak to Miss Bright, please?" It had been so long since Eleanor had called this number she had called, years ago, on a regular basis. She wondered how Helene would react to the sound of her voice.

"I'm sorry, but Miss Bright isn't available right now. Can I take a message?"

"Do you know when she'll be back?"

"Not for a couple of days."

"Oh. So she's out of town?"

"Not exactly. Miss Bright is in the hospital."

"Oh?"

"Who did you say you were again?"

"My name's Eleanor, Eleanor Day. I'm with Dr. David Long's practice."

The pause on the line told Eleanor the woman had no idea who Dr. Long was. Not so surprising, since it had probably been years since the two had seen one another.

"Well, Miss Bright is at St. Francis. Maybe you could try there."

"In Evanston?"

"Yes."

"Thank you." Eleanor hung up the phone and wondered what was wrong with Helene. She looked up the number for St. Francis and punched it in quickly. After being connected to the main desk, she asked to speak to Helene Bright.

Her voice was a surprise, not the voice she had remembered at all. This woman, her voice little above a croak, sounded much older than even Helene Bright would have been. She sounded weak and very, very tired.

"Helene? This is Eleanor Day, from David Long's office?"

"Yes? Eleanor, how are you?"

"I'm fine. I hope everything's all right with you?"

"Well, I've been better. Is there something I can help you with?"

"I had a call a little while ago from a detective. He told me his name was Ed Comparetto and that he was working for you. He wanted David's home address, said it was important." There was a pause. "So I gave it to him." Another pause. "I hope that's all right."

"I really couldn't care less, Eleanor, if you did that."

"Is he working for you?"

Eleanor listened to silence for a moment or two. "Yes, Eleanor, he is."

"Would you know why he needed David's home address?"

"I'm sure I don't... Well, now, wait a minute. Yes, yes he might have been tracking something down for me and wanted to get it done today."

"Oh."

"So," Helene's voice suddenly took on a slightly more animated, cheerful tone. "I don't think you're in any trouble. You haven't done anything wrong."

Eleanor sighed; this was all she needed to hear. "Thanks a lot, Helene. It was good talking to you again. And best wishes for a speedy recovery."

Helene hung up the phone. Strange. Why would Ed Comparetto be calling David Long's office? She hadn't spoken to the man in years. Not since... Well, she'd rather not think about it.

Then a chill gripped her, wrapping its icy fingers around her heart and squeezing. *Timothy, oh God, Timothy.*

Even though it made her ribs hurt, Helene reached over and dialed the number she still remembered, even though it had been years since she phoned it.

After four rings, Helene heard David Long's voice. The sound of it filled her with revulsion; she had never hated someone so much. Remorse rose up in her like a physical pain. She should have done more...

"You've reached the residence of Dr. David Long. I'm not available to take your call right now, but if you'd leave your name and number, I'll get back to you right away. If this is an emergency, please call 555-8790 and my answering service will page me. Thank you."

Helene didn't hang up; she disconnected from David Long's number and punched in 0 for the switchboard.

Her heart was pounding.

Chapter
Thirty-seven

IT HAD BEEN years since he had done this. Not since he was a teenager had Ed stood beside a roadway with his thumb out. He hoped the crashed car behind him would tug at the heartstrings of some good Samaritan.

Yet the cars whizzed by him, all with places to go too important for the drivers to stop and lend a fellow traveler some aid. He looked down at his watch and saw that his time was almost up. He thought of Dorothy in the witch's castle in *The Wizard of Oz* and knew just how she felt. A wave of nausea rolled over him as he watched another car pass him, without even slowing, and realized how the most innocent of events could conspire to create a true tragedy.

Just as he was thinking these grim thoughts, a beat-up VW bus pulled over to the berm, kicking up gravel, its taillights glowing in the grey light of the day.

Thank God, Ed thought running toward the old orange vehicle. *Thank God.*

Just let me make it before it's too late.

"WELL, MY LITTLE homo pal, it seems your time is almost up. Maybe your boyfriend doesn't give a fuck if you live or die."

Peter wished he could see Bright, wished he could speak to him. He felt so helpless, lying here on this dirt floor and waiting for his life to be taken. He couldn't even curl into a compact ball to protect himself. There was nothing he could do.

And even if Ed did show up on time, what guarantee was there that Bright wouldn't just kill them both?

If Peter had been a religious man, he would have prayed, begging forgiveness for his sins. Now was the time...

THE VW BUS dropped him off at David Long's driveway. Ed thanked the driver, a man close to fifty, with his long salt-and-pepper hair snaking down his back in a braid.

He hopped from the bus and sprinted up the brick driveway, shouting as he ran: "Bright! Bright! I'm here. It's not too late."

Timothy watched from David Long's kitchen window. "Perfect," he whispered as Ed Comparetto came into view, arms pumping and screaming for him. "Perfect. I've got you just where I want you."

Timothy enjoyed the look of terror on Ed's face for a few moments before heading toward the door off the kitchen.

ED PAUSED, LOOKING around the driveway. No one was in sight. The only sounds were the twittering cries of the birds in the trees. All the windows in the big house were dark; there was no movement behind any of them.

His heart thumped wildly. What if this was yet another ruse on Timothy Bright's part? What if he and Peter weren't here at all? What if, as he stood here, gasping for the cold air that surrounded him, they were somewhere else, and right now, Timothy was readying a blade for Peter's throat?

What if Peter was already dead?

Ed tensed as he heard the creak of a door opening and then a slam as it closed.

Ed turned and as he did so, Timothy Bright moved into view. Ed sucked in his breath. How could someone so small, so elfin really, have caused all this mayhem?

Bright stood before him, grinning, about fifty paces away.

"I see you made it. And not a moment too soon. I was just about ready to filet your boyfriend." Timothy pulled a butcher's knife from behind his back; he held it before him as a child might hold a new toy. There was the same delight in holding the object and, if one didn't know better, the same absence of malice.

"Where is he?" Ed croaked, still out of breath, the adrenalin pumping through his veins, shooting his blood pressure up, causing his heart to pound and the sweat to run, in spite of the chill in the air.

"All in good time, my pretty, all in good time." Timothy approached Ed until he was within a couple of feet from him. He ran the dull side of the knife along his palm and then grinned. "We had a deal. Remember? We were going to make a trade: you for him."

"Right." Ed could barely speak, so dry were his mouth and throat. "So, I'm here."

"I want to be sure you don't have any little tricks up your pathetic sleeve."

"I don't; I swear. Now will you let him go?"

"Slow down there, pardner. You seem to forget who's running the show here."

Ed bowed his head. In spite of the rage seething within him, he said, "I'm sorry."

"That's better. Now, the first thing I need from you are any weapons you've brought along." Timothy stared at Ed, forcing him to meet his gaze.

"I don't have anything, I swear."

"Your word is about as good as mine." Timothy giggled and deepened his voice. "I'm going to have to frisk you. Put your hands in the air."

Ed closed his eyes as he felt Bright's hands begin to wander his body, patting him down, rubbing, pausing at his crotch. The touch was sickening, having all the appeal of a cockroach skittering across one's chest.

"What kind of a dumb fuck are you?"

"What?" Ed was confused.

"You call yourself a cop and you show up here without even so much as a pocket knife?"

"They call it anticipation, Bright. Now, will you bring Peter to me?"

"Once again, you're out of line. What are we going to do about that?" Without waiting for a reply, Timothy went on. "I'm in charge; things will happen when I deem them ready. Do you understand?"

Ed bit his lip, hard, to keep from saying something that might jeopardize Peter's future. That is, if Peter was even still alive. "Yes," he whispered the "s" coming out sibilant, a hiss.

"Come with me." Timothy turned in the direction of a stand of pine and maple trees to his left. Ed could see the white outline of a small structure in the woods. He started to move toward it.

"Wait a minute. You don't think, even for a moment, that I'm going to give you complete freedom of mobility?"

"Of course not." Ed continued to eye the little structure in the woods. That had to be where he was holding Peter. If he could just...

Without considering his actions any further, Ed took a breath and began sprinting through the woods, finding a small cobblestone path that led to the little out building before him. He reached it, listening as Timothy's harried footsteps fell behind him.

Ed threw open the door and gasped in horror. Peter lay on the floor, ankles and wrists bound so tightly Ed could see the purple bruises beginning to form above the hemp. He was blindfolded with a black bandanna, a piece of duct tape stretched across his mouth.

But worst of all, what appeared to be a concentration camp victim lay beside him, perfectly still, the once-handsome features appearing to be cast in alabaster, so pale were they. The skin already had a bluish tinge to it, and the body had the stiffness that described the onset of rigor mortis.

He slammed the door shut just as Bright approached and looked wildly about for something to hold it shut long enough for him to get Peter unbound. The two of them, he thought, could handle Bright, no matter what weapons he had.

Holding his shoulder against the door while Bright banged against it, Ed continued to search through the detritus for something with which to bar entrance to Timothy Bright. Near the back, in one corner, stood an old wheelbarrow. Its red coat of paint was dull, dulled further by dust and cobwebs. Spots of rust, like some sort of cancer, dotted its surface.

But how could he get to the wheelbarrow and continue to keep the door blocked from Bright's entrance? Moving toward the wheelbarrow would give Bright the second or two he needed to get inside.

And then what would happen?

TIMOTHY BANGED AGAINST the door, hard, not caring how much it hurt his shoulder. This bastard was ruining his plans. He couldn't let that happen. He hurled himself against the door once more, muttering to himself, whimpering at the pain the jolt sent through his shoulder. This maneuver looked so easy in the movies. Why wasn't it working now?

He answered himself: *maybe because the guy on the other side has about fifty pounds on you and is much, much stronger.*

Fuck that! Timothy grunted and threw himself at the door again.

He was not about to let this happen.

ED STARED OVER at Peter. "Peter! Peter, I'm here! Things are going to be okay." Ed hated to lie, but he had no degree of certainty that things *would* be all right.

In response, Peter mumbled through the duct tape.

Ed leaned hard into the door. His shoulder was aching; he didn't know how much longer he could hold off Bright's onslaught. He pressed his aching shoulder hard against the door and reached out with his foot to snag the wheelbarrow. If he could just reach it, he could wrap his foot around the bottom and tug it toward him.

It wouldn't work. The wheelbarrow was still at least a foot beyond his reach, no matter how much he stretched.

Besides, would the wheelbarrow even hold? It was a stupid idea: one good shove and Bright would be inside before he had even the smallest chance of unbinding Peter.

IT WOULDN'T BE long now, Timothy thought with glee, not long at all until he was inside. He could feel the fight being put up on the other side beginning to wane.

This was going to be so sweet. Leave them all dead and he could run away to a place where no one had heard of him. He could begin his life anew, now that all his wrongs were reversed.

And sweetest of all would be letting the blood flow from that pansy little weasel who called himself a hero...

ED HAD ALMOST missed it. But there it was, on the dirt floor. Such a small thing, really, but it just might work.

Ed positioned his hip against the door as he stooped over to pick up the rusty hoof pick lying there on the earth floor. All he had to do was grasp it, scoop it up, and slide it through the metal handle of the door. And of course, then pray it held long enough for him to set Peter free.

Oh God, why had he brought this innocent man into this situation?

Ed grunted and stooped further, extending his fingers outward to grasp the pick.

His hip wasn't enough. He felt a great rush, then the door pushed open, letting it a draft of cold air and...

Timothy Bright, whose small frame filled the doorway. He laughed triumphantly as Ed stumbled backward into the shed.

TIMOTHY WANTED TO use some cliché movie line, like, "Trapped like rats," but was afraid that would lend too comic an atmosphere to the scene, as if he weren't playing seriously. And he was.

Dead serious.

Seeing the carnage he had already wreaked gave him a feeling of triumph. He wished he had a photograph to memorialize the dead man who had defiled him, the terrified, angry expression on Ed Comparetto's face, and the bound and gagged form of his lover.

Too sweet.

"Comparetto. Don't move an inch. You do and there will be no negotiating. It'll be over. You've already demonstrated to me you're not to be trusted." Bright moved in closer to Ed. "Back up against that wall there and sit your ass down on the floor."

Ed complied.

"Now put your hands together and lift your wrists to me. I'm sure you've played this little game before."

ED DIDN'T KNOW what to do. Something with sharp teeth gnawed relentlessly at his gut as he slid slowly to the floor, his back against the wall. He couldn't let Bright bind him like this; it would remove any leverage.

"Wait a minute, man. You said you wanted me out here for a trade. Before I let you tie me up, you need to let *him* go."

Bright shook his head back and forth, as if he was encountering a misbehaving child. "You just don't learn, do you? It's no wonder the police department booted your ass."

"What do you know about that?"

In reply, Bright only grinned. "Anyway, I'll remind you once more: I call the shots. When you do as I've said, I'll let your little friend go."

"No dice, Bright. That just won't work. What assurance do I have?"

"None." Bright stood smiling at him and again, Ed noticed how pale his eyes were, almost feral. "You don't get it, do you? You don't have any negotiating power here."

"Where does that leave us, then?"

"It's going to leave you with a gaping hole in your chest if you don't do as I say. Now, I'm getting tired of this shit."

"Me too." Ed was gaining confidence during this exchange. Bright was just a little guy, a weak little man. He had no muscular development. So what if he had a knife? Ed knew a little about how to subdue an armed assailant. He just might be able to fight him off...

Just as these thoughts were gathering momentum and giving him confidence, Bright moved toward Peter. Ed saw what was happening and started to get up from the floor to a crouch.

That movement was all it took. When Bright saw Ed begin to get up, he was on his knees with lightning speed. Just as quickly, he lifted a whimpering Peter, positioned himself behind him, and then, in a deadly caress, wrapped his arm around Peter's neck, positioning the blade at Peter's throat. When Bright spoke, his voice was no longer high-pitched and giggly, but low, barely above a whisper, and it had all the menace of a growl. "Whatever you're thinking, don't do it. Sit back down. One more movement from you and I'll cut him. I swear to God I will."

Ed had no doubt of the man's intentions. He was a killer. Ed flashed on the gory bathtub where he had found Bright's first victim. No, Bright would not hesitate to kill Peter.

He lowered himself back down to the dirt floor, touching Peter's bound hands as he did so.

"Isn't that sweet? Just keep your fuckin' hands to yourself."

Ed placed his hands in his lap. There was no choice; he had to let Bright bind him.

GOOD, TIMOTHY THOUGHT, *I've finally got this little macho asshole cowed. It was even a little easier than I thought.* He could feel Peter's back against his chest, the heat transferred, the sweat causing Peter to adhere to Bright. The sensation was not at all unpleasant and Timothy found himself getting aroused. He wanted so much to stick Peter, to watch as his life force pumped out of him, to experience the contortions as another young man fought valiantly against the unstoppable: his final demise. *Such delirious pleasure.*

Timothy found he didn't want to move away from Peter. It felt too good being this close. He enjoyed the feel of the sweat-soaked bound body pressed hard up against him, the muscles in his back bunched with tension, the tangy sour smell of his sweat and fear in the air.

Why not do it? Bright wondered. So what if Ed Comparetto was there? By the time Ed got up to intervene, Timothy would have already sunk his knife home into the little faggot's throat. Bright realized he might have a fight on his hands, but there would be nothing Comparetto could do to stave off his lover's death.

Timothy pressed the blade close to Peter's throat, sinking it in deep enough to cause the skin to dimple inward and finally, to cause a small crimson line to form there. Peter winced and his body bucked, which aroused Bright all the more.

"What the fuck are you doing?" Comparetto's voice was shrill; he was as alarmed at the sight of the blood as Timothy was aroused by it. He started to get up again, and Timothy growled, "Don't fuckin' move, asshole. I've got it already going in. You make even the tiniest motion and it goes in all the way."

The altercation had caused Timothy's excitement to ebb. He needed to take care of Comparetto now, while his buddy wore a razor-thin smile on his throat. Timothy slid out from behind Peter, rubbing against him as he did so. He scrambled to his feet and moved to stand in front of Comparetto.

MUTELY, AND WITH resignation, Ed lifted his hands to Bright. "Go ahead, you bastard. Just get it over with."

Ed watched as Timothy stooped to pick up the coil of rope that had been on the floor the whole time. Ed wished he had thought to at least kick the rope into a corner. Now, there was nothing he could do to prevent what was coming.

Timothy lifted the rope and, grinning, knelt down beside Ed. As he reached out with the rope, Ed joined his hands together and brought them up suddenly, with all the force he could muster, square into Timothy's face.

Timothy gasped in surprise and pain and went reeling over backwards.

"You son of a bitch!" Within a second or two, he had righted himself and was bearing down on Ed, the knife held aloft.

They all froze as the sound of a siren ripped through the night.

Chapter
Thirty-eight

HAD THEY BEEN asked, both would have admitted it was a boring job. Working for the Lake Bluff police department had all the excitement of doing laundry, or watching TV. There was little for them to do, other than the occasional domestic disturbance or moving violation.

So it was with some interest Officers Dobrowski and Michaels made their way up the brick driveway to Dr. David Long's home. Both officers were young, in their twenties, and still fresh enough to find excitement in a variation in their day-to-day responsibilities, no matter how small that variation.

The call had come over their radio ten minutes ago. The dispatcher had told them that an intruder had been reported at Dr. Long's house. The caller had not identified herself, but Caller ID had shown the call had come from St. Francis Hospital in Evanston.

Strange.

As Officer Jim Dubrowski pulled up in the circular drive that fronted the house, he said, "Doesn't look like there's much going on here."

"Yeah."

The place was so quiet as to appear deserted.

Dubrowski switched off the siren, but left his lights flashing. As he and Michaels exited the car, a figure came out of the woods to their left.

"Look at that guy," Dean Michaels whispered to his partner. "He looks like a kid."

A small blond man strode toward them, smiling. Dubrowski noticed that the man seemed to grow older with each step he took toward them; his small stature and fine, straight blond hair gave him a very deceptive appearance of youth.

"Good afternoon, officers. Is there something I can help you with?"

"Hello, sir," Michaels said. "We've had a call reporting an intruder on the property. Are you Dr. Long?"

The man laughed. "Good Lord, no. The doctor is in the house, sleeping. He's been ill."

"And who are you sir?" Dubrowski asked.

"My name's Peter Howle." The man paused. "I work for Dr. Long. Y'know, handyman, butler. They used to call me a gentleman's gentleman." The man grinned.

Dubrowski nodded. "And you don't know anything about an intruder?"

"No. I can't imagine where such an idea would have come from." The man made circular motions in the driveway with his toe. "I've been here all day, and there hasn't been a thing out of the ordinary." He smiled at them. "Not that there ever is. It's pretty quiet back here." As if to demonstrate, the man paused and listened to the wind whistling through the treetops and the far-off knocking of a woodpecker.

"Well, if it's all the same to you, sir, we'd like to just have a look around the place, just to make sure." Michaels said, recalling the dispatcher's alert. She had said that they were to use caution on this call.

The man shrugged. "Y'know, I told you already: there's nothing out of place here. There aren't any intruders. Who made this call, anyway?"

Dubrowski's reply was curt. "Anonymous."

"Well then, there you go. It's probably someone playing a prank."

"Probably, sir. But we'd still like to take a look around," Michaels said.

"I can't let you do that." Suddenly, the man grew serious. Gone was the lighthearted smile that had accompanied almost every statement up until that point.

"And why not?" Michaels took a step toward the odd little man.

"Because, as I told you, the doctor is very ill. I can't have cops tramping around here, waking him up and upsetting him."

Dubrowski offered: "We'll be very quiet and make this as brief as possible." He noticed how the man's gaze kept venturing back to his right, where a small dwelling of some sort stood among the trees. The nervousness was evident on his face. "What's out there?"

The man followed his pointing finger to the white building in the woods. He laughed. "Nothing. The doc used to have a horse, and that's where he kept it. Nothing in there now but rusting old tools, cobwebs, and mice."

"Then you won't mind if we at least check that out. It could be a good hiding place for an intruder."

"No! I mean yes, I would mind." The man laughed again, and

his laughter was giving him away. "I was just out there myself, tidying up." He shook his head, staring down at the ground. "Believe me, the only intruders out there are field mice. And as soon as I set up some traps, even they won't be doing any intruding."

"Sir, we'd like to have a look. May we?" Michaels put on his best official tone.

"No, you may not. Now, I've told you, the call was a prank. It always has been very quiet here and today is no exception. Now, you've paid your visit and I suggest you get on your way."

Suddenly, everyone froze as what sounded like a cry came from the little white dwelling.

Dubrowski asked, "What the hell was that?"

And the man, again, laughed. "My dog, Sheba. She probably found one of the aforementioned mousies."

Michaels started toward the woods. "We're takin' a look."

The man grabbed him. "Wait a minute! This is still the United States, isn't it? You have no right to barge into people's private property."

"So what are you saying? You gonna make us get a search warrant? Because believe me, mister, we will." Dubrowski already hated this asshole. A search warrant would not be easy to obtain under circumstances like these, but this Howle guy didn't know that. Dubrowski looked the guy over and then paused, narrowing his eyes.

The guy had blood on his hands.

"What's that?" he asked.

Howle looked down at his hand and flicked at the blood, as if surprised it was there. "Nothing," he said, way too fast. "Cut myself bundling some wire's all."

Dubrowski nodded slowly. "You know, we could say we have probable cause..."

Michaels nudged him. "Let's just go get the search warrant."

Dubrowski stared at him, dumbfounded. "What?"

"We'll call the judge, have it written up right away." Michaels turned to Howle. "And then we'll be back, if that's how you want us to do it."

The man smiled at them, but there was only malice in the smile. "That's how I want you to do it."

"Fine. C'mon, Jim." Michaels started back toward the squad car, with a confused-looking Dubrowski following.

"JESUS CHRIST," TIMOTHY whispered to himself. "Close call." He was sweating profusely. God knows what the happy couple had gotten themselves up to in his absence. He appreciated the fact that Comparetto was bright enough not to try anything stupid. Making some sort of move could be very stupid indeed if Comparetto considered the jeopardy he would be placing his brothers in should he try to make trouble.

Timothy hurried back to the stable. There would be no more games. He would dispose of these problems as quickly and efficiently as possible and then...then maybe it would be time to move on. There were plenty of faggots online in other cities, all just waiting for him to come into their lives and put things to right.

"WHAT THE HELL did you do that for?" Dubrowski asked when they got back in the squad car and were driving back down the brick driveway. "Didn't you think the situation there was a bit odd? And how the hell are we going to get a search warrant based on an anonymous call about a fuckin' intruder?"

"Calm down, Jim. We were getting nowhere with that guy. I wasn't about to stand there all day and argue with him. Of course, I noticed something was up, that's why I did it."

"Huh?"

Michaels sighed. His partner wasn't always the brightest. He steered the car across the road and parked it on the berm. "We're going to do a little covert operation."

"Huh?"

"We're gonna sneak back up there. Through the woods there." Michaels indicated the trees with his finger, hoping his partner would catch on. "Then we'll see what this dude is up to, once and for all. I'm dyin' to get a look in that little building in the woods. Ten to one, he's up to no good there."

"Yeah, you're probably right."

The officers got out of the car, waited for a charcoal grey Mercedes to pass, and crossed the road. They disappeared into the woods, their guns drawn.

ED LOOKED UP when Bright came back. He had pulled the duct tape from Peter's mouth just moments before and had had to shush him when he cried out at the stinging pain.

Bright was not smiling. He gripped the knife so tightly in his hands his knuckles were white.

Ed stood. "Now, listen."

"Shut up!" Bright shrieked, his voice coming out high-pitched, a woman's wail. He charged Ed and plunged the knife into him.

Ed dropped, face first, into the dirt.

Chapter
Thirty-nine

"BE CAREFUL," DUBROWSKI whispered to his partner as he watched him edge toward the little building in the woods. Dubrowski was behind him, covering him, and fear gripped his guts. He knew the fear was unreasonable, but something, intuition maybe, told him something very bad was going down inside the little building.

"OH NO," PETER moaned as he witnessed the stabbing. His stomach wrenched; he breathed deep to avoid expelling the bile rising up inside him. "Please, God, no."

Reason deserted him as Bright came toward him, the knife held aloft, his face alive with passion. "Now, I'm gonna put it to you, pretty boy. Put it to you like you've never had it." Bright dropped to his knees and was just about to bring the knife down when he stopped suddenly, the color draining from his face.

Both men looked down to see what had caused the interruption. Ed grasped Bright's ankle and yanked. Ed's face had gone sickly white, and the effort he was exerting to hold on to the guy's leg and pull had caused beads of sweat to pop up all over his face.

"You son of a bitch!" Bright cried. "Why the fuck don't you just die? I should have done away with you in the woods when I had the chance."

Bright snatched his leg away from Ed's grasp and kicked at his wrist. "My fault, my fuckin' fault for being so goddamn careless. Well, it won't happen again." Timothy scrambled to his feet. He turned and with one large swooping motion, readied the knife to plunge into Ed's back.

"Hold it right there!"

The voice shocked all three of them. With the command, the door flew open so hard it banged against the wall behind it. The two Lake Bluff officers stood in the doorway, filling its frame, their guns drawn.

Bright stared at them open-mouthed for only a second. Then he was heading toward the single window in the stable. He leapt at it, and the sound of the shattering glass combined with the report of Michaels' gun. Immediately the small confines of the space filled with the smell of cordite.

And Bright was gone, out the window.

"Let's get him!" Dubrowski cried, and the two officers disappeared from the doorway to make their way around the shed and into the woods.

Peter stared at Ed, who was scrambling to get to his feet. He held his hand against his side; blood seeped through his fingers. "What are you doing?" Peter asked.

Ed felt so weary, so very weary; he barely had the strength to put breath behind his words. Aside from that, he felt very cold. He wondered if he was going into shock.

"I've gotta go with them."

"Are you crazy? You've been stabbed, Ed."

"I have to see this through." Ed was on his feet and loping toward the door, wincing with each step.

"At least untie me and let me come with you."

"No time. I'm gonna fuckin' put an end to this! Now!"

Peter watched helplessly as Ed dashed through the door, gasping.

He wondered if he'd ever see him alive again.

HE NEVER THOUGHT he would think of it as a good thing, but now Timothy was grateful for all the summertime games the good doctor had subjected him to as a teenager. It now allowed him a good command of how to maneuver through these woods, giving him a distinct advantage over his pursuers.

And his pursuers were not far behind. He could almost feel their fetid breath on his neck as he crashed through the brambles, running first left and then right, dodging trees and the occasional bullet, the sound of which practically caused his heart to stop.

"Stop! Stop, Goddammit, or we'll kill you, you son of a bitch!"

No, Timothy thought, *no one's getting killed here unless I say so.* Ahead was a gully that was filled with brown, muddy water from the recent rain. Timothy gulped in some air and leaped.

He just managed to clear the small chasm, and wanted to stop and see if the cops had the same luck, but there was no time. He sighed and would have laughed, had he had the breath, when he heard the splash and their mumbled curses.

Just what I needed, just what I fuckin' needed, Bright thought as he sprinted deeper into the woods. He veered to the left and crashed through a briar patch, one in which he suddenly remembered the good doctor pushing him down in and holding him, like a frightened rabbit, while he fucked his ass dry.

But now these thorned yellow weeds offered him protection. He could no longer hear the police behind him and assumed they had gone off in another direction.

"This was meant to be," he whispered to himself. "It had to be." He knew that not too far ahead lay Route 41, and he could escape to freedom.

"GODDAMMIT!" MICHAELS SAID to his partner. "Where the fuck did he go?"

The two men surveyed the woods around them. They saw nothing, heard nothing. They had the choice of countless directions in which to go, and all of them were unsafe bets.

"What do we do now?" Dubrowski asked.

"How the fuck should I know?"

ED HAD SEEN everything. He had been several yards behind the cops when he saw their spectacular fall into the gully. He groaned and hoped they weren't hurt.

He watched as Bright disappeared into the woods. "Lithe little fucker," he whispered to himself.

He did not give chase. He figured he had gotten well enough acquainted with Mr. Bright to be able to figure a thing or two out about him.

Ed would take a risk. Jumping the gully and trying to catch him was a risk. But it wasn't as big a risk as what he was banking on.

Ed turned and retraced his path back through the woods.

"FUCK." TIMOTHY LET his hand slump to his side...again. It was no wonder no one would pick him up. His hands were cut from bursting through the window; his legs were bloodied and dirty, his pants torn from running through the woods; scratches marred his boyish face. Plus rain had begun to fall: suddenly and without warning, the skies turned dark, there was a pitchfork of lightning on the horizon to the east, a cackling *boom*, and then the rains came. Torrential. Water so heavy, it blinded him; the cars sent up splashes and sprays. This had to be one of the unluckiest days of his life. Timothy trudged a little further up the road, the rain chilling him, making him shiver.

Why had he been so cursed?

He paused, letting the water drain in rivulets down his face. One thought kept nagging at him, pulling at his psyche, teasing him, taunting him.

He had always hated unfinished business. And Peter Howle was still lying inside the stable, he assumed, shivering and cold, and listening to the storm outside.

Could he make it back? Cut through the woods and slip inside before the police returned? He knew the woods around David's house better than anyone.

He looked behind him and saw the opening. There was a trail that led directly back into the property. Once upon a time, on hot summer afternoons, David would take him horseback riding; they used the trail behind him often.

Going back would mean taking an incredible risk. On the other hand, the police could be a while, searching through the brush, trees and rain for him. And killing Peter Howle would take so little time, so very little time. All he had to do was slip through the door, *sans* the words of wisdom he would have liked to use, plunge the knife home, and get back out.

He could do the deed and be back on his way before anyone came back.

No. Doing that, going back, would just be stupid. It would be like walking into a trap. But those idiots who called themselves authority had been unable to outwit him so far. And the Lake Bluff police force was even more incompetent than Chicago's.

What would be the harm in just going back and discreetly checking to see if the coast was clear? He could hide himself in the foliage, take a look, and if no one was around, go in and fuck Ed Comparetto up royally.

Timothy turned from the road onto the trail. Rain beat on the treetops. Even though there were no leaves, the trees gave him a little protection from the downpour. It didn't matter anyway; he was sopping wet as it was.

Timothy hurried along, his brisk walk every so often breaking into a run. The run would continue until he got winded, then he would slow again to a speedy walk.

Within minutes, the stable was in view once more. He looked with amusement at the shattered glass and the door hanging open. It appeared no one was around. Just to be safe, Timothy turned slowly, peering into the darkening woods to see if a white face stood out, if a cop uniform clashed with the trees, the brown and green.

"Now or never," he whispered to himself.

He sprung out into the open, heading for the door. He looked around him the whole way there, casting glances over his shoulder, expecting to see Mr. Comparetto or one of Lake Bluff's finest spring out at him.

But there was no one. And Timothy knew this was an omen, telling him he was doing the right thing. Just as there was always a feeling of rightness about taking the lives of those other filthy boys...

He pushed the door back and leapt inside.

"Hello, Timothy."

Timothy gasped to see Peter Howle standing before him. Gone were the ties that had bound him, the duct tape that had gagged him and the cloth that had blinded him.

"What the hell?"

He was about to turn when he felt a strong pair of arms encircle him, one holding him in place around his waist, while the other shot out to grab his wrist. Timothy stared down in horror at the hairy-knuckled hand which now gripped his wrist...gripped it tighter and tighter, until the hand no longer felt human, but like some sort of vise.

He couldn't stand it. The knife dropped to the damp floor.

Timothy writhed, sending his elbows, with savage force, into the stomach of whoever was holding him. One blow caused a gasp of air to be expelled from his attacker. There was a loosening in his attacker's grip and Timothy found himself free.

"Jesus Christ!" he cried, whirling.

Ed Comparetto stood staring at him, a grin beginning to play on his lips.

"It's over, Timothy. Don't make it hard on yourself."

Adrenalin surged through Timothy. He was not about to let this happen. With an animal lunge, he leapt at Ed, sending him to the floor. Timothy, on top of him, joined his hands together and was about to bring them down on Ed's face when he was once more grabbed from behind.

Another pair of strong arms, this time Peter Howle's, encircled him in an unrelenting embrace, pulling him backward.

Timothy struggled to free himself, kicking at air. He felt Ed Comparetto wriggling out from beneath him and knew there was nothing he could do.

He went limp, falling back into Peter Howle's arms. He turned his head to one side and saw David lying on the floor. His eyes were open, and the blue was filmed over with a milky white substance.

"Stop staring at me!" he shrieked. "This is your fault."

"What the hell's going on?" The officers from the Lake Bluff force barged in at last, and Timothy looked up at them. There was nothing to do; their guns were drawn.

"I'm alone," Timothy whispered to no one. "I'm just fucking alone. Why couldn't you leave me that way?" He closed his eyes and let himself fall back into Peter Howle's arms. "Just hold me, okay?"

Ed leaned back on his haunches, never expecting things to end so perfectly. Or bizarrely... Timothy Bright was now the one hanging on. Peter's face was a mask of confusion as Timothy gripped his hands. Peter looked to Ed for some idea of what to do. Ed shrugged and turned to the officers.

"You can take him in. You better cuff him."

"No shit," Dubrowski was already getting out the handcuffs and readying them.

LATER, AFTER GIVING their statements, Peter and Ed drove south on Route 41. The sky was purple on the horizon, the last bit of light dying.

"I'm sorry," Peter said. The two had said nothing for most of the ride.

"You're sorry? I think you stole my line."

"No. I didn't have enough faith in you."

"There's no reason you should have. Anyone else wouldn't have stuck it out as long as you did. Anyone else would have written me off as crazy."

"Well, I'm glad I didn't."

"So am I."

"I think that if I had understood —"

"Shhh. Let's not talk about this now."

The two rode on in silence, neither saying anything until they reached the northern boundary of the city and traffic began to get heavy.

"What do you say we just go home and go to bed?" Ed didn't know how his question would be taken, but before he had a chance to ponder what his lover would think of it, Peter responded.

"That sounds wonderful. But we have to get that cut taken care of." Peter touched Ed's side gently; the blood had already dried.

"It was just a glancing blow; a flesh wound. I've got some hydrogen peroxide at my place." Ed steered off the exit at Touhy and merged into the line of headlights heading home.

The End

Coming Soon!

In the Blood

A Tragic Vampire Love Story from Rick R. Reed

Chapter
One

NO ONE CAN hear the screams, the cries for mercy, and the shrieks of agony. It is as though the house is alive and it clamps down in reaction to the turmoil going on inside. One would never guess from its calm exterior that blood drips from its walls and those unlucky enough to enter have a good chance never to emerge again.

This house appears to be empty. Dignified. Crumbling testimony to the wealth that once existed on Chicago's far north side. It sits like a boulder on a corner, empty eye-socket windows facing Sheridan Road and beyond it, the expanse of Lake Michigan. The lake is dark now; white-tipped waves crash against the shoreline, breaking at the boulders, a crescent moon bisected and wobbling on its black and churning waters. The house has borne witness to these waters, moody and changeable, always fickle, for more than a hundred years.

The house is fashioned from white brick, yellowed and dirty. Nothing grows in the yard, save for a few straggling weeds that refuse to give in to the barren soil.

The house is dead.

And so are its inhabitants.

THE DEAD ARE inside and reveal a surprising likeness to living creatures. They can move and speak just like the rest of us. They have wants and needs. They go about fulfilling these wants and needs with the same kind of intensity and purpose as the rest of the world. One could even say they have jobs, even if their occupations would be deemed illegal and certainly immoral by almost everyone.

But look beyond these superficial similarities and you'll feel chilled. Touch their flesh and it's cold. Lay your head at their breasts and hear…nothing. Look into their eyes and find yourself reflected back in a black void that you just know, if you linger too long in its embrace, you'll be sucked in and it will be all over for you. Grab one of their cold wrists and it feels like stone, marble to be exact. There is no pulse.

But tonight, they are a merry band of three. Like the living, they are filled with anticipation. An evening out awaits them. They will, like so many others getting ready for a night on the town, meet others, exchange knowing glances and a mating dance of words. They will sup, but not on the gourmet offerings of the city.

Most houses born of this period contain many rooms, perhaps more than necessary. Whoever designed this house had the presence of mind to create wide-open spaces, breathing room. Enter the double front doors and you come directly into the living room. Or is it a drawing room? A great room? No matter. What you do not enter is a vestibule or a foyer as other houses of this period would contain. The walls are parchment colored, but right now, that color is indiscernible to the human eye, lit as they are by dozens of flickering candles. Water stains mar the walls and give to them a *trompe l'oeil* elegance, a look of almost deliberate aging. The floors are dark, their hardwood planks, tongue and groove, blackened by the lack of light and dust accumulated over many years. Along one wall is a fieldstone fireplace, its mantel tall as a man, its hearth cold and empty.

There is no furniture in this huge room. No chairs. No tables. No bookcases or desks. No divans or chaise longes.

What does occupy the room, other than these three lifeless, yet curiously beautiful souls, is art. Paintings of every period lean against the wall and hang from their crumbling surfaces. Here is one after the style of Rubens, there another that looks pre-Raphaelite, here a Picasso...Jackson Pollock...Monet...Keith Haring....Willem de Kooning....Mark Rothko...Barnett Newman...plus the works of a legion of unknown artists, in every style and medium imaginable. The walls are crowded with it. The room is a gallery assembled by someone with vast resources, but tastes that go beyond eclectic. The only common theme running through these works is that all are unique. There is a respect for form, for color, for technique. Most of all, there is a certain indefinable quality that manages to capture the human spirit in its delicacy, in its discontent, in its hunger...

Perhaps it's the hunger that appeals to them.

And the floor is a cocktail party of human sculptures. Men and women carved from marble, granite, and alabaster, cast in bronze. There are later figures cast from polymers, smooth acrylic, welded metals.

It is eerie...this empty house that has become museum or mausoleum.

Or both.

But art is what the dead crave. It sustains them...that and something else...something more warm and vibrant, but they are too genteel to admit to such hungers. Like animals, they simply feed when they are hungry and discuss it as little as possible.

The walls also contain long, leaded glass windows, through which, appropriately enough, a full moon sends its pale rays, distorted and laying upon the darkened wood like silver. The leaded glass has become opaque, obscured by layers of dust, grime, and accumulated smoke.

And we can see the creatures now, gathering. Listen: and hear nothing save for the creaking of ancient floorboards.

First let us consider Terence, broad shoulders cloaked in a pewter-zippered latex vest open just enough to display the cleft between smooth and defined pecs, tight leather jeans, and biker boots. Blond hair frames his face in leonine splendor: thick, straight, and shining, it flows to just below his shoulders. Glint of silver on both ears, studs moving like an iridescent slug upwards. Terence is the second oldest of the three. His skin, like the others, has the look and feel of alabaster. Dark eyes burn from within this whiteness and present a startling contrast. Terence is a study in symmetry; his wide-set eyes match each other perfectly, his aquiline nose bisects dramatic cheekbones and his full lips speak volumes about sensuality and lust. Stare into Terence's eyes and gain a glimpse — quick, like a jump cut in a movie — of cobblestone streets, horse-drawn carriages and the grime and elegance that was London in the late 1800s. Shake your head and the image disperses and you are left thinking it's only your imagination conjuring up these images. After all, what does this post-punk Adonis have to do with the British Empire in the time of Oscar Wilde? Besides, Terence's smile will have you thinking only of the present. And the present is what Terence lives for…the pleasure he can find, the communion of flesh and blood, seemingly so religious and yet sent from Hell. He throws back his head and does a runway model turn, for the benefit of his companion, Edward, who rolls his eyes and snickers. "Don't look to me to be one of your adoring minions."

Let's shift our focus to Edward. Edward is musculature in miniature, stubbled face and a shaved pate. Leather vest, black cargo pants tucked into construction worker boots, no jewelry save for the inverted cross glinting gold between shaved and defined pecs. On his bicep, a tattooed band: marijuana leaves repeated over and over, rimmed with a thick black line. Edward's look would be comfortable in the leather bars along Halsted Street and he is the only one of the three who prefers the embraces of men. He is relatively young, a newcomer to this scene of death and the greedy stealing of life. Watch him carefully and you will detect a hint of uncertainty in his handsome, rugged features. Melancholy haunts his dark eyes, which, unlike Terence's, are not symmetrical: the left is a little smaller than the right and crinkles more when he laughs, which is seldom. Curiously, though, it is Edward's features that look most human…because it's humanity that lacks perfection and Edward hasn't been of this undead world long enough to adopt its slick veneer of beauty that's too perfect to be real or wholesome. Look into Edward's eyes and you'll see a beatnik Greenwich Village, a more personal vision: an artist's studio which is nothing more than a cramped room with bad light with canvasses he worked on night and day, brilliant blends of color and construction for which Edward had no name, but one day would be called Abstract Expressionism.

Shake your head, and — as with Terence — these images disperse. There's nothing there, save for this macho gay clone boy with eyes that still manage to sparkle, in spite of the thin veneer of sadness and remorse deep within them.

And last comes Maria, on silent cat feet, moving down the stairs. A whisper of satin, the color of coagulating blood: rust and dying roses, corseted at the waist with black leather. Black hair falls to her shoulders, straight, each strand perfect, sometimes flickering red from the candles' luminance. Dark eyes and full crimson lips. Maria stands over six feet and her body, even beneath the dress, is a study in strength: muscles taut, defined, like a man save for the fact that the muscles speak a hypnotic feminine language: sinew locked with flesh in elegance and grace. Feline would not be going too far were one to describe her. There is the same grace, the same frightening coiled up power, perfect for the hunt, perfect for surprising and making quick work of her prey.

She pauses, turning slowly in front of the men, her_men, waiting for an appraisal. And, unlike Terence, this move does not seem vain, but more her due.

The men applaud softly and Maria stops, dark eyes boring into theirs. They do not see the watery streets of Venice, but you would, if you dared to engage her gaze for long. Dark canals and mossy mildew-stained walls, crumbling stairs at which black water laps, an open window through which one hears an aria. Smell the mildew and the damp.

The three take seats on the dusty floor, bring out mind-altering paraphernalia.

Terence, first: "Whom will we lure tonight?"

And Edward, eyes cast downward, the candle flames reflected off his bald and shining pate, sighs.

It is Maria who touches him, her hand a whisper, but with the tightness of a claw against his shoulder, forcing him to look up into her eyes. "I know it's hard. But eventually you'll come to understand, to be like Terence and enjoy what is natural."

Edward laughs, but there is no mirth in it. "Natural? You call what we do natural?"

"We are God's creatures, just like the ones we prey upon. Just as an owl preys upon a mouse. We have needs and we do what we must to satisfy them….or else we die."

"We're already dead," Edward says.

Maria picks up a glass cylinder and looks at it critically for a moment. "Legend looks at us that way. That much is true." At the top of the cylinder is a small bowl, which Maria stuffs with sticky, green bud. The smell of marijuana is redolent in the air, mixing with the burning wax of the candles. "But I prefer to think of us as another species. A different kind of animal."

Edward stares at the silver light coming in through the long leaded glass windows. It has been more than fifty years since he first met Terence in a tiny, basement bar in Greenwich Village. Fifty years since he transformed himself into this new kind of animal Maria is now trying to make him think he is, to excuse their killing, the mayhem they wreak wherever they go. The heartbreak and the bloodshed, the latter so delicious, and so damning. Will he ever become callous enough to view what they do and what they are, like Maria? Will he ever be able to look at one of their victims, convulsing before them on a grimy floor, surrendering to death, and see them as merely sustenance? He'll never believe it.

The most curious thing about his transformation is this: time has taken on completely different dimensions.

Five decades have passed like five days. It makes eternity easier to bear, he supposes.

"If that's what gets you through the night, Maria, fine. And as for being like Terence one day, well, that's a hell I hope to never visit."

His last comment elicits a snort from Terence, who seems to either find everything humorous or everything sexy. He lives for pleasure. Sometimes, Edward wishes he could be like him. Terence has no conscience. It would be easier to be so ignorant.

"Here." Maria hands him the glass cylinder, the thing that in a head shop would be called a Steamroller, and Edward fishes in his vest pocket for a disposable lighter. He fires it up and holds it to the little ashen bowl topping the cylinder, watching as it grows orange and holding his hand over the open end of the tube. It fills with smoke. When Edward removes his hand, the blue-gray smoke rolls toward him, into his open mouth and he longs for the oblivion he knows it will bring. He holds the smoke deep in his lungs and then exhales. It doesn't take much of this stuff to change his mood, to make him forget, and for that, he's grateful.

He hands the cylinder to Terence, who locks his hand over his and stares into his eyes. "You always were so beautiful," he whispers.

"You always were such a liar."

And the merry band of three becomes silent and a little less merry. They know the truth: Terence is a liar and had it not been for his charm and deceptions, Edward would not be with them tonight.

No, Edward would not be with them. He would be a man in his seventies by now, either a bum or a respected abstract expressionist painter; in the movie of his life, someone short but muscular would play him; the title of this film would not be *Pollock*, but *Tanguy*. Instead, Edward was no longer an artist, no longer a human being really. No, he is now a creature who has made stealth and superhuman attunement his artistic expression. He thinks, with a dark snort, that all he draws now is blood.

Maria's cold, satin flesh takes hold of his forearm; the slight pressure of her nails: the gentle touch of a bird of prey's talons. Even with his own kind, Edward thinks, one can't be too careful.

She knows he is not attuned to the night, but is depressed and resigned to the hunt. He has never fully realized the joy of taking sustenance. Maria stares into his black irises with her own pitch orbs, and smiles. She licks her lips and raises her nose to sniff. "Mmm. Can't you smell them, Edward? The sharp, hot tang?" She closes her eyes in a kind of rapture, breathing in deep. The smell of people wafts through the hot summer air, as much a background as the bleating horns, exhausts, and squealing brakes from the cars on Sheridan Road.

Edward allows Maria to lead him to the front door. *Puncture or perish* is the joke he whispers to himself.

Terence waits at the curb, his big Harley churning and revving. He grins and one can see, even from yards away, Terence's eyes sprinkling with anticipation.

Edward thinks as he descends the wide flight of stairs, Maria clutching his arm, that Terence is the luckiest of the three because he feels no remorse.

He has no heart.

In the Blood will be available September 2007

FORTHCOMING TITLES

published by
Quest Books

Redress of Grievances
by Brenda Adcock

In the first of a series of psychological thrillers, Harriett Markham is a defense attorney in Austin, Texas, who lost everything eleven years earlier. She had been an associate with a Dallas firm and involved in an affair with a senior partner, Alexis Dunne. Harriett represented a rape/murder client named Jared Wilkes and got the charges dismissed on a technicality. When Wilkes committed a rape and murder after his release, Harriett was devastated. She resigned and moved to Austin, leaving everything behind, including her lover.

Despite lingering feelings for Alexis, Harriet becomes involved with a sex-offense investigator, Jessie Rains, a woman struggling with secrets of her own. Harriet thinks she might finally be happy, but then Alexis re-enters her life. She refers a case of multiple homicide allegedly committed by Sharon Taggart, a woman with no motive for the crimes. Harriett is creeped out by the brutal murders, but reluctantly agrees to handle the defense.

As Harriett's team prepares for trial, disturbing information comes to light. Sharon denies any involvement in the crimes, but the evidence against her seems overwhelming. Harriett is plunged into a case rife with twisty psychological motives, questionable sanity, and a client with a complex and disturbing life. Is she guilty or not? And will Harriet's legal defense bring about justice – or another Wilkes case?

Available July 2007

Face of the Enemy
by Sandra Barret

Helena 'Dray' Draybeck is a military brat finishing her final year of fighter pilot training at a Terran Military space station. She's cocky about everything except her dismal track record with women. Dray is driven to be a top pilot like her mother, but someone at the space station does not want Dray to succeed.

Jordan Bowers is the daughter of a high-ranking ambassador. She wants a career as far away from politics as possible. As one of the best cadets in the fighter pilot program, Jordan captures Dray's attention in more ways than one. But Jordan won't let anyone get close to her. She hides a terrible secret that could end her own career and turn Dray against her.

When an explosion on their training station turns into a full-fledged attack, Dray and Jordan are put on the fast track to active military duty. But Dray's enemy sabotages her assignment and her chances with Jordan.

The threat of war pits Dray and Jordan against family, questionable allies, and an enemy neither is prepared for. Can they build something more than friendship, or will war and family secrets tear these two women apart?

Face of the Enemy is a stand alone novel set in the Terra/Nova universe, where chip implants and DNA manipulation are commonplace, and bigotry drives an interstellar superpower.

Available November 2007

OTHER QUEST PUBLICATIONS

About the Author

Rick R. Reed's published novels include *A Face Without a Heart*, *Penance*, and *Obsessed*. Short fiction has appeared in numerous anthologies, the most horrific of which was collected in *Twisted: Tales of Obsession and Terror*. *In the Blood* and *Deadly Vision: Book One of the Cassandra Chronicles* will be published by Regal Crest under their Quest imprint later this year. He lives in Miami with his partner and is at work on another novel.

Printed in the United States
123797LV00005B/31-60/A